The Thousand Year Journey of Tobias Parker

The Thousand Year Journey of Tobias Parker

A Novel

Terry Tarnoff

AVIAN PRESS

San Francisco

To see a video companion to this book, please visit www.terrytarnoff.com.

Cover design by Tina Tarnoff

ISBN 978-0-9888585-2-7

Second Edition, 2017

For my mother,
who knew what was what

ACKNOWLEDGMENTS

My deepest thanks to Michael Danzig for his years of friendship, advice and encouragement; to Michele Mortimer for her wise and insightful editorial suggestions; to the Meyer & Norma Ragir Foundation for its generous financial support; to Michael Tarnoff for helping make this possible; to Tina Tarnoff, who aided, abetted and added immeasurably to this project; and to the endlessly odd and inspiring denizens of North Beach, who make every walk through the neighborhood an adventure.

—Terry Tarnoff

Seventy-seven percent of this book is true.
Twelve percent is questionable.
The rest is utter nonsense.

Some names have been changed to protect the innocent.
Some names have been changed to protect the guilty.
Some names haven't been changed at all.

The Thousand Year Journey of Tobias Parker

Prologue

Every once in a while I look into the mirror and see my father. He's in there, all right, and I don't mean in the mirror; no, he's in me, in my brain. It's like he's taken over for a moment and he's thinking about composing a letter or maybe a short story or some kind of political diatribe, and then he's gone. This happens every so often—I look into the mirror, I see my dad, he thinks about something, and then he disappears. It's a weird feeling, like a wake-up call from the dead, but it's very real and I know he's there. My father always wanted to be a writer and, if I remember correctly, his father did, too. For reasons not completely clear to me, I have followed this path with such zeal and determination that I've actually made a career of writing, although it's a career that's left me so penniless one might question if it's a career at all. Still, I suspect that my father is in the mirror to check up on my progress, almost as if he's got a stake in what's going on. Me, him, his dad, maybe we're all connected in some way, and I don't just mean genetically; no, it's more mystical than that, it's like we're on some kind of family mission and I'm just the latest to try and work it out.

Every family has its own particular mission which is passed down through the generations, father to son and mother to daughter. We fight the same battles as our parents and become shaped by the struggle, as if cast from the same mold. I have no idea why anyone in my family wanted to become a writer except that they must've had something they wanted to say. I have no idea why I wanted to become a writer, either, and even less idea of what I want to say. Was it actually my family's destiny to struggle all those years so that I could become a screenwriter who never got a movie produced? To write nine screenplays that are sitting in the basement of some Hollywood production company holding up folding chairs? This was our big mission?

The men in my family wanted to be writers back at a time when I'm not even sure they knew what writing was. They wrote and wrote, decade after decade, generation after generation, and sank deeper into the abyss. That's how my family saw this issue of mystical genetics. Mystical was for rich people. For them this urgent, insane desire to write was a curse. My dad had it his whole life. After being consistently thwarted he descended into a deep, dark depression. Then he lost his mind. Then he entered a nursing home. Then he lost his memory. Then he got happy.

Me, I got the bug early. At the age of twelve, I delivered newspapers for a weekly publication that had no discernible audience, no point of view and no reason to exist. Since delivering the papers took so little time, I doubled as a gofer for Emma Hound, who wrote a column about bake sales, restaurant openings and pot luck dinners. Emma weighed three hundred pounds. "Want to know how I got my name?" she'd ask every time I saw her. "You ate a Saint Bernard?" I wanted to say, but before I'd get the words out she'd say, "Because I *am a* hound, get it? A newspaper hound!" We'd laugh and laugh until the cows came home—an expression

I've never understood—and then she'd complain that they didn't have enough material to fill the pages and couldn't even get people to write letters to the editor. When I said that *I* could do it—hell, I could write *anything*—she said it wouldn't look good to have some kid writing letters, but then I proposed using fake names and she agreed to give it a try.

And so began my career as an imposter/writer. It's not often that you can throw your journalistic ethics out the window at such a tender age, but I was an imposter/writer on a mission. I was paid a penny a word—an amount I've yet to match as a screenwriter—and I began filling the pages with letters from dozens of civic minded, if imaginary, neighbors. Emma was thrilled, the publisher was thrilled and my dad was thrilled. He saw before his very eyes the possibility of the family curse being lifted once and for all.

My dad always supported the idea of my being a writer, even when I took up screenwriting and piled up one failure after another. But the newspaper game seemed to be the most promising to him and he kept suggesting that I keep that avenue open as a fallback plan. "Dad, I can't write fake letters to the editor for the rest of my life," I'd say. "Why not?" he'd reply. I never had a really good answer to that but eventually he got on board the screenwriting bus, even if he never quite understood what exactly it was that I did. He did know, though, that screenplays were 120 pages long and every time I'd call home it would just be a matter of time before he'd ask what page I was on. I lived and died on character development. He lived and died on page count.

My father was eighty-five when he entered the nursing home. At first he was okay, then he got both better and worse by losing his memory. He'd just sit there with this goofy grin on his face and laugh every couple of minutes. It really wasn't right—him being happy—but there was nothing I could do about it. There wasn't much left to talk about since he'd forget the beginning of a sentence before he got to the end, and our conversation consisted of mostly interjections and conjunctions—

"Good!"

"Hah!"

"Or!"

"But!"

The last time I saw my dad, he'd just turned ninety. I came in from San Francisco and when I looked at him I knew I'd never see him again. We sat there for several hours just kind of staring at each other, sharing the occasional laugh over a leaf blowing against the window or a cloud passing by. When it came time to leave I bent down to hug him goodbye and he turned his cheek and kissed me full on the lips. This was completely out of character since my family didn't kiss on the lips. I think that came from my mother's side, something about germs being the kiss of death, but when we kissed I felt something pass between us, or rather from him to me. It was something from deep inside his chest that tasted of electricity and nerve endings. It was the taste of gravity. The kiss lingered a moment, then I pulled away. My dad had the biggest grin on his face I'd ever seen. His eyes danced in their sockets and the hair on his neck stood up. And then he yelped—it was like a falcon's yelp, high and sharp and primal—and it hung in the air like lightning over a desert.

I never saw my dad again. He died several months later. I returned to San Francisco, finished the screenplay I was working on and sent it off to Hollywood, where it languished with all of my other projects. Then several years later I set out to write a novel, hoping a change of form might help me to understand what this insane writing quest was all about. I decided to mix fact with fiction and actual people with fanciful characters and real events with preposterous lies in order to arrive at what surely would be an even greater truth. In it I would discover what had driven my family's thousand year search. After all, the time had finally come. I knew that I would leave no heirs, that I was the last of the line and that it was incumbent upon me to fulfill my family's quest. And so it begins...

Chapter 1

I want to meet him. I want to meet That Guy, that fucking, fucking guy, and tell him to bug off. I walk the streets of San Francisco, up Stockton, down Broadway, right on Columbus, past City Lights Bookstore—where Lawrence Ferlinghetti never published any of my books—across Kearny, down to the Sentinel Building—where Francis Ford Coppola never directed any of my movies—back up Columbus, past Wolfgang's—where Bill Graham never promoted any of my bands—I'm walking and walking, up through Chinatown, back to North Beach, around the side of Telegraph Hill, down to Levi Plaza, up through Grace Marchant Gardens, up, down, up, down, where the hell am I walking, nowhere, that's where, it doesn't matter if I turn right or if I turn left, if I go up Russian Hill or down Nob Hill, it's all the same thing, there will be houses, trees, people, dogs, and I'll either smile or I won't, and they'll either respond or they won't, and—what's this?—*hmm*, there's that girl again, the one with the big mound of hair, the one I keep seeing all over the place, she's just across the street, that's odd, that's twice in one day I've seen her, she's across the street but she doesn't appear to see me, she just keeps walking and I just keep walking, okay, fine, but now I turn a couple of corners and guess what, I see her again, only this time she's right in front of me, what should I do, should I stop her, should I overtake her, should I follow her, no, better not, better not to even let her see me, she'll think I'm stalking her, wait, there she is again, she's everywhere I look, did they clone her, are there seventy-five copies, all with their hair swept up into magnificent butterfly's nests of planned messiness, each of them avoiding me, each turning their head the other way, each pretending I don't exist, damn, maybe I *don't* exist, I hadn't thought of that, maybe I've gone completely invisible, sure, first I lose sight in one eye, then comes the synesthesia, then comes the stupid dreams, then I start hearing voices, and now I go completely invisible—

I've been invisible as a writer for years now, ever since I wrote a thriller about a biographer who misses his deadline for a book about Frank Lloyd Wright. That's the part Hollywood didn't get. Why Frank Lloyd Wright? What's Frank Lloyd Wright got to do with anything? The biographer is being chased through the back streets of Prague, his wife's been murdered, his life's in danger, why in God's name do you need Frank Lloyd Wright?

Because I'm an asshole. I've found a way to sabotage every screenplay I've ever written. I've broken every rule, stretched every boundary and defied every convention. None of which has anything to do with that woman across the street, of course, except for the fact of the spectacular architecture of her hairstyle, how the swoops and swirls take form and function and turn them on their head. Okay, say something why don't you, throw me a zinger right down the middle of the plate, toss me something I can knock out of the park. "What's the matter, cat got your tongue?" I yell to her across the street.

The woman looks startled. She turns, stares at me for a moment as if trying to remember who I am, then backs away. "Are you crazy?" she answers with an icy gaze.

"Yes, I'm crazy," I yell to her, "crazy like a fox!"

At which moment, a small red fox falls from a tree and lands at my feet, dead.

The fog fully engulfs the city and I can't see much farther than across the street. I make it up to the corner, where neighborhood weirdo Bernard is waiting for me. "Aaaak! Aaaak!" he screams out, and I know it's too late to escape. Bernard can't talk and can't hear but he can see like a hawk and he tracks me down at least once a day to hit me up for spare change. Bernard is Chinese of indeterminate age—I'm thinking Ming Dynasty—and he's incredibly short, not dwarf-short or little-person-short, but cute-short, like I could put him in my pocket and take him out to look at his little pants and little shoes and little shirt every once in a while. Still, Bernard's cuteness only goes so far and it's a good thing he can't hear because if he could I'd tell him to bug off, that these daily contributions are pushing me into bankruptcy, that, in fact, I've heard he's got a nice-enough place to live, probably nicer than mine, and that my little donations are giving him something I myself haven't had in at least seven years—a steady income. But Bernard just stares at me with such thoroughly hopeful eyes that I'm forced to pay up immediately. What I'd really like to do is buy one of those extra-sharp eyes off him and transplant the whole mechanism onto my optic nerve. But no, that probably wouldn't work anyway, so instead I give him a quarter and he gives me a Nazi salute.

I don't get the Nazi salute. There's no way Bernard is a Nazi and there's no way Bernard thinks I'm a Nazi, so what's with the stiff arm? It's one of the many mysteries of Bernard

I may never unravel.

The fog is really rolling in now. What the hell is fog, anyway? It's just clouds too lazy to get up in the sky, so why don't they call it low clouds, or lazy clouds, or disappointing, unfulfilled, out-of-work clouds—instead of some whole other genus? Why does everything have to be so complicated? I return Bernard's Nazi salute and move off through the low clouds to higher ground.

Higher ground is where I live, up on the top of Telegraph Hill. I head up the path to my cottage and run into Barbara, a Visigoth warrior-princess who lives in the bushes. Barbara has thick legs and thick arms, her hair is matted, and her face is caked with mud. She wears a burlap bag, wraps her feet in deerskin and carries a sharp, pointed stick for hunting. If this were the Pleistocene Era I could probably dig a chick like Barbara. She'd be good in battle and would be an excellent forager. But for now I'm just trying to keep things on an even keel and have established a kind of détente, no easy task given that Barbara is good for exactly thirty seconds of conversation and not one second more. After that it's a ten-car pile-up, a crunching, scrunching, fender-bender of wordplay I avoid at all costs.

"Have you seen the newspaper today?" she says, blocking my way along the path.

"Not yet."

"Wagner's coming to town."

"Wagner, the actor?"

"Wagner, the composer. They're performing *The Ring* at the Opera House."

"That's good," I say, having no idea why a Wagnerian opera would be good for me or anyone else. Opera has a way of getting inside my head and blowing out all the nerve endings. I like things on a smaller scale, like a nice little character-driven movie with two actors, three rooms and a bunch of shadows flickering on the wall.

"Balcony tickets are still available," she says, dropping a not-so-subtle hint.

My internal clock begins ticking. We're well past twenty seconds. "Sure, sure, I'll look into it," I lie, feigning interest. "I know a guy."

"It's Wagner, you know."

"So you mentioned." We're getting dangerously close to the red zone. I try to push past Barbara but her heft keeps me pinned against the edge of the path. The clock keeps ticking... *twenty-eight... twenty-nine...* "Listen, I—"

"*Der Morgen kommmmmmmmmmmmmt!*" she warbles with a piercing soprano as she tosses back her head and throws out her arms to embrace the sky. Her voice echoes off the hill, shakes the windows and sets off a half-dozen car alarms.

I make a break for daylight and escape down the path before a hundred knights in shining armor respond to her Wagnerian call to arms. If there's one thing I don't have, it's room for an army of singing soldiers. That's because I live in what might best be described as a shoe. It's a very old shoe in a state of total disrepair. There are patches everywhere, as well as breaks, cracks, dips, sways and odd little protuberances that rub uncomfortably and squeak on humid nights. The eyelets, which I vaingloriously refer to as skylights, are worn and fractured, leak terribly and are thoroughly beyond renewal. So too, the tongue, lip, sole, heel, instep, seam and toe guard. The shoe is much too small, at least for me. It barely allows me to breathe, much less stretch out. It's a size ten shoe I'm trying to wrap around a size twelve life.

I'm about to open the door when I see the shadow of a man scurrying past my window. There's something strange in his movements, almost simian, as if his arms are too long or his legs too short, and as the shadow blends into the vertical expanse of the house next door he appears to be climbing straight up as if he has suction cups on the bottom of his feet—*why, he's half-ape and half-spider!*—and then, just like that, he's gone. This is a very bad sign. It can only mean that an alien expeditionary force has set up its forward base in my backyard. Or that an escaped orangutan is plotting a final showdown with circus sharpshooters right outside my door. Or that That Guy is back, that fucking, fucking guy who is committed to ruining my good thing up here.

There are six houses at the top of Telegraph Hill and five of them are abandoned and boarded up. They're about to be torn down and replaced by condos but that's been going on for eight years now, what with permit problems and lawsuits and construction delays, and with any luck it'll go on another eight years. I, the one tenant who was too disoriented to move out in a timely manner, somehow wound up staying on as the caretaker of a parcel of land that needs no taking care of. It confirmed for me something I've long suspected: When faced with life's greatest challenges it's best to curl up into a fetal position and do absolutely nothing. I've codified this into my Law of Diminished Expectations, which states:

> WHAT WILL BE, WILL BE,
> UNLESS IT WON'T BE.

My only real job is to make sure that no homeless people set up camp in the abandoned houses, a job that takes me exactly seventeen minutes a week, fourteen minutes of which consist of trying to figure out which key goes into which lock. It's no little irony that if I were not the caretaker of this three-million-dollar plot of land on the top of Telegraph Hill I very likely would be homeless myself, so what I'm really doing is keeping the buildings safe from me.

I enter each apartment, look around carefully and confirm that yes, indeed, I have not moved in. I leave, feeling much safer. Until That Guy showed up. That fucking, fucking guy.

It started innocuously enough. I was walking down the pathway late one night and noticed a fire burning in the top-floor unit of the Big House. The Big House is what I call the three-story structure that dominates the parcel of land like a hulking fortress. The top floor of the Big House has a breathtaking view of the Golden Gate Bridge, Alcatraz Island and Russian Hill and, I was fairly certain, should not be on fire. Then I noticed the shadow of a man and it appeared he was holding some kind of prong that he slowly waved back and forth over the fire. That was all the reason I needed not to go up there. A prong can be an extremely dangerous weapon, especially when wielded by a crazed, drunken homeless person, so I fled to the safety of my cottage. The next morning, though, right around eleven, I was up there like a ferocious bulldog. There were telltale signs of human presence, all right. I found empty beer bottles, a box of matches and a little pile of kindling. The middle of the floor had a darkened, sooty spot that smelled of barbecued hot dogs and a gooey, yellow streak of what appeared to be hot, spicy mustard. I checked the doors and found that the locks were intact and hadn't been tampered with. There were no broken windows, no floorboards loose, no signs of forced entry whatsoever.

If it was a mystery I wasn't about to let it ruin a perfectly fine morning. I glanced out the big bay windows, amazed as always by the magnificent view, and watched the low clouds rolling in under the bridge. A ship was heading in, one of those big container ships from China, and it occurred to me that I never saw any crewmen on those ships. No, there were just stacks and stacks of containers but no crew; it was a ghost ship, the latest in a long line of ghost ships with hermetically sealed containers containing, well, what exactly? Always the same number of containers, always neatly stacked, always hermetically sealed, always the same route—under the bridge, around Alcatraz, over to Oakland, ghost ship after ghost ship, and they never return, no, they only head east, then disappear into the Oakland headlands where they are never seen or heard from again, and that's when I noticed a pane of glass being held in place by an odd system of strings and pulleys—*aha!*—a pane of glass just big enough for a man to remove, slip through and replace, but only if such a man were somehow able to scale a three-story vertical expanse, why, he'd have to be half-ape and half-spider to attempt such a feat, he'd have hundreds of little suction cups embedded into his feet. I left him a note:

> DEAR SIR. PLEASE DO NOT BREAK INTO THIS HOUSE AGAIN AND BUILD ANY FIRES. AS YOU MAY KNOW, FIRES IN ABANDONED HOUSES CAN BE VERY DANGEROUS. WHILE YOU'RE AT IT, PLEASE DO NOT BREAK INTO ANY OF THE OTHER HOUSES, EITHER. THANK YOU FOR YOUR ATTENTION TO THIS MATTER. BEST REGARDS.
>
> P.S.: I REDEEMED THE DEPOSITS ON YOUR BEER BOTTLES AT THE CORNER STORE.

There are people who make a living redeeming bottles or, as I prefer to think of it, make a living out of redemption. They dive through dumpsters, garbage cans and landfills and collect enough bottles to build an entire city of glass. I've been thinking a lot about redemption these days, and it occurs to me that a glass cottage might be good for my soul. What do I care if everyone can see right through me? It's not like I've got anything to hide. Then I remember that I only have six months to live and it seems I should be able to find a more useful way to spend my last days on earth. The construction of a glass house, after all, seems both overly ambitious and painfully transitory at the same time.

That night I was dismayed to see little flames reflecting in the glass of the third-story apartment of the Big House. The sight of those flames and the danger they implied immediately sent me into a somnambulant swoon from which I didn't awaken until noon the next day. But then, in a flash, I headed up there and nailed that window so tight even light couldn't sneak through. I left another note:

> HELLO, AGAIN. MAYBE I DIDN'T MAKE MYSELF CLEAR THE OTHER DAY, BUT THE DRINKING AND BUILDING OF FIRES IN THIS APARTMENT HAS TO STOP OR I WILL BE FORCED TO TAKE MORE SERIOUS ACTION. YOURS VERY TRULY.

The next night there was another fire and the following morning I found another pane removed. I left another note:

> LISTEN UP, ASSHOLE, THIS IS REALLY UNCOOL. IF YOU DON'T STOP, I'LL CALL THE COPS. NO FOOLING.

Actually, I *was* fooling. I'd never call the cops, not if I was being attacked by blood-thirsty banshees on a Leap Year full moon, but that night there was another fire and I did a complete 180 and called the cops after all. I specialize in 180s. I've gotten so good at changing my mind I can literally turn on a dime. That's right, toss a dime out there and I'll do a 180 so fast I'll leave you a nickel change.

Now, I have a very calm exterior. This gives the impression that I'm not easily rattled, that I think things through and make good decisions. People gravitate to me in crisis situations, wishing to anchor themselves to a calm port in the storm. What they don't realize is that at the first sign of trouble I simply teleport to some pristine spot where no harm can befall me. It might be at the edge of a babbling brook where a woman is sitting close enough for me to reach over and put my arm around her. She has a butterfly's nest of hair and as I pull her close I feel her breasts against my arm, they push a little each time she takes a breath, and now we're kissing, her tongue is pushing and her breasts are pushing and now my hand moves down along her waist and I reach inside her skirt and her hips are pushing, her tongue, her breasts and her hips are all pushing, and the banks of the river are pushing, the hill is pushing, the tree is pushing, the sky is pushing, everything is pushing, our clothes are flung all over the place, pants, shirts, shoes, socks, they're hanging from branches, they're stuck in the bushes, they're floating down the river, and that's when Patrolman Keith Kuiper appears at the foot of the Filbert Steps, Keith Kuiper, a raw rookie with a hot temper, a bad attitude and a rumpled uniform, and when I meet him outside the Big House it's like gasoline meeting a match, my calmness and his trigger-finger nervousness combining into an unholy grail of miscommunication and misinterpretation.

"Is that where he is? Up there?" yells Kuiper when I meet him at the door.

"Yeah, but keep it down," I whisper. "We don't want to tip him off."

"What do you mean?"

"We want to surprise him, don't we?"

"I'll decide who gets surprised."

"Okay. Let's go."

"I'll decide when we go. Follow me."

We edge up the staircase, me on my tiptoes, Kuiper stomping his boots so that the whole house shakes. Halfway up the second landing, I notice him pulling out his service revolver. "Hey!" I whisper urgently. "What are you doing?"

"I'm sure as hell not walking into a pitch black apartment and taking a bullet in my chest from some homeless fire-bug."

"No, wait a minute! Nobody's shooting anybody. That's not why I called you guys. I just want to get him out of there."

"What if he's under a blanket?"

"What's wrong with being under a blanket? I get under a blanket every night."

"What if he's under a blanket and I tell him to put his hands up and he doesn't? How do I know he doesn't have a gun under that blanket? How do I know he doesn't blow my fuckin' head off?"

"Why would he have a gun? He's making *hot dogs.*"

"Uh-uh, the guy makes one false move, the guy just twitches wrong, I'm takin' him out. Now get outta my way."

"No! Wait! You can't shoot him!"

"You got a better plan?"

"I'll go first."

"You'll go first?"

"Yeah, I'll go first."

Kuiper fastens his gun into his holster. "Okay. You go first."

We bang our way up to the third floor, argue some more and fling open the door. I stand there waiting to get a bullet in the chest or a poker in the eye but all I hear is Kuiper screaming: "Stop or I'll shoot!" The guy's already halfway down the side of the building—*why, he's half-ape and half-spider!*—and Kuiper nearly knocks me right out the window as he storms down the stairs waving his pistol.

By the time I get down to the Filbert Steps the place is crawling with cops. Kuiper has phoned in a Code Something and half the force surrounds the hill. A big burly sergeant with a speckled walrus mustache grabs me as I go flying down the stairs. "We'll take over from here, laddy," he says with a thick Irish brogue. An hour later they capture the guy five blocks away with a jar of mustard, a prong and a fox fur wrapped around his neck. The cops tell me I have to go downtown to press charges.

"Press charges? I don't want to press charges. I just want the guy to stop breaking into the apartment."

Kuiper takes a long, hard look at me. "Wait a minute. I ran after this guy, I risked life and limb, and you don't want to press charges? What are you, some kind of asshole?"

Yes! Didn't I already tell you? I'm a *total* asshole! I've found a way to sabotage every screenplay I've ever written. I've broken every rule, stretched every boundary and defied every convention.

"I'll be seeing you around, pal," says Patrolman Kuiper as he slowly runs his fingers over the barrel of his service revolver. "Don't double-park anywhere, okay?"

Chapter 2

I double-park outside Dr. Gerald Gold's office and slip inside his clinic for the deranged. Dr. Gold is a gastroenterologist, a specialty so hard to spell I figure he must be pretty good at whatever it is he does. Not that I'm overly impressed. I trust doctors about as far as I can throw them. I figure that Dr. Gold, being old and frail, is probably good for a toss of five, maybe six feet, depending on what he had for lunch.

Dr. Gold, whose name is one mere consonant from God, dispenses his opinions, prescriptions and admonitions like edicts from above. Me, I barely believe in gravity, so I take it all with a grain of salt. "Stay away from salt," he says. It's a little game we play, me and Dr. Gold. He asks questions I don't answer, gives instructions I don't follow, prescribes medicine I don't take and sends bills I don't pay. The fact is, I don't want to know anything about my body. Somehow I got all the way through high school and college without ever once studying biology, anatomy or physiology. Consequently, I'm not entirely sure how babies get made, what eyebrows are for, or what happens to our feet when we die. I just want to be a little bit handsome and be done with it. Isn't that enough?

Apparently not. My problems all began on a cold Tuesday morning when I glanced into the mirror and discovered I'd gone blind in my left eye. Oh, I could see a few shadows and some reflected light, but I had experienced what the silver-tongued wordsmiths of the medical profession refer to as an anterior ischemic optical neuropathy. It's basically a stroke to the optic nerve but doctors have to gussy it up into something as incomprehensible and numbing as ether. It was caused by stress. Or lack of sleep. Or too much sleep. Luckily nothing much happened for the next several weeks, but then I awoke one morning to a strange phenomenon that left me happy, sad and incapable of tapping my foot and finger at the same time: I began *seeing* sound. It started when my alarm clock rang and I saw a hundred purple boxes vibrating out in concentric circles from my forehead. Then someone slammed a door and I saw an array of crimson triangles spiraling up out of my cranium and exploding against the heavy sky. Then it started raining and the sound of the drops plunking against the rooftop appeared as a thousand tiny cactuses rubbing against the skin of a silver balloon. Much as I enjoyed the lightshow in my mind, I figured it was time to get a professional opinion.

That was mistake number one. Mistake number two was throwing a dart at the phonebook in order to pick a doctor. Mistake number three was not fleeing the instant I stepped into his office. Dr. Gold's waiting room reminds me of the waiting room at Midas Mufflers. There are three uncomfortable chairs, a forlorn rubber plant and a bunch of undecipherable charts of internal organs that may be human or may be automotive, since to me they look exactly the same. Dr. Gold has an assistant who's always sick and keeps running to the bathroom down the hall. Whenever she leaves, the phone invariably rings. Sometimes I answer and tell whoever it is to call back later. Sometimes I pretend to be Dr. Gold's assistant and schedule an appointment. Sometimes I pretend to be Dr. Gold himself, dispense some medical advice and save somebody a costly visit. My mother always wanted me to be a doctor and I think she'd be proud if she could see me now.

I enter the inner office where there are more charts of what are either heart valves or piston valves, plus assorted cylinders, pumps and hoses. I swear, the internal workings of a human being and a Buick LeSabre are indistinguishable—

"How many fingers am I holding up?" says Dr. Gold the moment I sit down. I figure this is some kind of joke, like a cartoon version of what a doctor's supposed to be.

"I'm not even sure how many hands you're holding up," I counter. It's a good response, maybe not Tracy and Hepburn, but good nonetheless.

Dr. Gold pushes an old-fashioned pair of tortoise shell glasses up the crown of his nose and shines a pinpoint of light into my one good eye. *"Hmm,"* he says, after a long moment. It's a noncommittal utterance, something you might expect to hear at an autopsy or a banker's convention, not the affirmation of life I was counting on. He moves the light to my other eye, then hovers there with a shaky hand. *"Um...hmmmm,"* he finally intones with a touch more confidence. "Your condition seems to have stabilized."

"Finally," I say, breathing a sigh of relief. "Some good news at last."

"Not really. It's a lousy condition."

I sink back into my chair. "How much longer do I have?"

"How long did I give you last time?"

"Six months."

"When were you here?"

"A month ago."

Dr. Gold does some quick calculations. "I'd say you've got five months."

"That's about what I figured."

"I've done some research into your condition," he says, again pushing his glasses higher up his nose. "What I came up with is rather intriguing. You have a rare aberration of the brain called *synesthesia*."

The word hangs in the air like a toxic cloud, then slowly dissipates in little droplets over Dr. Gold's forceps and tongue depressors. It sounds serious.

"It sounds serious," I say.

"Synesthesia is a mixing of the senses, as if the wires in the brain somehow got crossed. You see what you should hear. You hear what you should see."

"That's what my mother always told me."

"It takes different forms. In some cases somebody might taste a piece of chocolate and see the color red. Or smell a rose and hear a symphony. Or look at a number and see a burst of purple. It's a condition found most frequently among people in the arts. And among the very intelligent. And among demure, left-handed English women."

"I'm not really in the arts. And I ain't all that smart. And I'm definitely not demure, left-handed, English or of the feminine persuasion."

"Look, approximately one in every twenty-five thousand people has synesthesia but they all appear to be born with it, all except you, that is, because you seem to have *contracted* it as if it were a bad cold."

"Which makes me what, an aberration to an exception?"

"In your case it appears to be an outgrowth of the blindness, although I've found nothing whatsoever in the medical literature to suggest that one might cause the other. The fact is, nobody knows what causes this syndrome or how to cure it or even if it really exists."

"Oh, let me assure you, it exists all right."

"There are some researchers who think that synesthesia is nothing but the product of an overactive fantasy life."

"What do they think I'm doing every morning? Putting my fingers in the electric socket?"

"It's an interesting case," says Dr. Gold as he pushes his stool back and gets up. "I'm going to keep my eyes and ears open. I suggest you do the same."

"That's it?" I say, surprised that our consultation is over already. I want to get my money's worth, after all, even if I have no intention of ever paying him.

"Sometimes in cases like this you get a change after the first few months. But at this point—" he says, his voice trailing off with a noticeable lack of enthusiasm.

"You're saying I shouldn't hold my breath," I offer, filling in the blanks.

"Holding one's breath rarely solves a serious medical condition."

"Unless it's hiccups," I say, invoking an old home remedy having absolutely nothing to do with the present situation.

"Yes, unless it's hiccups," says Dr. Gold, not getting the joke which, after all, isn't really much of a joke at all. "Still, I want to monitor your condition—"

"Yeah, yeah, of course," I say, slowly getting up.

Dr. Gold leans against his examination table, waiting for me to gather my things. "How's the writing?"

"Same as always."

"Have you seen last week's box office?"

I was waiting for this. My conversations with Dr. Gold invariably turn to the box office, as if I've got the slightest interest in the latest Hollywood blockbuster. "I don't read the trades," I say with my usual weariness. "It's just numbers. What does the size of the box office have to do with the quality of a film?"

Dr. Gold has heard all of this before. He puts his arm around my shoulder and escorts me into the hallway. "Your condition concerns me," he says. "I want to give you some advice."

Here it comes. I turn to him slowly. "What?"

"Write action-adventure."

Of *course* he'd say that. I've got a doctor who prescribes writing advice rather than medicine. Doesn't he realize I'd rather have brain surgery than write action-adventure? What am I supposed to say to this guy? That I'm really more into nuance and character? He'd never understand.

"I'm really more into nuance and character."

"Just think about it, okay?"

"Sure thing."

A car door slams and a dozen pine cones circle out from my hippocampus. A foghorn blasts a warning from the Bay and a black and white chessboard radiates across my forehead. A bus screeches to a halt and a hundred hooks and ladders tumble off the ledge of my eyebrows and sink into a pool of tears. I've always been a bit trapped in my head anyway, but now I'm in full-bore examination of what's inside my brain, outside my body and anywhere in between. There's an infinity of thoughts and perceptions in there and I need to grab hold of every one of them while I've still got the chance. I head home, watching every step, listening to every heartbeat, touching every leaf.

My path takes me through Washington Square Park, an odd trapezoid of land that would be exactly one square block were it not for Columbus Avenue, which veers off at a diagonal like a drunk on a late night binge. Across the way, at 666 Filbert Street, is Saints Peter and Paul Church, a stately cathedral famous for having been the wedding place of Joe DiMaggio and Marilyn Monroe. That Joe DiMaggio and Marilyn Monroe actually got married at City Hall is rarely mentioned—good lies die hard in North Beach—but who cares anyway? The marriage lasted about a minute and a half and then went to hell in a hand basket.

That's another expression I've never quite understood—
what exactly is a hand basket and why would anyone go to
hell in it?—but it seems strangely appropriate considering
my surroundings. There's a statue at one edge of the park of
a fireman reaching heroically for the skies. Every once in a
while someone climbs up the statue and places a fifth of
whiskey in the fireman's hand. Then someone else, maybe a
drunk on a late-night binge on Columbus Avenue, climbs
up and removes it. This has been going on for as long as
anyone can remember, or for two years now, whichever is
longer. A block down is the Green Street Mortuary, where a
uniformed marching band plays dirges to the dead, and a
block from there is the Central Police Station, where Keith
Kuiper puts on his rumpled uniform, straps on his gun and
comes out looking for me to jaywalk or trespass or sneeze
too loud.

As I head through the park I notice that the woman I
keep seeing everywhere is sitting on a bench, staring
straight ahead as if in deep contemplation. Her hair is
swooped up in kind of a planned messiness, a perfectly
balanced butterfly's nest that swirls around, then drops into
a modified pony tail that brushes against her shoulders. I
wonder who she is and why I keep running into her. This is
a big city after all, not big like New York but big enough to
get lost in and remain anonymous. There are people I don't
see for years, some of them living just across the street, but
this woman keeps reappearing so often that it defies coincidence, no, she keeps showing up wherever I go, always with
that butterfly's nest of hair, always remote, always pretending she doesn't see me. It's time to find out once and for all,
yes, indeed, I'll simply pass her on the path, casual and
nonchalant like one of those shadowy guys in a black and
white film from the forties, I'll play the patsy who just
happens to be walking through the park and she can be the
mysterious stranger who follows him into a cold, dark alley

and changes his life forever, okay, this should be good, I'm getting closer, five'll get you ten that the minute I pass her she'll get up and follow me, okay, I'm almost in front of the bench, I'll just give her a little glance as I pass by—

"There are police in this park," she says in a flat, distant monotone. "Do you want me to call them?"

"That won't be necessary," I say, with forced nonchalance.

"Then stop following me." She stares at me coldly, then gets up off the bench and saunters down the path. I notice how gracefully she moves for a tall girl, how her hips sway and how perfectly balanced is her walk—

Doooiiinnnggg—doinng-doinng-doooiiinnnggg—

The church bells of Sts. Peter and Paul Cathedral suddenly send a shock wave up through my medulla oblongata and into my cerebellum. It's noon in North Beach and I'm directly in the line of fire for the full cacophonous assault. A dozen hideous spirals of shocking pink at the vomit end of the spectrum bore right through my cranium as the steeple erupts. No wonder Joe DiMaggio and Marilyn Monroe never got married at this church; the wedding bells are so discordant they'd make any couple deaf and infertile. Can't someone get the priests to tune the goddamn bells to a pure *A*—which means 440 cycles/second, not 434, not 443, but 440, got it?—so that we can have a little consonance in North Beach instead of dissonance? That's all I'm asking for. A little consonance.

My cottage was built after the San Francisco Earthquake of 1906, when half the city burned down and the Army Corps of Engineers came in and constructed thousands of identical cottages to house the refugees. Now, eighty-three years have passed, the refugees have long since moved on, and I'm the last of what once had been ten thousand lost souls. No matter that I didn't actually move in until many decades had passed and thus, technically, couldn't really be considered a refugee at all. Refugee, to me, is more a state of mind and what better place to seek refuge than in a rumbling, crumbling shack that threatens to disintegrate with the next gust of wind? There are only twenty-six refugee cottages left and everybody thought mine was one of them until we discovered that it deviated from the original architectural plans and therefore didn't qualify as a historical landmark which would give it preservation status and allow me to live there forever or until I die, whichever comes first. It actually deviated in a great number of ways, chief among them being that the quality of construction was so bad even the army found it uninhabitable. No, it really wasn't up to the choleric, grief-stricken, panic-inducing standards of post-apocalyptic San Francisco but for me, right now, it'll do just fine. I enter:

The bedroom. The bedroom is my multifunctional living space and therefore could also be called the living room, the family room, the study, the den, the library or, more likely, the bulging, sagging, collapsing, imploding tomb that will bury me alive the next time there's the slightest gust of wind from across the Bay. The bedroom is a trigonometry puzzle of angles and curves that could only have been conceived of by a drunken architect. Nothing really makes sense, not the intersection of the walls and the ceiling, or the doorway and the window, or the fireplace and the floor. The wood is rotting, the brick is crumbling and the sheetrock is swollen with so much moisture it sweats at night. The bedroom is built atop jagged rocks without the benefit of a foundation. When it rains a river rises above the rocks and seeps up through the floor, which makes no sense whatsoever since water, as everyone knows, is supposed to flow down a hill, not up. To add insult to incomprehensibility, my mattress acts like a giant sponge that slurps up any moisture the instant water begins to rise, leaving my sheets damp on good days and completely soaked on bad days, which puts the "dank" into the cold, dank cottage I call home. The cold comes from the original 1906 space heater, which is located under a window that won't close and lets all of the heat escape. The heater is affectionately known as a "granny killer" because of its tendency to blow back the gas and flame from the pilot light into a massive fireball that will consume anyone within knitting distance. Sometimes, when I'm in my bedroom, I find myself strangely short of breath. I enter:

The bathroom. I step into the shower and discover something horrible growing out of the wall. It looks suspiciously like bowtie pasta—what the Italians call *farfalle*—a three-quarter inch piece of off-white flour that's been scrunched together and twisted in the middle into a tiny cravat, something that you could put on a little doll cut-out, or on a little toy diplomat or on Bernard. I lean in a bit closer and realize that the bowtie is alive and that concerns me because it doesn't look at all like any living thing I've ever seen before. That's right, an entirely new variety of intergalactic consciousness has decided to make its terrestrial debut in my shower stall and suddenly I'm short of breath, the closer I get to the farfalle, the shorter my breath, and now it begins changing color, it's got a pink glow, well, sure, that makes sense, it's regenerating my blood corpuscles into its own genetic structure, it's sucking the life out of me molecule by molecule, and now it's growing, yes, it's growing while I'm shrinking, it's pulling me apart cell by cell and reconstituting my chromosomes into some kind of alien parasite that won't be satisfied until it's taken over every last tissue in my body, ah, of course, I was waiting for this, now it's got a voice—see how fast these things mutate?—but it's not my voice, no, that would be too obvious, it's got Patrolman Kuiper's voice, and now my breathing is really getting bad, I'm not sure I'll make it, I try to pull away from the wall but the farfalle has me in its grip and it says: "I'll be seeing you around, pal."

I leap from the shower to the stone floor, which shakes and vibrates just enough to make me worry that it will collapse but doesn't shake and vibrate quite enough to make me actually do anything about it. The floor is a disaster, which is as it should be since to be anything less than a disaster would make it completely out of place with everything else in the cottage. The floor was never completed and there are big, gaping cracks that attract all manner of flotsam and jetsam and make cleaning impossible. Every time I go into the bathroom I remind myself to buy some grout so that I can fill in the cracks, and every time I leave the bathroom I forget all about it. This has been going on now for twenty-one years. I enter:

The kitchen. The kitchen slants at a very odd angle. Walking through the kitchen is a lot like being on a boat in choppy waters. Sometimes while navigating from the stove to the refrigerator I lose my balance and fall down. That's when I see the gap between the floor and the wall, although to call it a gap doesn't really do it justice. It's more like a chasm or a gulf or a continental divide, a space large enough for wildlife to enter, make a nest, procreate, give birth, live, die, rot, fertilize, osmosify, regenerate and start all over again. Water seeps in during the winter rains, dust blows in during the arid summer months and a vibrant ecosystem sets in for the duration. The kitchen has one feature worth noting and that's the door, a dramatic entryway that is curved at the top and inlaid with twelve windows in the shape of a rainbow. No one has ever seen a door like this before and rumor has it that it was shipped over from nineteenth century Europe, the only likely origin for such fine craftsmanship. That anyone would ship over such a door to put on a post-apocalyptic cottage in San Francisco is ludicrous, of course, but it's the best explanation I've heard so that's what I tell everyone. The only problem with the door is that anyone can simply knock out the bottom panel of glass, reach in and undo the lock. This happens every few months and is one of the reasons I have nothing of value left in my cottage. Actually, that's not technically true. The door has some value. If someone were to break the window, undo the lock and steal the door, *then* I'd have nothing of value. But for now, I'm cash poor, door rich. Things could be worse.

Chapter 3

The Jains, a religious sect in India, extol *The Doctrine of Maybe,* a philosophical principle that has always intrigued me. It's kind of like something I've long espoused—*The Law of Maybe Yes, Maybe No*—which reduces things to their basic nature and concludes, for example, that maybe the priests will tune the goddamn bells and maybe they won't. The Jain system, on the other hand, is a bit more complicated than mine and is therefore worth exploring. The Jains say that reality is always in a state of flux and is never fully knowable, so anytime you think you know something you're just fooling yourself. What you think you know, in fact, is true in certain ways, false in certain ways and unknowable in certain ways. Toss this altogether and there become seven possible permutations of any one idea—what the Jains call *Sevenfold Paralogic*—in which anything is a) Maybe true; b) Maybe false; c) Maybe unknowable; d) Maybe true and false; e) Maybe true and unknowable; f) Maybe false and unknowable, and—here's the kicker—g) Maybe true and false and unknowable.

For example let's take Bernard and his Nazi salute. Now,

maybe it's true that it's a Nazi salute in which case maybe Bernard's a Nazi. Maybe it's false that it's a Nazi salute in which case Bernard almost certainly is not a Nazi but might have something seriously wrong with his arm. Maybe we'll never know if it's a Nazi salute since Bernard is too cute and cuddly to ever be taken seriously as anything but a Nazi toy soldier. Maybe it's true that it's a Nazi salute and false that Bernard is a Nazi in which case we might ask what exactly Bernard has to gain by acting like a moron fifty years after the end of World War II. Maybe it's true that it's a Nazi salute but we'll never know if Bernard is a Nazi because he's a clever little bastard hiding behind a ruse of being a deaf mute. Maybe it's false that it's a Nazi salute and uncertain whether or not Bernard is a Nazi since no real Nazi would be so unbelievably stupid as to go around giving the Nazi salute. And finally, maybe it's true that it's a Nazi salute and false that it's a Nazi salute and unknowable if it's a Nazi salute, which makes my head spin so much that I fall into a narcoleptic swoon from which I don't recover until Barbara jolts me awake with a refrain from *Tristan und Isolde* three days later.

My desk is very neat, some might say insanely neat, with everything precisely in its place. The phone is in the far left corner, angled five degrees from an imaginary median so that when my agent calls with news of a deal I can most efficiently pick it up, make sure it's not a wrong number, make sure it's not a hoax, make sure it's not a friend putting on a British accent, make sure my agent is calling me and not one of his real clients by mistake, make sure he's not drunk, make sure I'm not drunk, reconfirm all of the above, faint, hit my head on the keyboard, revive, run through the whole thing one more time and then realize that, yes, it *was* a mistake, he *is* drunk, he *did* mean to call someone else, and why am I bothering him at this hour? My agent, whom I will call Bobby Littman since his name is Bobby Littman, was once one of Hollywood's top deal makers. He arrived from England in the '60s at the time of the British invasion, but whether it was with the Beatles in the 1960s or with the Redcoats in the 1760s has never been entirely clear. I keep meaning to have my contract carbon dated to find out exactly which century it was drawn up in.

Had I never met Bobby Littman my life would have been immeasurably easier. I would have long ago realized that I had no aptitude for screenwriting, would have abandoned this ridiculous quest and would have gotten a real job at a real company in a real city. Instead Bobby Littman called me very late one evening, said he'd just read the script I had sent him and promised to sell it the very next morning. That's exactly what he did. He sold it the next morning. And then it sat on some company's shelf. And then it sat on some other company's shelf. And then Bobby started drinking. And then I started having strange dreams. And then everything went to hell in a hand basket.

There's a message light urgently blinking on the phone. Due to the sporadic electricity flowing through the decaying wires of my cottage it appears to be some kind of hysterical Morse code. I decide to take a chance and discover that it's Victoria, Bobby's assistant, reminding me that it's time for my semi-annual-agent-client-check-up, an event I both look forward to and dread. I look forward to it because it's a rare chance to actually see Bobby face to face. I dread it because I'll have to look Bobby in the face and explain to him all of my failures of the past six months.

I leave San Francisco International at noon, land at LAX seventy minutes later and arrive on Camden Drive in Beverly Hills just in time for my two-thirty appointment. Camden Drive is the perfect address for a man of Bobby's stature. It's only fitting that Bobby should perform his magic on this most British of all American streets, just one block from Rodeo Drive, and it's only fitting that I should be waiting twenty minutes before being allowed into his inner sanctum. It's what I call the *Rule of Twenty*, which states that all meetings in Hollywood shall commence exactly twenty minutes after your arrival, regardless of whether you're early, late or bleeding to death from a gunshot wound.

The office is in a classy two-story brick building and there's mahogany everywhere. The waiting room is dominated by a bookcase that stretches from floor to ceiling and would fit perfectly in a London barrister's office. Set into the shelves are small brass plates with the engraved names of Bobby's exceptional client list, some current, some former, some dead, but all of them represented by an impressive pile of film scripts. Bobby, after all, isn't just a talent agent or a literary agent, he's a "star" agent who handles elite actors, writers and directors, and there they are, in impeccable alphabetical order, David Bowie, John Cassavetes, Lee J. Cobb, James Coburn, Mia Farrow, Christopher Isherwood, Cheryl Ladd, David Lean, James Mason, David Niven. There must be twenty-five names in all and I glance over to see if I'm still there. Oh, yes, I'm there all right, the illustrious Tobias Parker, just before Nicolas Roeg and Ken Russell, and that only deepens the mystery since I'm not a star anything unless you consider an asterisk a star, in which case I might star as a footnote in one of Bobby's hallucinations.

"Mr. Parker?" calls Victoria from the doorway of her office exactly twenty minutes after my arrival. Her voice has the maple syrup smoothness of Kensington High Street. "Mr. Littman will see you now."

Bobby looks beautiful today. His hair is slicked down, his eyes are sparkling and his skin has a healthy glow. Even though it's still early afternoon he's wearing a pinstriped suit, a cuffed French shirt and Fleet Street loafers with tassels that could get you killed anywhere east of Figueroa Street.

The walls are full of celebrity photos—Bobby laughing with Gene Wilder, Bobby hugging Peter Ustinov—plus movie posters, awards, citations and the painting of a rabbi reading the Torah. I can't take my eyes off the painting. The rabbi looks like Bobby.

"You like it?"

"Uh, yeah, it's—"

"A guy on Fountain Avenue did it for me. You don't think it's too much?"

"No, no, it's just right."

"I'm getting older. I figure it can't hurt to cover all the bases." Bobby leans back in his oversized leather recliner and taps the mahogany desk with his freshly manicured nails. "Did I ever tell you the Christopher Plummer story?"

"A couple of times."

"It was when I first came to this town. The swinging sixties. London was too small for me. I needed to conquer the colonies. I needed a big client, somebody with a name to put me on the map. Who better than Christopher Plummer? He was a fellow subject of the Queen, a guy ready to break out big, he could be a pal. So I orchestrate events to meet him, it's at a bar, I buy him a drink, then I buy him another drink, then I buy him another drink, then I introduce him to a couple of birds who just happen to wander through, then more drinks, more birds, more bars, night after night this goes on, for three weeks we're painting the town red, eating, drinking, screwing, every morning we see the sunrise, and now it's time to formalize the relationship, I get a contract drawn up, we meet on a Sunday afternoon and I say, 'Christopher, I would be deeply honored to represent you in your soon-to-be burgeoning career,' and he says, 'Bobby, you're the greatest guy I ever met, the finest friend I ever had, but you can't be my agent.' My head is cracking right down the middle. 'Why not?' I ask him. 'Because I need an agent who's going to work for me,' he says, 'not some guy who's out *partying* all night long—'"

"That's a good story, Bobby," I say. It's a story I've heard at least five times, but it's just part of the living legend to whom I am attached in perpetuity or until one of us dies, whichever may come first. I take strange comfort in the fact that Christopher Plummer turned down Bobby's offer, as it connects me to a famous Canadian actor who will never appear in any of my films. Bobby's got a ton of stories, most of them ending badly.

"This script of yours, I'm gonna get it made, you know."

"Yeah, I know."

"It might take a month, it might take a year, it might take ten years, but I'm gonna get it made."

"I'm glad to hear that."

"Meanwhile, what are you doing, just sitting up there waiting for your ship to come in? A writer writes."

"A caretaker takes care."

"How about you take care of me by writing something that everybody in town wants, something big?"

"I'm not good at the big stuff. I'm more into nuance and character."

"Yeah, yeah, we're all into nuance and character. I'm the biggest character you'll ever meet. You want to write about me?"

"Nobody would believe it—"

"No, of course not. You want to write about something that hits people between the eyes, something set in the Civil War or in the trenches of France or in the ruins of Rome. Give me something biblical, for God's sake, something Babylonian, something with muscle and sweat, something Schwarzenegger could star in, or Gibson, or Seagal, give me something where I can fly first class for twelve hours to some exotic location and they put me up in the Maharaja's Suite and send up little puff pastries for breakfast."

I shift uncomfortably in my chair. "Nothing really rings a

bell at the moment."

"Did I ever tell you about the time Jack Nicholson came to see me? He was standing right there, right where you are, he had on shorts and a T-shirt and a seersucker jacket. He wants me to be his agent, he's dying for me to be his agent, he's begging me to be his agent, and what am I gonna do with this crazy kid? 'Jack,' I tell him, 'I'm gonna do you a favor, a huge favor, you'll thank me one day. This script of yours, it has some potential. You do a couple of rewrites, then I turn it over to a pro for a couple more rewrites, who knows what happens? Maybe somebody bites. Stranger things have happened. But this acting idea? No, Jack, that's not gonna fly, not here, not in Hollywood. This is the movies we're talking about. Guys like Christopher Plummer. You want to act, go to some community theater in Calabasas, you can act all day long. This is the movies, Jack.' Poor kid. I never saw anybody so down in the dumps. I told him to go to Musso and Frank's and get himself a nice mushroom omelet. So what happens? A couple of years later, he's onstage at the Academy Awards, he's just won best actor for *One Flew Over the Cuckoo's Nest*, and he says—get this—'*to the agent who told me I'd never make it in Hollywood*'—and I'm in my living room, I'm on my hands and knees, I'm praying to God, please, Jack, please-please-please, don't say my name, don't ruin my life, and Jack says, '*to that agent, I say, this Oscar's for you...*'"

"That's a good story, Bobby."

"How many scripts have you written?"

"Nine."

"How many have I gotten optioned?"

"Four."

"How much money was involved?"

"Not much."

"How many have been made into movies?"

"None."

"What does that tell you?"

"I need a new agent?"

Bobby turns to the photos on the wall. "I make people famous. That's my job. Some of my clients were already famous when they came here. I made them more famous. The years pass. Some of them died. Some of them left me. Some of them I left. Some of them left me and came back and left me again. So, I've made a couple of mistakes. We all make mistakes. Plummer, Nicholson, the Beatles."

"The *Beatles?*"

Bobby suddenly looks grave. "Yeah, I turned down the Beatles. I didn't have time for them. David Niven needed attention." Bobby stares off into space, the name Niven stuck to his lips like an old, uncancelled British stamp. "Now, do you see my point?"

"Not exactly."

"The point is, I'm still here. 409 Camden Drive. The rent gets paid. The lights work. The toilet flushes. Thirty years I'm in this crazy town. You win some. You lose some. Some you win *and* you lose and you don't even know which is which. But one thing I've got, going all the way back to my days at William Morris and MGM, one thing I've got is an eye for quality. And that's why, when I send a client out there, the producers know what they're getting." Bobby grabs a film script off the mountain of projects on his desk and waves it in the air. "You know what this is?"

I look at him uncertainly—

"*This* is a Bobby Littman," he says with pride. At which moment, the painting of the rabbi falls from the wall, bounces off the bookcase and hits Bobby squarely in the head. "Christ!" he bellows, flinging the painting across the room.

"I'm just not sure I'm cut out for Hollywood," I say. "I don't see things as a neat, little, three-act play."

"The moment you walked through that door, your life

became a three-act play. Do you think anybody was born to this? No! Of course not! We adapt to the process. You're still in Act One, the set-up, the starting line, and if you want to know what it's all about I'll tell you what it's all about: None of us has any idea whatsoever what it's all about. That's the secret, straight from the horse's mouth, nothing makes sense because nothing makes sense. I'm a mirror and you're a mirror and we're just two reflections talking to each other. It's not about reality, it's about the illusion of reality. It's not about writing, it's about the illusion of writing. Understand?"

"Not a word."

"Good." Bobby glances up to where the painting hit the bookcase and sees that a book is teetering on the edge of the shelf. "Get that damn thing off of there before the whole case falls down!" he bellows. I pull down an old, tattered copy of what appears to be a British encyclopedia. The title is so worn I can barely read it. "Now, open it," he says.

"Where to?"

"Anywhere. Just open it." I pull back the covers and run my thumb over the jaundiced-looking pages. The dust alone seems to be a couple of hundred years old and I feel queasy just breathing in the infectious passages. These are pages that stood up to the test of time and lost, beaten back by history's heavy hand. The book flutters open to page 453 and I stare at the photo of a rough-hewn sword which is sitting in the glass case of what appears to be a museum. "What does it say?" asks Bobby.

"*The Spear of Longinus,*" I say, reading the caption. "*Reputed to be the weapon of a Roman centurion that pierced the side of Jesus on the cross.*"

"Never heard of it."

"Me, either."

Bobby sits there a moment, the slightly sour expression on his lips slowly sweetening. "Still, it's got a certain ring.

Spears are always good. And you can't go wrong with Jesus. Talk about a built-in audience. What is it, from some battle he was in?"

"I don't think Jesus was a soldier."

Bobby thinks it over a moment, then motions for me to go on.

"A legend surrounds the object: He who possesses the Spear has the power of ultimate good or ultimate evil. Over the centuries it has been in the hands of Constantine, Otto the Great, Charlemagne, and Hitler."

"Hitler?" says Bobby as he leans forward in his seat. "Now we're getting somewhere."

"It resides today in the Hofburg Museum of the Hapsburg Palace in Vienna, Austria."

"Vienna, huh? That's where they make Sacher Torte, the best damn pastry in the universe. You have a piece of Sacher Torte, you can die a happy man." Bobby stares at me for a long moment, then gets up and walks across the room. He's strangely quiet, reverent almost, and all I can hear is the little rustling sound of his loafers on the carpet. He picks up the painting, dusts off the frame with his sleeve and kisses the rabbi's forehead. "Thank you."

"You're welcome."

"Not you! What am I thanking *you* for? I'm thanking the higher forces. They speak through me sometimes, like I'm a finely tuned vehicle of transmission. It's almost humbling. This, young man, is what we've been waiting for."

Now, I haven't been a young man in decades, but in Hollywood you're always a young man until you get your first movie produced. Only in Hollywood can a young man die of old age, but this is not the moment to quibble, no, Bobby's been touched by the holy spirit and it's best not to gum up the works with actuarial charts. I pick up the book and take another look. A bug from the Austro-Hungarian Empire crawls across the page. It appears to be wearing armor. "I really don't know about this—"

"Of course you don't know about this. That's why I'm your agent. To tell you what to think," he says, impatiently tapping his fingernails on his desktop. "No, no, the muses have spoken. Your path is laid out. All you have to do is follow it."

"Listen, Bobby, there's a medical situation I haven't mentioned—"

"Medical situation? What am I, your doctor? You look fine, take my word for it. Mix in a little more orange juice with your vodka, that's my prescription. Works every time. Keeps the cheeks rosy and the liver pink."

Victoria buzzes from the hallway. *"Mr. Littman? Paramount on Line Four."*

"Gotta take this," says Bobby, reaching for the phone. The whole thing, of course, is an obvious ruse since there's no way that Bobby's phone has four lines. Maybe in the old days, when he was on top of his game, but now he's lucky if it's not a party line. My guess is he's got a piece of string he pulls to signal Victoria to end the meeting. Or a lamp cord. Or a sun dial. Before I can say a word, he's shaking my hand. "You've got Dr. Littman's seal of approval," he says. "Now get back to San Francisco and start writing!"

"Um... about what?"

"The Spear, for Christ's sake! Do I have to draw you a map? Figure it out. Get in there and give me the nitty-gritty. Work some magic. Make me proud. Give me a Bobby Littman!"

And with that, the desk, the bookcase, the painting, the chair, the telephone, the encyclopedia and the Austro-Hungarian Empire fade to black. Next thing I know I'm back out on Camden Drive, shading my eyes against the sun. It's just like a movie, only without the credits. What a town.

Chapter 4

The drive in from the airport is slower than usual, giving me plenty of time to think about what I may be getting into and how, exactly, to get back out of it. Is this really how I want to spend my last months, pursuing yet another of Bobby's misguided ideas to its illogical conclusion? I'm already dead and buried as far as Hollywood's concerned; do I really need to formalize the contract? No, it's time to give up any idea of leaving my mark on the silver screen or on the pages of a manuscript or in the grooves of a record. I'll just pass into the ether having done nothing particularly of note but not leaving too horrible a mess either. Nothing lost, nothing gained, just another life passing through the firmament. That's not so bad when you think about it. Most people leave a trail of muck that takes decades of scrubbing before it fades from view.

I can see Telegraph Hill and Coit Tower from the freeway. If I squint I can even see my little cottage nestled into the hill. Coit Tower juts into the sky, kind of like an exclamation to my tiny point of a cottage which lies just beneath. Even from here my wobbly shack looks like it's about to collapse. Especially with a million tons of concrete hanging right over its roof.

Barbara is waiting for me when I get to the top of the Filbert Steps. We have an unspoken agreement that whenever I leave town she takes over as caretaker of the realm. That means that my job, which consists of doing nothing, gets passed to someone else whose job is to do nothing, twice removed. It's complicated, this workaday world. "I saw that guy hanging around this afternoon," she says.

"What guy?"

"The guy with the suction cups on his feet."

My jaw tightens. It's him again. That Guy, that fucking, fucking guy. "What did he want?"

"I don't really know. I saw him climbing up the side of the house and told him he'd better watch out, that you'd be angry."

"What did he say?"

"Nothing. He just laughed it off."

I clench my fists and glance up at the third-floor apartment. Unbelievable. He's back for more. Is he completely crazy? Doesn't he understand that my patience has its limits? Realizing that my conversation with Barbara is getting dangerously close to thirty seconds, I hurry for the gate but it's too late. Barbara makes some kind of crazy hand gesture to a eucalyptus tree as a narrow band of sunlight peeks through the fog.

"There are secret prisons across the bridge in Sausalito," she whispers.

"Yeah?" I say, playing along.

"The vortex is expanding."

"I was afraid of that."

She puts a finger to her lips and whispers to me: "Be careful. The hills have ears."

"Mum's the word," I whisper back.

We exchange knowing glances and I slip through the

gate. The smell of hot dogs hangs in the air.

By the time I get home there are seventeen urgent messages from Bobby telling me to call him immediately. I figure I must've broken something in his office or made off with a prized pen or left the toilet seat up. As I run through the possibilities I notice an array of dust particles floating through my room, each speck stirred up and agitated and in its own orbit. Such is the effect of Bobby Littman's voice, even when recorded. I've always thought that the dust of one's home is like tea leaves—you just need to know how to read them—and these floating oracles tell me that maybe it really *is* time to fulfill my family's legacy and discover what has driven us to become writers for all of these years. Either that or I picked up something from that mildewed book in Bobby's office and he's warning me to register with the Bureau of Infectious Diseases.

Victoria puts me straight through and Bobby excitedly tells me he's passed the project on to one of Hollywood's top producers, a producer so famous, so powerful and so hush-hush he can't even tell me who it is. Then he tells me that this Producer Who Shall Remain Nameless is head over heels about the idea and is ready to finance the whole thing. Then he tells me we're in like Flynn, another expression I don't understand, and he explains that Errol Flynn was a legendary lover and that to be in like Flynn is to be in, indeed. Then he tells me a story about James Coburn. Then he tells me a story about Mia Farrow. Then he tells me the same story he told me this afternoon about David Niven except with a different ending. Then he tells me how putting the Spear and Jesus together is pure genius, how the Producer Who Shall Remain Nameless is ready to send me to Vienna to do research, how I've got five days to come up with an outline, and how the idea is king in Hollywood, to which I respond that I have no idea what the idea is, that putting the Spear and Jesus together is not an idea, it's a random accident, and a dumb one at that, but Bobby, who is nothing if not quick on his feet, tells me that the Spear is all-powerful. And a curse. It's everything. And nothing. It saves civilization. Or ends it. And with that we're in business, me and Bobby and the Producer Who Shall Remain Nameless, and the fact that I may be dying suddenly doesn't seem quite so important anymore. Not when Hollywood calls. After all I've got a movie to write, and a big movie at that. Leave it to Hollywood to put things in perspective.

That night, for the first time in ages, I sleep like a baby.

Now comes the hard part: I've got five days before my flight to Vienna and I have to use every minute of it to learn whatever I can about the Spear. The North Beach library provides me with the perfect setting from which to launch my academic assault, mostly because it's just down the street. I usually keep research at arm's length, preferring that my inspiration not get influenced by actual facts, but this time I dive right in. I discover that the Spear holds one of history's great mysteries, that great battles have been fought over it through the centuries, and that it has an occult history dating back two thousand years. I turn up at least a dozen references to legends surrounding the Spear which leads me to wonder why, if this object is so famous, has nobody ever heard of it? Isn't this the weapon that pierced the side of Jesus? Doesn't it promise transcendent powers to its owner? I read on:

THE SPEAR WAS IN THE HANDS OF THE HOLY RO-
MAN EMPIRE FOR A THOUSAND YEARS. IT WAS USED
AS AN OBJECT OF CORONATION. WHEN NAPOLEON
INVADED GERMANY, THE SPEAR WAS TRANSPORTED

TO VIENNA, WHERE IT WAS PLACED UNDER HEAVY
GUARD AT THE HOFBURG MUSEUM. HITLER HAD A
VISION THAT HE WOULD ONE DAY POSSESS THE
SPEAR AND RULE THE WORLD. THIRTY YEARS LATER,
HE LED HIS ARMY INTO VIENNA, WENT STRAIGHT
TO THE HOFBURG, REMOVED THE SPEAR AND
CARRIED IT BACK TO NUREMBERG. THE GERMANS
POSSESSED THE SPEAR THROUGHOUT THE WAR. IT
IS SAID TO HOLD MYSTICAL POWERS. THE ALLIED
ARMIES WERE IN A RACE TO RECOVER IT. THE SPEAR
CHANGED HANDS ONE LAST TIME, ONLY MINUTES
BEFORE HITLER'S SUICIDE.

I cross-check dates, locations and names and then, in the
footnotes of some beat-up paperback, I find reference to a
German historian named Walter Horn—the man who
actually retrieved the Spear from the Nazis—and then I
discover that he later taught at the University of California,
retired, moved to Point Richmond—*a little town I can see
right from my window!*—and quite possibly is still alive.
That's when my breathing starts acting up again. Maybe it's
the farfalle in the shower or the dust on my bookshelf or the
anxiety of doing research, but I suddenly discover that the
slightest thought of the Spear causes me to gasp and go blue
in the face.

I decide to try and find Walter Horn even if it seems impossible that the man who recovered the Spear could be
living just across the Bay. What are the odds that it's the
same guy? What are the odds that he's still alive? What are
the odds that he'd even see me? My investigation leads me
from phone books to post boxes to social security offices, all
of which turn up nothing. Then I drive over to Berkeley and
visit the University of California where, after a few slip-ups
and missteps, I locate a tiny office on the third floor of
Dwinelle Hall which is shared by Professor Esteban Fielding

and—yes, indeed—Professor Emeritus Walter Horn who, it turns out, comes in once in a blue moon for a game of chess but otherwise is long retired. I explain to Professor Fielding that I'm engaged in important research and must see Professor Horn but that gets me nowhere, then I tell him I may only have several months to live and that barely elicits a yawn of sympathy, and then I tell him that I'm a client of Bobby Littman, that my screenplays share a shelf with Peter Ustinov and Gene Wilder, and that, who knows, maybe we could use him someday as an on-set consultant for some series or another, and that, as always, does the trick. I walk out of there with Horn's home phone number, which I immediately call. I ask the old man for a meeting, provide my academic credentials, give a little synopsis of my project and am rudely advised to take my Hollywood bullshit to the commercial marketplace, not to the halls of academia. I call back, get a busy signal, call again, get an answering machine, call again, get hung up on and call again, pretending to be a heavy breather. Horn finally gives in and agrees to a meeting. Address in hand I follow his incredibly intricate directions to Point Richmond, where I take Western Avenue up over the hill and down past three oak trees, turn right on Washington Street, turn right on Crest Lane, turn right on Belvedere Place, turn right again on Western Avenue and— very funny!—wind up right back where I started. I call again, tell Horn that I'm going to start knocking on every door in the neighborhood until I find him, we argue some more, I get some new directions, and either by hook, crook or utter coincidence I wind up at 47 Cypress Point where I ring the doorbell, tell him I just want to ask him a few questions and have the heavy redwood door slammed on my foot. We battle like footballers on the two yard line until finally, amid a flood of shouts, shoves and threats, I manage to produce evidence of my seriousness and sincerity, that being a bottle of Goldschlager Schnapps, and that loosens not only my foot, but also the lock, the door and ultimately, his tongue.

"*Ja,* vell, there I vas," he says over a barren kitchen table once the schnapps has coated his larynx, "I was a young professor at the University of Heidelberg and one day we are called to the auditorium for a speech by some crackpot, a real nut with a bad haircut, and my friends and I are getting a good laugh at all the idiots with their straight backs and stiff salutes. *'Heil Hitler!'* they yell at every stupid remark and we just sit there laughing until a few of them see us and then it isn't so funny, but we trick them in the end, we salute right along with the crowd, *'Heil Hitler!'* this and *'Heil Hitler!'* that but what we really are shouting is: *'Drei Litre!* Give us three liters of beer to wash away our tears!'"

Horn leans back in his chair, lost in thought as if he'd been transported back fifty years. He looks good for an old man, almost too good with those pink cheeks and strong arms and a booming voice that makes me cower at the table as if he might rap me over the knuckles with a ruler or yank my ear for not paying attention. I pour him another drink.

"Soon after, I have had enough and I flee my homeland— you think that is so easy?—and arrive in London with this eighty-pound German accent. Let's see you get a date with this burden in 1943! Soon I go to the British army and offer my services but they keep looking at me like I'm some kind of Mata Hari, so I go to the Americans instead and they don't care where I'm from—such is their lack of sophistication, they probably think I am from Liverpool or Manchester!— and straight away I am assigned to the Monuments and Fine Arts Branch of the Third Army—"

"—because you're an art history professor—"

"—because I am an art history professor. Who better to help track down the art work that the Nazis are looting from every museum in Europe? It soon turns out that I have

talents as an interrogator and when the army begins to
reconquer Europe I am called in to turn the screws on these
thieves and opportunists. Just days before the end of the
war a ragtag band of soldiers is brought before me. Soldiers?
It is laughable! They are conscripting seventy-year-old men
who don't know a gas mask from a Halloween mask. I ask
them the cursory questions—'what do you know about art
collections and lost paintings and looted museums?'—I tell
you, these are plumbers and carpenters, not curators, and I
am doing all I can to stay awake when one graybeard says
he knows nothing about art but has learned of a very
interesting dehumidifying machine that has been installed
in the caverns beneath the castle of Nuremberg. Who could
care about such a thing?"

"Nobody."

"Yes, nobody, unless one knows that Nuremberg is the
center of Nazi culture, that the absolute finest art is brought
there to be displayed at the Church of St. Katherine and that
the Allied armies are at that very moment preparing to
attack. Why would the Germans build such an installation
inside the caverns, if not to store art?"

"Maybe they were planning to hide out down there. They
could've been storing weapons or supplies."

"Please, do not interrupt," he says, shooting me an impatient look. "So I send a telegram to the Army High Command
warning them to stay clear of the hill. This, of course, they
are unable to do, being witless soldiers, and they manage to
drop a bomb right on the side of the hill and blow away the
entrance to an underground tunnel. At the end of the
tunnel they come upon a big steel door and thank God they
at least have the sense not to blast right through it—I tell
you, many times I was ready to quit—can you imagine the
damage? No, they are wise enough to call in their masterful
interrogator and illustrious art expert, this very man whom
you have forced yourself upon in his quiet moments of

retirement. Have you no respect at all for an old man's wishes?"

"Of course, I do."

Horn suddenly leans forward until his face is only inches from mine. All I can see are his wide, piercing eyes and his dancing eyebrows. "How did you find me?" he demands.

"I told you, your name is in a book—"

"*Ja, ja,* this is an old story, many names are in many books, I want to know why you have chosen this particular name at this particular time in this particular place."

I lean back as far as my chair will allow but Horn's face moves right along as if it were attached by invisible thread. I feel a bead of sweat forming on my forehead. Is it the heat? The humidity? The guilt? "It's like I said on the phone, I'm working on a screenplay—"

"Hah! Do you really expect me to believe that?"

The guilt fully kicks in. I uncontrollably jump in my seat and feel my palms sweating. The fact is, I've never felt so guilty in my life. I need to confess. I *want* to confess. My guilt is like a ten-foot tapeworm curled around my intestines and Walter Horn is pulling it out inch by inch through my esophagus and trachea and larynx. He's got my guilt on a hook and he won't let go. "All right!" I scream to him. "I admit it!"

"Tell me!"

"It was a big mistake!"

"Confess!"

"I never should've become a screenwriter!"

Horn slowly backs away, watching me beneath one upraised eyebrow. As he sinks into his seat the eyebrow settles into an uneasy stasis, momentarily satisfied but, I suspect, not for long. "It is the final days of the war," he says, his stare never wavering, "and the handwriting is on the wall. Heinrich Himmler is in charge of the artwork and he wants to hide the most important pieces from the invading armies.

The Nazis know the game is over but they hold onto the hope that someday the party will revive, and what better way to rally the forces than around these artifacts? Himmler puts the mayor of Nuremberg, a wretched little man named Willi Liebl, in charge of the caverns. He gives him a key to the door and the combination to a separate lock. Liebl in turn gives a copy of the key to one of his aides and tells the combination to another. When the Allies attack, Liebl shoots himself, leaving his assistants as the only ones who know how to get in."

I reach for the bottle. "More schnapps?"

"One of them, a fool named Gerhardt, is captured by the Russians. The other, a bigger fool named Weber, is captured by the Americans. I interrogate them both and convince them that the other has confessed. That's all it takes. They babble like babies. Gerhardt tells me where he buried the key and Weber blurts out the combination to the lock. A few days later I walk down the tunnel with General Dwight David Eisenhower and General George S. Patton. I have committed the combination to memory and dig away a brick next to the door, just like Gerhardt has told me. Behind it I find the key to the lock. Seconds later we walk into a room filled with priceless relics. The first thing I see is a two-foot spear with a gold shaft and an iron blade. I pick it up, feel its weight and balance and rest it in my palms. It's the Spear of Longinus, all right, of that there can be no doubt. I hand it to Eisenhower, who holds it for a moment, then raises it into the air just slightly, like a reluctant warrior. 'Now it is ours,' he says. Moments later, in a Berlin bunker, Hitler shoots himself in the head. The exchange is complete. Some months later the Spear is taken back to the Hofburg Museum, where it has been to this day."

"Amazing."

"There is nothing amazing. It is history. Something had to happen. This was it."

"Meeting Eisenhower and Patton, that's not everyday stuff—"

Horn suddenly lunges across the table. "So, you think *I* have the Spear!"

"What?"

"Isn't that why you're here? To abscond with the weapon? What do you think, that it is under my bed?"

"No, no, of course not. Why would I think that?"

"Because every occultist in the world knows this story and half of them think I took the real Spear and replaced it with a fake!"

"I've got no idea what you're talking about—"

"Would you like to look in my closet? Or maybe in the tool shed? Is that where you think I'm hiding it?"

"Listen, Professor Horn, I'm sorry, but I'm just a—"

"Lowly screenwriter? Do you really expect me to believe that? It's the oldest joke in the book."

"Yeah, well, glad you feel that way, but that's the sad truth of it. I'm on a new project. Something different for me. It's, well—"

Horn waits impatiently. "Yes?"

"Action-adventure."

Horn looks at me with a mix of pity and incredulity, then bursts out laughing. "Well, that's a good one, isn't it? Who will play me in your little film, Sylvester Stallone?"

"You never know."

"*Ja*, I can see it now. *Rocky and the Spear.*"

"It's got a certain ring."

Horn gets up and leads me to the door. "Be careful pulling out of the driveway."

"I didn't realize I was leaving."

"Tell your friends to stop calling me. Tell them to stop following me. Tell them I am an old man with bad hearing and a failing heart. Tell them to leave me alone."

"Yeah, okay. Thanks for meeting with me."

"Think nothing of it. I certainly didn't."

"Okay, well, keep the schnapps."

"*Ja, ja,*" he says, maneuvering me onto the stoop. And with that, Walter Horn closes the door in my face.

Chapter 5

It's cold in my cottage, cold and damp, the perfect climate for some ancient disease to resurrect itself—tuberculosis, perhaps?—and wouldn't it be just what the doctor ordered if yet another incurable disorder were to join my ever-growing list of maladies? TB, after all, thrives on wet and dreary conditions. It prefers dark cottages, dank basements and ceilings that drip. It likes whiskey, not wine; wool, not cotton; black and white photography, not color. It's the kind of disease you cuddle up to late at night when the lights are down low. You whisper sweet nothings into TB's ear and TB blushes and moves in a little closer and slaps you across the face—

Okay, I can't sleep. I've got Walter Horn on my brain and I can't help feeling a little sorry for him as he struggles with the bitter aftermath of his life. Does he really think there's an army of occultists out to steal the Spear? Does he really think I'm one of their chief operatives? Incredible. Is this all that awaits us in our final years? Is this the reward for service to our country and for enriching the minds of the young? Is this the culmination of our noble efforts, leaving us with nothing but anger, resentment and suspicion?

Okay, I *really* can't sleep. Directly above me, a family of somnambulant raccoons claws around in my ceiling, precipitating a synesthetic meteor storm of dancing rhomboids, squiggly pretzels and marching teacups. That I live in the middle of San Francisco and have a troupe of tap-dancing raccoons in my house seems only natural—could I expect anything less?—but what exactly are they doing up there? Why are they pacing back and forth all night? What are they planning?

I can't live like this. If man was meant to be nocturnal he'd have red, beady eyes and a furry backside, he'd have a fondness for grubs and larvae, he'd have cloven hoofs and a flat snout. When the sun begins to rise I feel a tickling sensation on my toes and discover that a patch of ivy has grown through the wall and is making its way for my throat. This has been going on for years now, ever since the cottage became engulfed by an imperialistic strain of ivy that declared war on my human habitat. The ivy grows up, over, around and through the walls if I don't keep it properly trimmed, but I *can't* keep it properly trimmed, not even a little, because the ivy has a mind of its own, a very stupid mind with only one thought, and that thought is: Take over the universe. I'm in no mood for this, certainly not after another sleepless night in my involuntary nature preserve, so I decide to cut the ivy down to size.

I roll out of bed, not figuratively, as if this were some clichéd example of bad writing—and I assure you, I am *not* a bad writer, not after having four screenplays optioned in Hollywood—no, I roll out of bed quite literally because my low ceiling leaves me no other choice. I dress quickly, grab a few necessities and hurry outside to the patio, a hundred-square-foot tract of broken bricks I've designated as the safe area the next time there's an earthquake. This is a little drill I do once a week to keep me on my toes. Everything seems to be in order. Coit Tower is still there, the Big House is still there and nothing appears to be on fire. Thank goodness for small favors.

I locate an old pair of garden shears and examine my living conditions. Surely one can learn volumes from his surroundings. After all, isn't the manifestation of one's existence imprinted on the walls of his home? If so my life is even shakier than I thought. No sooner do I snip off a few branches than the whole structure begins to disintegrate. First a shingle loosens, then a beam supporting the window frame, then the window itself, and then everything begins creaking—the walls, the ceilings, the corners—the whole cottage is ready to collapse!

I call Dominic Martinelli, the landlord's handyman, and he shows up a couple of hours later with a tape measure, a notebook and a pencil behind his ear, as if that's going to do any good. He inspects the eastern side of the structure, checks the door frames and windows and eyeballs the general stability of the walls and roof. "You know what's holding it up?" he says, rubbing his chin.

People who rub their chins scare the hell out of me. Carpenters rub their chins. Car mechanics rub their chins. Doctors rub their chins. "The ivy?"

"No, I don't think so."

"Well... what then?"

"Nothing."

"No, really."

"No, really. There's no physical way this cottage is still standing. You see that central beam over there? It's gone. Betcha termites took it out twenty years ago. And the load-bearing corner beam? It's gone, too. I figure all the corner beams are gone."

"No, really."

"No, really."

"Then how can we fix it?"

"Fix it? You can't fix it. There's nothing to fix. Where you gonna pound a nail? You pound a nail, the house falls down for sure."

"No, really."

"No, really."

Modern physics can't explain what's holding up my cottage. This cottage doesn't adhere to the laws of nature. It exists in its own special world where anything goes, a world where water flows up, raccoons dance the night away and the shower stall calls my name.

The shower stall calls my name. I walk into the bathroom, glance at the floor and remind myself to buy some grout so that I can fill in the cracks between the stones. Then I look into the mirror and see my dad. He's shaking his head, disapproving as always, as if to remind me that I'm living like a shepherd on some medieval hillside. He's joined by my mother who makes a brief appearance as well, which is rare and tells me I must've upset the whole clan. She's more of a shimmer than a face, more a feeling than a thought, like maybe she's feeling chilly or something and she kind of laughs it off and then she's gone.

Dad reassumes his position at the center of the mirror so that he can give me what for. And what *is* the what for? That's the question that keeps haunting me, even more so than my dad himself. It's that damn mystical genetics idea, the idea that every family on Earth has a destiny to complete, a specific task that's passed through the generations until it's finally accomplished, from father to son to grandson, a particular piece of a grand puzzle that we're all putting together, and that my family's destiny is to be writers and I'm here to write the final chapter, that I'm the end of my family's line.

"Go on, go on," says Dad, which is easy for him to say

even if it requires him to animate six hundred facial muscles he hasn't used in years. The fact is, he never figured out what's the what for and now there's nothing he'd like more than to pass it off on me to solve the riddle so that he can ride my coattails into the sunset. The problem is that I don't know *how* to go on. This business of mystical genetics is a complete mystery to me, something better left to the deep thinkers and enlightened savants of the outer realms. As far as I'm concerned we might be nothing more than blobs of ancestral space junk that are floating around the universe for no good reason whatsoever, mere flotsam and jetsam of the Big Bang, the accidental discharge of an energy burst that went horribly wrong. Kind of like the crud in between the cracks of my bathroom floor. But that's for other people to figure out. The Jains, for example. The Jains would probably call my little riddle something clever like the *Sevenfold Paradox of Non-Being*, but the Jains shame me with the breadth and depth of their knowledge and leave me in their dust.

"C'mon, give it some elbow grease," says Dad, employing one of his favorite expressions, one that I always found particularly irksome. What the hell is elbow grease, anyway, and how exactly is it supposed to help me figure out this mental conundrum? Do I rub it over my forehead and wait for a brainstorm?

Doooiiinnnggg—doinng-doinng-doooiiinnnggg—

The wind off the Pacific catches the church bells of Sts. Peter and Paul Cathedral and delivers their discordant hymnal straight to my cranium. It's the perfect distraction and allows me an escape from the mirror, the bathroom and the cottage itself. After all, how can I be expected to work like this with each new incantation sending fluorescent waggledaggles zinging around my gray matter? I march straight down the Filbert Steps, past the auto repair shop, past the Italian bakery, past Washington Square Park and directly to 666 Filbert Street, where Father Richard Indelicato is snoozing fitfully in his office. It's no joke, this address, which is a total joke in itself since the Catholic Church could've convinced the city to number it 660 Filbert or 670 Filbert or 6,000,006 Filbert if they damn well pleased. "Listen, this really has to stop!" I say, bursting through the heavy oak doors of the rectory.

Father Indelicato jerks awake with a look of exaggerated innocence that only the truly guilty can muster. "Is something wrong?" he says, feigning concern.

"The bells are driving me insane!"

"What bells?" he says, smiling thinly. His lips seem overly moist and the slightest smile threatens to dislodge a drop or two of sputum onto his chin. *Speculum speculorum sputum.*

"The *church* bells. Don't you realize they're completely out of tune?"

"I think you're wrong about that. We're very concerned about the consistency of the pitch and the overall quality of the peal."

"Then why do they sound like they're about to shatter into a thousand pieces of broken glass?"

"Are you a member of the church?"

"What's that got to do with anything?"

"I don't remember seeing you at services," says Father Indelicato, narrowing his eyes and looking at me more closely. "Are you Catholic?"

"Not even close."

"I see. Therein lies the problem."

"Oh?"

"Only a true Catholic can appreciate the celestial harmonies of the church spire. It is the music of the angels."

"Look, I don't want to take on the entire Vatican but I'll file a complaint—"

Father Indelicato eyes me nervously as he finally understands that he's dealing with more than a disturbed neighbor. *Lux hominum lunaticium.* "Would you like to see the steeple?" he says, trying to ingratiate himself with me for reasons not entirely clear. "There's a narrow stairwell, if you're not afraid of heights."

The priest catches me off guard. The fact is, I've always wondered what it looks like inside a steeple. Is it lined with bird nests? Are there bats hanging in the belfries? Hunchbacks swinging from rafters? "Yeah, well, sure, I guess—"

I find myself following him up along a marble staircase from the rectory to the vestibule of the church. My every footstep echoes down the empty corridors while his thin-soled black Italian loafers shuffle noiselessly along the polished floors. I feel strangely self-conscious, like an intruder in a forbidden world. We pass an open door of the chapel where a twenty-foot Jesus stares down from a wooden cross. It's a powerful image exerting both strength and weakness, hope and despair. I can almost reach over and touch the plaster skin stretched tightly over his emaciated frame. I find myself drawn to a slight indentation on the statue between the third and fourth ribs where a drop of blood trickles down over the abdomen. "If you gaze long enough upon this image, all of your problems will miraculously disappear," says Father Indelicato.

I figure that's a pretty good trick considering I can't even get the clanging of the bells out of my head. God knows, that would be miracle enough. Still I keep staring at that drop of blood and imagine for a second the incredible act of brutality that accompanied it. "The Spear," I say, more to myself than anyone else.

Father Indelicato glances at me out of the corner of his eye: "What Spear?"

"The Spear that killed Jesus on the cross," I say, pointing to the ribcage of the statue. "The Spear of Longinus."

Indelicato turns back and faces me. "Yes, of course. The Spear of Longinus. It's an important relic. There are many stories."

"Oh? Tell me."

"Why?"

"Because I'm interested."

"Because you are interested?" he says, caught off guard by my strangely direct answer. Father Indelicato shrugs his shoulders and continues down the corridor, savoring the rare chance to preach to the unconverted. "Well, you see, Longinus was a Roman Centurion in the Jerusalem brigade. He was summoned by Pontius Pilate, the Governor of the territories, to see to it that Jesus died before sunset. It was Friday afternoon, after all, and the law of the land demanded that there be no crucifixions on the Sabbath. Of the three men executed that day two expired by afternoon, but Jesus continued to breathe on the cross. Pilate was worried they might have to postpone the execution so he ordered Longinus to break the legs of our Savior with his Spear and put an end to it."

"It seems like kind of a strange way to kill somebody."

"If one cannot hold himself up on the cross with his ankles, his lungs collapse and he dies of suffocation."

"I see." We come to a narrow doorway that is nearly camouflaged by ornate carvings of the apostles. Above the door is a placard that skewers my attention:

EVIL IS DONE HERE

It's an interesting slogan, open to several interpretations. I'm not sure whether to feel relieved or threatened. I lean toward the latter, especially when Father Indelicato gives the door a sharp rap which loosens it from its moldings just enough for him to get his hand inside and unlatch a hook. "But there was a second reason that Pilate ordered Longinus to break his legs—"

The door swings open and we slip inside to a steep and

narrow staircase that seems to rise straight into the sky. "Which was?"

The priest begins the long climb up the stairs, not answering for a moment. He glances back at me over his shoulder. "You say you are not Catholic and yet here you are in the heart of the cathedral. Perhaps you have been brought here for a reason."

"The bells, remember?"

"Yes, of course. The bells." He continues his upward journey. "There was a prophesy in the Old Testament that the Messiah would die with no broken bones. Pilate knew that once the Centurion broke his legs, Jesus' followers would give up their claim that he was the one they were waiting for."

I follow Father Indelicato high into the steeple, losing track of the number of steps. That I am counting the steps at all is a sure sign of anxiety. I often count things when I'm trying to escape an unsavory situation, be it the minutes left in a school day or the miles left in a boring journey or the pages left in a screenplay. "This is much higher than I thought."

"I hope you don't have vertigo."

"That's about the only thing I don't have."

"Why are you so interested in the Spear?"

I was afraid of this. The priest has a suspicious nature and is trying to get me to divulge some nugget of information. He's a lot like Walter Horn that way. Priests and old German interrogators have a lot in common. "I'm doing research on a project."

"What kind of project?"

"Uh... a film project."

Father Indelicato turns and furrows his brows. I feel especially insecure standing a few steps down from him on the stairs. He could nudge me with an elbow and I'd fall like a hundred-pound sack of sacraments. He fixes me with a stare. "Longinus was said to be quite feeble and nearly blind. You'll need someone old to play him. Peter O'Toole could do it if he doesn't overact."

Good God, *everybody's* a film critic! "Sure, Peter O'Toole would be great."

The priest continues up the stairs. "When Longinus arrived at the cross he looked into the eyes of Jesus and was overcome by an overwhelming feeling of compassion. So moved was he that he decided to put Jesus out of his misery. With an act of bravery and defiance he plunged his Spear into our Lord's chest instead of breaking his legs. At that very instant a drop of blood spurted into Longinus' eye and immediately restored his eyesight. It was the first miracle after the Savior's death. Longinus fell to his knees, begged forgiveness and became a Christian convert on the spot."

We head higher into the steeple and I feel my breathing getting weak again. I can see the giant clapper of a bell just above me and I stop for a moment to gather my breath. "What about the prophesy?"

"That was the most amazing miracle of all. When Jesus' followers pulled him off the cross they discovered that the Spear had passed between his third and forth ribs without breaking a bone. It confirmed everything from the Old Testament."

"Old legends die hard."

"Prophesies are not to be taken lightly," says Indelicato in clipped tones. "Nor is the Spear. It's a very important artifact. The Spear, the Holy Grail, the Shroud of Turin, they are all objects of veneration."

"But nobody talks about the Spear," I remind him. "Most people haven't even heard of it."

"Many things get lost in history."

"This didn't get lost. It's in Vienna."

"So I've heard." Father Indelicato waits for me at the top of the stairs. I arrive next to a steel gate that creaks slightly in the wind. "Now, about our bells—" The priest opens the gate and we lean out over a two-hundred-foot drop that leads to a black chasm below. Fourteen giant bells sway back and forth like iron monsters stalking their prey.

"Jesus Christ!" I whisper under my breath.

"Do you know what goes into the making of a bell? Do you know what care is taken to perfect the pitch?"

I back away from the deep pit. "No, not really—"

"Do you know about prime tuning, partial intensity and true harmonics? What about quint, tierce and hum? Have you studied strike notes, splashes and superquints?"

"Look, I just care about harmony. I just want to hear a couple of notes blend together and not make my teeth rattle."

Father Indelicato turns on me with what, for lack of a better word, I can only describe as a demonic grin. "Harmony? Is that what you want?" he hisses at me. He glances at what appears to be either a very cheap Rolex or a very expensive fake and sprints like a madman for the stairs. "I'll give you harmony!"

Before I can move away from the gate a mechanism on the side of the steeple begins clicking—*tick-tick-tick*—and then the clicking stops and a big, crude ballbuster of a clapper swings by and crashes into the side of a bell and sends a shockwave of sound into my toenails, up through my chest cavity and into my cranial recesses. It wipes out my chakras, lays waste to my spinal column and rearranges my DNA sequence. It rubs off my fingerprints, changes my signature and alters the pigment of my skin. It grabs my throat, pummels my soul and delivers me into another incarnation where Monk plays the soundtrack, Fellini holds the camera and Dali spins the turntable. I descend the stairs, teetering and tottering, my fingernails digging into the walls as one clapper after another swings by and nearly decapitates me. I head for the rectory, eyes ablaze, and register a written complaint in the strongest possible terms:

> DEAR SIRS. PLEASE BE ADVISED THAT THE BELLS OF
> STS. PETER AND PAUL ARE AN AFFRONT TO THE
> NEIGHBORHOOD AND A BLIGHT ON MANKIND.
> PLEASE MAKE THE NECESSARY REPAIRS IMMEDIATE-
> LY OR FACE LEGAL CONSEQUENCES OF THE MOST
> SEVERE NATURE. I'M NOT KIDDING THIS TIME.
> YOURS VERY TRULY, TOBIAS PARKER.

As the incessant throbbing rattles the cage of my body, I feel my bones rubbing together like dice in the hands of a compulsive gambler. I drop my note into the church suggestion box and get the hell out of there before the clock strikes four. Who knows what sonic terror Father Indelicato has up his sleeve?

Chapter 6

The clock strikes four. I wind my way through the streets of North Beach and get far enough away from the church to only suffer a mild tympanic attack. I find myself outside the Café Vienna, a little dive on the other side of Broadway known for its coffee, beer and old world charm. It's a place I've been meaning to visit for ages and this seems like the perfect time to go inside and get a feel for the city I'll be calling home in just a few short days. I've never been to Austria, after all, and my only real image of the place is from *The Third Man*, an old black and white movie that left an indelible, if dated, impression on my mind. I don't think the Allies still occupy Vienna or that there's a black market in penicillin anymore or that zither music is all the rage. Nothing stays the same, after all, not even old Europe.

The Café Vienna blends into the surroundings of Pacific Avenue, half-hidden between a furniture store and an antique shop. A wood clapboard sign on the sidewalk lists the day's specials—potato soup, potato dumplings, potato salad—and the faded scrawl suggests that those specials haven't changed in at least a month. Above the doorway yellow pin lights illuminate a veranda that's just big enough for three tiny tables, some metal stools and a menu holder. The front window is covered by heavy velvet drapes, giving the place a slightly musty feeling even from the street. Next to it the front door is slightly ajar, giving a sense of welcome to prospective customers, if not the outright enthusiasm a fully open door might imply. Perfect. I walk in.

A long, narrow triptych of the Danube River extends the length of the room, interspersed with photographs of St. Stephen's Cathedral, the Vienna Opera House and the Austrian National Theatre. On the opposite wall are portraits of Mozart and Schubert and a painting of the Hofburg Palace in an ornate, gilded frame. As I stare at the artwork I try to imagine if this is the Vienna that Freud and Jung awoke to each morning, with shadows and fog and a chill damp wind that cuts right through the little curlicues of smoke rising from the ovens and chimneys. Did they walk along the cobblestone back alleys to the bakery just across the way? Did they ride in a carriage past the Schönbrunn Palace toward the old Haas House? Did they wander through the Naschmarkt with pretty assistants on their arms?

There's a skylight in the café right over the counter and a big blue umbrella that diffuses the light. A tropical plant grows out of an oversized clay pot, its leaves puffed up with almost comical self-importance, as if they were the café's central attraction. It's a casual restaurant, a lunch place really, with self-service and a pared-down menu. There's a woman behind the counter and a smattering of customers reading newspapers and sipping coffee. She's making a sandwich and has her back to me, unaware that I'm even there. I could reach right over and make off with a spoon or a fork or a sliced cucumber and no one would be the wiser. Why I would want such an item, of course, is beyond me. I repress the urge to load up on artificial sweetener and clear my throat instead. The counter girl glances up from her sprouts and onions and turns slightly to acknowledge my presence. Her hair is swooped up in kind of a planned messiness, a perfectly balanced butterfly's nest of hair that swirls around then drops into a modified pony tail that brushes against her shoulders. "Coffee?" she says, with just the hint of an accent.

"Yes. Please."

The swoop of hair exposes her neck, which is long and thin and shows a delicate, porcelain-colored skin. It occurs to me that in all my years as an unsuccessful writer I'd at least never sunken to descriptions such as "porcelain-colored skin," but her skin *is* porcelain-colored, so what am I going to say? More importantly, putting together the hair and the skin I realize that this woman is strangely familiar, and when she turns to face me full on, she realizes the same thing, too. "Oh, it's you," she says through pursed lips.

It's her all right, the mysterious woman from the park, the one who thinks I'm following her all over North Beach even though it's quite possibly she who is following me. What are the odds of walking into an Austrian restaurant and finding her, of all people, working behind the counter? This is going to require an explanation, and a fancy one at that, but I'm at an absolute loss for words—

"Large or small?" she says with noticeable irritation.

I don't much like the fact that she's standing next to a pot of boiling-hot coffee. These Austrians have famously short tempers and even shorter fuses. One wrong word and I could find that pot of coffee scorching me from head to toe. She impatiently brushes a strand of hair off her forehead and I see her eyes for the first time. They're such a dark brown that they barely allow light to escape. She has the kind of eyes, you look into them and maybe you never come back. "Large will be fine," I say, diplomatically.

She turns quickly and walks to the back counter, her

every movement restrained as if to maximize energy effi-
ciency. Still, she seems to hesitate a moment as if she's not
quite sure where everything is. She finally locates a large
mug, pours my coffee and returns to the counter. She places
the cup next to the cash register and studies the keys for a
moment, then shrugs and hits a key arbitrarily. "A dollar
sixty-three."

I watch with growing interest as she fumbles with the
machine. "Is this your first day or something?" I say. "You
seem new here."

She looks at me out of the corner of her eye as if gauging
the inherent risks of engaging in conversation. "No," she
finally responds. It's like she doesn't really want to commit
one way or the other, as if it were information that could
one day be used against her. "I have been here a few days."

"A few days," I repeat, as if confirming some secret code
that's never to be revealed. Your secret is safe with me, I
indicate with a quick nod.

"Anything else?" she says, quickly closing any window of
opportunity and drawing the shades on further conversation.

"Uh, no, that'll do it," I say.

I give her two dollars. She gives me thirty-seven cents
change. I casually move my hand over to the tip jar and
pour the entire amount in. It's a nonchalant gesture, as if it
were only natural that I would put in whatever amount of
change she gave me. That's right, it wouldn't have mattered
if the change was from a five-dollar bill or a ten or a twenty,
it all would've gone straight into the tip jar. I hope she
understands that. I'm really very generous and it's only my
complete lack of money that prevents me from acting upon
that generosity. It just so happens that I only had two
dollars today but the fact of the matter is, I'd give her a
thousand dollars for that cup of coffee and not bat an
eyelash. That's right, I wouldn't give it a second thought.
And do you know what I'd expect in return? Nothing. Not

even a thank you. Not a single thing. Nope, it's all yours, a thousand-dollar tip for a cup of coffee. Big deal.

She stands there, composed and impenetrable, her back straight, shoulders level, gaze unwavering as I pull my hand away from the tip jar. It's almost as if she expected me to take something *from* the jar rather than put something in. "Milk and sugar are on the counter," she says, avoiding all possible eye contact. Still, I can't help but notice that she has incredible eyebrows. They're long and thin and swoop down at just the right angle to her temples. Looking at those eyebrows I realize something: I like her. She has an intelligent face. She's very pretty. I think she likes me, too. She feels drawn to me even though something holds her back. It's an odd kind of chemistry we have: it pulls and repels at the same time.

I head for the side of the restaurant and take the first available table. It wobbles slightly on the uneven floor, as does the chair, giving the distinct impression of being on a boat crossing the Danube. That's what I like, a restaurant so authentic you can get seasick just sitting there. I lean back beneath the painting of the Hofburg Palace and gaze upon the Heldenplatz and its statues of Archduke Karl and Prince Eugene on horseback. Panning the canvas I note several Gothic towers which empty onto a vast square filled with art nouveau sculpture. As I look more closely at the palace I can almost see in through a window to the Schatzkammer, the museum room where the Spear of Longinus is displayed. It's so near it's as if I could touch it.

"I'd like to go there."

I glance up and see the counter girl changing the linens on a table nearby. Did she say—"I'm sorry. What's that?"

She glances over as if disturbed from some deep reverie. "I didn't say anything."

"No, no, just now, you said—"

She looks unhappy with the intrusion and responds more

firmly. "I didn't say anything."

Okay, she didn't say anything. Fine. Except that she did. She's a strange one, that's for sure. "You're from Vienna?"

"Germany. East Germany."

East Germany? There's something very sexy about that. "Oh, and now...?"

She shrugs and shakes out the linen: "Now I'm here." I watch her for a moment as she smoothes out the tablecloth, rearranges the salt and pepper shakers and heads back to the counter. I try to put her out of my mind as I glance across the restaurant to a photo of the Palais Schwarzenberg, the grandest of all Austrian hotels, and wonder if that's where the Producer Who Shall Remain Nameless is going to put me up. I wouldn't mind going there with that counter girl—God, she's sexy—yes, we'll stay on the top floor of the Palais Schwarzenberg and watch the sunset over the Danube, then we'll take a cruise down the river and that's when we'll kiss, the boat swaying gently in the waves, right there in the middle of the Danube the boat will sway just enough to slide her closer to me, she'll look up, a little embarrassed perhaps, and that's when we'll kiss, swaying gently in the currents of the river—

An eerie, scratchy sound fills the room as if someone were playing a saw with a knife. I glance over to see the waitress punching in a couple of buttons on the jukebox. Is she actually playing zither music? Fantastic! "I'm leaving for Vienna in a few days," I call to her over the jarring sound. "I'm researching a screenplay."

"So?"

"I just thought you might want to know."

"Why would I want to know?"

"It's... just conversation."

"I am very busy."

I glance around the restaurant. It's completely empty. "Yes, I see." I quickly finish my coffee and get up to leave.

Better not to overstay my welcome, such as it is. "Maybe we can talk about it sometime," I say.

"I don't think so."

I stare into her eyes and there's nothing—no expression, no hint of recognition, no nothing. I turn away, head for the door and glance back one last time. She's at the sink, washing a cup, unaware of whether I'm there or if I've left or if I was even ever there in the first place. It occurs to me that if this is what Vienna is like maybe it's not too late to switch my ticket to Warsaw or Bratislava.

The moment I step out onto the sidewalk a big black Oldsmobile with tinted windows pulls up at curb and parks right next to me, its engine idling. I glance inside to see who it is but all I can make out is the reflection of my own face in the glass, and that's when my breathing problems start in again, worse than ever. I gasp for air and wheeze and feel my face flushing but the Oldsmobile just sits there, quiet and menacing, as if taking my measure. I hear a familiar cry from across the street—

"Aaaak! Aaaak!" Oh, God, not now. What the hell is Bernard doing over here? This isn't his turf. This is Pacific Avenue. Bernard never goes south of Broadway. It's out of his range. "Aaaak! Aaaak!" he repeats, making a bee line for my pocket.

I try to get away—from Bernard, from the café, from the Oldsmobile—but when I take a few steps the whole street seems to move right along with me. The car edges forward, Bernard closes in and even the café seems to slant in my direction as if trying to get a closer look. The bare outline of a face bleeds through the tinted glass of the car. It looks like an old man, a guy with thick jowls and a receding hairline. It could be a stock broker. Or a lawyer. Or a professor. Yes, of course, Walter Horn would drive a car like that—what's more professorial than an Oldsmobile?—but does it makes any sense that Walter Horn would follow me to San Francisco? Maybe he's come for some potato soup at the Café Vienna. Or he's got a schnapps connection down the street. Or an old chum from the war lives in the neighborhood. Maybe, maybe, maybe. I could maybe myself right around the block. Where are the Jains now that I need them?

But what if it's not Walter Horn at all? What if it's one of those occultists he kept rambling on about? Hell, you could fit a dozen occultists in a car that big, twice that many if they were Bernard's size. The fact is, anybody could be staring at me behind those black windows, anybody at all, and now my breathing really gets bad, my lungs vibrate like a giant tuning fork as I struggle for air and edge down the sidewalk—

"Aaaak! Aaaak!" says Bernard, thrusting out his palm for spare change.

"Yeah, yeah," I say, digging for a quarter even though I just left my last penny inside the restaurant. Wouldn't you know it, I find two bits stuck in the folds of my pocket. Bernard looks impatient, like I'm using up too much of his time. "I swear, if I find out you've got a penthouse somewhere I'm getting all this back with interest," I tell him. Bernard zeroes in on me with those hawk eyes of his and I dig a little deeper. I want that optic nerve of his so bad I can almost taste it. "You're not lost, are you? You know how to get home?"

"Aaaak! Aaaak!"

"Okay, good." I drop the quarter into his hand and Bernard gives me a Nazi salute. Very nice. I hope the East German waitress doesn't see that through the window. She could get the wrong idea.

The Oldsmobile follows alongside us as we head down the sidewalk. I pretend not to notice but when we approach the intersection, the car flashes its headlights three times in some kind of signal. I turn quickly but before I can catch a sign or a shimmer or even a shadow, the driver jams on the gas and screeches off down the road.

As the car goes left, Bernard goes right and disappears down Columbus Avenue. The whole thing is a mystery. The car, the café, the quarter. Where does Bernard go with that quarter? Nothing costs a quarter these days. A dime stamp at the post office costs more than a quarter. Does he have a big bag full of quarters—*my* quarters—that he's going to redeem one of these days for some serious cash? What would a guy like Bernard *do* with serious cash? Hell, I'm the guy who needs cash, enough cash to buy an optic nerve and get back to twenty/twenty vision, instead of just twenty. That's what I've got. Twenty vision. Bernard's got perfect vision, plus all of my quarters. He's an enigma wrapped in a mystery wrapped in a coin purse. What the hell is his story, anyway?

In which Bernard is shown to be a complicated character of many sides and an even bigger knucklehead than previously imagined.

Interlude

Bernard walks along Pacific Avenue, then heads up Columbus as fast as his small feet and short legs will take him. He flips the quarter between his fingers, feeling the embossed image of George Washington on one side and the outstretched wings of an eagle on the other. Washington and the eagle are like two old friends you can always count on, Washington always facing left, his hairline receding, his nose strong and patrician; the eagle fierce-eyed and resolute, its talons sharp, its wings all-encompassing.

Bernard passes a florist's shop and stops to inspect his reflection in the window. He's wearing khaki pants, a floppy sweatshirt with a hood, and sneakers that squeak in the rain but somehow stay white no matter what soils them, a phenomenon he doesn't fully grasp. There's a lot Bernard doesn't fully grasp, such as what he's actually doing on Columbus Avenue, why he's staring into that window and how he even got into this country in the first place. He vaguely remembers boarding a freighter some years ago and sailing out of Hong Kong harbor for ports unknown. It was one of those big container ships with stacks and stacks of identical, hermetically sealed containers and precious few crewmen. Was Bernard one of those crewmen? Or maybe a ship's mate? Or, who knows, maybe even the captain? He doesn't remember. All he knows is that he had an old monocle he bought in a Kow Loon antique shop and a fresh change of clothes from one of those big department stores on Nathan Road. And the only reason he even knows that is because the monocle is still tied around his neck and he's been wearing those clothes ever since.

Bernard sees his reflection superimposed on a bromeliad inside the flower shop and he imagines himself swinging from vine to vine in a tropical jungle. He looks for all the world like Tarzan with a monocle. "Aaaak! Aaaak!" he calls to his reflection in the window.

"Aaaak! Aaaak!" the reflection calls back.

Bernard continues down the street and stops to see what's new at the optician's shop in the middle of the block. There's a sign in the window announcing a special on Veri-lux lenses, a chart showing the difference between reflective and non-reflective coatings, and a display of Calvin Klein frames. If there's one thing Bernard doesn't need it's glasses. Even the monocle is just for show, something to make him look like a distinguished nineteenth-century Prussian general or a bank teller from an old Western. He catches the attention of an optician inside, holds the monocle up to his eye and erupts in a burst of laughter far out of proportion to the comedic quotient of the situation, which is zero. The optician rolls his eyes and motions for Bernard to beat it. Bernard waves to him and slips into a crowd of tourists heading for North Beach.

Next on his rounds is Tosca, a neighborhood saloon and Hollywood hangout that Bernard frequents from time to time to soak up the ambiance. The top of Bernard's head and the bottom of the bar are exactly the same height, which allows him to move unseen and unimpeded through the darkened recesses of the room. Nobody seems to notice him or care that he's there, which is fine since Bernard doesn't have any idea that he's rubbing knees with Sean Penn, Sam Shepard, Nicolas Cage and other exiles from the studios down south. They're there to escape the public eye, but he likes the 1940s feel of the place and imagines himself as a handsome antihero from an old Chinese film noir. In the movie in his mind he saunters inside, lights a match with one hand and takes a deep drag on a mentholated Kool. A fan turns slowly in a corner of the room, barely pushing through the thick air while the silhouette of a dancer reflects against the wall like a Balinese shadow puppet in an opium den. A waitress walks by, her legs stretching to the sky like the limbs of a banyan tree, and Bernard tips the brim of his satin skull cap. She keeps moving, pretending not to notice, but she turns at the last moment and catches his eye. Bernard takes in everything with his sharp vision and engraves it into his memory: a guy slowly moving his hand inside the folds of a woman's kimono; a bored beauty leaning against a cushion and looking cool as mint leaves on a Shanghai afternoon; a bartender pouring mai-tais while keeping an eye on the beaded curtains for any sign of trouble. Bernard slides off his stool, disappears among the ankles and knees, then moves sharply along the bar. Someone turns up the music and Chinese opera blasts from the sound system, nearly peeling the mascara off the waitress's eyes. She begins to faint but Bernard catches her before she hits the floor and cradles her head in his arms. She blinks her lashes open and looks up in wonder at the handsome man with the monocle in his eye. Bernard flashes her a chop suey smile.

Bernard's movie fades to black and he heads next door to Specs, an old Beatnik hangout that invariably lures him inside. The joint is crammed with an array of South Pacific masks—a bunch of junk, really, the kind of stuff that has no value to collectors—but they remind Bernard of a childhood that has been otherwise erased from memory. Is he the son of a Sulawesi headhunter left by accident on the coast of the South China Sea? Is he the last of a long line of Mongolian tomb robbers abandoned along the ancient trade routes? Is he the descendant of a race of master wood carvers exiled to the barren deserts of central Asia? Kerouac once stared at these masks, and Ginsberg and Corso, too, but Bernard has never heard of any of them and would be unimpressed if he had. Bernard has no time for philosophical ruminations and even less for the spoken word since the only thing he can hear is an odd kind of cooing inside his own head. He salutes a Polynesian ancestral figure and backs out through the swinging doors.

Next up is Pearl's Jazz Club, yet another establishment from an earlier era. The place harkens back to the days of big band jazz and sometimes the music's so loud Bernard can feel the bass and drums being propelled right into his feet. The rhythms pulsate up his legs and make him want to move his body in ways he'd never imagined. Sometimes it's a hop, sometimes it's a swing, sometimes it's both at the same time, and it transports him to a primal moment from early childhood. He imagines his tiny fingers on a soft breast, his lips searching for a tender nipple, the taste of warm milk on a chill winter night, the feel of supple hands combing the little knot of hair from his forehead. Bernard does a funny little jig, then shakes it off and moves along up the street.

At the corner of Broadway is a place that has changed hands so often Bernard passes by just to see what's there today. It's been a bank, a restaurant, a bar, a dance club, a Burger King and an election headquarters, and that was just last week. He figures it's good—this constant change—as it keeps the blood circulating. And circulating is what it's all about for Bernard, circulating through the neighborhood, circulating through the bars, circulating through the endless nooks and crannies that only he can fit into as he tries to remember what exactly it is that he's looking for.

Bernard feels the quarter in his pocket again, warmer now as he rolls it over in his hand. His good friends Washington and the eagle come alive in his fingers, their flesh and blood pumping, their hearts beating, their heads craning leftward as if searching for something. Bernard passes a tobacco shop, a taqueria and a pizza joint, then picks up his pace past a newsstand, a Tunisian kababery and a video shop. He finally stops when he feels the warm glow of five hundred flashing light bulbs on his skin. It's a lightshow at the happy end of the rainbow—red, pink and orange—an incandescent wonderland that veritably calls to him, *come, Bernard, come right in, it's been a long time, come out of the fog and the cold, comecomecomecomecome.* The voices in his head combine into a celestial hum as the angels beckon him across the lobby. He's swept along in a heavenly trance until he locates a private booth where he slides his quarter into a slot and pushes the mechanism with all of his might. A curtain opens upon a velvet room draped with brocade pillows, satin sheets and silk scarves. There's someone lying on a bed—oh, God, it's her!—and Bernard can't take his eyes off the enchantress inside, not even for a second, as she struts past his window in spiked heels, studded collar and motorcycle cap. He feels his left hand reaching into his pants as he stares at the leather and lace, he feels taller now as she bends down in front of him, he feels taller and stronger and harder, and as she spreads her knees to expose the magic between her legs, Bernard's right arm begins rising as if it were spring loaded, it keeps rising and rising in a glorious salute to the swastikas tattooed on her inner thighs.

"Aaaak!" he cries out to anyone within hearing range of the Lusty Lady Strip Club.

Aaaak, indeed.

Chapter 7

The top of Telegraph Hill is a showplace of elegant mansions, tasteful hideaways and understated pied-à-terres. Thrown into the mix is my crumbling empire of six houses and a piece of land that would be worth more if the buildings simply blew away. It's strange to be living in a house that's worth minus money especially when next door, on the other side of an impenetrable wall, is the spectacular Waverly Wellington mansion. Waverly Wellington is a blue blood socialite, owner of an extraordinary Asian art collection, and entertainer to the stars. Gregory Peck flies in from L.A. a couple of times a year and stays with Waverly. So does Princess Lee Radziwell, who's the sister of Jackie Kennedy and apparently prefers the cool San Francisco summers to the Hyannis Port heat. Princess Lee Radziwell has more spare change in her purse than I have in my entire checking account, Gregory Peck makes more at a charity appearance than I will in a year, and Waverly, well, Waverly is so rich he's gone completely invisible, at least to me, although that might have more to do with the fact that I've gone blind in one eye than with

him procuring some magic potion for millionaires to avoid
their neighbors. Whatever the case, I haven't actually ever
seen Waverly Wellington—not in twenty-one years now—
or Gregory Peck or Lee Radziwell either, but their presence
hangs over me like a silk top hat on a tattered scarecrow.
That's because whenever they come to visit *I* get robbed.
Thieves must read the society pages because the moment
someone famous shows up, the neighborhood begins
crawling with guys named Ray in wraparound sunglasses.
Unfortunately the security around Waverly Wellington's
mansion is so daunting it discourages any would-be thieves
who, not to make a total waste of the day, knock off my
cottage instead, which has no security whatsoever.

Today is just such a day. I come home from an afternoon
of vicarious travel to find my door wide open and swinging
in the breeze. Shards of broken glass from the bottom
window pane crackle under my feet as I rush inside to see
what disaster awaits. What's left to steal? The stereo's long
gone, plus the TV, the stained glass lamp and the leather
notepad holder I gave to my dad for his ninetieth birthday,
then inherited when he died a few months later. Next door,
there are priceless Cambodian Buddhas, Tibetan thankas
and Burmese bronzes, and these jokers have to come in here
and rummage through my bedraggled personal effects? I
step inside and take a quick accounting of the room: bed,
lamp, suitcase, pillow, desk, box, chair. Strange, it's all
there. In fact, it's *more* than all there. That box, the one
sitting on my desk, I've never seen it before—

I walk over and gingerly inspect it. It's brown cardboard,
perfectly square, about sixteen inches on each side. The flap
is sealed with extra-strength fiber tape and there's a pink
plastic cord tied around the circumference. The surfaces are
completely bare except for a little smudge of dirt on one side.
The top flap has a red and blue label at the upper left corner,
neatly affixed and equidistant from the edges as though it

were applied professionally. This leads me to wonder: Do they have machines that apply labels to boxes? Or people who do it all day long so they can just eyeball it and make it look perfect? Or somebody so careful that he used a ruler to precisely center the label at exactly a predetermined width and length from the edges? None of which, of course, is even remotely relevant to the issue at hand, which is that there's a strange box sitting on my desk with a label that says:

DO NOT OPEN

Do not open? Are you kidding me? What's *that* supposed to mean? I quickly step away from the box and a host of worrisome images floods my brain: It's a bomb. It's a severed head. It's a fruit cake. It's Bernard. It's unprocessed uranium. It's the beating heart of an alien fetus. It's a vial of anthrax stashed inside a tube of mercury wedged inside a sheath of asbestos. It's my last nine film scripts from Bobby Littman. It's a hand basket.

I flee for the patio and watch from a safe distance to see what happens. Nothing happens. At least not yet. But something's *going* to happen, that's for sure, because nobody breaks into a house and leaves a box just to be cute. No, I'm getting out of here as fast as I can. I head up the path looking for a clue, even though I can't even imagine what a clue would look like. I hear a strange brushing sound, something like deerskin on brick, and look up to see Barbara at the head of the path walking around in a spiral of progressively smaller circles. I've seen her do this before, usually after a big rain or before a lunar eclipse. She'll walk like this until the circle gets so small she'll have to take baby steps and then she'll finally bump into herself and the exercise will be over. "Hey! Barbara!" I yell to her. "Have you seen anyone suspicious-looking around here in the last couple of hours?"

Barbara stops her perambulations, purses her lips, then glances high into a eucalyptus tree and thinks for a moment. There's something medieval about eucalyptus trees and Barbara seems to take comfort in the scraggly branches and porous bark. "Yes," she finally says. "A guy."

"What'd he look like?"

"Tall, I'd say six feet at least."

Okay, that eliminates Bernard... by a good three feet. Not that I ever really suspected Bernard but you can't be too careful, especially with a guy who may have Nazi tendencies. Nazis can't be trusted, that's one thing we've learned. You don't want to loan your car to a Nazi or give him the routing number to your bank account or offer him your time share on the Costa del Sol. My mother warned me when I went off to Europe: Don't date any Nazis.

"He had long hair. Thick and curly."

That eliminates Patrolman Kuiper. Kuiper's got a buzz cut you could file your nails on. Kuiper's got the kind of hair, you just run it through a tree mulcher and use it to fertilize a snail farm. Kuiper's got the kind of hair, you toss a match up there and just burn it off. Not that I really thought a cop would break into my cottage but with Kuiper who knows? The guy is nuts. But that could only mean—

"Now listen, Barbara, think hard about this. Was he real wiry, with long arms and maybe suction cups on the bottom of his feet?"

"Maybe yes, maybe no, maybe I don't really know—" she begins wailing, as if she's about to break into song.

The clock is running. We're at twenty seconds and counting. "Think, Barbara, think—"

"He had a long nose, long and thin." Let's see, six feet tall, long thick curly hair, long thin nose. Hey, wait a minute—

"Barbara, that's me!"

"You *said* suspicious-looking," she says, rocking with laughter. Okay, that was a good one. Barbara's got a pretty good sense of humor for an antediluvian hunter-gatherer. Maybe we could share a hot bowl of primordial soup one of these nights and do mastodon pantomimes. She finally catches her breath, then places her fingers over her forehead and rubs her third eye as if she were tuning in to especially sensitive psychic data: "Wait. There was someone else. A woman."

"A woman?"

"A woman with unusual hair. She might be a butterfly."

"*What?* Where was she?"

"Out on the steps. Earlier in the day."

I hurry for the gate. I look right. I look left. I look up. I look down. There isn't a butterfly in sight.

I walk the steps. Up Greenwich, down Montgomery, around the cul de sac beneath Julius Castle, past the art deco building where Hitchcock shot *Dark Passage*, over to Napier Lane where Philip Kaufman shot *Invasion of the Body Snatchers*, up Varennes where Peter Weir shot *Fearless*, then back along the Filbert Steps where none of them shot any of *my* screenplays, no, of course not, better to bring in some Hollywood hack than to commission a real life North Beach bohemian who could tell it like it really is.

I find myself in Jack Early Park, twenty square feet of iron and concrete that overlooks the Bay from atop a narrow staircase, and what better place to contemplate the enormity of recent events than in the smallest park in San Francisco? I find my mind slowly emptying out and the hundred conflicting thoughts that usually jockey for position are falling back into a slow simmering ratatouille of mindlessness. Who exactly was Jack Early and what's with this stupid park? It's more a sliver of grass than a park, a sliver of grass offering no amenities whatsoever except for a stool large enough for one person and enough leg room to almost, but not quite, stretch out. A plaque says that Jack Early was some guy from the neighborhood who took care of this little patch of dirt and when he died they called it a park and named it after him. Same thing with Grace Marchant and her much bigger parcel of land on the Filbert Steps. This is a neighborhood that respects gardeners, that's for sure. Gardeners and Beat poets. Two very solitary jobs, I might add, that extol beauty while keeping mostly out of sight, hiding from the sunlight.

I wonder if Jack Early knew Grace Marchant. I'll bet he did. And I'll bet he envied the enormous square footage she controlled while he was puttering around in his forgotten compost heap. Maybe the neighbors compared Early's Liechtenstein to Marchant's France and snickered behind his back. I suspect that Jack Early despised Grace Marchant with every fiber of his being, but he simply couldn't show it. Gardeners don't emote that way. They hold it in. Like fertilizer. They let their emotions churn and slowly burn a hole in their stomachs while secretly fantasizing about laying waste to that obscene fuchsia fanfaronade on the other side of the hill.

The point is, I may have to walk these streets forever. It's not safe to return home, that much I know, not with that box waiting there for me. Who would leave a box on my desk? The East German waitress? She was spotted outside my house but does that make any sense? What have I ever done to her except leave a lousy tip? Is that reason to kill a guy? To be fair there are other culprits afoot, all with their own twisted motivations to see me dead: ex-girlfriends, former neighbors, past writing partners—lunatics all—and any one of them could be responsible for the box. The question is, which of them would be foolish enough to return to the scene of the crime? I believe in that—that crazed criminal impulse for self-destruction—and I swing back around the Filbert Steps to a spot hidden in the rocks from which I can view the entire area.

Immediately I see Bernard lurking around the bushes, catlike and sneaky. At first I think it *is* a cat, but no cat could be that small so it must be Bernard. Then Barbara appears at the gate. She glances up and down the Steps, does some kind of secret hand signal to the trees, then disappears back into the eucalyptus grove. A moment later paint chips shower down from the walls of the Big House and I see That Guy, that fucking, fucking guy, slipping into the recesses of the third floor balcony. Next, I see Patrolman Kuiper walking his beat, even though his beat is half a mile away. He twirls his nightstick, smashes it violently against the gate to my house, then smashes it again for good measure. It appears as if everyone I know has returned to the scene of the crime, no big surprise since everyone I know is a potential criminal. Watching this group of odd- balls I realize that I need to start hanging out with a better class of misfit. Gregory Peck, perhaps. Or Princess Lee Radziwell. I hope they know that my door is always open.

I stay hidden in the rocks of Telegraph Hill until late afternoon, then do a 180 and return home after all. What else am I going to do, walk the streets forever? What happens when I get tired? Do I cozy up to Barbara in the bushes? No, it's better to meet my fate head on. I open the door and find that the box is still there on the far side of my desk, just in front of the phone and next to the lamp. It doesn't seem to have moved, which I take as a good sign since a moving box would connote consciousness or intent or motive. Therefore it seems altogether reasonable to assume that the box itself is not alive. It's not—like the farfalle in the shower—an alien life form come to suck out my breath and spit my shadow into the ether. Okay, I already feel a bit better. The box itself is unlikely to kill me.

What's *in* the box is really the issue. What I'd like to do is pick up the box and give it a good shake. That way I could figure out how much it weighs and see if it rattles or clangs. Unfortunately, shaking the box could trigger any number of cataclysmic events so I decide to smell the box instead. The box smells like, well, cardboard. At first this feels reassuring—better cardboard than nitroglycerine—but then I'm overcome with the image of colorless, odorless toxins and I quickly back away. Colorless, odorless toxins seem infinitely worse than colorful, odiferous toxins. They could be slowly releasing into the air like time-released arsenic and this duplicitous lack of olfactory sensation only makes the box seem that much more menacing. I feel myself unraveling. The toxins are getting to me. I'm at the end of the road. At an impasse. In desperate need of guidance.

If the box truly is deadly maybe I need to rethink my 180 by doing another 180, which, depending on your mathematical proclivities, is either a 360 or a zero. Then again, it may be that I'm overreacting to the situation since I am, admittedly, prone to the odd overstatement and embellishment. The fact is, maybe I've misconstrued this whole situation and should learn to love and embrace the box. Then again, maybe the box really has it in for me but hasn't decided when to unleash its evil, in which case there might still be time to get the box to change its mind. Maybe I can develop a relationship with the box and show it that I'm not such a bad guy after all. Maybe I owe the box an apology.

Okay, time to pull myself together. I've got a box sitting on my desk. It says *Do Not Open*. It smells of cardboard. Someone broke in and left it here. That someone could be almost anyone. I can't leave my cottage because I have nowhere else to go. I can't do any more 180s because I've used up all the angles. Oh, God, where are the Jains now that I *really* need them?

Chapter 8

"**D**er *Morgen kommmmmmmmmmmmt!*"
A hundred honeycombs dance across my forehead as I awaken to a piercing bellow that emanates from the bushes near my cottage. The sun rises slightly, sneaks a peek over the horizon, then retreats again, scared off by Barbara's impossibly high C's. I glance over at the desk and see that the box is still there, bothering no one and everyone at the same time. The box occupies the prime spot of real estate on the desktop, totally disrupting a surface which must be kept incredibly neat at all times. My desk must be incredibly neat because my brain is incredibly messy and I need to be able to look at something in the universe that makes sense. It's the same thing with my sink. I need to wash my dishes immediately after using them or face consequences too dire to consider. Having a neat desk and a tidy sink doesn't necessarily make me a better person but it would make my mother happy, so it can't hurt either. This obsessive neatness, Dr. Gold once told me, is symptomatic of synesthesia so I feel justified in my quirks except for the fact that I acquired synesthesia in recent months

whereas I've had a neat desk and spotless sink for as long as I can remember. It almost makes me wonder if my neatness might be the *cause* of the synesthesia, but that idea is too messy even to contemplate.

I head for the bathroom, where I toss some water on my face, brush the sleep out of my eyes, remind myself to buy some grout and immediately forget all about it. Before I can make my escape an urgent plea emanates from behind the mirror. "Wait!" calls out my dad. "Aren't you forgetting something?"

"What?"

"Have you seen my watch?"

"What watch?"

"The watch I gave you for your graduation. Your grandfather's watch."

"That old pocket watch?"

"It needs winding."

"Okay. Fine. I'll wind it."

"You won't forget?"

"Didn't I just wind it the other day?"

"That was eighteen years ago."

I pause a moment for comic effect. "And it's run down already?"

"It's a good watch. You should carry it."

"Yeah, chicks love it when you dig around in your front pocket looking for the time."

"Always with the jokes."

"You know me, Dad."

"I sure do, Son."

I get out of the bathroom before Dad goes into one of his long rants. I feel bad for him, trapped behind the mirror and all, but these little conversations of ours are rarely fulfilling. The fact is, he's got precious little to add to the dialogue and, if memory serves me right, our discussions weren't all that great when he was on *this* side of the mirror. What was he thinking, coming out here to spend his eternity? Of all the billions of possible destinations, did he really have to pick this dump?

A long time ago my father bought a little parcel of land in a cemetery big enough for four people. I never totally forgave him for assuming that neither of his sons would leave any offspring who might also want to be buried in the family plot. I mean, the guy was always tight with a dime but couldn't he at least spring for a little extra acreage just in case one of us had our own families? Nope, four plots, he insisted, and that was that. Dad was hardly the prescient type but in this case I guess he knew something. He knew that he'd have no grandchildren and that four plots in the cemetery would be sufficient. Maybe he already knew that I, the youngest son, was going to be the end of the line for our noble dynasty, leaving me and me alone to resolve our family destiny. Hence the predicament in which I now find myself.

My mother became the first to take up residence, a chilling event that I still haven't fully reconciled. I can still hear the sound of the dirt falling from my shovel onto her casket, that cold, hard Midwestern dirt that seems dead itself as it lies dormant in the interminable winter. When my dad moved into the plot right next to her and I heard the cold dirt from my shovel settling against his coffin, I started noticing a pattern. Then my brother took his space and there became little doubt who was meant for that last spot, a meager, ugly little piece of land in Milwaukee of all places, a piece of land overlooking, well, a cemetery! *This* is going to be my final resting place, this barren, windswept, miserable piece of acreage along the side of Blue Mound Road? Talk about a road to ruin! I spent my entire youth trying to get as far away from Milwaukee as possible and this is what they've got in mind for my eternity? Milwaukee? My nine years there *were* an eternity, wasn't that enough, how many dues do I have to pay, are they really going to bury me on the side of Blue Mound Road, where does Blue Mound Road even go, for God's sake—*Waterloo, that's where, Waterloo, Wisconsin!*—I've never been to Waterloo but if I ever do go there, it'll be the *real* Waterloo, the one in Belgium, not some little township in south-central Wisconsin, okay, so they want to bury me on the road to Waterloo in that godforsaken deep freeze of a winter overlooking the Miller Brewing Company, yeah, if you squint you can see a smokestack on the skyline where they roast hops and stink up the whole west side of town, this is just great, I'm going to smell of stale beer for an eternity, I'm going to be a frozen, drunken stiff on the road to Waterloo, this is what they've got planned for me, this is my grand destiny, this is the culmination of my family's unknown, sacred mission. Oh, God, what is life anyway but a withered pomegranate on the windswept dunes of a parched desert, a dried-up coconut on the sun-baked sands of a desolate beach, a trampled grape on the skeletal limbs of a decomposing vineyard. Is this really all there is?

The telephone rings, never a good sign this early in the morning since everyone I know sleeps until noon. Bad news, like a soprano's solo, always arrives in the morning so that it can ruin your entire day. I warily pick up the receiver to the unmistakable voice of Bobby Littman, agent to the stars. Bobby, of course, being Bobby, has to interject a little shred of false hope into the conversation. "I've got good news and bad news," he says. "Which do you want to hear first?"

"The good news."

"Just kidding. There is no good news. The bad news is that you can forget the Sacher Torte."

"What do you mean?"

"The trip to Vienna is off. The Producer Who Shall Remain Nameless decided to go there herself. She said she needed a break from Hollywood and figured she'd check out the museums and coffee houses herself."

"*What?*"

"Yeah, tough luck, kid. Anyway, don't let it get you down. This crap always happens in Hollywood. It's good in a way. It strengthens your intestines for when the *really* bad news comes."

"This isn't bad enough?"

"This is nothing. Thirty years I've been in this crazy town. Who knows anymore what's up and what's down? Half the time what's up *is* what's down. I just roll with the punches and let the cards fall where they may. Like when I got Peter Ustinov to play Alfred Hitchcock in his life story. Is that casting, or what?"

"Bobby, please, no stories right now."

"What's the matter, you've got an appointment or something?

"No, it's just... I never even saw that movie."

"Of course you never saw it. It never got made! Who's going to put up twenty million dollars to see Peter Ustinov play Alfred Hitchcock? The point is, we got paid and Peter didn't even have to get out of bed. Which is a good thing. Peter was so fat he *couldn't* get out of bed."

I wait for Bobby to have a good laugh at his own joke, then interject a moment of levity. "You didn't send me a box, did you?"

"A box? Why would I send you a box? Am I in the box business?"

"No, it's just that—"

"Now, listen, we need a story about the Spear. No more excuses. It's a good thing this trip got cancelled. What were you going to learn in Austria that you can't learn right where you are? Screw Vienna. Stick to what you know."

"That's the problem. I don't really know anything about

the Spear."

"Then find out, damn it. Do some legwork."

"Actually, I met this professor—"

"Good, good. Listen, I gotta go. You're not my only client, remember? Figure it out. Give me something big. Put something in the mail. Everybody's waiting."

I walk the streets, up-down, up-down, it doesn't matter if I turn right or left, if I go quickly or slowly, I'm just trying to clear my head, that's what I tell myself anyway, but this is a head that might be beyond clearing, it's a head that's been filled to overflowing and then tamped down and compressed like a recycled garbage bag. Okay, so the trip to Vienna is off. No fancy hotel room. No evenings strolling along the Danube. No Sacher Torte. Oh, God, how I wanted to indulge myself in Sacher Torte, with its double layer of rich dark chocolate, apricot filling and a delicate dollop of whipped cream on the side. To eat Sacher Torte in Vienna is to have arrived, and not just to a city but to a station in life, but I'm not going anywhere near Vienna, I'm going absolutely nowhere unless you count these all-too-familiar streets of San Francisco, these streets that bear the footprints of a destitute screenwriter searching for any idea at all that will salvage this project. I need to think but that's becoming more and more difficult these days, what with the crossed wires of my lower cortex and all those forms and figures loop-de-looping around my retina. Sometimes it seems like the simplest thoughts get rerouted through a maze and what comes out is a big spaghetti of confusion. And so I walk the streets, up-down, up-down, I look at doors and windows, gutters and streetlights, I look between the cracks of sidewalks and the limbs of trees, at sneakers strung over telephone wires and boots abandoned on the street, I search for an idea, a *big* idea, an idea that tips the

scales and breaks the bank, something powerful and gut-
wrenching, a war or a plague or an invasion, because the
fact is I never knew what I was going to write about in
Vienna, maybe that's why the trip fell through, the cosmos
was telling me not to put the cart before the horse, but
c'mon, let's get real, who am I fooling, I don't have those
kinds of ideas, I like little stuff, a man and a woman meet on
a bus, he's got amnesia and she's a compulsive liar, they
wind up in a beach bungalow where he pulls down the
shades and she turns on the radio, a foghorn echoes in the
distance, he takes her hand, she comes a little closer, he
can't remember what he's doing there, she tells him they're
married, a black and white shadow creeps across the wall, a
violin plays an eerie tune, two wallabies play badminton in
the kitchen while singing the Australian national anthem—

I walk up Pine, across Mason and down through the side
streets of Chinatown to Portsmouth Square. Clotheslines
crackle in the breeze. Shirts and pants and blouses and
skirts dance side by side, most of them weathered from too
much starch, their hems frayed, their creases worn and
irregular, their elbows and knees threadbare. Still they
dance, too old to generate much enthusiasm, too tired to
fight the wind. I keep on walking, past the Chinese Hospital,
across Columbus and down to the Transamerica Pyramid, I
keep on walking, aimless, directionless, I walk without
thinking, I let my feet decide where to go, yes, let the feet
decide, they've been around the block, let the feet choose
the path and let the feet pay the consequences, I'm tired of
being in charge, let some other body parts pull the weight
for once, today the feet, tomorrow the spleen, and off we go
on a circuitous route along the outer edge of the Financial
District and through Jackson Square, up past the architectural bookstore where I learned about Frank Lloyd Wright
and down some one-way street, I'm not even looking
anymore, I'm not paying attention, I'm just letting my feet

do the walking and that's when I come upon, irony of ironies, the Café Vienna. Wasn't I supposed to be on an airplane any day now headed for the *real* Café Vienna where a shy Austrian waitress would ask me if I liked my coffee *espresso oder melange?* No, this is the final straw, this is a conspiracy of unseen forces pulling my strings to see how far I can go before I snap, okay, fine, you want to see it, here it is, *zing-zing*, I'm snapping, I'm snapping right here on the street for all to see, my cranial fluids are bubbling and flowing out of my ears and down my cheeks, oh, yes, I'm snapping, a fruit fly buzzes by and gets caught in my oozing resins and fossilizes right before my eyes, I'm snapping all right, in a million years they'll sell me as a piece of amber in a Baltic second-hand shop, I'm snapping like it's going out of style, I'm snapping like there is no tomorrow, I'm snapping like a bebop poet in a bar that never closes.

I enter the Café Vienna ready to blow my lid. She's there again, the East German waitress, wiping down the counter with a faraway look in her eyes. What's she thinking about? A boyfriend she left behind in the old country? A mother's reprimand? A grandfather long deceased? She blinks a few times before realizing I'm even there. "Back so soon from Vienna?" she says with what I take as a little hint of sarcasm.

"Yeah, well, the trip to Vienna didn't pan out in the end."

"Hmm."

"What's that supposed to mean?"

She shrugs. "It is as I expected."

As she expected? What does she think I am, some kind of delusional nut walking around the streets? I've had four scripts optioned in Hollywood, for God's sake—

"Coffee?" she finally says, forcing the syllables from her lips.

"Large," I respond.

She fills a cup and places it on the counter. "One sixty-three."

Her monotone completely takes the wind out of my sails. What's the point of wasting a passionate rage on a cold, unfeeling automaton? I give her two dollars. She gives me thirty-seven cents change. I drop it into the tip jar. She says nothing. "You're welcome," I say, taking my seat beneath the painting of the Hofburg Palace, my world class snap cruelly nipped in the bud.

The painting is so realistic I can almost walk right into the big square outside the castle and sit among the statues of Austrian heroes. I imagine myself crossing over the Josefsplatz and the Michaelerplatz to the Imperial Apartments and the Spanish Riding School. From there it's an easy walk through the ornate, gilded halls to the Imperial Court Chapel and the Treasury Room. Inside the Schatzkammer I find what I'm looking for, the Emperor's Crown of the Holy Roman Empire, the bejeweled Orb and Scepter and there, in a heavily guarded glass case, the Spear of Longinus—

"To be honest, it's nice to see you again."

I'm pulled out of my reverie to see the waitress on the other side of the room filling a water jug with ice. It feels as if I've been away for ages. How long have I been sitting here like this? How long has it been since she spoke to me and gave up waiting for a response? It worries me sometimes how lost I can get in these stories, how I can walk right into a painting on the wall and enter a whole other universe, a dream world of spears and heroes and ancient empires. "Yes, it's nice to see you, too," I call over, hoping she won't think I've been ignoring her.

"I'm sorry," she says, glancing up. "Did you say something?" She looks completely distracted, as if she'd forgotten I was even there.

Here we go again, just like the other day. She says something, I respond, and she pretends not to know what I'm talking about. I decide to ignore the whole thing and return to the painting—

"I guess you're too busy to talk," she says.

I glance up again. "No, no, not at all."

She turns back to me with a strange look, a look I've never seen before. *Everyone is so busy these days.*

Now, maybe I'm crazy or maybe the light is weird or maybe a dust storm just blew through town, but she didn't seem to move her lips just then, not even a little. Maybe she's a ventriloquist. Sure, that makes sense, she's an East German ventriloquist working in an Austrian restaurant in the Italian section of San Francisco.

The waitress leans her arms on the counter top and brushes a hand through her hair. *Am I disturbing you?*

Okay, that time she definitely didn't move her lips but, c'mon, there's no way she's a ventriloquist—who the hell is a ventriloquist these days? Nobody! It's a lost art. There hasn't been a good ventriloquist since Señor Wences on the Ed Sullivan Show, and even *he* moved his lips. But if she didn't say anything, and she's not a ventriloquist, it can only mean—

Ah, finally.

—that she's reading my mind—

Yes... yes...

—and I'm reading hers—

Now, you're getting it.

—and we're communicating telepathically.

Wunderbar!

I turn and look into her jet black eyes. Okay, what's going on here? Is this some kind of practical joke?

I think I am much too practical to be a joker.

I see. So, unless I've finally lost my mind—a distinct possibility—you're telling me that I've established psychic contact with somebody who won't even give me the time of day?

Weird, isn't it?

Uh-huh. Sure. That makes sense. And what if I go over and talk to you at the counter, what if I demand that you talk to me? What if I make a scene?

Go right ahead.

I accept her challenge and make a bee-line for the counter. "You mean, like this?" I say in a loud, clear voice.

The East German waitress lurches a bit, as if surprised someone is there. "I'm sorry... like what?"

"You know exactly what I'm talking about."

Her sullen expression darkens as she narrows her eyes and fixes me with a stare. "Did you want a refill? Refills are seventy-five cents. You can only have one refill. Then it's full price again."

"Listen, I'm getting tired—"

"No, *you* listen. This is my job. I work here. If a customer asks a question I must give an answer. That's what the manager tells me. 'Try to be friendly,' she says, but she doesn't really mean it. Who cares if I'm nice? You won't order another coffee? You won't come in again? The world won't end, will it?"

"No, probably not," I say, backing off. I gather my things, then head quickly for the door. I catch the waitress' reflection in the window. She's standing at the counter. Folding some napkins. Staring at herself in the mirror.

What the hell is going on in this place?

Chapter 9

I return home from the Café Vienna, open the gate, step onto the pathway and get slapped across the forehead with a handful of mashed-up twigs and leaves. "Tonight's the night," says Barbara as she rubs eucalyptus balm on my forehead and invokes the tree spirits of the ninth circle. I figure it's either one of Barbara's homegrown headache remedies or an old trick from the medieval forest dwellers to get unsuspecting caretakers to take them to opening night of the opera. There's something especially ominous in her tone, even though there's pretty much always something ominous in Barbara's tone. It's the way she speaks, as if every little mumble were laden with layers of monumental importance. Some people are just like that. They bundle up their voices in wool and wear them like heavy winter coats.

Okay, so tonight's the night. I run through a list of possibilities through my increasingly woozy state of consciousness: Tonight's the night the box blows its lid and unleashes flying frogs from the sky. Tonight's the night That Guy smashes through my ceiling and slathers hot mustard all over my face. Tonight's the night Patrolman Kuiper storms the compound with a posse of mutant lawmen and strings me up from the pepper tree on the patio. Tonight's the night—

"Tonight's the night we've been waiting for. Tonight is Wagner's *Parsifal*."

"Wagner the actor?"

"Wagner the composer. *Parsifal* saved my life. He kissed my lips and offered me redemption."

"I really wish I could join you—"

"He opened my eyes and elevated my spirit."

"—it's just that I'm awfully busy tonight—"

"He filled my heart and expanded my consciousness."

"—what with this and that—"

"You must allow *Parsifal* into your life."

"—and the other—"

Barbara leans back and unleashes an operatic incantation which blasts through the clouds and knocks the radio transmissions out of the sky. Now, I like opera as much as the next guy—granted, not much of an endorsement—but my tastes run to the more pedestrian stuff like Puccini and Verdi, not the interminable epics of Wagner and Barbara. As she reaches deeper for an impossibly high C it feels like the whole of Telegraph Hill is cracking, first the bedrock, then the shoulders and ledges. The entire neighborhood is in danger of being leveled by a category five aria. "The children, Barbara," I entreat her, "think of the children."

"*Parsifal* will change everything," says Barbara as she transfixes me with a hypnotic stare.

I feel my resistance slipping. The eucalyptus balm leaves me feeling lightheaded and incapable of further battle. "Okay," I say, surrendering my dignity, my manhood and, worst of all, the rest of the evening.

"You won't be sorry," says Barbara, doing a couple of joyful steps from the nymph's dance to the autumnal equinox. She holds her fingers together in an isosceles triangle and does a quick twirl. "Let's hit it."

As Barbara and I head for the entrance of the Opera House I'm already sorry. The Civic Center is buzzing with excitement as a parade of limousines drops off the bejeweled elite of San Francisco society. I always feel uncomfortable in the presence of people who have actual lives, but Barbara's potion has left me in a kind of netherworld where I both want to flee and just curl up in some rich lady's handbag. It's strange. I barely remember putting on my thrift store suit... the drive over here is but an indistinct memory... and where did I get this tie?

Barbara is powdered up and nearly presentable in that layered look of hers that's all the rage these days. I suspect that Dior and Lagerfeld had something in mind other than untanned animal skins and untreated fur, but Barbara has always been a provocative dresser. She's accessorized her burlap dress and deerskin boots with an orange parachute wrap, a nice touch that freshens up her medieval look. Maybe that's all she needed, a little touch of modernism to fluff up whatever century she's in.

We join the promenade along the carpeted entryway trying to blend in as best as we can, then veer off toward the side of the building. "Say nothing," says Barbara as she leads me along a leafy path through the bushes. It's an unnecessary warning since I have no intention of saying anything to anyone in this crowd and, I suspect, the feeling is mutual. We come upon the stage entrance to the Opera House, where several women in flowing gowns and horned helmets are sharing a cigarette. A stagehand guarding the door mistakes Barbara for a medieval chorister and waves her right through. "Stage left in twenty minutes," he says, checking his scene sheet. Barbara pulls me alongside but my vintage 1940s film noir detective suit apparently isn't convincing as a tenth-century tenor. "And you are?" says the stagehand, stopping me with a firm hand.

"Understudy," says Barbara, zapping him with one of her patented eyeball shazaams. It's amazing what the hypnotic stare of an urban forest dweller can do. The stagehand motions us right through.

We move quickly along a brightly lit hallway that opens upon a confused maze of costume closets and scenery workshops, then take a shortcut through an empty dressing room. We maneuver around a mountain of lighting rigs and sound boards and find ourselves directly behind the proscenium. Barbara sneaks a peek through the curtain, then leads us down a couple of darkened hallways and through a doorway. Next thing I know we're sitting in a private box overlooking the orchestra pit.

"Are you kidding?" I whisper to her, looking around for the first usher who will give us the boot. "These are the best seats in the house."

"Nobody ever uses them," she says, cool as a pickled cucumber. "Just act like you belong."

I run my fingers over the plush velvet upholstery and notice a brass plaque that's discretely set into the armrest. "This is the Governor's box!"

"We're liberating it."

"What if he shows up?"

"He won't. He's touring China."

We take our seats, hoping to get lost in the shadows. "I hope this show is worth going to jail over."

"Oh, it is, it definitely is."

The stage is elaborately set with a rocky forest clearing, a painted lake in the background and a path leading off to a medieval castle. The path eventually gives way to a doorway which opens onto the great hall of Monsalvat Castle. I open the playbill to a synopsis of *Parsifal, Act I.* I figure if I've got to ruin a perfectly good night in this torture chamber, I might as well find out what all the hubbub is about. I turn a few pages and run through the action, if you can call it that. Good God, can these guys talk! They've got problems with their king, problems with their castle, problems with their crops, problems with their health, and as for medicine, well, medicine is whatever leaf you choose to rub on your wound, and that's how it starts as the lights come up on the stage.

King Amfortas has a wound that won't heal and Gurnemanz, an elderly knight, is praying for his recovery. I keep flipping back and forth between the synopsis and the events onstage as Amfortas is carried to a lake for his morning bath, screaming in pain. Now, me, if I'm screaming in pain from an open, oozing wound, there's no way I'm getting dipped into some rancid body of water, but this the tenth century we're talking about and gastroenterologists with advanced degrees in film criticism have yet to make it to the Spanish Pyrenees. But help is on the way, if you can call a crazy old hag named Kundry help. She wears snakeskin and goat carcasses and rides wildly into the forest on a demented horse, and what does she have, why, leaves, of course, special leaves she picked up in Arabia and pounded into a balm and now she leaps off the horse, flashes Amfortas a toothless smile, hands over the potion and falls fast asleep.

I turn to Barbara. She's fast asleep.

Gurnemanz tells us—in an ear-shattering basso profundo— the story of how Amfortas got his wound. The King was entrusted with protecting the most important icon in all Christendom, the Holy Grail, and he carried a magical weapon that wielded great power over the evil forces, a Spear that was never to leave his side. Evil lurked everywhere, especially in a castle down the road where a black magician named Klingsor plotted to gain the Grail. Klingsor had come up with a magic potion which allowed him to turn his decrepit castle into a fragrant garden and transform his old hag of a maid into a beautiful seductress. When Amfortas came to visit one day Klingsor called forth the young maiden, who not only seduced the King but got him to drop his Spear in the lush garden. Klingsor immediately swept in, grabbed the weapon, stabbed Amfortas in the chest and ran off with the Spear.

What the synopsis explains in a few paragraphs it takes Wagner two hours to stage. There are long interludes of shrieking and sobbing, not to mention prayers, incantations and a chorus of forty knights singing to the heavens.

The gravely injured Amfortas finally manages to escape from Klingsor's castle but has lost his Spear, a disastrous blunder for the Protector of the Grail. Now, only "a pure and innocent fool" can cure the King by recovering the Spear and touching it to his wound. And what is this Spear now in the hands of Klingsor? The Spear of Longinus, the Spear that stabbed Jesus on the cross.

I feel dizzy. The Opera House is full to capacity and the heat is rising into the tiny balcony where I'm trying to digest this most remarkable "coincidence." This opera to which I have been mysteriously dragged is a story about the Spear of Longinus? The Spear that resides in the Hofburg Museum in Vienna? The Spear that was recovered by Walter Horn under the castle of Nuremberg? The Spear I'm writing about? *My* Spear? I read the synopsis with more interest, glancing between the notes and the stage.

A holy swan is shot out of the sky and Gurnemanz's squires go to investigate. They drag a young idiot with a bow and arrow into the clearing. The brash youngster doesn't realize the sin he's committed, doesn't know where he is and doesn't even know his own name. Kundry, waking up from a long sleep, says he is Parsifal, the son of a dead knight, and Gurnemanz decides to take the young man to the castle, where an important ritual is about to be held. Along the way Parsifal notices that they are moving quickly without their feet even touching the ground. Gurnemanz tells him that in the magical realm of the castle, time becomes space. Parsifal

has no idea what he's talking about. Time? Space? Of what do
they speak?

In the castle, the knights are gathered for the unveiling of
the Holy Grail. It's a celebration that provides spiritual
sustenance to the knights, but the grief-stricken Amfortas
says that by losing the Spear to Klingsor he has sinned too
greatly to reveal the Grail. When his father insists that he
perform the magical ritual Amfortas finally uncovers the chal-
ice and the room is bathed in light. Parsifal, not even realizing
what the holy object is, picks up the Grail and brings it to his
chest as if it were a common cup. Gurnemanz can hardly
believe his eyes and boots the wandering fool out of the castle.

The lights come up to a standing ovation and we follow
the crowd out into the lobby for the intermission. It turns
out we're only halfway through Wagner's longest opera, five
full hours of pain and suffering. As we pass through the
crowd I hear mention of this mezzo-soprano and that
baritone, of this oboe and that clarinet, and my eyes glaze
over. When I eventually refocus on the lobby I discover that
Barbara has disappeared, poof, just like that, leaving neither
trace nor track. How I could manage to lose Barbara among
five hundred sophisticates dressed to the nines is completely
beyond me—I mean, Barbara is barely dressed to the ones—
and where exactly could she go during this brief intermission if not to some clearing in the bushes to freshen her
face, powder her mange and fuss with her deerskin?

I have a moment to collect my thoughts and I return
again to the fact that I'm presently in the San Francisco
Opera House immersed in an opera dealing with the Spear
of Longinus, a happenstance beyond chance, a coincidence
beyond belief, and it occurs to me that someone is pulling
my strings and everyone else's as well, that we're all players
in some big overblown opera in which no one knows his
role. A week ago I was coming to terms with my impending
mortality, now I'm on the trail of a story about a Spear I

never even heard about until my agent got hit over the head by a painting of a rabbi. Bobby Littman, as usual, is the source of all of my problems. Oh, God, why did he have to read that screenplay I sent him years ago? Couldn't he have just thrown it away like every other agent in Hollywood?

The lights dim in the lobby, a chime rings twice and everyone returns to their seats. Everyone but Barbara, that is, Barbara who has disappeared and left me high and dry and completely alone in the Governor's box, and the only question is how long it will be before the police burst in to arrest me. If only Patrolman Kuiper could see me now!

The curtain opens to reveal a dark castle and a tower where Klingsor, the black magician, sits in front of a magic mirror. Reflected in the glass is the image of Parsifal projected on the wall. He's wandering around the countryside and Klingsor realizes this is the "innocent fool" who could ruin his plans to finally capture the Holy Grail. He prepares his seductress to cast her web. And who is this seductress? Why, Kundry, of course, the witch who was sneaking around Amfortas and whom Klingsor has the ability to turn into a young, ravishing maiden.

When Parsifal shows up inside the castle Klingsor transforms his shabby patio into an enchanted garden and Kundry emerges as the beautiful flower maiden. She tries to seduce Parsifal but he resists her charms. Finally she plants a kiss on his lips, but Parsifal feels the sting of Amfortas' wound and cries out in pain. He pushes her away and Kundry flies into a rage. She tells him her own story, how a thousand years ago she laughed at Jesus on the cross and was cursed to spend an eternity being reborn as a miserable witch. The only thing that can lift this curse is the kiss of an innocent fool, which Parsifal alone can provide. But Parsifal has a vision of his true mission, which is to maintain his purity and return to Amfortas' castle as a Knight of the Holy Grail. Rejected again, Kundry screams out for help from her master. Klingsor rushes into the garden and flings the Spear at Parsifal. The Spear miraculously stops in midair over Parsifal's head, who makes the sign of the cross and watches as the castle crumbles and the garden withers around him.

The third act begins twenty years later outside Amfortas' castle. Gurnemanz is still alive, but barely. Kundry is still alive, but regretfully. Amfortas is still alive, but begrudgingly. His father has just died and is being buried by the knights on Good Friday.

The knights are nearly in open revolt. Amfortas no longer reveals the Grail to them and they're starving to death, both physically and spiritually. Parsifal, who's been wandering the forest all these years looking for the castle, finally shows up. Gurnemanz recognizes the Spear of Longinus that Parsifal is carrying, remembers him as the young man from years ago and realizes he is the innocent fool, after all. Amid singing, chanting and rejoicing, Gurnemanz declares him to be King of the Grail, Kundry washes his feet, Parsifal touches the Spear to Amfortas' wound... and Barbara rushes out onto the stage.

"Dienen... dienen!" she sings in a mellifluous soprano. "To serve... to serve!" She pushes the singer playing Kundry out of the way and begins drying Parsifal's feet with her hair. The cast exchanges confused glances, then recovers quickly and goes on as if nothing happened. The audience, half-numb from five hours of Wagner, doesn't appear to even notice that snakeskinned Kundry has been replaced by deerskinned Barbara, one hide-bound soprano apparently being pretty much interchangeable with another.

Parsifal heals Amfortas with the Spear, then unveils the Grail and rejuvenates the knights to their rightful duties as protectors of the realm. The Grail fills the castle with light as the knights kneel in prayer. The new Kundry collapses dead at Parsifal's feet, free at last from her curse. A white dove descends from the dome of the castle and hovers over Parsifal's head. The light shines bright. The curtains close.

The opera is over. Five hours of my life have disappeared. Babies have been born and people have died. The sun has set in the west and risen in the east. Three species of spiders have gone extinct. I depart the Governor's box in a daze beyond dazes. Barbara meets me outside the Opera House and we hail a cab. She's quiet on the way home and I'm all out of words. What, after all, is left to say? I'm living next door to a two-thousand-year-old woman who's been reincarnated as a Wagnerian soprano and I'm going to start asking questions? I don't think so. We're way past thirty seconds. We're so far past thirty seconds, it's not even funny.

Chapter 10

It's probably time to acknowledge what any discerning observer would have realized long ago: I am prone to the occasional exaggeration. I do this mostly for humorous effect, not to pad my résumé, so to speak. Most of what I write is true but not everything, since that would limit my exaggerations, and exaggerations with limitations are barely exaggerations at all. And so, in case anyone might take me a bit too seriously, I would like to correct any misapprehensions right now and state unequivocally that I do *not* live in a shoe. What I live in is a cold, dank cottage that is crumbling around my head and puckers on wet nights more than any ten shoes ever could. Also the woman who lives outside my cottage is most assuredly not two thousand years old, Bernard is not really smaller than a cat and my agent is not actually an eighteenth century vampire. The guy with the suction cups on his feet I'm not so sure about.

It rains, a howling, yowling squall of rain that exhorts the river beneath my cottage to rise up and flood my room. I flee for lower ground, not the advised course of action for such meteorological events but this is my cottage we're talking about, where up is down and down is downer. I find myself outside the North Beach Library although I have no memory whatsoever of planning such a journey. There must've been a reason my feet took me here, something preternatural, some mysterious force directing me to an unknown destiny. Why fight the forces? The forces are going to win in the end, everybody knows that. You fight the forces, you get clobbered.

The library is as good a place as any in the rain. It's dry, it's warm and they rarely throw you out for overstaying your welcome. The rain unfortunately also brings in the crazies, not the least of whom is Patrolman Keith Kuiper, who is drying out his billy club in the Crime & Punishment section. I give him the slip and head for Medical Sciences. This seems like a good opportunity to investigate Dr. Gold's diagnosis that I have a rare aberration of the brain. It's not that I don't trust Dr. Gold, but the fact is, I *don't* trust Dr. Gold, not for a second. I open a medical dictionary and discover that "synesthesia is a rare aberration of the brain."

Kuiper saunters by and eyes me from across the stacks. His uniform is more rumpled than usual—does he sleep in it? Does he even take off his gun at night?—and he just keeps staring at me, waiting for me to slip up. What am I going to do in here? Whisper too loud? Abuse the Dewey Decimal System? Cross aisles before looking both ways? The guy is nuts.

I do a 180 and slide over to the Mysteries but the only mystery is how long it will take Kuiper to find me and, sure enough, there he is, rubbing his hand on the wood handle of his revolver. Okay, fine, if that's the way you want it, the chase is on. We cat and mouse it through Cookbooks, Biographies and Religious Studies. Kuiper nearly nabs me in Psychology (hah!) but I pull a triple 180 and slide melliflu-ously into Classical Music. All the heavyweights are there, Beethoven, Mozart, Zappa, and up on top is a whole shelf for the Top Puncher of them all, the Muhammad Ali of the Scales, the King of the Ring, the Big Bopper of the Opera, Wilhelm Richard Wagner. The shelf is sagging from the heaviness of the collection, if not the music itself, and all his masterpieces are lined up in a row—*Tristan und Isolde, Die Meistersinger von Nürnberg, Das Rheingold, Parsifal*—and here comes Kuiper, billy club in hand, and I grab every reference book I can find on *Parsifal*—a grand total of two—and march right over to the reading table to further my knowledge of this most arcane of operas.

I finally understand why my feet brought me to the library. It's about time I embarked on an honest day's work or even a dishonest half-day's work or at least a couple minutes of something resembling work so that I can pretend to be moving forward on this project. I page through chapter after chapter, reading theories that Hitler, the evilest character of the twentieth century, is actually a reincarnation of Klingsor, the evilest character of the tenth century. Surely it can't just be a coincidence that a thousand years passed from the time of Jesus to the time of Parsifal and another thousand years passed from the time of Klingsor to the time of Hitler. And surely it can't be denied that the battle between good and evil keeps repeating itself over the centuries and that the Spear of Longinus is somehow always involved. Can anyone refute that Parsifal, Klingsor and Kundry are all reincarnations of their earlier selves, that Hitler died only hours before the passing of the Spear from the Nazis to the Allies, and that the location of the real Spear is argued to this day?

Kuiper watches me with squinty, nervous eyes, waiting breathlessly for me to bend back a cover or rip a page or shed a loose eyelash. I can outlast him, at least I think I can, as I try to make sense of the myriad of coincidences that have pulled me into the middle of this story that I myself seem to be writing. After all, that's what I'm doing, isn't it? Researching a screenplay that Bobby Littman shoved down my throat on nothing more than a whim? Who knows anymore? Kuiper finally tires of my lawful behavior and flees the library in search of someone with mismatched buttons or untied shoelaces or whatever else is on today's menu of misdemeanors and malfeasance. Why doesn't he arrest Bernard for conduct unbecoming a human? Or Barbara for impersonating a sorceress? Or That Guy for climbing without a permit?

It's too dangerous to go home and it's too dangerous to stay in the library. A box keeps me away from one table, the threat of arrest from another. I need a neutral corner, a table where I can think in peace and not worry about the consequences. Isn't there one place even, somewhere warm and friendly and just a little bit out of the way? Isn't there a place of refuge where I can rest my weary bones? A sanctuary from the building storm?

"Coffee?"

"Black."

"One sixty-three."

The East German waitress gives no indication whatsoever that she knows who I am. Does she remember me from yesterday or the day before? Does she realize that I almost left her a thousand-dollar tip for a cup of coffee? And how about those telepathic conversations? Did they even happen or were they just the latest in my series of brain malfunctions? I have no way of knowing, none at all, because she's an unemotional lump of molecules without an ounce of human feeling. Molecule Girl, that's what I'll call her. Day after day I come in here and always it's the same thing: I order, she pours, I sit, she stares, I leave, she cleans. I don't even know her name, yes, that's today's mission, I'll find out her name and let things unfold naturally. First comes her name, then her phone number, then her address, then our first walk in the park. It'll be a full moon and her cheeks will be flushed with excitement, our hands will touch, I'll turn to her and stare deeply into her eyes and then we'll kiss. But first, her name. I feel strong today, strong and focused, all I need is to secure a glance, yes, behold, Molecule Girl, you have met your match, I am Atom Smasher, the white knight of organic chemistry, no woman can resist my charms, I will excite your electrons and provoke your protons, indeed, it's all written in the Periodic Table of the Elements:

DESTITUTE WRITER + UNEMOTIONAL WAITRESS =
COSMOLOGICAL LOVE BOMB

It'll be history in the making. They'll name whole new galaxies after us. We'll circle the heavens unto eternity, an undying, never-ending, magnificent romance that will light up the sky. Giddy with confidence, I capture a beam of light from her eyes and ride it in like a surging wave—

"What's your name?" I inquire.

She stands there a long moment as if considering all the possible negative consequences of an honest reply. "Sabine," she finally shrugs.

"That's a nice name."

"It's French."

"That's what I thought."

"My sister, too, she has a French name."

"That's unusual, isn't it? To give German children French names?"

"I suppose."

"What was the reason?"

"No reason."

"Your parents just decided—"

"No reason."

She retreats to the counter and I think things over. Okay, that wasn't bad. We had a little conversation. I got her name. It's a start. At least I think it is.

I'm glad you came in today, says a muted voice from across the room. I look over to see Sabine on the far side of the café emptying some leftovers into the garbage. I'm not really certain if I understood what she said.

"Huh?" I say.

"Huh?" she responds, as if I were disturbing her from some very important work.

"What did you just say?"

"I just said 'huh.'"

"No, no, before that."

"I said nothing."

"No, you said you were glad I came in today."

Sabine raises an eyebrow almost imperceptibly. "I said no such thing."

Okay, we're back to the ventriloquism. Or the telepathy. Or, worse yet, some kind of disembodied voice in my head, an extraterrestrial free agent whose sole purpose is to mimic and mock me. The fact is, I've been feeling lightheaded and feverish and I should probably go straight to Dr. Gold to tell him about these spontaneous hallucinations—

Oh? Is that what you think it is?

Uh-oh.

Spontaneous hallucinations? That's a good one.

I know this isn't really happening. This is just some weird echo inside my brain, something to do with the synesthesia. After all, if I can see sound, why couldn't my thoughts echo back, but with her voice attached?

That's ridiculous.

Yeah, definitely, it's just an echo.

Is it? Don't you wish we could meet somewhere and talk things over? Like in the park? Under a full moon?

You heard that?

What were you planning to do in the park? Hold my hand? Kiss me? Pull me into the bushes?

No! I mean, I don't know, I didn't get that far.

You can't be trusted, can you? It's just as I suspected.

Sabine adjusts a ring on her finger and walks right past me to the door. The stone is an oversized piece of turquoise that hints of late night liaisons in the tropics, of high romance under the moonlight, of daiquiris and limes and bottomless glasses. It's all quite perfect—the ring, the pants and the blouse are all coordinated for maximum effect—but the beauty of it is in its understatement, to anyone else it might seem the height of modesty, none of those belly shirts for her, no stomach piercings or tattoos across the small of her back, in fact, the only tattoo she has is a small tasteful one on her arm and it's a monotone tattoo at that, nothing garish, just a simple black geometric pattern, Toltec perhaps, something totally obscure written in a lost language, it's probably operating instructions on how to get through to her for the next Toltec time traveler who happens upon the Café Vienna, but even then it's understated, yes, even her message to the Toltecs is subtle—Toltecs! Fucking flesh eaters! Blood drinkers! For *them* she's got time!—understated or not, she's not fooling me for one second, I know what's in her mind, she's setting me up, she's leading me on and orchestrating her plan, and what *is* that plan, why, to win me over, that's what, she wants this to be a romance for the ages, a romance they'll write about, it has to have obstacles and pitfalls and heartbreaks so that I'll appreciate it all the more when she finally gives in to me, but for now she has to play it cool, icy cool, so that she doesn't give away too much at once, yes, the message is there to read, it's all in those flared corduroy pants and black blouse and pink hair clip—

Sabine returns from outside, where she's put up the Happy Hour sign to induce wayward strangers into the unhappiest café in town. Oh yes, it's going to be a wild time from 4:00 P.M. to 5:00 P.M. at the good old Café Vienna.

Wine! Beer! Fun!

Do you like my shoes? comes a voice as Sabine passes my table. Hmm, was that her real voice or her telepathic voice? Hard to tell. I'd better play this carefully—

"They're nice," I say, the words tiptoeing out of my lips uncertainly.

Sabine turns slowly and eyes me with suspicion. "What are nice?"

"Your shoes."

She looks down as if to remember which pair she has on. "They're just shoes."

"Well, I think they're very special shoes."

"What do you mean, *special* shoes? Will they make me jump over the moon? Will they make me run like a gazelle? Will they make me dance like a ballerina? They're just shoes like everybody else has. Old brown shoes."

I'm encouraged by the conversation, which for the first time has included complete sentences with subjects, predicates and even several action verbs. I gingerly follow up with an innocent inquiry. "So, what do you do for fun?"

The light from the overhead skylight gets sucked straight into Sabine's eyes and the room gets darker—the ceiling, the walls, even the windows, everything is getting darker as if a thunderstorm just moved in from the Ruhr Valley and is about to knock out the power. Her eyes swallow the light and the air around her looks as if it's about to collapse on itself. "This is my fun," she says darkly, pointing to the containers of tuna fish, cucumbers and sprouts on the counter.

"What about music? Or movies? Don't you go to the movies?"

"I'm not interested."

"Lots of movies have been shot right in this neighborhood. All the way back to Hitchcock. Do you like Hitchcock?"

"Not really."

"How can you not like Hitchcock? Everybody likes Hitchcock."

"Not me." Sabine leans over the counter to a bank of switches and lowers the lights even further. Is this it? Happy Hour? A car alarm rings in the distance. A bus coughs up a black cloud of smoke. A kid skateboards down the sidewalk. Only fifty-five minutes left until things get back to normal.

"Maybe I'll have a glass of wine."

"You? Mr. Coffee?"

"Sure, why not?"

"Red or white?"

"You choose."

She shrugs her shoulders and brings over a glass. I take a sip of wine and sit back in my chair. It feels good. A nice pinot noir, a quiet café, a friendly waitress, yes indeed, it feels good to be alive. I take another sip and feel a slight rush of heat to my brain. It's strong, this wine, and very tasty. I feel my face flushing slightly and unbutton the top of my shirt. It's warm in here, maybe a bit too warm. I feel a bead of sweat forming on my forehead and take another sip of wine. It goes down easily, as if being sucked directly into my blood stream, and I can almost feel the corpuscles expanding as they latch onto my oxygen molecules. The fact is, I'm having some difficulty breathing. Actually, I can't seem to get any air at all. My lungs are vibrating like when I get too close to the farfalle in the shower but this is worse, this is really bad, the fact is, I really can't breathe at all, I'm gasping for air, I'm inhaling as hard as I can, and now it's getting bright in here, I mean it's *really* getting bright in here—did the waitress turn the lights back up? Is Happy Hour over already?—the lights are getting bigger and bigger until there's nothing else I can see, they're blinding me, oh, God, I'm fading, I'm fading right into the light, it's white and shiny and bright as hell—

⚬⚭⚬

I awaken to a bright light shining into my one good eye and leaving a comet-like glimmer in the other. It takes me a moment to realize where I am, a moment longer to realize what happened and no more than ten seconds to attempt a mad dash for the door. It's too late. Dr. Gold holds me down on his examination table as he pokes around my eyeball.

"I see sound," I say.

"You have synesthesia," he says.

"I see all kinds of colors," I say.

"Don't drink red wine," he says.

"I see strange geometric patterns," I say.

"Write action-adventure," he says.

Dr. Gold is wearing his usual tortoise shell glasses and lab coat. For him it's a day like any other. For me it's a total muddle. "How did I get here?" I ask him, trying to piece together today's events.

"Somebody dropped you off in a taxi."

"I was in a café... I couldn't breathe..."

"You went into anaphylactic shock. You're lucky to be alive. If it wasn't for that young woman—"

"Sabine? Is that who saved me? Is she here?"

"No, no, she left immediately. She was very concerned about the meter running."

"How did she know to come here?"

"She found my card in your wallet. Pretty quick thinking, if you ask me."

"Did she say anything?"

"She said to give you a message."

"Really? What?"

"Thirteen eighty-five."

I lean up on my elbows and try to clear my head. "What do we do now?"

"I could put you in the hospital and run a series of tests but I doubt we'd learn much. Your blackout could've been initiated by a blood clot or a stroke or hypertension. Worst case, maybe a brain tumor, but I doubt it. We could take an MRI and waste five thousand dollars, but of course you don't have five thousand dollars so why even bother discussing it?"

"Yeah, why bother?"

"Then again, I suppose we could check for sensitivities to allergens but that takes a long time, and, well—"

"Yeah, I know, I don't have a long time."

"Look, just try to relax. Get a good night's sleep. Stay away from red wine. It has sulfites. That's the biggest cause of anaphylactic shock. If you're allergic to sulfites, they'll shut your bronchia tight as a drum. Stick to white if you have to drink."

"So, I can just leave?"

"It's like I told you, it's a progressive illness. The wires keep crossing and short-circuiting. I don't know where it'll hit next. It's a degenerative condition. Go home. Take a hot bath. Put on some soothing music. Light a few candles. Make yourself a nice dinner. Just kick back and enjoy the warmth and security of your home."

"Um, do you have any idea where I live?"

"You know what I mean. You need to relax. Get things back to normal. See things for what they are."

I take Dr. Gold's advice seriously. He's not a bad guy even if he's just throwing darts at his medical charts, hoping he hits upon an answer. As I try to focus my one good eye I can't help but notice that there's an unusual bug crawling out of his ear. The bug has sixteen legs, four eyes and is carrying a very tiny travel bag. The thing maneuvers itself onto the arm of Dr. Gold's glasses, moves across the top of the lens and settles in on the bridge of his nose. The little critter digs into its bag, pulls out a bottle of suntan lotion and leans back with a copy of *Sports Illustrated* magazine. I feel better already. I take a couple of deep breaths and relax the muscles in my neck and shoulders, happy that things are indeed returning to normal. "Thanks, doc," I say, slowly getting up from his examination table. "You know where to send the bill."

"Yes," says Dr. Gold, glancing from me to the wastebasket and back to me again, "I most certainly do."

Chapter 11

Sometimes a cigar is just a cigar. I think Freud said that. And sometimes a cigar is a runaway freight train roaring through an alpine tunnel of love. I think I said that. After all, the romantic instinct isn't easily quashed, even if life itself is being snuffed away. What is life anyway but a big chemistry experiment in which every action has an equal and opposite reaction? In other words, who knows what's going to happen in this test tube of life, this Petri dish of love, this swirling, churning concoction I'm brewing up that just might explode at any instant? Yes, Molecule Girl, I'm back, it's me, Atom Smasher, I'm back with reinforcements, I've got a whole arsenal I'm ready to unleash—love bombs and valentine mines, hormones and pheromones, love potions and massage lotions—that's right, I'm rejuvenated and reinvigorated and ready to write the next act of our incredible saga.

Molecule Girl turns on her jet pack, zooms high over Washington Square Park and alights in the bell tower of Sts. Peter and Paul Church. She opens her hand basket and a small brown raccoon sticks its head out. "Are you ready?"

she says.

"Ready steady," says Brown Raccoon.

Atom Smasher arrives in the shadowy recesses of the campanile and launches himself a hundred feet across the airy chamber. He grabs onto a heavy steel cable, causing a clapper to vibrate against the bells and the sound waves to pound into the sides of the chamber. Just as the sound is about to explode all around her, Molecule Girl dives straight into the surge and begins riding the sound waves as if they were mere swells on a placid lake. Atom Smasher follows close behind and so does Brown Raccoon, who protects Molecule Girl's outer flank with daring zigs and zags. The bells begin tolling wildly as the sound waves bounce off the walls of the tower like laser particles—*zing-zing! zing-zing!*—they keep building as Brown Raccoon holds on for dear life, Molecule Girl fights the wind and Atom Smasher is thrown hither and yon.

Molecule Girl looks right. She looks left. She's trapped. Suddenly Brown Raccoon appears above her in the rafters. He's swinging on a rope with one single bell. "Ready?" yells Molecule Girl.

"Ready steady," cries Brown Raccoon. He grabs the rope and descends at lightning speed into the abyss of the chamber. The bell rings—*clang-clang! clang-clang!*—but it's not 440 cycles/second—it's 434, or maybe 448—it's dissonant, for God's sake, not consonant!

Father Indelicato appears at the top of the spire, shaking with laughter. Atom Smasher holds his ears and falls back against the base of the tower, his powers neutralized. Molecule Girl gives a thumbs-up and powers on her jet pack. Brown Raccoon returns her signal and jumps into the hand basket. With the church bells tolling wildly they fly off into the cool, clear, crepuscular sky.

I awaken on a park bench barely able to hear out of my left ear. I should probably be alarmed by this latest malady but I'm almost getting used to the degeneration of my body. After losing vision in my left eye I also lost depth perception until my brain found other ways of creating the illusion of distance. Now, it's like that with my hearing. I'm not entirely sure where sound is coming from but I can almost feel my brain adjusting to the new, declining circumstances. It's as if the whole left side of my body is going. My left arm feels a bit weak and my left leg, too, and half my memory might just as well be gone as well because I'm not really sure when things happened anymore, or *if* they happened. It's not just short term memory or long term memory, it's *half* memory. I can remember half of my mother, half of my father, half of my brother, I can remember half of the house I grew up in and half of my friends and half of my summer vacations.

Memory's a funny thing. My dad had an incredible memory. He could remember things that no one else could remember. I think that's what drove him crazy. He retained all-too-vivid memories of a bad childhood, of losing his mother, of having to support his family, of not having money to continue with school. It was all a big pile of regret that haunted him and kept him awake at night. He'd pace the house when everyone else was asleep and I'd hear the little cracks in the floorboards. They'd start beneath his bedroom, then move into the hallway, the living room and the kitchen. It was almost as if the house was coming alive with each step he took. What kind of a house cracks with every step? A haunted house, that's what, a house haunted by my father. Soon *I* couldn't sleep and I started thinking about my own memories. It wasn't long before both of us were up all night, thinking and pacing. I wondered if maybe the same thing was driving our thoughts. Something mystical. Something genetic.

Then something funny happened to my dad. He lost his memory. Right down to the dark gray roots. Oh, he remembered his name and he knew he was in Milwaukee and he remembered that he didn't like asparagus, but that was about it. His childhood had been wiped clean—his mother, his father, his poverty, his hunger—the whole thing was gone. And suddenly, at the age of eighty-eight, he got happy. No more pacing. No more thinking. No more regrets. Actually there wasn't much of anything left and I began to wonder what his life meant at this stage. If you wipe out someone's past, is there anything left at all? Isn't life the sum total of everything that has ever happened to us? If that's gone, what's left? Happiness?

I can't deal with this idea. It's not fair that my father should lose his memory and wind up happy. What kind of a message is he sending? That we can't be happy until we've forgotten everything that ever happened to us? How am I supposed to lead a sane and productive life with this as my model? The funny thing is, now that I've lost half of *my* memory, I actually do feel better. I lean back on the park bench, half-blind, half-deaf and half-happy. That's when Father Indelicato sits down next to me and ruins the whole thing—

"I hope the bells haven't been disturbing you," he says with a hint of sarcasm.

"By my calculations they're off by at least six cycles per second. That's well beyond any accepted definition of dissonance, don't you agree?"

"One man's dissonance is another man's celestial harmony."

"Yeah, and one man's lemonade is another man's chopped liver."

"You're Jewish, aren't you?"

"Lapsed. I don't attend services, I don't observe the high holidays and I hate gefilte fish."

"But you're funny."

"Yeah, I'm funny."

"Jesus was a Jew."

"You know what his problem was?"

"I don't believe Jesus had any problems."

"Sure he did. He wasn't funny. Nobody likes a Jew who isn't funny."

"You're not suggesting—"

"I'm just saying that if he'd mixed in a little comic relief with all the sermons, he wouldn't have pissed everyone off. A couple of one-liners could've saved him a lot of *tsuris.*"

"*Tsuris?*"

"It's Yiddish. It doesn't exactly translate."

Father Indelicato is quiet for a moment as he sits back against the bench. A Jack Russell Terrier yaps in the distance. A Chinese woman does Tai Chi. A tourist lines up a photo of the church. "How's your Spear research going?"

"Good. It's all coming together."

"It's interesting, a Jew—"

"—lapsed—"

"Yes, a lapsed Jew writing about such things. Maybe there is a deeper meaning."

"Oh?"

"Maybe you are searching for something to replace your lost faith. Maybe I have something to offer you."

"I could use a couple hundred bucks to see me through the month."

"The Catholic Church doesn't lend money. We offer something of much greater value. You complained of health issues when I last saw you. Tell me about them."

"You don't want to know."

"I do. Confess, my son."

"Well, it all started when I awoke one morning with blurred vision. Turns out I'd had an anterior ischemic optic neuropathy—a stroke, basically—that wiped out ninety percent of my left eye. A short time later I developed synesthesia, a kind of blending of the senses where simple sounds get translated into wild optical patterns in my brain. Then I started having these really strange dreams, not strange because they were so remarkable, but strange because they were so unremarkable, as if all the good stuff was being sucked out of my memory. Then came breathing problems, either because I live in a cold, dank cottage or because there's an alien presence growing in my shower, and that led to anaphylactic shock, caused either by stress or red wine, not to mention the onset of hallucinations that led to my imagining that I was communicating telepathically with a German waitress, which, of course, makes no sense whatsoever, all of which led my doctor to giving me five months to live even though he has no idea what's wrong with me, and that barely even touches on these visions I have of guys with suction cups on their feet and women dressed in burlap bags and cute little Nazis and cops with chips on their shoulders and hermetically sealed container ships and strange cardboard boxes that suddenly appear on my desk, but the funny thing is, the crazier it gets and the sicker I get and the closer I come to completely falling apart, there seems to be this odd benefit, this weird side effect where I somehow get the feeling that I'm actually getting smarter, that I'm on the verge of some great discovery, that the less I can see and hear and feel, the more I understand about this whole crazy world we're living in, why, it's almost as if I'm getting ready to put the pieces of the puzzle together and finally see what the big picture is all about."

"Very good, my son. I want you to say three Hail Marys and pray for forgiveness."

"When are you going to tune the bells?"

"The bells are in no need of tuning."

"Well, we have a problem, don't we?"

"Apparently so."

"Tune the goddamn bells, Father, or I'm filing a complaint."

"You wouldn't dare."

"What've I got to lose? Eternal salvation? I'm working on my own plan."

"That's blasphemy."

"Too bad," I say, gathering my coat. It's time to get out of here before things fly out of control. At which moment, a white swan falls out of the sky and lands in Father Indelicato's lap, dead. The priest leaps up, startled, then plucks a long plume from the soft underbelly of the swan's stomach, shoves it behind his ear and storms off. On the other side of the park I watch some kids scampering along the path with toy bows and arrows. A whole new generation readies itself to wreak havoc and cause mayhem. Stories repeat. Myths emerge. Screenplays unfold.

Parsifal Unleashed

Opera by

Richard Wagner

Screenplay Adapted by

Tobias Parker

FADE IN:

EXTERIOR. THE PLAINS OF MEDIEVAL EUROPE – DAY
An arrow zings across the screen. A thatched hut catches fire. A tool shed explodes. A group of horsemen rides full speed across the plains, the galloping hooves of their steeds kicking up a great cloud of dust. In the distance, silhouetted against a foreboding sky, a hulking black castle is perched high in the hills.

INTERIOR. CASTLE – DAY
Doors slam in the wind. Cooking pots gurgle and steam. A woman moans in the distance. Klingsor, a black magician dressed in the flowing robes of a sorcerer, gazes out from his turret. He's thin and wiry—as if he were half-ape and half-spider—and watches the horsemen with a sly, twisted smile.

KLINGSOR
At last! How long I have waited!
At last they come!

EXT. THE PLAINS – DAY
Amfortas, King of the Knights of the Holy Grail, leads the charge on a white horse that bears the insignia of the Holy Roman Empire. He's strong for an old man, with broad shoulders and a rosy complexion. In his hand is an ancient-looking Spear that glistens in the light. In his other hand is a flask from which he drinks. He calls out a battle cry to his troops in a thick German accent.

AMFORTAS
Drei Litre!

The horsemen spread out across the plains. They toast him with their own flasks, then charge the castle with their jousts and lances at the ready.

HORSEMEN
Drei Litre!

INT. CASTLE – DAY
Klingsor watches from his vantage point high above the plains, savoring the moment. He turns to Kundry, an old hag dressed in burlap and deerskin, her hair matted into a hideous mess of knots and gnarls.

KLINGSOR
Are you ready, old witch?

Kundry flashes him a toothless smile and unleashes a bellowing soprano that nearly cracks right through the walls.

KUNDRY
Der Morgen kommmmmmmmmmmmt!

EXT/INT. CASTLE – DAY
The horsemen burst through the door and gallop into a deserted courtyard. They ride from corner to corner, finding no one.

HORSEMEN
Where is he?

Amfortas looks around suspiciously, then calls out to the castle walls.

AMFORTAS
*Have you fled your evil
kingdom, Klingsor?*

High in the turret, Klingsor mixes a potion of oil and powder into a gooey mess. He whisks it in a jar until it takes on the texture of pancake batter, then crumbles in some special spices.

KLINGSOR
*A dash of taro root and
a pinch of cobra skin...*

He rubs the potion into his hands, then holds his fingers in the shape of a triangle over Kundry's head.

KLINGSOR
Mingle, spirits of the deep...
mingle, spirits of the trees...

Kundry's skin begins to transform. Her boils and moles are replaced by the creamy skin of a young maiden. Her teeth glisten, her eyes sparkle and her hair is swooped up like a perfectly balanced butterfly's nest that swirls around, then drops into a modified pony tail that brushes against her shoulders.

YOUNG KUNDRY
How's that for an old hag, my majestic sorcerer?
Too bad you've gone bald between the legs!

Klingsor glowers at her, then sprinkles some magic powder out the window and onto the courtyard.

KLINGSOR
Enough talk! Now, go to him!

EXT. COURTYARD – DAY
The cracked and untended courtyard transforms into an enchanted garden. A dozen seductresses enter from the wings and approach the horsemen.

HORSEMEN
What's this?

SEDUCTRESSES
Welcome to our garden, handsome strangers.
Let us pour some wine and greet the night.

Amfortas looks upon their arrival with suspicion.

AMFORTAS
Careful there, knights. There is evil afoot.

Young Kundry, the most beautiful maiden of them all, appears on a pathway amid the lush flowers and sidles up to Amfortas.

YOUNG KUNDRY
Come, Amfortas, ease your worries. Let me
unburden you of the weight of your armor.

AMFORTAS
How do you know my name?

YOUNG KUNDRY
Everyone knows the great
King of the Holy Grail.

AMFORTAS
Then surely you know that I am
never to relinquish my Spear.

Young Kundry runs her fingers through his hair and whispers into his ear.

YOUNG KUNDRY
Don't delay, Amfortas, the night hastens.
Who would you rather hold in your
arms, me or your weaponry?

She kisses his lips and Amfortas wavers for a moment. He drops the Spear to the ground and embraces the young maiden. The Spear clangs against the floor.

AMFORTAS
You are beautiful beyond words.

CLOSE-UP ON KLINGSOR
watching from above. He sees the Spear falling to the ground and clenches his fists in victory. He climbs down the walls, the suction cups on his feet making sickening fwopping sounds, as he races across the room and grabs the Spear.

KLINGSOR
At last! It is mine!

Amfortas looks upon Klingsor with horror and pushes Kundry away.

> AMFORTAS
> *Oh, God, what have I done?*

> KUNDRY
> *You're in for it now, Amfortas.*
> *Let's see how mighty you are*
> *without your precious weapon.*

Klingsor wields the Spear like his personal plaything and stabs Amfortas in the chest.

> KLINGSOR
> *Suffer, old fool!*

> AMFORTAS
> *I deserve to die!*

MUSIC SWELLS.

AERIAL SHOT –
The horsemen in full retreat. Amfortas slumped over his horse. The countryside burns.

EXT. FOREST – DAY
Trumpets announce the arrival of the King. Knights straggle into a clearing as the King's guard carries Amfortas into his castle. Gurnemanz, a scholarly knight wearing old-fashioned tortoise shell eyewear, delivers a medical report.

> GURNEMANZ
> *It is grave. Our king suffers*
> *a terrible wound.*

A young Squire nervously rubs his hand along the handle of his sword. He has a hot temper, an abrasive manner and wears a rumpled uniform that looks like he's slept in it all night.

> SQUIRE
> *Let me at the villain who has injured*
> *him. I will avenge Amfortas,*
> *you've got my word.*

GURNEMANZ
Hold your ire, young squire. Legend tells
us that no one but a pure and guileless
fool can do battle with Klingsor. And
only a touch from the Spear upon his
wound can cure our good King.

SQUIRE
What then in God's name
are we to do?

GURNEMANZ
We must wait. And pray.
And hope for a sign.

INT. AMFORTAS' CASTLE – DAY
The King is brought in on a stretcher. He's bleeding and half-delirious. He reaches out to Titurel, his father, with shaking hands.

AMFORTAS
Father! I have sinned!
Let me die here and now!

TITUREL
We are sworn to protect the
Holy Grail! This we shall do!

MUSIC SWELLS.

EXT. CLEARING IN THE FOREST – DAY
Parsifal, a young man with an open face and a carefree attitude, walks through the forest. He carries a bow and arrow, much like a writer might carry a pen and pad.

PARSIFAL
Oh, glorious day, open your heart
and give me sustenance.

A white swan hovers in the air, its beautiful wings flapping in the soft breeze.

PARSIFAL
What's this? So soon my prayer is answered?

Parsifal pulls back on the bow and lets the arrow fly.

EXT. FOREST – DAY

Gurnemanz and the Squire hear a commotion in the distance. The Squire hurries off to see what it is, then returns holding the dead swan. An arrow pierces its neck.

GURNEMANZ
What! Who has done such a thing?
What kind of man could be so cruel?

SQUIRE
What kind of fool would break the law of the land?
Does he not realize that the killing of a holy
dove is a crime of the highest order?

They hear someone whistling beyond the bushes. The whistling comes closer until Parsifal finally enters the clearing. He sees the swan lying on the ground.

PARSIFAL
Ah, there you are!

As he bends down to pick it up, Gurnemanz and the Squire grab him.

GURNEMANZ
What ho! Who goes there?

PARSIFAL
It is only I, a poor and simple wanderer.

SQUIRE
I shall arrest you for your
grievous misdeed!

PARSIFAL
But surely I have done nothing
but to slay this wild swan.

GURNEMANZ
And what, pray tell, did this swan
do to deserve such treatment?

PARSIFAL
I was hungry, that is all.

Gurnemanz picks up the swan and holds it for Parsifal to see.

GURNEMANZ
Look at what you have done.
You have destroyed one of
God's most noble creations.

Parsifal looks deeply into the face of the swan. A tear falls from his eye.

PARSIFAL
I did not understand.
It is truly a thing of beauty.

The Squire grabs Parsifal roughly by the scruff of his neck.

SQUIRE
And now you shall pay the price.

Gurnemanz pulls the Squire aside and talks to him outside of Parsifal's earshot.

GURNEMANZ
Wait. There is something about this boy.
SQUIRE
Yes, he is an absolute fool.

GURNEMANZ
But there is another quality
about him, a certain purity—

SQUIRE
Gurnemanz, surely you don't
suppose he could be the fool
for whom we wait—

> GURNEMANZ
> *I don't know. We must*
> *find out for sure.*

Gurnemanz turns to Parsifal.

> GURNEMANZ
> *Come, you are hungry. A feast*
> *at the castle awaits. Today is*
> *the day of great celebration.*

> PARSIFAL
> *A feast? For me? To celebrate*
> *my arrival? You really are too*
> *kind, dear sir.*

The Squire shakes his head with bewilderment.

> SQUIRE
> *An unbelievable fool...*

EXT. THE PLAINS – DAY
Gurnemanz, Parsifal and the Squire make their way for the castle in the distance.

CLOSE-UP ON PARSIFAL
noticing that the trees pass by quickly, and so too the road. He glances down to see that his feet are not touching the ground. It's as if time and space have disappeared.

MUSIC SWELLS.

EXT. CASTLE – DAY
An unruly patch of ivy covers the outer walls. The roof sags and the windows protrude at odd angles. Kundry stands near a tree, her hair as wild as a horse's mane. She prepares a balm over an open fire and sings in a high, piercing soprano.

> KUNDRY
> *Der Morgen kommmmmmmmmmmt!*

A stone pillar at the top of the castle cracks into pieces. A piece of tile falls to the ground. An urn is ripped asunder. Parsifal, Gurnemanz and the Squire approach Kundry. Parsifal, seemingly unafraid of her, pauses a moment.

PARSIFAL
Tell me, old woman, have I seen you before?

Kundry grabs his hand and laughs wildly.

KUNDRY
Many have seen me before.
Only you shall see me again.

Parsifal sees that Kundry has placed a mixture of twigs and weeds in his palm.

PARSIFAL
What is this, another gift for me?

Kundry seductively wraps her unruly mane above her head in a kind of butterfly's nest of hair.

KUNDRY
Give this balm to the King.
It will soothe his pain.

Parsifal takes the balm in his hand, unfazed by her words. He heads for the castle, carefree as a child.

PARSIFAL
Everyone is so kind in this fair land!

The Squire watches from a few feet away. He whispers into Gurnemanz's ear.

SQUIRE
Truly, an unbelievable fool...

GURNEMANZ
I fear it is so.

Chapter 12

I sit beneath the painting of the Hofburg Palace in the Café Vienna in a daze. This is not the usual daze brought on by my synesthesia or the daze of one of Barbara's potions or the daze of just living, no, this is the daze of writing, a magical state that allows me to escape time and space and float off into some alternate universe. I study the intricate detail of the painting and imagine myself in the courtyard of the Hofburg Palace. The sky is cobalt blue with just a wisp of a cloud moving in. It looks like winter, maybe November, an hour or two before sunset. I can almost see myself hurrying across the Heldenplatz, down the halls past the Treasury Room and into the Schatzkammer. The Spear is there, a solitary presence inside a heavy glass case. I move closer in, so close that my breath leaves little clouds of condensation on the window. The clouds expand with each exhalation until all I can see is the silhouette of the Spear fading into the background—

"So, you're back," says Sabine from behind the counter. She's wiping the dust off the leaves of the exotic plant that sits beneath the skylight and gazes at me out of the corner of her eye.

It takes me a second to process her words and a second longer to return to the present tense. The present is tense, all right, and the past imperfect. As for the future I barely dare venture a guess. "I owe you my life," I say with due gratitude.

"You owe me for the taxi."

"That was amazing, what you did."

"I had to close the café."

"Most people would've just called nine-one-one."

"It was Happy Hour."

"I'm feeling much better now. You'll be glad to know that the doctor said—"

"Fifteen minutes we were closed. Alena was not happy. She's the boss."

"Yes, well—"

She shrugs.

The incident from the other day obviously did nothing to ingratiate myself with Sabine. If anything it only added another layer of ice to our already extremely frosty relationship. Still, any conversation is better than nothing and I decide to seize the opportunity to melt the ice patch that stands between us. "You know, I was thinking about how I've been coming here for a while now and how you've been working here all that time and how I really don't know anything about you."

"What do you want to know?" she says after a long moment of silence. "My favorite color? It's black."

"Yes, I've noticed how you often wear black. It looks very good on you—"

Sabine narrows her eyes and continues on in her low monotone. "My favorite day of the week? Tuesday. Favorite month? November. Favorite time of day? Three-thirty. Favorite temperature? Twenty-seven. Favorite TV show? The weather. Favorite Olympic event? Hurdles. There. Now you know me."

"I just thought we could talk a little."

"I'm tired of talking. People come in all day and they want to talk. Why should they care what I think? *I* don't even care what I think. Whatever I think today, I'll think something else tomorrow, so what's the point? Last week I thought I liked the whole wheat bread. Today I can hardly look at it. Yesterday I liked cheddar cheese. Today I hate it. It all makes me tired."

"There's more to life than bread and cheese."

"Yes, there are sprouts."

"Take me for example, I'm a writer."

"So?"

"So I spend most of the day fantasizing, turning nothing into something."

"And I am a waitress. I spend my whole day turning something into nothing."

"Well, being here, I wouldn't exactly say that's nothing."

"You're not the one making sandwiches."

She leaves me speechless. Sabine has a way of taking a conversation and turning it into a court deposition in which every word can—and mostly like will—be used against you. Better to stick to my own confabulations, like that incipient manuscript beckoning me from the tabletop. There are ten pages so far, not bad considering that I had nothing at all just a day or two ago. Ten pages of a screenplay equals about ten minutes of film time and ten minutes of this film equals about ten million dollars, give or take an extra puff pastry for Bobby's breakfast. Bobby will be thrilled to find out that I'm setting the film in the plains of Spain, just as soon as I build up the courage to tell him that I'm adapting a Wagnerian opera into a big budget Hollywood action film. What's he going to tell me, that Hollywood wants *soap* operas? I already know that. Hell, I've got my own soap opera playing out right in front of me. It's called *Nothing Happens* and is set in the rapacious world of sprouts and cucumbers. Which leads me back to another ill-advised attempt at conversation—"So, do you remember that screenplay I was working on?" I call over to Sabine behind the counter.

"The one where you were supposedly going to Vienna until somebody pulled the plug?"

"Uh, yeah. Turns out the story for the film was right under my nose the whole time. It's amazing how things happen sometimes. Things just drop into your lap when you least expect them."

"Not for me. I expect nothing. I am rarely disappointed."

"You have to be open to it. Take this story. I'm adapting a Wagnerian opera to modern sensibilities as a medieval action-adventure."

"Hmm."

"I know it sounds crazy but it's like everybody in the neighborhood walked right off the pages of the opera and straight into my script. A woman who lives in the bushes... a panhandler on the street... a cop on the beat—they're all a perfect match! Why, even *you* are a character in my screenplay."

Sabine drops her sponge to the floor and glances up with a startled look. "Did you say—"

"Don't worry, it's a very positive portrayal. For a harlot, I mean."

Before Sabine can say anything—or throw a knife at me—a woman enters the cafe and heads for the counter. She's dressed in skin-tight lycra pants, four-inch heels, a feather boa and a shiny jacket that looks sewn right onto her body. She's dangerously top-heavy with what could only be augmented breasts, since nature simply doesn't allow for torpedo-shaped anniversary balloons to come shooting out of one's chest. I figure she's either a stripper from Broadway or the optician's new assistant, in which case half the neighborhood might need to get their eyes checked. "Can I help you?" says Sabine.

"I'll have a tuna fish sandwich to go," says Chesty Larue or whatever name it is she goes by.

"Everything on it?"

"Forget the sprouts."

"Happily. Name?"

"Helga."

"I'll call you when it's ready."

Helga takes a seat at a table just across from mine and waits patiently. I pretend to return to my script but what I'm really doing is trying to gauge Sabine's reaction to my bombshell. After all, not every woman gets told she's the model for a character in somebody's movie, even if she's just one in a cast of crazies that have emerged from the nooks and crannies of North Beach. That's something I still don't understand, how almost everyone I know has become the perfect personality upon which to base my characters. Barbara's not just like Kundry, she *is* Kundry. So, too, Walter Horn makes a perfect Amfortas, Dr. Gold steps right into Gurnemanz, Patrolman Kuiper doubles as the squire, and That Guy almost demands to be Klingsor. Like I said, it's as if a Hollywood casting director dropped the whole bunch of them in my lap. All that leaves is Parsifal, the one character who baffles me. I have no idea whatsoever who to cast as the fool. As for Sabine I figure she'll either be flattered or insulted by her caricature. Oh, yes, she'll either like the idea or hate it. Embrace it or reject it. Like they say in the lunch trade, wheat or white, mustard or mayo—

"You like her, don't you?" says Helga.

"Sorry," I say, glancing over at the woman at the next table. "Did you say something?"

"I see the way you look at her. She's very attractive."

"No, no, I'm just drinking my coffee—"

Helga sees right through me. I suppose that's one of the benefits of her line of work, the ability to peg a customer's

desires with the slightest glance. "Have you ever tried a compliment?" she says. "Women love compliments, you know."

"Believe me," I finally mutter, "I've tried."

"Maybe not hard enough. You have to massage the words
a little, loosen up the syllables."

"Some people can't take yes for an answer."

"Some people don't know that no means no."

Maybe Helga is onto something. Maybe she isn't. Maybe
she's both onto something, not onto something and onto
something unknowable. She should meet the Jains, who
could join her backstage and consider all the permutations
and hypotheticals until the strippers come home. Whatever
that means.

"Helga," Sabine calls out. "Sandwich is ready."

Helga gives me a suggestive wink and heads for the
counter. "What's the damage?" she asks Sabine.

"Six dollars, sixty-seven cents."

Helga drops a ten dollar bill on the counter and takes the
brown paper bag. "Keep the change," she says, staring into
Sabine's eyes for just a second too long. It's like she's
waiting for something or searching for something or expecting something to unfold.

Sabine looks uncomfortable under Helga's gaze. She adjusts the ring on her finger and almost imperceptibly
straightens her back. "Anything else?"

"Not just now," says Helga. She folds over the lip of the
paper bag three times, drops it into her purse, smiles
enigmatically at Sabine and saunters out of the restaurant.

Sabine watches as she disappears through the door, then
steps out from behind the counter and resumes wiping
down the plant. She turns the pot to balance its shape and it
occurs to me that everything about Sabine can be described
in terms of shape. The shape of her eyes. The shape of her
head. The shape of her hands. The shape of her shoes. The
shape of her pants. Oh, yes, especially her pants. Who ever

saw such a crazy shape? They're beyond shape. They're what happens when shape gets stretched into shapeless and then gets stretched some more. They're pants Charlie Chaplin might wear on a date at a skating rink. They're pants worthy of a compliment or two. "Hey, nice pants!" I call over to her.

Sabine glances up from the plant with a sponge in her hand. "They're just pants."

"No, they're very unusual. Something about the legs."

"The legs are square."

"Yes. That's it."

"And very short."

"Yes, square and short."

"I made them."

"By accident?"

"What do you mean?"

"No, just how they're so unusual. I thought maybe you didn't follow the pattern or something and they came out looking like that by accident."

"Do you think I'm an idiot?"

"No-no, not at all. Some of the greatest discoveries came out of accidents. Einstein, Copernicus, Newton, they were all screw-ups."

"I am not accident prone. And I am not a 'screw-up.'"

"I didn't say that. Of course you're not. You're elegant and graceful."

"And you're rude and distasteful."

"Hey, wait a minute—" I get up and head for the counter, trying to salvage my latest disaster of a conversation. Sabine will have nothing of it. She's already waiting for me next to the cash register as if I was nothing but the next faceless customer to come walking through the door.

"Coffee?" she asks.

"Large," I reply.

"One sixty-three."

INTERLUDE

In which the mystery of Sabine deepens, her family's destiny figures into the equation, we learn the color of numbers, Karl Marx gets the boot, and the wall comes tumbling down...

Interlude

Sabine awakens on a chill, foggy morning, a Wednesday morning to be precise, although precision is one of the qualities she'd just as soon weren't so large a part of her life. She'd rather awaken a bit blurry, at least once in a while, not quite sure what town she's in or what day it is or what she did last night. But imprecision or equivocation or any kind of soft-edged gray zone of uncertainty is not a part of Sabine's disposition. On the contrary she knows without looking that it is Wednesday, it is 7:30 A.M., and it is time to get up. She pulls back her duvet cover, folds it over twice and sits up in bed. It's a large bed, larger than she needs, and one side is completely unwrinkled. Sabine's a careful sleeper and is able to lie in one position for eight hours with barely a turn. It's another quality she's not particularly fond of, this precise sleep pattern, even though it allows her to make the bed with a simple pull of the sheets. She swings her legs over the side and her feet automatically slide into the well-worn slippers that are always there, always in the same spot, always pointing the same direction. Her hair is still up in a magnificent butterfly's nest of swoops and swirls and even a full night's sleep has barely moved a strand out of place. Sabine slips into a forest green kimono, ties a satin scarf around her waist and steps into the living room.

The living room is covered with a wild array of tropical plants occupying every imaginable space—spider plants hanging from the ceiling, aspidistra growing up along the walls, elephant ears potted along the floor, Buddha's hands draped along an end table, anthurium, calathea and fittonia winding down from shelves, heliconia bursting out of vases, protea and scarab ferns hanging from wall mounts, sago palms and umbrella plants folding out into a thick canopy— and Sabine blends right into the landscape, a veritable efflorescence wandering through her own private rainforest. She's comfortable here, more comfortable than can be imagined because it was in just such a room that she spent her childhood, a room of horticultural excess created by a mother desperate to escape the gray confines of East Germany. Her mother, Gudruna Westerburg, would have much preferred to wander the jungles of New Guinea or the savannas of Tanzania or the plains of Argentina than to be held a prisoner of circumstance in that dry, lifeless land. It's a desire Gudruna shared with *her* own mother and her mother's mother, too, this desire to roam without worry in a magical garden of endless plants and trees.

This shared love of the great outdoors—albeit trans- planted indoors—has led Sabine to wonder if part of her life might be outside her own choosing, if some kind of family destiny could be shaping her future and if some unseen hand might be awakening her each morning. She suspects that something in the blood or the spleen or the bone marrow might be driving all the women of her family, some preternatural design that manifests itself in unruffled sheets, green kimonos and well-worn slippers. After all, didn't her mother, too, have fluffy slippers and a loose robe and sheets that were crisp as the wind?

Sabine surveys the apartment, taking inventory of her assets to make sure nothing disappeared in the night. It's a task made easier by the fact that she knows exactly where everything is located, whether it be the spoons in her utensil drawer, the different colored threads in her sewing kit or where each blouse hangs in her closet. This compulsive orderliness stands in stark contrast to certain deficiencies in other areas, such as a complete inability to perform the most basic higher mathematical calculation. Sabine might therefore know the exact location of three sewing needles on her desk but she has no conception that they are forming a perfect isosceles triangle. She has a remarkable memory, yet confuses her left hand with her right. She has no sense of direction, yet managed to travel halfway around the world without once getting lost. She has no conception of time, yet understands the inevitability of every family's multigenerational destiny.

Sabine walks to the kitchen counter, where the flour jar, sugar container and spice tins remind her of her family's grocery store in the little town of Parchim, East Germany. She is inextricably transported back to a moment in her childhood when her mother is teaching her how to count. There are flash cards spread out next to the pickle barrel with all the numbers from one to ten. "Now, repeat them to me," says her mother.

"White, yellow, green, red..." says Sabine without hesitation.

"No!" says her mother with great alarm. "Look at them again!"

Sabine studies the cards a moment. "White... yellow... green... red..."

Her mother grabs the cards and pushes the big black numerals close to the child's face. "Are you blind? Anyone can see these numbers! They are blue, gray, pink, black! Now, tell me again."

"White, yellow, green, red!"

"You are an impossible child!"

There was good cause for alarm. Sabine's mother remembered the same argument she had with *her* mother and her mother's mother and so on back through the ages, for the Westerburg women shared an unusual quality, this ability to see numbers as colors, and it inevitably caused a stir. That's because they were in total disagreement as to what color those numbers actually *were*. It was an argument best left within the family since no one else saw anything but big black lines, but it caused increasing dissension between Sabine and her mother. Sabine's father, a gentle bear of a man, was of no help since he long ago assumed the role of family conciliator in his desperate attempt to keep a lid on things. He was more like a father confessor than a father, someone guaranteed to give solace but no solution to the problem at hand.

"Papa, what are these colors?" asks Sabine, flashing the cards his way.

He looks at the black numerals and smells trouble. "Um, what does your mother say?"

"She says blue, gray, pink, black."

"Then that is what they are."

"But Papa—"

"Go play! Be like the other children!"

Sabine learned to keep the colors to herself even though every day at school was like walking through a kaleidoscope. There were numbers everywhere—on the walls, on the blackboards, on the doors, on the pages of the books—but only she could see the rainbow of colors, and the colors made her happy. She felt sorry for her playmates who lived in a quotidian black and white world and couldn't begin to understand the vibrant patterns around them. At home, though, trouble—like the ever-present coffee pot—was brewing. "Every family has a battle to be fought through the ages to its final conclusion," Sabine says one day to her stunned mother. "I am the end of that battle."

"What are you talking about?"

"It ends with me. I will not have children. Soon I will move far away."

"You are seven!"

"You will see. I will find a place where there are all the colors of a rainbow. And they will be *my* colors."

By the time of her thirteenth birthday Sabine had finally had enough. Six long years had passed since she'd informed her mother of her plans and now the time had come. She dyed her hair green—or three, as she insisted to her mother—and they argued violently through the night. The next morning she ran away from home, moved into a squatter's house at the edge of town and began a new life. Leaving home was easier than she'd imagined and leaving school was easier still, her deficiencies in geometry blessedly irrelevant on the streets. The only thing she really missed were the sewing classes but they always ended too soon and the machines were usually broken anyway. But the squatter's house was only a way station. Soon she fled to Berlin, where she awaited the destiny she knew lay thousands of miles to the west.

The years blurred into a socialist gray that surrounded her until she awoke to the spring of 1989. Things were stirring all over Eastern Europe. Statues of Marx were falling in Warsaw, protesters were marching in the streets of Budapest and even the German Democratic Republic arose from its torpor. One night Sabine walked alongside the Berlin Wall and could almost hear it creaking under its own weight. Soldiers patrolled the streets, fumbling nervously with their rifles as shadows danced along the cobblestone streets. A waltz drifted out of someone's apartment and Sabine suddenly found herself surrounded by a half-dozen people. They danced in the moonlight—she right along with them—closer and closer to the Wall they came, so close she could see the imprint of a hundred tiny suction cups running up and over the concrete. An old man suddenly appeared in the shadows and beckoned her closer, and then something crazy happened. The Wall cracked open right before her—it was like an earthquake—and she knew that destiny was calling to her just as surely as the Wall had held her in. It was a destiny that told her she was special, that she was the end of the line, the culmination of countless generations of searching and questioning. Sabine slipped right through the Wall—she stepped from East to West and took the deepest breath of her life—and when she turned back it was as if nothing had happened. The Wall stood there stark and foreboding, its steel rods and barbed wire looming ominously as an insult against the sky, and absolutely nothing had changed at all, except that she was free. The Wall was behind her now. The dancers were gone. The old man was gone. She understood that it was time to leave the land of her forbearers and seek the mountains and oceans of the New World. It was as if she had to find an entirely new beginning in order to bring it all to an end.

Sabine sits at her tiny breakfast table and glances out at Telegraph Hill Robes, a strange little shop that's located just across the street. It's a funny business, these robes. People wear them at health spas in Napa, so there must be a need. But just robes? Couldn't they at least sell loufas and sandals and maybe even a bar of soap? No, it's a specialty shop. Like everything in America it's either very simple or very complex.

She pulls out a sketch pad and draws the figure of a tall, graceful woman. She sketches in a loose-fitting blouse, some layered shoes and a pair of strange-looking pants. The pants are tight at the waist, then drop down with one leg extremely wide and the other extremely narrow. "Who would wear such pants?" Sabine asks herself. The answer is easy. Nobody. She glances at the clock even though she knows what time it is. It's time to put away her dreams of spectacular clothing designs and make her way to the Café Vienna. It will be another day of boredom and little consequence, of that she is sure. There are things in this life guaranteed to disappoint.

Sabine passes the old Italian bakery that's always closed and wonders about this place, too. They sell nothing but focaccia when they are open but they are never open so one might ask if they sell anything at all. Is focaccia so popular that they sell out early in the morning before she even gets there? Or is it so unpopular they figure it's not even worth opening the doors? Sabine likes focaccia, although she's not so sure she'd open a bakery selling nothing but an obscure Italian flat bread that no one can spell.

She heads up Filbert Street to the top of Telegraph Hill, where a tiny green cottage has been boarded up for months. She glances through the cracks of a gate and notices a strange-looking woman who steps out of a grove of eucalyptus trees and seems to follow her every move. She's seen her before, this woman in the primitive clothes and deerskin boots, she's seen her in deep conversation with a whole host of chimerical characters. Farther up the Steps is Pioneer Park, a little swatch of land at the base of Coit Tower where Sabine sometimes watches the sunset and takes in the incredible view. On the other side of the hill is Grace Marchant Gardens, where the cottages harken back to the San Francisco of a hundred years ago. The eastern slope of Telegraph Hill is sheered away as if a giant jaw had taken a voracious bite out of its midsection and spat it out in disgust. That's exactly what happened a century earlier when giant earth movers relentlessly chipped away at its edges to create landfill for the Bay. At the base of the hill is

Levi Plaza, world headquarters of the giant clothing empire. Levi's carved a park out of the dirt and imported their own waterfall, a big rock edifice that strangely mocks the sheer escarpment of Telegraph Hill. This is the America Sabine will never understand, how in the midst of such natural beauty, a city can lose all sense of shape.

She turns up Pacific Avenue to Jackson Square, the old part of San Francisco. This was the original settlement, the Barbary Coast, and the dead voices of gold miners and merchant seamen and Chinese prostitutes still hang in the air. Now it's mostly design studios, architectural firms and antique shops, but they all have one thing in common, a profound love and devotion to the idea of shape. They fall on their knees before the altar of shape, they sing their praises to the glory of shape, they proclaim everlasting fealty to the temple of shape. In this uncertain world it's the one thing Sabine can understand as she enters the Café Vienna, where Alena is looking at her watch. "You are early," she says.

"Five minutes."

"Do you expect to leave early, too?"

"No, I will leave at six, like always."

"So the five minutes are free?"

"I suppose they are."

"Then will you take out the garbage? It is too big for me to lift."

"I can do it."

"You are strong for such a skinny girl."

"I'm not skinny."

"For a German."

"Yes. For a German."

Five minutes later Alena leaves. This is the time Sabine likes best, when she's alone. She racks the cups and glasses, grinds the coffee and gets the ingredients ready for lunch hour. There are tomatoes to be chopped, onions to be sliced and sprouts to be washed. Then the self-serve table needs straightening, the pitcher of water refreshed and the cream container and sugar dispenser topped off. Next comes a quick sweep of the floor and, if time permits, wiping down the leaves of the tropical plant that grows beneath the skylight and threatens to topple the big blue umbrella with its puffed up self-importance. The music is on, of course—there's always music at the Café Vienna—and it adds a bit of brightness to Sabine's day. The Austrians are a happy people—certainly happier than the Germans—and it comes out in their lighthearted and fanciful melodies. Everything in the café is geared toward happiness—the food, the beer, the music—and she knows she's lucky to have landed a job there.

Sabine takes her spot behind the counter. It's a small space, big enough for two people, but they squeeze in three on busy afternoons. Now there's plenty of room, especially when she moves the plastic buckets into their proper positions. She looks around the café and sees that it's empty. No customers. No Alena. No one to watch her or question her or make demands. She swings her arms, cautiously at first, then more vigorously. She feels light, so light she might just float away. She could float right through that skylight and just keep on going, free as a bird. After a moment, Sabine stops herself in embarrassment. A darkness falls over her. Something is missing from her life, that much she knows. There's a big gaping hole that runs right through her solar plexus, a hole so monumental, so all-consuming, so overwhelming, she can't even see it. Why is she in this city again? All she remembers is that she ran away from home many years ago because the numbers were all the wrong colors—

"Are you all right?" comes a voice out of the blue.

Sabine is startled to see Helga standing there. It's hard to tell if she's just ending a long night's work or beginning a hard day's night. "Yes-yes. I didn't see you come in. Can I help you?"

"The usual."

"Umm—"

"Tuna fish," says Helga as she taps her long fingernails against the side of the cash register. "No writer today?"

"What do you mean?"

Helga flashes Sabine a knowing smile. "I've seen him in here before. I've seen the way he looks at you."

"I have no idea what you are talking about."

Helga shrugs her shoulders and laughs. "Tell me, what is your name?"

Sabine barely conceals a frown. "I don't understand why everyone suddenly must know my name."

"I'm not everybody."

Sabine considers the woman standing across from her and mulls over her options. "The manager says... *ach*... my name is Sabine."

"You have a French name but a German accent."

"Yes, yes, the parents—"

Helga pulls a flyer out of her purse and hands it to Sabine. "We're having a meeting tonight. Maybe you'd like to come?"

Sabine glances at the paper, then hands it back. "I'm not interested in politics."

Helga slides it back to her across the counter. "Just think about it, okay?"

Sabine returns it more firmly. "No, really."

Helga pushes it back once more. "Maybe you can look at it later."

Sabine gives in and shoves the flyer under some napkins. "Wheat or white? Mayo or mustard?"

Helga takes a few napkins off the pile, winks at Sabine and dabs her lipstick. "Surprise me."

⚬⚭⚬

It's 4:00 P.M., the second of Sabine's favorite times of day, because that means it's Happy Hour and the place will be empty again. She's surprised that no one comes in for Happy Hour since beer is a dollar off and includes three complimentary pizza squares that she adorns with party toothpicks. But Happy Hour is as dead as a doornail—an expression she doesn't understand. Aren't all nails dead? And screws, too?—and the pizza squares are almost always thrown away.

One man comes in sometimes, that writer, a tall man with long curly hair and a long thin nose. He always orders coffee, always sits at the same table and always stares at the same painting. Sometimes Sabine thinks he actually disappears into the frame and just leaves his body there to keep the seat warm. She decides to make conversation before he gets lost in the wallpaper. "Coffee?"

"Large."

"Happy Happy Hour."

"Huh?"

"I said, 'Happy Happy Hour.'"

"Why twice?"

"You didn't hear me the first time."

"No, why do you say it twice? Isn't one Happy Hour enough?"

"One Happy Hour is more than enough. A few more Happy Hours, we will be out of business." Sabine is surprised by her little joke. She stifles a laugh.

"That's a good one," he says, flashing her a hopeful smile. Sabine gazes at the floor.

He goes back to his writing, or whatever it is he's doing, and Sabine returns to the counter. She hears a slight ringing in her ears, an irritating condition that has developed recently. Not that she's unused to strange phenomena emanating from her brain. Those colored numbers from her childhood never went away but it's been so long since she talked about it, it's almost as if it doesn't exist anymore. But there are other things, voices mostly, that are like radio broadcasts from another century. Especially when that writer comes in. It's as if his voice and her voice echo off the walls all of their own accord. She's not sure if she's the transmitter or the receiver.

Happy Hour ends, the pizza squares get thrown away, the dinner waitresses arrive, the writer leaves and Sabine retraces her route up and over Telegraph Hill. She never varies the route since this one has always worked and there's no good reason to change it. It's another facet of the precision she wishes she could alter, but it's in her blood, this precision of her mother and her grandmother, years and years of precision that, God willing, are finally about to come to an end.

She turns into Washington Square Park and sits on the same bench she always sits on whenever the weather allows. The park is full of unusual characters, any one of whom might break into song or dance as the whim arises. Today it's a violinist, an elderly lady who plays the sad, sad notes of a sad, sad instrument. Sabine knows these lugubrious tones all too well as she herself was forced into lessons by a teacher who decided that violin would be her instrument of choice. Choice in East Germany was a funny concept as it always seemed to be in the hands of someone else, but she was too shy to argue anyway, so what's the difference?

Sabine follows a path out of the park as church bells clang and a cable car tour bus slows down at the corner. It's a ridiculous idea, this cable car tour bus—is nothing real in this country?—and especially annoying since the driver insists on barking through a microphone even though only two passengers are aboard: "To your left is the famous Sts. Peter and Paul Cathedral, where North Beach native Joe DiMaggio married Marilyn Monroe."

Sabine heads up the stairs to her apartment. A letter is in

the mailbox. She glances at the stamp, opens the door and tosses it onto an end table. Three other letters are on the table, all unopened. They're from her mother. She puts on the kettle and ponders again how she ever came to San Francisco. One day she was in a little town in the northeast of Germany—a town where her ancestors lived for ten centuries, a town where the numbers were white, yellow, green and red—and then one day she was here, in search of a rainbow. She puts on her forest green kimono and satin scarf and settles into her magic garden. A butterfly flutters in from outside, makes a few dips and twirls, then alights on a wisp of Sabine's hair.

It's been another day, not especially good, but certainly not bad. Soon enough, it will all add up to something. This thought warms Sabine through the evening as she drinks her last cup of coffee and slips into her well-worn slippers. She pulls out her sketch pad and adds a few lines. Soon enough, it will all be revealed.

Chapter 13

Day and night blend into an ambiguous yellow haze. The sun sets, the moon rises and I'm not sure if I can even tell the difference anymore. The only constant is that box, the one sitting on my desk, and there it is, well-rested from another night of doing absolutely nothing. Doesn't it get bored just sitting there hour after hour? Doesn't it have any dreams or aspirations? Doesn't it ever get hungry or sick or lonely? C'mon, box, do something just to let me know you're there, cough a little or sigh sarcastically or shudder with annoyance, c'mon, give me a little something to work with, a little soft shoe, a few bars of Cole Porter, a Marx Brothers routine. The box responds to my pleas with nary a sniffle. Okay, tough guy, you just hang in there. But just remember who you're dealing with. I'm a guy you don't want to push too far. When I snap, the whole place gets shredded.

When I was seven years old I ordered a Captain Midnight decoder ring and waited the standard three weeks for delivery. Three weeks is an impossibly long time for a seven-year-old, which got me to wondering why it takes three weeks to deliver anything. I mean, they get the check, they put the ring in a box, they send the box and that's that. It should take one day, two at the most. Unless they are selling so many Captain Midnight decoder rings that hundreds of thousands of orders are piling up into a great mountain of paperwork that itself needs decoding. Or they are selling so *few* Captain Midnight decoder rings they make each one to order, which at two-and-a-half bucks a pop seems to be a very lousy business. Now, for a seven-year-old, three weeks is enough time for an entire universe to be born, expand, contract, blow up and regenerate itself into some whole new dimension. Three weeks is not three weeks, it's twenty-one mornings of staring at an artist's rendition of the ring that saved the world, it's twenty-one afternoons of rushing to the mailbox to be disappointed yet again, it's twenty-one sleepless nights of creaking floorboards, wondering if Dad is pacing the house waiting for *his* ring.

My dad was born in the Pale, an area that Russia, Ukraine and Poland set aside for Jews to develop their comedy routines. A "pale" is the bottom wedge of a fence post and taken together all those wedges became one very large fenced-in area beyond which Jews were not allowed to go. Those countries might have maintained their racial purity but I'll tell you one thing: It wasn't funny *beyond the pale*. Ever met a funny Ukrainian?

My dad's family went beyond the Pale when they left the little village of Boguslav when he was two years old. When I think of Boguslav I imagine potato fields and cabbage patches and sheds filled with rye. They were big on rye in the Pale. They had rye bread, rye cereal and rye whiskey. What they didn't realize is that rye can become infected with ergot, a particularly virulent mold spore that drives people crazy. I suspect that's what happened to my dad's family. They ate too much rye bread and went nuts. Why else would they have moved from Boguslav to Milwaukee?

They could've gone to Paris, for God's sake. Or St. Moritz. Or Gstaad. We could've been a family of ski bums! My dad had an unhealthy appetite for rye his entire life and was extremely unstable. I, on the other hand, avoid rye entirely and am one of the most well-adjusted people I know. Draw your own conclusions.

Cut to today. I say "cut to" because I still hold onto my dreams of becoming a successful screenwriter and using terms like "cut to" keeps me in the game. A week ago I made an appointment to see Dr. Gold. Today is that appointment. Do you know how much time elapsed? Not even a minute! I made the call, I blinked and now here I am. All of which goes to show, well, what exactly? That time is relative? That time simply appears to move faster as we get older? I don't think so. No, of all the things we can count on in this universe, time is not one of them. Contrary to popular opinion time is not a constant. The fact is, time doesn't just seem to move faster as you get older, it *does* move faster. Much faster. The older you get, the faster it moves. When time starts moving so fast that you can barely distinguish one thing from another, watch out. You're about to die.

"Time is moving so fast, I can barely distinguish one thing from another," I tell Dr. Gold. "I'm seeing things, hearing things and saying things that make no sense—"

"I've done more research into your condition," he says, "enough to make some preliminary findings. Come, look at this chart." I follow Dr. Gold to the other side of the room to one of his dreaded anatomical visual aids. He points to what appears to be a half-cooked cauliflower. "This is the limbic system," he says, "a sub-cortical ring of tissue that encircles the brainstem. It's the primitive part of the brain and handles your basic emotions." Then he points to a region several inches higher on the cauliflower stalk. "This is the neo-cortex, the center of analysis and reasoning. Now, what do you think would happen if certain functions of the more developed part of your brain were in fact being processed by the lower cortex?"

If Dr. Gold is trying to be subtle, he's failing miserably. I catch his drift, all right, and it's as understated as an eight-foot snowdrift blowing in off Lake Michigan. "Wait a minute," I say. "Are you saying that I'm incapable of higher reasoning?"

"I prefer to think of it as a tendency to exhibit irrational behavior."

"What's that supposed to mean?"

"Take your writing, for example. You persist in thumbing your nose at the box office while insisting on nuance and character. Doesn't that strike you as somewhat irrational when you can't even pay your doctor bills?"

Much as it hurts me to get with the program, I acknowledge to the doctor what I can barely admit to myself: "You'll be happy to know that I'm working on something a bit more mainstream at the moment."

"Oh? Are there explosions?"

"As many as I can account for in the tenth century. They were mostly into bows and arrows back then."

"Dipped in oil, I believe, and quite capable of causing quite an inferno," says Dr. Gold with an enthusiasm entirely unseemly for a practitioner of the healing arts. He comes more alive as he leads me to another chart and another cauliflower. "Now here we have the cranium of an adult male. It's fully hardened, a process that doesn't occur until the late teenage years. Before then the skull is malleable and allows the cranial fluids room to expand. There are theories that the hardening of the cranium corresponds to a rigidity of thought patterns, that as one gets older his capacity for creativity and originality becomes physically constrained." Dr. Gold guides my index finger to an area on my forehead corresponding to the third eye. It's strangely soft, as if my finger could slip right inside. "Right here," he says, "right above the eyes, is where the action is."

"This is exactly where I see all of those vibrant patterns whenever I hear a loud noise."

"Embrace them, that's my advice. Your synesthesia is telling you something. You need explosions. The bigger the better. Take the light show in your brain and put it up on the screen." Dr. Gold puts his arm around my shoulder and leads me to the door. "You don't have forever, you know."

"Yeah, I know," I say as our eyes meet in a rare moment of understanding.

"This is an area deep inside the brain we're discussing," he says. "The only way we'll ever understand the science behind it is a post-mortem examination. Would you be interested?"

"Would I get to die first?"

Dr. Gold smiles. I smile. It all fits the profile. After all, rumor has it that Dr. Gold runs a black market operation in body organs and has been seen carrying a shovel through the cemetery on dark, moonless nights. It's a good rumor, one I started spreading a couple months ago after I started seeing him.

I wave a tenuous goodbye and head down the hall. The moment the receptionist sees me she hurries for the bathroom, as if on cue. The phone rings. I pick it up. "Dr. Gold's office," I say in my most officious voice.

Some guy goes on and on about a minor congestion issue. I try to listen but find myself digging around in my front pocket instead. My grandfather's watch is in there. What the hell did my grandfather need this watch for? The thing never kept the right time anyway. Did they even have time back then? Who cared if you were five minutes late? No, time is not a constant, that much I know—

"*Let me ask you something,*" I say, taking on the sober, know-it-all demeanor of a general practitioner. "*You don't drink red wine, do you?*"

Time is nothing more than an artificial construct, something they came up with back in the middle ages to keep us from asking the real questions—

"Um-hmm, just as I suspected."

I think that's what I'm here for, why I was put on earth. To ask the *real* questions—

"You don't live in a cold, dank cottage, do you?"

It's Friday, which means I have to go to work today. It's not easy, this deviation from my well-oiled schedule, but every Friday morning I succumb to the harsh reality of my diminished economic state and don the tools of my trade. I slip into a pair of sneakers, some old jeans and a moth-eaten shirt, and commandeer an absurdly large key ring from my kitchen drawer. The keys are brass and nickel amalgams that were produced in some kind of reverse alchemy to be worth less than the raw metals from which they were made. What value, after all, could keys have when they grant entry to fourteen apartments in six houses whose aggregate value is less than zero? One might expect there to be fourteen keys to fourteen apartments but, in fact, there are thirty-four keys to fourteen apartments, given that some units have double locks, some triple locks and some no locks at all. Eleven of the keys don't match anything and serve only to create mismatches, redundancies and obfuscations. Every Friday morning I remind myself to remove the extra keys and every Friday afternoon I forget all about it.

There are places in the world where the size of your key ring is a sign of your wealth. It's at times like this that I wish I were a resident of Azerbaijan or Turkmenistan so that I could show off my key ring and revel in my great good fortune. The residents of these far-off lands must be a very trusting people. Couldn't you just buy a bunch of keys and pretend to be a man of means? That's what I would do. I'd have so many keys I'd need a donkey to carry them all. They'd make me Mayor. Or Governor. Or Locksmith General.

Behind my cottage is another cottage that even the raccoons won't enter. I have a ritual in which I toss the key ring into the air, let it land on the patio, then try whichever key points at the door. It's a ritual based upon an arcane belief that the cosmos wants me to succeed as a caretaker and will guide me in my efforts to do my job, but the fact is, the cosmos couldn't care less about my job and is only wasting more of my time by encouraging this ridiculous performance. I try the key in the lock. It doesn't work. I try another. I try a third. I swear at the key ring and kick the door. I try several more keys and realize how much easier this would be if I didn't have all those extras clogging things up. And how utterly inefficient it is that not a single key has a tag or tape or color code to indicate where it goes. Who could perform such a service? Aren't there professional key taggers or color coders out there somewhere? And shouldn't I, as caretaker, be able to hire such a person? I'm a writer, for God's sake, do I have time for this? I try all thirty-four keys and none of them work. I start again, more carefully this time, and somewhere around the fifty-third attempt I feel the sensual easing of the bolt, the click of the tumbler and the release of the latch. I open the door to a sweltering, shaking, deathtrap of a room, perform my famous one-eyed optic scan and slam the door before any air escapes.

Next I check on Bill Bailey's old cottage. Bill was a merchant seaman who lived in the front cottage for longer than anyone, including Bill, could remember. Bill's life could fill a book. In fact, it did fill a book that he wrote when he was well into his eighties. It's the story of how he fought with the Abraham Lincoln Brigade in the Spanish Civil War, was arrested for vandalizing a Nazi ship in the New York harbor and became a communist labor organizer on the San Francisco waterfront. Somehow this rough and tumble life created such a grizzled character that Hollywood came calling whenever they needed a tough old Irishman with a heart of gold. He played Bruce Dern's father in *On the Edge* and a security guard in *Guilty by Suspicion*. That bit of casting was an inside joke between him, Irwin Winkler and Robert De Niro. Imagine, Bill Bailey as a cop? He'd never seen anything but the business end of a billy club and had no idea how to stroke it, twirl it or God forbid, bash someone over the head with it. No, Bill was a stand-up guy and when he died a thousand people attended his funeral. I glance inside his little cubby hole of a cabin and whistle a few bars of *Won't You Come Home, Bill Bailey* just as I always do, then stop in embarrassment. The song, after all, is about another Bill Bailey but the fact of the matter is, I wish Bill were still here. I miss him.

I move on to the Big House and this is where the keys become a massive headache. There are four apartments on three floors and the keys simply don't match. I long ago made a secret pact with the Big House to check the apartments on a more relaxed basis in order to save wear and tear on all of us. I figure if I can't get into the apartments no one else can either, so why mess around? The only apartment I feel irrevocably committed to checking is the one on the top floor since I want to make sure that That Guy hasn't moved in with a hot dog stand. I move up the stairs judiciously. Homeless drunks can be very cantankerous in the morning and there's no need for me to surprise him, or him me. "Yoo-hoo, it's me," I call out. If my voice doesn't warn him, my twenty-eight attempts at opening the door surely do. Finally, I enter and am elated to find everything in order. There are no signs of fires, mustard stains or windows broken out. Maybe he's gone south for the winter.

A strange cracking sound interrupts my reverie. I take a closer look around the apartment and find nothing unusual, just a mop and bucket in the kitchen, a broken curtain rod in the bedroom, an empty toilet paper dispenser in the bathroom and a paint brush and roller in the living room, but then something draws my attention to the window sill and I notice some fingerprints in the dust, ten to be exact, and then I notice something even stranger, which is that the fingerprints appear to be *moving* slightly, and that doesn't seem right, no, the only way fingerprints would move is if they were attached to fingertips and that's when I realize that That Guy is hanging outside the window three stories above the ground. He's back! That Guy, that fucking, fucking guy, has come back to ruin my good thing up here! At that moment a wholly unnatural sound emanates from the deepest part of my chest cavity, a prehistoric sound that is part growl, part whoop and part snarl. I uncoil my body and leap like a marsupial in a mosh pit, landing at the window just in time to grab nothing but a handful of dust. Is he completely insane? Doesn't he remember what happened last time? Doesn't he remember Patrolmen Kuiper and his band of North Beach Irregulars chasing him through the streets? Doesn't he remember the police lights and the sirens and the drawn guns? Does he really think that my refusing to press charges is an open invitation to come back? What am I running here, a bed and breakfast for halfwits?

The guy shimmies down the outer wall and disappears around the corner into a maze of pipes and moldings. I fly down the stairs and out onto the Filbert Steps only to see a few branches shaking in the breeze and eliciting the faintest smell of spicy mustard and pickled relish. I follow in a rage, hoping both to find him and not to find him since I have no idea whatsoever what I'd do if I actually trapped this most nimble of lunatics in a corner or at the end of some alley. What would I do, coax him out with a sharp stick? It's not really my style. Then again maybe I could try being a bit more civilized, sure, I could bring him something, maybe a peace offering, I could gain his trust and then talk sense to him and explain why roasting hot dogs in a fire trap dwelling is considered, well, as the French would say, *jejune*, yes, he's sure to respond to a more sophisticated appeal, I could bring him something to eat, maybe a banana and a grain of salt or whatever it is that appeals to the palate of a half-ape, half-spider, no, wait a minute, I am *not* bringing him any culinary delicacies, he really *will* think it's a bed and breakfast and he'll start demanding clean sheets, okay, that leaves only one option, the police, yes, I'll call the police and tell them he's back, the guy they chased all over North Beach with the mustard jar is back and this time I'll press charges, oh yes, I'll press charges all right, I'll press charges like they were going out of style, it'll be like a reverse fire sale, double everything, five will get you ten, that sounds about right, ten years in San Quentin, the *real* Big House, let's see what they think of your hot dogs over there, asshole!

I'm about to dial nine-one-one when I do a 180 and hang up: What if Patrolman Kuiper shows up? *Of course,* Kuiper would show up. Kuiper goes to bed every night just dreaming of coming up here. I can see him now, he'd be in battle fatigues, grenades strapped around his waist, an M-16 in his hand, a twelve-inch knife between his teeth, yeah, Kuiper would come up here blasting, all right, and we all know exactly who he'd be looking for. The guy is nuts.

The whole thing gives me pause, pause enough for the intruder to get away, which seems like the proper strategy, yes, I'll chase him just fast enough not to catch him, and that's what I do, I half-run and half-walk after the half-ape and half-spider until I reach the bottom of the Filbert Steps, where I am blinded by two bright headlights that are flashing on and off in the distance. It takes a moment for my eyes to adjust, a moment longer to reestablish depth perception and another moment still to notice that a large Oldsmobile with darkened windows is idling at the corner.

I've seen that Oldsmobile before, outside the Café Vienna, and wonder what it's doing over here. "Mr. Horn?" I call out from across the street. "Is that you?"

The Oldsmobile lurches into gear and pulls out onto the street. I follow after it for a few steps, trying to get a look inside. When I get too close it pulls forward a few feet, then slows down until I approach again. Each time I near the trunk the car edges forward and we keep moving like this down the street, as if engaged in a cross-species game of tag. Finally, either out of sheer boredom or a realization that we must look pretty stupid to anyone watching from the sidewalk, the wheels spin wildly, kick up some rocks and screech away. I watch as the Oldsmobile disappears down the road.

It doesn't take a genius of deductive reasoning to realize that the appearance and disappearance of That Guy coincides quite remarkably with the appearance and disappearance of the Oldsmobile and it is therefore altogether reasonable to postulate that they could have disappeared together, in which case this supposedly homeless firebug either owns or has access to a very spiffy set of wheels, much spiffier than mine, and this very same firebug also appears to have a connection of some sort to Walter Horn, the cranky professor who may or may not be the owner of the Oldsmobile in question and that, as far as bedfellows go, is about as strange as they come, I mean, what could these two misanthropes have to talk about—the history of abandoned buildings? The metallurgy of pre-and-post-war house keys? The etymology of the hot dog and its impact on Euro-American cross-cultural relations?—c'mon, I could barely get a word in edgewise with the old coot, what's this half-wit wall climber got to offer, unless, that is, they're not friends at all, in which case the Oldsmobile might not belong to Walter Horn but to a neighbor or a cohort or maybe even one of those crazed occultists he was so suspicious of, but what kind of an occultist drives an Oldsmobile, occultists drive Volvos, everybody knows that, four-door Volvos with crash resistant trunks that fit thirteen months worth of black candles, chicken feathers and enough goat blood to quench the most devilish of thirsts, no, the Oldsmobile is a mystery, that's for sure, unless these are patriotic occultists, the buy-American kind, oh, great, right-wing occultists, the scariest of them all, they're probably connected with Nancy Reagan, that's all I need, Nancy Reagan and her coterie of crazed astrologers camped out outside my cottage, I always thought there was something suspicious about those old-lady bags and white gloves of hers, no, wait, I may be jumping the gun here, I have no evidence whatsoever that Nancy Reagan is involved with the homeless firebug next door, even though, when you think about, it has a certain kind of crazy logic, no, I'm just going to file this under suspicious behavior, the kind that seems to be surrounding me on all sides, but I'll tell you one thing, if I ever *do* find Nancy Reagan prowling around up here, I'm giving her the old heave-ho, right then and there, white gloves or not.

Chapter 14

The Green Street Mortuary Marching Band plays a somber fugue as it moves slowly across Columbus Avenue and up Stockton. Seven trombonists, trumpeters and drummers in matching navy blue uniforms march by in a wobbly progression, their brass buttons, silver epaulets and gold braids sucking in the light and providing gloom to what had been a perfectly sunny day. Behind the band the son of the dearly departed carries an enlarged photo of a handsome man wearing a black suit from the 1940s and an overstarched white shirt. The frame is wrapped in garlands of flowers, Buddhist prayer candles and flags from the Republic of Taiwan. Then come family members, friends and well-wishers, all dressed in formal attire, and a few stragglers who might be part of the procession or perhaps just got caught up in the moment or maybe simply love a good parade.

"Aaaak! Aaaak!" comes a cry from behind the casket and for a moment I think that Bernard might be trapped inside. The thought of Bernard being buried alive is simply too awful to contemplate and I take a couple of quick steps toward the procession before realizing that not only is Bernard not in the casket, he's not even aware there's a funeral going on. Bernard, in fact, is somewhere *under* the casket trying to squeeze his way through the mass of mourners in his desperate attempt to rendezvous with my pocketful of spare change. Sometimes I find it quite embarrassing to count Bernard among my friends. "Aaaak! Aaaak!" he beseeches over the trombones as he finally breaks free of the procession and rushes over with his hand out for a handout.

"Bernard! Shut up!" I whisper urgently, not that it matters whether I whisper or scream since Bernard can't hear me anyway, but I'm hoping he can at least read my lips with those perfect eyes of his. "Listen, how about you sell me your left optic nerve for a quarter?" I say, reaching into my pocket.

"Aaaak! Aaaak!" he says, which certainly sounds like a yes to me.

"We'll just go over to my doctor's office, do a quick transplant and be out on the streets before dinner."

"Aaaak! Aaaak!" he says, pointing to my pocket with growing impatience.

"Yeah, okay, relax." I pull out a handful of change and give him two dimes and a nickel.

Bernard examines the coins and nearly flips out. "Aaaak! Aaaak!"

"What's the matter? Dimes and nickels aren't good enough?"

"Aaaak! Aaaak!"

"Bernard, I don't *have* any quarters. This is the same thing."

"Aaaak! Aaaak!"

"Now, listen, two dimes and a nickel... a quarter... they're *both* twenty-five cents."

Bernard looks at his hand, stares into my one good eye

and shudders with rage. And then he throws the coins at my feet and storms off.

"Screw you, Bernard. You hear me?" I yell after him.

Bernard doesn't look back. He disappears into the funeral procession as the band continues its dirge. The guy can be a real dick, that's for sure. No apologies, no Nazi salute, no nothing. Just try to get another quarter from me, Bernard, just try it.

I never really thought of myself as a primitive, but Dr. Gold has opened up all sorts of new possibilities and it's something I could easily get used to. After all, my living conditions are already primitive so the adjustment shouldn't be much of a stretch. Maybe it's no coincidence that I'm surrounded by people like Barbara, Bernard and That Guy. One is a direct link to prehistory, one never evolved and one is half-ape and half-spider. Maybe they just naturally gravitated to me, sensing a psychic kinship. And then there's Sabine. There's something raw and primitive about her, too. I think she'd appreciate the rustic qualities of my charming bungalow if only she'd venture a visit to the top of the hill. The million-dollar view alone is worth the trip. She might like my place, maybe even find it oddly appealing. After all, how much worse could my meager circumstances be than life in communist East Germany? Hell, the entire East German secretariat would swoon at such palatial digs, the poor bastards. No, I've got nothing to be ashamed of, that's for sure. And anyway, with a little luck she'll be so blinded by the view she won't even notice the cracks, holes, recessions, wobbles, shimmies, puckers and other construction errata that comprise the miracle of my existence.

"It's charming," she'll say.

"Do you really think so?" I'll reply.

"Oh, yes, it's absolutely you," she'll say.

And we'll laugh and laugh until the cows come home.

Pity that my stereo, along with most everything else in the cottage, was stolen long ago. It would help immeasurably in my attempt to romance Sabine. So much so, I decide to pull out all the stops and avail myself of the generosity of Circuit City, a noble establishment that allows customers to bring anything back for a full refund, no questions asked. Fifteen days to test your purchase at home to see how the bass and treble respond to your particular acoustics. Fifteen days to see how the speakers match the décor. Fifteen days to see if the dials cast the proper romantic glow. Who knows? I might be so successful that I'll even decide to keep the stereo and figure out a way to pay for it. It'll be my little reward to myself for maintaining such admirable persistence. I go with the Onkyo TS-DX474, a handsome unit that looks more expensive than it really is. It's black—Sabine's favorite color—and has all the wires and connectors I'll need to tie back the ivy that's taken over the corner of my room. I head for home loaded down with boxes, struggling to get up the Filbert Steps without dropping the whole thing. It's a balancing act, this life. I should've been on the old Ed Sullivan Show spinning plates on a stick. Right after Señor Wences, the crappy ventriloquist—

"Hey! Where do you think you're going with that?" comes a voice from down the hill. It's a harrowing voice full of spite and venom, a voice that cuts to my spleen and sends a chill down my spine. Am I going to get robbed right here? Right in broad daylight? Right on the Filbert Steps? Can't I at least get the thing hooked up before they break the bottom window pane of my finely crafted nineteenth century European door and steal me blind? No, this is unacceptable. I decide to ignore the voice and keep walking.

"Hey! You! You got trouble hearing?" calls out the sinister intruder with even greater urgency. As a matter of fact I *do* have trouble hearing but I'm guessing that's not what he means. No, this is the classic robbery situation where the perpetrator threatens the victim, where one false move can lead to untold consequences and where a sensible response is the only option, and had this been any other time in my life I'd just give in, I'd hand over the stereo, the speakers, the wires and my wallet, too, if that's what he wants because nothing is worth losing your life over, but then I start thinking about the present value of my life and I start thinking about the value of the stereo, and what should be a very simple decision suddenly becomes very complicated because the fact of the matter is, it's a toss-up, my life and this piece of electronic junk are of approximate equal value in the current marketplace, in fact, the stereo has a better chance of adapting to its surroundings than I ever will—what can go bad with a stereo, a couple of crossed wires? Hell, I'm the *king* of crossed wires—no, I've had enough, this is it, I'm not giving in to this guy, I'm not stopping, I'm not running, I'm just going to keep on walking up the Filbert Steps as if nothing is happening, and that's when I hear a trigger cocking—

"Stop or I'll shoot."

I turn to see Patrolman Kuiper in full combat position—gun drawn, arm steady, barrel aimed directly at my forehead. I can feel the cranial fluids pounding against my skull, struggling to expand. "Go right ahead," I say defiantly. "Save me an MRI."

"What are you, some kind of asshole?"

Yes! Didn't I already tell you? I'm a *total* asshole! I've found a way to sabotage every screenplay I've ever written!

"I've got you this time, buddy. Who'd you rip off for the sounds?"

"I just bought all this stuff."

"Sure you did. And I'm the Queen of Sheba."

"Listen, Officer—"

"No, *you* listen. I want you to drop your hands real nice

and easy."

"I really can't do that—"

"Drop 'em!"

I drop my hands. The boxes go flying down the steps. One of them hits Kuiper's arm. The gun goes off. A small squirrel falls out of a tree, dead.

"Don't touch anything!" Kuiper yells. "This is all being confiscated as evidence."

"Make sure you confiscate the receipt, too."

"Oh, I'll confiscate the receipt, don't you worry about that. Let's go, buddy, you've got an appointment at Central Station."

The holding cell at Central Station isn't all that bad. With running water and a secure front door it provides many of the amenities lacking from my own home. It occurs to me that if Sabine were to visit me here I'd have far less explaining to do about my living situation than I would in my cottage. She might even admire my minimalist approach to interior decorating. Patrolman Kuiper, the itinerant manager of this little bed-and-no-breakfast, does everything he can to make my stay uncomfortable. After threatening to send me up the river—what river? The one that flows under my cottage? Go right ahead!—he leaves me alone to think about things. That's what I'm doing right now: I'm thinking about things. He's even supplied a pencil and paper with which to write my confession. Sure, Officer, I'll do that right away. Just as soon as I finish this screenplay I'm working on.

I transport myself to the Hofburg Palace. It feels cooler today, as if winter is approaching. I hurry across the Heldenplatz, make my way through a group of tourists and slip into the Schatzkammer. The Spear sits behind the two-inch thick glass, out of reach and impermeable. I look at it more closely and walk around the case to view its different angles. The weapon is about a foot-and-a-half long, crudely crafted from raw iron and roughly hewn in some workman's open pit. Still, it's strangely compelling to gaze upon. The mid-section of the Spear is covered with a gold sheath, two crosses are inscribed into the base and silver bindings are woven across the shaft. I stare into the case and can almost see horses riding up in the distance...

Parsifal Unleashed

Part II

EXT. CASTLE – NIGHT

A burning arrow thwangs from a crossbow. It rises through the air, soars over some trees and lands on the turret of Amfortas' castle. A few seconds later another dozen arrows light up the sky, *zing-zing, zing-zing.* One of them lands in a vat of oil on the parapet of the castle. The vat explodes in flames and sets the wall on fire. Servants rush out from the courtyard to put out the flames.

EXT. MOAT – NIGHT

Klingsor's Black Knights let go with another volley of arrows, then slip away into the forest.

> BLACK KNIGHTS
> *Let it burn to the ground!*

EXT. CASTLE – NIGHT

More explosions. Flames engulf the rim of the castle. A monk, his robes afire, falls from the upper reaches of the castle to a terrible death.

EXT. FOREST - NIGHT

Parsifal, Gurnemanz and the Squire hide among the trees as the Black Knights make their escape through the woods. Parsifal whispers to the Squire.

> PARSIFAL
> *The castle is under siege!*

> SQUIRE
> *Quiet, fool! Do you wish to see the morning?*

> PARSIFAL
> *Sure, I'd like to see morning. I'd even like to see the afternoon if it were possible.*

> SQUIRE
> *I warn you, fool. Watch your tongue.*

Gurnemanz sees that the Black Knights have fled. He leads Parsifal and the Squire to the path.

GURNEMANZ
*The King awaits. It is the holiest of nights, the
ceremony of the Grail. The Grail will give
food to those whose hearts are pure.*

PARSIFAL
I am awfully hungry.

SQUIRE
*Don't count on it.
Only the chaste shall eat.*

MUSIC SWELLS.

EXT. CASTLE – NIGHT
The servants pass bucket after bucket of water from the
cistern to the walls of the castle. Everyone lends a hand as
they attempt to fight the fire. Finally they douse the flames
and bring the fire under control.

INT. CASTLE – NIGHT
The Knights of the Holy Grail gather around an immense
table in the Great Hall of the Castle. They look troubled.
The soft chanting of boys' voices wafts down from the upper
chambers.

BOYS
Faith endures, oh, Lord, faith endures...

Four Squires lead a solemn procession carrying a holy shrine
into the room. Behind them King Amfortas is carried on a
litter by a group of Knights. He holds his hand to his wound
and looks to be in great pain.

AMFORTAS
Please, God, let me die...

EXT. CASTLE – NIGHT
Parsifal, Gurnemanz and the Squire enter the gates of the
castle. They are suddenly transported—as if by magic—right
across the courtyard.

ANGLE ON PARSIFAL
flying across the screen. There is wind in his hair. His
clothes ripple slightly.

HIGH ANGLE ON COURTYARD
passing below. Parsifal alights on the ground. He is bewildered.

> PARSIFAL
> *We have scarcely moved,*
> *yet we have traveled so far.*

> GURNEMANZ
> *In the Castle of the Grail, Time and*
> *Space become the same thing.*

> PARSIFAL
> *How can this be? Time does*
> *not exist? It is not possible.*

> GURNEMANZ
> *Wait until you get older.*
> *Then you'll really see.*

> PARSIFAL
> *But who is this Grail of whom you*
> *speak? Will I meet him at last?*

The Squire looks upon Parsifal as if he truly is an idiot.

> SQUIRE
> *The Grail is not a person!*
> *Have you not an ounce of sense?*

INT. GREAT HALL – NIGHT
The Squires place the holy shrine on a stone table in front
of the King. The Knights of the Grail stand behind the
feasting table.

> KNIGHTS
> *Let the bread and wine flow!*

Titurel is seated behind the King. He whispers into his son's ear.

TITUREL

You must lead the ceremony, my son.

AMFORTAS

I cannot! I am too great of a sinner!

Amfortas faints from pain. Titurel gathers himself from his own feeble state and shouts out over the hall.

TITUREL

Uncover the Grail!

The Squires uncover the holy shrine and take out a crystal chalice. The Holy Grail shoots out great beams of light across the hall.

A SERIES OF SHOTS
The castle is lit with an explosion of colors. The walls throb with a hundred purple concentric circles. The pillars vibrate with an array of chartreuse geometric cones. The ceiling pulsates with spiraling crimson triangles.

TITUREL

The Lord greets us!

Amfortas recovers slightly and picks up the Grail. He blesses the bread and the wine. Gurnemanz joins the Knights at the table. He calls to Parsifal.

GURNEMANZ

Come. The feast is on.

Parsifal, overwhelmed by the spectacle, is unable to move. He stands off to the side staring at the incredible light show on the walls.

KNIGHTS

*Partake of the bread and
wine, brothers!*

The feast begins. Laughter rings out. The clinking of glasses and slurping of soup. Amfortas suddenly grabs his wound and cries out in pain.

AMFORTAS
Aaaaah!

The hall falls silent. Parsifal, as if in a trance, approaches the glowing chalice. Before anyone can stop him he picks up the Grail and holds it to his chest.

ANGLE ON THE SQUIRE
staring at him in unholy disbelief, stunned at his display of sacrilege.

SQUIRE
He has gone too far!

The Squire grabs the Grail away from Parsifal and carries the relic to safety. The Knights carry Amfortas out of the room. The Great Hall empties except for Gurnemanz and Parsifal. Gurnemanz is shaken by the events. He turns angrily to Parsifal.

GURNEMANZ
Why do you stand there? Don't you
understand what you have done?
Have you never heard of the Holy Grail?

Parsifal shakes his head with confusion.

PARSIFAL
I still don't get how Time and
Space can become the same thing.
Are you sure about that?

Gurnemanz roughly pulls him to a side door of the castle.

GURNEMANZ
You truly are a fool, and a very
stupid one at that! You are not
the one for whom we wait!

Gurnemanz shoves Parsifal out of the castle.

EXT. CASTLE – DAY
The door slams behind him and echoes loudly in the empty chamber. Parsifal, alone and confused, aimlessly walks the hills.

Chapter 15

The door to the jail cell slams behind me and echoes loudly in the empty holding area. I leave the Central Police Station with nothing—no stereo, no receipt, no apology, no nothing. Patrolman Kuiper tells me they're going to "run a check" on the serial number and then they're going to "run a lab" on the receipt and then they're going "run a background" on me. Sounds to me like I'm getting the big runaround. "Don't leave the country," he warns me, like I'm going to high tail it to Botswana over a hundred-and-fifty-dollar Onkyo TS-DX474. The guy is nuts.

I walk the streets. Walking never solves any problems but it rarely makes things worse so I take comfort in making sure the hills are still there, and the houses and the trees and the shops, too. Walking, walking, walking, but never getting anywhere, that's the story of my life. I check out the little alleys named after the Beat poets—Ferlinghetti, Micheline, Kaufman, Kerouac—and wonder when they'll name a street after me. I don't want any of these crummy dead-ends, either, I want a major thoroughfare, something that runs across town with a bus line on it and traffic lights at every corner. Market Street, for example, a name that means nothing, would be vastly enhanced as Atom Smasher Avenue. I could say to Sabine: "Meet you on the corner of Fifth and Smasher." That would impress her.

I mosey through Portsmouth Square, the open air a perfect counterpoint to the jail's cramped cells, the smell of freshly cut grass a stark contrast to the stench of stale urine, the park bench a welcome relief from the Central Station's institutional chairs. I continue on to the outer reaches of my domain on the edge of Chinatown, where I wander down Bush Street to Dashiel Hammett Place, backtrack along Grant Avenue and zigzag over the Stockton Tunnel. There are other parts of San Francisco but I never go there. No, this is my turf, one square mile in any direction from my cottage, one square mile that I have staked out as my personal fiefdom. In a sense I'm really the caretaker of this whole little corner of town. Living in its highest perch I am, in fact, one of the major assets to the community, a kind of moderating influence to creeping normality. I head up Columbus checking the shop windows to make sure everything's in order, checking Washington Square Park to make sure the bushes have been trimmed, checking the statue of the fireman to make sure the whiskey bottle's still there, and who should I see on the sunny side of the street but Sabine! She's walking that graceful walk of hers—back straight, shoulders square, chin up—she moves with elegance and purpose, steadfast in her direction, always moving toward some unspoken goal. I also have a goal, and that goal is to catch up to her and tell her about the stereo incident. It will give me an excuse to talk about music—maybe we've got something in common in that area—and then from music it's a quick jump to movies, art and literature— I'll bet she's a fan of architecture—I could slip in something about form following function, and what could be more functional than an exquisitely crafted nineteenth century

European door, the magical portal to my humble abode? Who knows, maybe she likes coffee. I'll make my special blend, pouring it by hand through filter paper, and she'll realize I take things slow and easy, that there's nothing to fear. That's the plan—first the door, then the coffee, then the view—look! She's slowing down at the corner. She's picking up the vibrations. She's feeling flushed. Her skin is tingly. The hairs on her neck are electric. And now she's locking into my thoughts. She turns. She sees me. Her eyes widen. They widen some more. And now she's walking again, only faster, past the church, past the library, past the wig shop, past the nail salon, but I'm keeping up with her, past the deli, past the truffle shop, past the tattoo parlor, and every inch of her body is screaming out, yes, follow me, this is all part of the dance, I must be won, I must be captured, come, gallant suitor, be clever and brave, and now she's walking even faster, almost running, but I keep pace, clever and brave, and then I feel something from deep down inside, it's like a great unleashing, a cracking open, a veritable eruption from the depths of my brain, it's a strange sensation but it feels like me, more me than ever before, the me who's been crying to get out, the me I barely recognize, the me that has been trapped in the dark, dreary lower cortex for a hundred and fifty thousand years and is finally exerting its true nature, and it is at that moment that my stride lengthens and I nearly fly through the air, I'm faster than ever before, fast and nimble and darting like a bird, and I catch up to Sabine and grab her arm and let out a falcon's yelp, a high-pitched ululating warble that comes from the avian part of my agitated limbic system, and she says: "One is white, two is yellow, three is green, and four is red."

And I say: "Yes!"

And she says: "If you add two and three you get blue."

And I say: "Yes!"

And she says: "The odd numbers are cold and the even are warm."

And I say: "Yes!"

A great rainbow of color fills the sky and I find myself thinking of nothing so much as a warm, cozy nest set high in the trees. I bite off a small gingko branch and offer it to her in a gallant gesture. I anticipate a feathery kiss, my lips and her lips and the little branch all mixed together in a primitive pool of raw savage impulse, but at that very instant a bus pulls up and opens its doors. Sabine, her eyes glazed over, steps inside, deposits her fare, moves to the rear and takes a seat. In the flick of a falcon's feather the doors close, the bus pulls out and I'm left standing there in a pungent cloud of diesel exhaust.

Okay, East German waitress, you have truly stoked the fires. You are a combustible mix of contrary impulses, a roiling stew of unpredictability, a towering inferno of caprice. I am impressed. I am overwhelmed. I am smitten.

The undercurrents of a Wagnerian leitmotiv vibrate from the bushes outside my cottage. I haven't seen Barbara since the opera and was hoping maybe she'd run off with the circus. More likely, the circus would've run off with her. "Be cool," she says with no hint of irony as she steps out from the eucalyptus grove.

"Be cool? Yeah, okay, I'll try my best."

"Have you been to those camps outside Sausalito lately?"

"Not yet."

"Turns out they're not prisons. They're concentration camps. I was over there last week, just past Bridgeway. There's an energy vortex you step into and it takes you right to the nerve center of the whole operation."

We're fast approaching thirty seconds. I open the outer gate—

"They're planning something big. I'm learning all about it. I'm cracking through."

"Be sure to let me know."

"I *am* letting you know," says Barbara, humming another turgid leitmotiv.

"All right. Thanks." I close the outer door and Barbara exits stage left into her undergrowth of bushes. The sun peeks from behind a cloud, sees that the coast is clear and rises a little higher in the sky. Okay, I've been warned. The vortex is expanding. That can't be good.

Can it? The fact is, I'm feeling good about things. My creative juices are flowing, the screenplay is progressing, the box is holding steady, Patrolman Kuiper is off on his rounds, the third floor of the Big House is intact, Barbara is lying low in her bed of leaves and Bernard is quiet as a titmouse. I'm feeling so optimistic I decide to send the beginning of my screenplay to Bobby even if, by so doing, I'm breaking one of the irrevocable Laws of Screenwriting, which states:

DON'T SEND ANYTHING TO ANYONE UNTIL IT'S DONE.

You only have one chance to get a first impression, after all, and that first impression is the only thing that matters. Nobody reads anything twice in Hollywood—do they even read it once?—and that's why placing my little half-baked masterpiece into an envelope might be considered pure lunacy. It's a decision born of equal parts desperation and hope, desperation because I feel my ticker winding down faster than my grandfather's clock, hope because there's still a chance to leave my mark on this world before I move on to the next.

I'm reminded of a journey I once took through the Himalayas. A friend of mine wrote to someone back home one day, then stood on a mountaintop and threw the letter to the wind, saying if it was meant to get there, it would.

Impressed by his faith, I wrote my own letter several days later and tossed it from the same spot. Being just slightly more practical, however, I at least affixed a stamp to my envelope, thinking it couldn't hurt. It turns out that my friend's letter got sucked into the jet stream and found its way to a cornfield in Iowa where a farmer picked it up and became his lifelong pen pal. My letter, weighed down by the Nepalese stamp, fell straight down the hill and was picked up by a beggar boy who steamed off the stamp, redeemed it at the post office and took in a movie with the proceeds. Now, *that's* magic.

But that was then and this—if I'm reading the correct page of the calendar—is now. I take an elevator up Coit Tower and pass a collection of socialist workers' murals that are painted on the walls. The tower was built during the Great Depression and I love that about San Francisco, that at the worst of times we build whimsical towers celebrating out-of-work workers. At the top of the tower is a small viewing area from which I gaze out upon a spectacular, panoramic vista of the Financial District, the Bay Bridge and thirty-seven other noteworthy points of interest. It's one of the great views in the world, and what better place to see if the cosmos has my back? With an optimism far out of proportion to any sense of reality I toss Bobby's envelope to the wind, general direction Hollywood, and watch as it flutters off into the southern sky. I feel strangely self-assured, knowing I didn't weigh it down with a bunch of unnecessary stamps. Never make the same mistake twice, after all, that's my motto.

Chapter 16

Several days pass. My erratic sleep is shattered by the sound of sandblasters cleaning Waverly Wellington's veranda and I'm assaulted by a spearing jolt of crimson triangles flooding my brain. The triangles are all shapes and sizes—some equilateral, some isosceles, some scalene—and they shimmer and throb to the grating vibrations of metal on metal. Moments later a crow flies overhead, unleashes an ear-jangling caw and sends a tumbling pattern of geometric cones bouncing off my retina. Then my alarm clock rings and a hundred tiny curlicues vibrate out of my retina in concentric circles until they break up at the edge of the horizon, like waves falling off a cliff.

The synesthesia is wearing me down as more and more sounds erupt into an onslaught of colors and shapes that reverberate incessantly whenever anything creaks, groans, coughs or whistles. What had once seemed like a fantastical alternative world of the senses now is nothing but an irritation. I try to suppress the whole thing but the brain, having a mind all its own, refuses to go along. You push down somewhere on the brain, it'll find a way to bubble up somewhere else. The brain is like a big water balloon rubbing against the pin cushion of a myopic seamstress.

The phone rings and the whole thing explodes. Triangles, cones, curlicues and pin cushions carom off my hippocampus like a game of eight-ball gone berserk. Under normal circumstances I wouldn't answer the phone before 2:30 P.M., but these are not normal circumstances, not with that box shaking nervously with each ring. What's it waiting for, for a timer to go off and level the whole hill? For the lake beneath my cottage to rise high enough to activate some kind of soluble toxic compound? For the sides to burst open and suck all the oxygen out of the air? I grab the phone before it rings me and half the neighborhood right out of existence. "Hello?"

"Young man," Bobby shouts into the phone, "this is the most sensational script I've ever read!"

"You got it?"

"The envelope had tire tracks and grease stains all over it, but I got it. What did you do, send it by Pony Express?"

"I just kind've tossed it out there—"

"Like I said, sensational, sensational! It made me laugh! It made me cry! It made me sit up and wonder why!"

"Why I'm not a household name?"

"No, why you didn't send me the rest of it."

"It's coming. I've just got to nail down the third act."

"No time for that now. I've already sent it to our producer. She wants to talk to you right away."

I pause a moment to let it all sink in. I'm talking to Bobby. He talked to the producer. The news is good. Is it possible? Am I really awake? Or is the cosmos puffing me up with some grandiose dream that will pop the moment I turn over. I turn over. Nothing pops. The phone is cradled on my pillow. "Bobby? You still there?"

"Of course I'm still here. What do you think I'm doing, blowing bubbles in the wind?"

"Look, I'll call her right away."

"Don't bother. She wants to meet you. You've got to get down here immediately. Grab the next flight."

"Are you kidding?"

"Do I sound like I'm kidding? Call Victoria the moment you get in. She'll give you directions. And remember one thing. Nothing happens without me. I'm the agent. You're the writer. Don't mix them up. Got it?"

"Got it."

"Okay, good. We'll have lunch at Musso & Frank's. Bring an appetite."

"Thanks, Bobby. Thanks for everything."

"I'm a miracle worker, young man, don't forget that. Now get moving. Make me proud."

The flight to L.A. and the drive to Santa Monica are uneventful, which I take as a good sign. I park outside a charming bungalow which reminds me of my own cottage except that it's comfortable beyond description and costs millions of dollars. An assistant greets me at the door and leads me to an outer office where I wait for the *Rule of Twenty* to run its course. I'm offered the choice of bottled water or coffee but decline both in my own exercise of power, designed to show that I know how to say no, even though I *am* thirsty. The office is done up in tastefully minimal style, another subtle declaration of power and success. To have so few things must've cost a bundle but I plop down on the sofa like it was my own living room. On the coffee table is today's *Los Angeles Times* and tomorrow's *Hollywood Reporter*. That they have tomorrow's news today confirms I am in the corridors of power and had better watch what I say.

Exactly twenty minutes later, the Producer Who Shall Remain Nameless enters with a black Labrador that may have been created on an animatronics sound stage. The behemoth bounds over the table, smashes into a lamp and topples a vase of flowers in his urgent quest to smell my crotch. "Good dog," I say hopefully, pretending to be perfectly comfortable with the idea that his razor sharp canines are just inches from my corpora cavernosa. I stare into his eyes and summon up trace memories of the dancing raccoons in my attic. That's right, doggie, *raccoons*, the kind with gnarly claws that could rip out your throat if you so much as breathe wrong. The Lab's ears droop and he backs off into the corner to chew on a pile of film scripts.

"So, Bobby tells me you're from San Francisco," says the Producer Who Shall Remain Nameless. "It's my favorite city in the world." Like any good screenwriter I'm sensitive to subtext, and the subtext of this greeting is that I'm already in trouble. San Francisco is every Hollywood producer's favorite town, and why not? It's a real city like Paris or London or New York and is the perfect destination for a long weekend. Maybe a little too perfect. Every Hollywood producer would rather live in San Francisco, but they can't because the film industry is in Los Angeles, and what she's *really* saying is, What makes you, a lowly screenwriter, think you can just zip in and out for a meeting while we're all stuck here in the stew fighting the fight every day? You think you can just drop in for a quick hello, then go back to your cable cars and sourdough and winding streets? No, that's not the way it works, not for me at least. Here's what I really think of you and your faggy little town: "I love the fog," she says.

"There's no such thing as fog. It's really just low clouds."

"Oh?" she says, looking at me a half second too long. I know exactly what she's thinking: *Another smartass screen-writer looking to impress; he's obviously hard to work with.* No, she doesn't appreciate my fog theory and is already looking for the quickest way to wrap up the meeting. "So how come we've never heard of you before?" she says, cutting straight to the chase.

"I've been kind of lying low," I say, trying to recover momentum.

"Believe me, I understand. Don't spread yourself too thin, that's what I always say. Keep it on the down low and play it close to your vest."

"Kind of like poker," I say, having no idea what I'm talking about.

"Exactly," she says, doubling down on the lousy metaphor. She leans back in her leather recliner and looks at me closely. "Bobby Littman is God, you know."

"I know."

"When Bobby sends over a script we drop everything. Nobody wants to miss out on a Bobby Littman script."

"That's what I've heard."

"A Bobby Littman script gets read before the ink dries. And let me tell you, this was one great read. It's a magnificent piece of work, something that's going to bring you a lot of attention. Are you ready for that?"

"Ready steady."

"How soon can you have it done?"

"Pretty soon, I guess. I'm ready to tackle it as soon as we have a deal."

The Producer Who Shall Remain Nameless taps her fingernails on the table, then shuffles some papers. "I'm sure you'll understand what I'm about to say," she says. "We don't enter into anything on spec. It's a longtime company policy. Our investment is the guidance we offer, the development process, setting up the deal. That's the payday."

It doesn't take a genius writer to read between her lines: *you should've taken the coffee, buddy, because that's all you're going to get.* I sink lower in the sofa. This is beginning to sound suspiciously like every other Hollywood meeting I've ever had. I'm going to talk about up-front money and she's going to talk about back-end credits. Just once I'd like to meet somewhere in the middle. "I don't work for free," I say with as much conviction as I can muster.

The Producer Who Shall Remain Nameless leans in a little closer across the table. "What do you think of Marty directing?"

"Scorsese?"

"And Leo starring?"

"Di Caprio?"

"And Willem as the antagonist?"

"Dafoe?"

There's another break in the conversation so that she can read my mind reading hers. She's upped the ante—at least so it would appear—and there's no way I can fold. The balloon in my brain rubs against the jagged edges of my cranium. The Producer Who Shall Remain Nameless studies my face and sees right through me. She tightens the screws: "Of course, I have a few issues with the script."

"Issues?"

She picks up the screenplay and holds it at arm's length, as if she might catch something from it. "You didn't think we were going to film straight from this, did you?"

"No, no, of course not," I say, feeling the sweat building on my forehead. It's a common physiological reaction we writers have to hearing the truth: *of course* I thought they were going to film it exactly as I wrote it. That's why I wrote it.

"Writing is rewriting."

"And acting is reacting," I say, making a point which escapes me, her and the dog. "But I see what you mean. I'll have to make some changes."

"Tell me something. How important is this Klingsor character to the script?"

"Klingsor?" I say, sinking deeper into the sofa. "Why... he's *crucial*."

"Because we don't want to go too negative. Negative isn't

selling these days."

"Klingsor's *more* than negative. He's the incarnation of evil. Without Klingsor there's nothing."

"Well, technically that's not true. Without Klingsor there's still something, it's just a slightly *different* something."

I feel my larynx tightening. "You did read the script, right?"

"Of course I read the script," she says as the screenplay slowly drips through her fingers onto the table. "Okay, not a problem. Klingsor or no Klingsor, it's a great read. We'll talk about it later."

A police car races by outside, its siren blaring. I see a hammer, a hundred nails and a coffin lid flying past my forehead. The Subtext Police swing into action: *It's all over! Come out with your hands up. The conversation is over. The negotiation is over. The meeting is over. Just get up real nice and easy and get out of there.*

But I can't. I'm paralyzed with hope and I can't move a muscle.

"Look, this is a great action-adventure film," she says. "Let's just make sure we don't lose the sophistication."

Did the words *sophistication* and *action-adventure* actually appear in the same sentence? Am I starting to hear things? If it's sophistication she wants, I've got nine other scripts in the car—

"That's why we're thinking of bringing in Jerry Karp to co-produce."

Did she just say Jerry Karp? *Jerry Karp?* She can't be serious. Had Will Rogers met Jerry Karp he would've said, "I never met a man I didn't like... until I met Jerry Karp." She wants to bring in the most abusive producer in Hollywood for sophistication? The producer of *Fatal Flaw, Bloody Birthday,* and *Die Or Else,* a guy I would run from like the plague were it not for one redeeming quality—

"He's into Frank Lloyd Wright, isn't he?"

"I think he owns a Wright house somewhere up in the hills."

"Yeah, sure," I say, warming to the idea. "Jerry Karp would be perfect." I feel things beginning to turn. "Listen, about the money—"

"I already talked to Bobby. He understands. Ask him what he thinks."

"Okay, it's just—"

The producer's face turns ashen as she feigns sensitivity and concern. It's the skin's natural reaction to unfamiliar emotion. "The last thing in the world we want is to go into something where everyone's not happy," she says. "Talk to Bobby. See what he thinks. If you don't want to do it—"

"No-no, I didn't say that—"

"It's a process. Bobby understands how it works. All you have to do is finish the script."

The phone rings. The Producer Who Shall Remain Nameless settles in for what promises to be a long call. I sit there uncomfortably for a few minutes until she finally glances up, surprised that I'm still there. She waves goodbye without making eye contact. The dog gives me one of those fake Hollywood smiles. I leave.

It's dark inside Musso & Frank's even though it's midday on a typically sundrenched Los Angeles afternoon. The chairs are dark, the booths are dark, even the light bulbs are dark, as if not to awaken any bad memories still lingering in the nooks and crannies of Hollywood's oldest restaurant. The walls are constructed of old forest redwood, very nearly petrified and so brittle that a tap in the wrong spot might bring the entire place down. These walls know things. They've eavesdropped on Louis B. Mayer, laughed with Sid Caesar and cried with Judy Garland. The waiters are as old as the walls, maybe older, and need walkers to make their rounds. It's really more of a triage center than an eatery, a place where old actors come to die, where an ambulance always awaits, where you're just one mushroom omelet away from being entered into the *Hollywood Book of the Dead.*

Bobby's already waiting for me at the corner table when I arrive twenty minutes late. He's holding court, flashing his beautiful smile, hobnobbing, embracing and glad-handing all the while nursing a cocktail that somehow never needs refilling. "So?"

"I think it went pretty well. She likes the script."

"Of course she likes the script. It's a Bobby Littman script, isn't it?"

"One of his best."

Bobby opens a menu he could recite in his sleep. "You hungry?"

"I could eat."

"Try the mushroom omelet. The canned mushrooms are fresh today."

"I'm leaning toward the tuna melt."

Bobby furls his eyebrows, shrugs and calls over a waiter. "Gibby, what am I gonna do with this kid? Give him a tuna melt, okay? Easy on the melt." He knocks back a healthy shot of vodka, then turns back to me. "Where were we?"

"The script. They don't want to pay."

Bobby's face turns to stone. "What do you mean?" he says, his eyes darting toward the kitchen as if to see if it's not too late to cancel the tuna melt. "You didn't talk about money, did you? You never talk about money. That's my job."

"There is no money. They don't pay for spec scripts. She said she told you."

"They *always* say that. Do you really think I'd ever agree to a client of mine working for free? You didn't say yes, did you?"

"I didn't say no."

Bobby looks at me with horror. "Listen to me. Writers write. Producers produce. Agents die of liver cancer. Now we'll have to go through with it."

"She said Marty will direct."

"Feldman?"

"And Leo will star."

"Nimoy?"

"And Willem will be the antagonist."

"Dafoe?"

There's a commotion at the maitre d's desk, the turning of heads and the sound of quick footsteps. A small man careens by, then stops abruptly in front of our table. He does a triple take and feigns stupendous surprise. "Is that Bobby Littman or have I died and gone to heaven?"

"Both," says Bobby.

"Can you imagine they got a joint like this in heaven? We shoulda been killers. Killers eat better in the afterlife."

"There's a guy at Paramount you could kill for me. Then we'd all eat better."

"Consider it done."

Bobby looks at him closely, feigning seriousness. "I didn't tell you which guy."

"Does it make any difference?"

"Not in the least."

The guy winks at me, then turns back to Bobby. "Who's this?"

"Doesn't matter. He's not produced yet. Kid, this is Mel Brooks."

"I'm a big fan," I say, duly impressed.

Gibby comes by and drops off my sandwich. The plate nearly tumbles off the table but Gibby doesn't seem to notice. Or care. "What you got there?" says Brooks, examining the plate from all sides.

"Tuna melt."

"Yeah? Is it good? It looks good."

I take a bite. "It's good."

"I'm gonna get me one of those. Tuna melt, you say? It sounds a little nutty, but fun. Is it fun? I want fun for lunch. I had serious for breakfast."

"It's fun."

"Okay, I trust you. You look like you know your tuna." Brooks takes one more look at my sandwich, then leans in a little closer. "Bobby Littman is God, you know."

"I know."

Mel leaves, Gibby leaves and Bobby takes another drink from his bottomless glass. The sun slowly moves across the sky, the shadows shift slightly and the lunch crowd slowly dissipates. The walls turn in, having gotten another earful. Deals were made. Deals were broken. Deals were both made and broken at the same time. Who knows what anything means in Hollywood? I'm either in like Flynn or out like Grout. I just hope I can still tell the difference.

I walk the Hollywood Hills, up Bluebird Avenue and down Flicker Place, across Skylark Lane and along Warbler Way, walking, walking but never getting anywhere, these hills aren't made for walking, they're made for limousines and town cars, police cruisers and security vans, no, to walk in L.A. is to invite suspicion and derision, it's an unnatural act, like honesty and generosity, it's a bold political statement, a dangerous deviation from the norm, it's anarchy in action, and still I continue on, weathering the squinty stares of passing drivers, deftly avoiding the headlong charge of taxis and minivans, I pass a thousand palm trees, their leaves yellow and drooping from exhaustion, I pass once-flamboyant flowers now disappeared in a crazed jumble of construction, I pass cracked fountains and empty swimming pools and untended waterfalls built for a town that fears its own architecture, oh, I am a stranger here, a stranger without purpose, a caretaker searching for an empty lot, a writer seeking an ending, I walk these hills dazed and disillusioned, a bit player in a never-ending movie where the last reel is always missing, I walk and walk and walk through a menagerie of streets, up Nightingale Drive and down Thrasher Avenue, across Oriole Lane and along Blue Jay Way—oh, this is a flighty town!—I continue up a wooded path, along a winding trail, and then I feel something stirring, the primitive bird inside me awakens and rustles in its nest, the falcon stretches its wings and unleashes an antediluvian call of recognition, behold, it beseeches the hills as we take wing over the peaks and valleys, soaring through the thin air of a depleted sky and plummeting through the downdrafts of gusty canyons, we circle a canopy of trees and glide through a thicket of branches, and then we swoop down a steep hillside and come upon Frank Lloyd Wright's temple to the ancient future, its concrete columns reaching for the gods, its bold terraces extending into the landscape, and I am smitten, smitten and infatuated, for this is a house that stretches the bounds of architecture, a house that might hold the key to the universe, a house that only a temperamental producer could own, and as security alarms shatter the thin night air, I straighten up and fly right—right the hell out of there—before Jerry Karp comes out blasting an eighteen-barrel bazooka and clips my wings.

INTERLUDE

In which Barbara concocts her potion, learns a new form of meditation, conceals some important state secrets, does the pagan hand jive, and nestles into her bed of leaves.

Interlude

Barbara grinds the nut of a eucalyptus tree and the leaf of a fennel plant into a thick paste that forms a residue along the inner lip of a stone cup. She adds a few drops of water gathered from the dew of early morning, then sprinkles in marigold seeds and a reddish powder rubbed from the stalks of wild salvia. She unearths a few grubs from the roots of a redwood tree and pounds their malleable bristles into a sticky dust that adheres to the walls of the cup and coats the mixture with a lattice of gooey film. She then sets the whole thing on a makeshift altar that rises out of the eucalyptus grove and waits for the morning sun to slowly bake the concoction into an all-purpose porridge, cleansing agent, hair tonic and healing balm. Another day begins.

A day of added responsibility. The writer has gone south on one of his hopeless forays into the world of dreams and illusion, leaving her in charge of the compound. At least she thinks he did. The fact is, she's rarely sure of what he's trying to say as he seems to be inflicted by a rare disorder of the brain that causes the first thirty seconds of conversation to be a mad jumble of verbal fits and starts. If she can ever get past his first half minute of gibberish things start making a bit of sense, but their discussions rarely last that long. He's obviously from that new generation of writers whose attention span is so short they can barely tell a coherent story. What do they call it, the MTV generation? Barbara reminds herself to find out exactly what that means.

She smoothes out her bed of leaves, fluffs up her bird feather pillow and sweeps the grove of fallen twigs and acorns. She covers the area with an orange parachute she found wrapped around a parking meter, then makes her first foray of the day down the path of the compound, through the gate and into the patio behind the cottage. She likes it back there. There's room to stretch her arms and appreciate the fine acoustics accorded by the strategic placement of crumbling cottage walls, turn of the century brick terraces and imperialistic ivy. It's enough to make her want to give voice to the feelings of freedom and elation growing within her chest: *"Der Morgen kommmmmmmmmmmmmmt..."*

Her mother claimed that Barbara came out of the womb singing and why not, it was a musical family, the mother an itinerant vocal teacher who gave birth either in the northern part of South Dakota or the southern part of North Dakota— she could never remember which—and her mother before her and her mother's mother, too, singers all, right back to their ancestral home in the northeast of Germany, they were a family of sopranos weaned on Wagner—they cooked to Wagner, they gardened to Wagner, they ate, drank and made love to Wagner—and so, too, Barbara, born on a cold winter morning with *Parsifal* playing on the Victrola, was infused with the spirit of ancient times, of warriors and sorcerers and knights-errant, and she carried with her a particular melody, Kundry's song of woe and regret, this Kundry who was the reincarnation of a besotted soul who had laughed at Jesus on the cross and was cursed to spend an eternity in misery, this tortured woman who for a thousand years was reborn as a sorceress and waited to meet Parsifal, the guileless fool who alone held the key to her salvation. Now another thousand years have passed and Barbara has made her way from the Dakotas to the Rockies to the Sierras, heading ever West until to go any farther West would take her to the East, and that's where she turned her attention, to the East, sitting day after day staring out over the Pacific Ocean, doing yoga in the morning and meditating at night, diving farther into herself until one day she simply never came back. Barbara meditated herself into some wholly new state of Other, the switch clicked on and never again went off, and the next day she traded in her jeans for burlap, her sneakers for deerskin, her studio apartment for a eucalyptus grove, and for the first time in a very long time things made perfect sense.

Barbara plies her trade, such as it is, in a little recess in front of a Natural Foods store on Grant Avenue. She wraps her abundant legs into a perfect yogic asana, straightens her back so that the chakras are open and flowing, and places her hand out in elegant approximation of a woman about to take tea. Except that's no tea cup in her hand; it's a stone jar used for collecting funds to help finance her agrarian reform project at the top of the hill. Some might consider it to be a beggar's cup but that is to miss the point because Barbara has never begged for anything in her life. No, Barbara's jar is more a suggestion box than anything else, a suggestion that we all stop for a moment and consider why concentration camps have been spotted outside Sausalito, why the energy vortex of the planet has been strangely realigned and why red foxes, brown raccoons, white swans and orange parachutes have been seen dropping from the sky.

Barbara is a fixture in the neighborhood and her disappearance one day causes considerable alarm. Rumors begin to spread of sirens, ambulances, stretchers and men in white coats, and then, on a cold North Beach morning, an altar appears on the window ledge of the Natural Foods store with a profusion of flowers, candles, cards, herbal supplements and photos of Barbara. That night half the neighborhood shows up for a memorial service in which the Green Street Mortuary Marching Band tosses away its usual dirges and breaks into a strutting, swaggering New Orleans parade—we come not to bury Barbara, we come to boogie her—a march that leads right up Columbus Avenue and past Broadway and straight into Specs where everyone sips from a final cup of Barbara's extra special hot and spicy primordial soup.

Days later Patrolman Keith Kuiper is making his rounds through North Beach when he comes upon someone occupying Barbara's old spot on Grant Avenue. It's bad enough that Barbara had stretched vagrancy laws to the limit, but a second homeless person in the same location? As he reaches for his handcuffs Kuiper is stunned to see Barbara herself looking up at him with a scrubbed face, brushed teeth and one of those popular Jennifer Anniston bouffant hairdos. "Hey, wait a minute," says Kuiper, "aren't you supposed to be dead?"

"I know!" says Barbara. "That's what everyone's been telling me!"

"You'd better have a good explanation for this," says Kuiper, his hand automatically moving to the wood handle of his revolver.

"It's pretty simple. Somebody saw something crawling out of my head the other day and called nine-one-one. Then an ambulance came and took me to the emergency room. Next thing I knew I woke up in a concentration camp in Sausalito where they kept asking me all these crazy questions. *'What's your name? Where do you live? Who's the president of the United States?'* Like I'm really going to give up state secrets!"

"How did you get back here?"

"It was easy. They took me down for a bath one day. I squirted under the bubbles and just kept going."

Kuiper can't figure out what to charge her with—self-identity theft? Impersonating a dead person? Public detoxification?—and storms off in search of a jaywalker or litterbug instead. Barbara heads for Washington Square Park, where the church tower across the street acts like a kind of lightning rod for the energy coursing through her spine. As she practices her yoga she sometimes feels like she just might leave her body behind and ascend straight into the sky. Barbara stretches her torso into a cobra position, balances on the tips of her fingers, holds the pose for a full two minutes and slowly pulls herself into a ball. She notices a familiar figure sitting on a park bench, this Butterfly Girl who appears sometimes at the compound, sometimes on the street and sometimes walking the hills. Barbara feels both pulled and repelled by the young woman, as if some kind of strange chemistry were at work. She reminds her of her younger self, when she was thin and pretty and had to hold off an endless army of suitors. It's hard now to even remember the feeling of being desired, the warmth of a caress, the brush of a stranger's lips on her skin. And yet, when she looks at this young woman on the bench, that's exactly what she feels. Why her? What's the connection? Are they cut from the same piece of cloth?

Barbara crosses the street and nearly runs into Father Indelicato, who is slowly making his way out of the big double doors of 666 Filbert Street. Priests always walk slowly, as if weighed down by the heavy silver crosses around their necks or the heavy black frocks draped over their shoulders or the heavy guilt of misdeeds hanging on their conscience—

"Hello, my child," he says. "I didn't see you at mass this

morning."

"No shit," says Barbara with her usual irreverence. "I'm on permanent leave. How's business these days?"

"Business?"

"You know, wafers and wine. I could give you a good deal on balm."

"I'm quite sure we have a sufficient supply."

"Not like mine."

"I can just imagine," says Father Indelicato.

"I'll bet you can't."

The priest shudders at the thought, then makes the sign of the cross and ambles off down the street. Barbara responds with her own pagan hand jive, a mix of finger pops and palm shimmies that puts the priest to shame. They each go off on their separate rounds, the priest to check on his flock, Barbara to inspect her own menagerie at the top of Telegraph Hill.

Barbara sings an evening aria to the woodland sprites, stretches to the yawn of ivy and settles into her eucalyptus grove for the evening. It's a crisp, cool night and she glances at the branches above to watch the moonlight dancing from leaf to leaf. How many nights has she spent just like this? A hundred? A thousand? A million? She feels old, as if the centuries were embedded in her bones. Her reverie is interrupted by a rustling sound in the bushes. She leans up on one arm, then glances around to see the nimble silhouette of a shadow darting along the gate of the compound. Barbara doesn't much like shadows which, by their very nature, are elusive, monochromatic and quintessentially shady. Especially when the shadow begins climbing the outer wall of the Big House.

It's That Guy, the one the writer doesn't like, the guy with the simian movements, the spidery arms and the suction cups on his feet. The truth is, Barbara doesn't like him either. He creeps around, appearing and disappearing at the strangest times, always with his face hidden in darkness. It's almost as if his body is able to alter its shape to the surroundings, elongating into narrow drainpipes, curving around balcony corners and stretching along the sharp edges of roofs. Sometimes she feels him calling to her, even though not a word is spoken. It's as if he exerts some strange control over her despite her feelings of revulsion at his very presence. How can such a man hold sway over Barbara, the Visigoth warrior-princess of the forest? What is it about him that makes her blood run cold, her soup go tepid and her voice fall silent?

The shadow disappears into the third story recess of the house. A moment later a flicker of light reflects off the windows of the top apartment. Barbara leans back in her bed of leaves and slowly dozes off to the faint smell of hot dogs cooking on a cool, quiet San Francisco night. It's been another day, a day neither good nor bad, a day of waiting for the forces to gather and bring things to their final conclusion.

Chapter 17

The ReTan Hotel on Whitley Street is the crummiest hotel in Hollywood. There's a one-armed guitarist in Room 103, a hebephrenic dancer in Room 212 and a somnambulant stunt man in the third floor utility closet. This is old Hollywood, twenty-five square miles of lingerie shops and memorabilia emporiums that any self-respecting screenwriter would avoid like the plague. Self-respect, of course, like bubonic fever, comes in all shapes and sizes and I figure if I can keep the swelling down I can live with it. The truth is, the ReTan Hotel wasn't my first, second or even fifth choice, but that's the compromise Bobby has reached with the Producer Who Shall Remain Nameless, so who am I to argue?

I've missed two weeks of San Francisco sunsets now, plus a like number of sunsets in the Southland. That's because the sun never really sets in Los Angeles, it just disappears behind a tattered curtain as the credits role. I've had breakfasts at the International House of Pancake Makeup, lunches at Denny's Cutting Room Floor and dinners at Duke's Canteen of Broken Dreams. How am I supposed to work like this? I'm half-buried in an urban dump of peeling wallpaper, dripping faucets and clanking steam pipes. I lie on a creaky bed and stare at a sagging ceiling, trying to figure out how I've managed to move from the most dangerous cottage in San Francisco to the most derelict hotel in Hollywood. How many failed writers before me have succumbed to these very walls? How many have been lost to wild leaps of imagination from which they never returned? It's as if a conspiracy of forces were gathering to toss my whole life back at me.

I try to turn away but I can't. My entire morbid history as a screenwriter is being projected in the cracks and crevices of the sheetrock. Whole scenes fly by, it's a blizzard of words, a veritable snowstorm of camera angles, lighting suggestions and snappy dialogue, the whole room is thick with plot points and character arcs, it's bloated with close-ups and intercuts, it's feverish with voice-overs and stage directions. Pages and pages are zooming by, pages of action, pages of adventure, pages of romance, and it's as if my entire literary life is flashing before my eyes. Every failed script is there, every synopsis, every analysis, every rewrite, it's all a big huge intergalactic encyclopedia of failure, the film noirs, the comedies, the thrillers, the first drafts, the second drafts, the polishes, I can't take it any more, the wasted years, the wasted effort, the wasted words, I've been pushed beyond all human limits and what is left but to let out a scream, a wailing, flailing cosmological scream that shakes the dust off the atmosphere and sends a shiver down the terrestrial planes. In a flash the room disappears into that most primitive part of space where the wires cross, the senses combine and dream life and wakefulness reverse. Joe DiMaggio and Marilyn Monroe do a soft-shoe across the stage. Five hundred cauliflowers roll down the aisles. A Toltec time traveler resets his watch. The curtain drops. Sleep sneaks in on little pterodactyl feet.

❦

I dream of Sabine. She's been in my thoughts ever since the day I confronted her on the street and finally understood that her own form of synesthesia is responsible for our deep psychic connection. Who, after all, but two synesthetes like us could have more in common at a primitive molecular level? Who could better understand the pure impulses of the brain's underworld? Who could be better transmitters of pheromones and receivers of telepathic messages? Whenever I think of her my hair stands on end. I feel ionized, as if I were a neutral charge in a world spinning with electricity.

Sabine and I dance upon a magic carpet. An entire symphony of motion surrounds her. Her hair, her hands, her hips, everything moves with elegance, charm and an ecology of ease. An unbelievable array of colors shoots through my brain and I see a kaleidoscope of incredible dancing images— *waltzing* images—we're waltzing under the twelve moons of the Hibiscus Coast, we're waltzing in the shadow of the Fragrant Mountains, we're waltzing on the shore of the Jasmine Sea. We're like two hot flames on a cool night that come together and move apart, back and forth, back and forth, my pheromones and her pheromones attracting each other, bouncing off walls and squeezing through steel. We're like flamenco dancers on the Andalusian Plains drunk on wine and paella. We're like Italian anarchists gone all soft and gooey at the Berlin Love Parade. We're like freewheeling clusters of sexual matter that meet in space and do the hugga-bugga. Our pheromones don't stand on ceremony, they don't play games and they don't take no for an answer. After all, it's a strange kind of chemistry we have, it pulls and repels at the same time...

Parsifal Unleashed

Part III

INT. AMFORTAS' CASTLE – DAY
The Holy Grail sits inside its shrine, dull, dark and lifeless. A deathly quiet surrounds the room. The camera slowly pulls back to include Amfortas, who lies in bed, his wound getting worse, his pain unbearable.

> AMFORTAS
> *Let me die, dear God, let me rest at last!*

> GURNEMANZ
> *Please, good King, try to*
> *hold on a little longer.*

> AMFORTAS
> *I cannot! Only the Spear can save me*
> *and only one man can wrestle the*
> *Spear from the forces of evil.*

The Squire pulls Gurnemanz aside and whispers into his ear.

> SQUIRE
> *What of the pure fool for whom*
> *we wait? Surely he must come!*

> GURNEMANZ
> *So it is written. Let us pray it is so...*

EXT. FOREST – DAY
Parsifal roams the countryside, lost and alone. He falls to his knees and looks to the heavens.

> PARSIFAL
> *Where do I go? How do I*
> *eat? Where is my home?*

A falcon appears above his head. Parsifal pulls out his bow and arrow and takes aim, then drops his weapon with shame.

> PARSIFAL
> *Forgive me, beautiful bird, I wish*
> *you no harm. I have lost my way.*

The falcon flutters down and lands on Parsifal's shoulder. The young man strokes its wings. The bird nuzzles into his chest, then slowly flies ahead, leading Parsifal deeper into the forest.

FALCON'S P.O.V. – BIRD'S-EYE AERIAL VIEW OF THE FOREST

> PARSIFAL
> *Where do you take me? Are you a*
> *sign from the heavens? I follow you,*
> *dear bird, but I know not where.*

INT. KLINGSOR'S CASTLE - DAY
The sorcerer's lair is dark and dirty, like a waiting room to hell. Klingsor paces back and forth, impatient, waiting for something. In his hand is the Spear of Longinus. He waves it through the air as if to vanquish an invisible enemy.

> KLINGSOR
> *Soon, the Grail will be mine!*

EXT. FOREST – DAY
Parsifal climbs a hill and sees a dark and dreary castle in the distance. The fortress rises straight up and disappears into a thick, soupy fog.

> PARSIFAL
> *What a strange and enchanting*
> *cloud cover...*

EXT. KLINGSOR'S CASTLE - DAY
Behind the castle great explosions rock the grounds.

ANGLE ON KLINGSOR'S ARMY
training in the field, shooting burning arrows into the sky and setting oil drums on fire.

> PARSIFAL (V.O.)
> *Look, little bird, even now they*
> *practice their arts and crafts.*

INT. KLINGSOR'S CASTLE - DAY
A Dark Knight, tiny as a tick, stares into a magic mirror, rubbing his hands with glee. Unable to speak, he mutters an alarm.

> DARK KNIGHT
> *Aaaak! Aaaak!*

Klingsor hurries into the room to see what the commotion is about. He pushes the Dark Knight aside and leers into the mirror.

> KLINGSOR
> *What's this?*

CLOSE-UP ON THE MAGIC MIRROR –
Parsifal is seen approaching the castle.

> KLINGSOR
> *It is him! The guileless fool! The one*
> *who is prophesized! Only he can*
> *capture the Spear and cure the King.*
> *Once I slay him, the coast is clear.*
> *The Castle of the Grail shall be mine!*

The Dark Knight excitedly raises his arm in a stiff salute to his master.

> DARK KNIGHT
> *Aaaak! Aaaak!*

Klingsor pushes past him and calls to a room higher in the castle.

> KLINGSOR
> *Kundry! Awake!*

INT. UPPER CHAMBERS – DAY
Kundry awakens in a bed of leaves. It looks like she's been asleep for months. Her hair is matted into a hideous mess. Her burlap dress hangs like a sack of potatoes. Her deerskin boots fall to her ankles.

KUNDRY
What does he want of me?
Pray, leave me alone!

INT. KLINGSOR'S CASTLE - DAY
Klingsor positions the Dark Knight at the window of the turret.

KLINGSOR
Watch for him with your hawk eyes.
I want to know the minute he arrives.
And wait until you see what we have
for Kundry! The one who can absolve her
sins is soon upon us. Too bad she must
destroy her only chance for salvation!

Klingsor cackles with glee.

ANGLE ON KUNDRY
arriving in a disheveled state.

KUNDRY
Why do you wake me from
the sleep of innocence?

KLINGSOR
You know nothing of innocence,
harlot! It is time to utilize
your greatest talents!

KUNDRY
No, I beg you, leave it to
others. I am old and tired.

KLINGSOR
Not for long. It is time
to do my bidding!

Klingsor dips his hand into a bag and pulls out a magic powder. He throws it into the air and watches as it slowly descends over Kundry's head.

KUNDRY
Not again!

INT. BELL TOWER – DAY
A discordant bell tolls in the castle tower. An Evil Priest rings the clapper with a crazed look in his eyes. He wears a heavy silver cross and a black frock.

EXT. KLINGSOR'S CASTLE – DAY
Parsifal holds his ears as he approaches the gate. The doors open and the Evil Priest slowly ambles outside. He is surprised to see the young man standing there.

EVIL PRIEST
What, ho?

PARSIFAL
The bells, are they not slightly off in pitch?

EVIL PRIEST
Certainly not. I have tuned them myself.

PARSIFAL
And this fortress, is it not taller than usual?

EVIL PRIEST
What if it is?

PARSIFAL
*And these walls, are they
not of provocative design?*

The Priest takes a long look at the young visitor. His tone mellows as Parsifal's earnestness wins him over.

EVIL PRIEST
Not everyone notices.

PARSIFAL
*I have been told that form
follows function. This fortress
challenges all of my assumptions.*

                    EVIL PRIEST
        And so it should. A fortress must blend into
        the surroundings. It should be of low profile
        when constructed in the plains and bold
        and expansive when built in the hills.

                     PARSIFAL
          Interesting. And yet, in your desire to
          break the rules, have you not simply
           created a whole new set of rules?

                    EVIL PRIEST
          You speak with the wildness of
           youth. What brings you here?

                     PARSIFAL
             Something calls me.

                    EVIL PRIEST
        Would you like to see the balustrades,
       cornices, dormers and porticos? I could
      show you the mortar work and fenestration.

                     PARSIFAL
           Maybe later. Is Klingsor in?

                    EVIL PRIEST
                 I'll see.

INT. KLINGSOR'S CASTLE - DAY
The Dark Knight notices movement at the base of the tower.
He calls to Klingsor.

                    DARK KNIGHT
                Aaaak! Aaaak!

Klingsor rushes to the edge of the turret and glances down.

                     KLINGSOR
            It is time, my fine witch!

He turns to Kundry and motions her to the garden.

KLINGSOR
Now, go. Your young man awaits.

CLOSE-UP ON KUNDRY
now young and beautiful. She is transformed. Her hair is
swooped into a perfectly balanced butterfly's nest that
swirls around, then drops into a modified pony tail that
brushes against her shoulders.

KUNDRY
I am crazy with desire...

Klingsor sprinkles his magic powder over the inner chamber
of the castle.

INT. CASTLE CHAMBER - DAY
The magic powder glistens in the air as it falls from the
turret, then slowly settles on the walls and floor of the lower
chamber. A lush garden blossoms amid the dark and
forbidding walls. Parsifal and the Evil Priest enter the garden.

PARSIFAL
Is it marigold I smell? The
perfume of an enchanted flower?

Kundry appears in the doorway. A flower is pinned in the
swirls of her hair.

EVIL PRIEST
Yes, but note the entablature between
the columns and the roof, if you will.

Parsifal gazes up at the broad expanse of the ceiling.

PARSIFAL
The columns are Doric, I believe.

EVIL PRIEST
Corinthian, actually. If you look
carefully above the plinth, you'll
notice the carved acanthus leaves.

> PARSIFAL
Yes, quite.

Kundry stands in the doorway. She brushes her fingers through her hair, trying to get Parsifal's attention.

> EVIL PRIEST
I'm especially drawn to the
arches. You see how the
haunches angle majestically
toward the center crown?

> PARSIFAL
Impressive, indeed. The pediment
over the doorway is also intriguing.

> KUNDRY
Ahem...

> EVIL PRIEST
And see how the tympanum
is exquisitely carved?

Kundry flies into a rage. She marches down into the garden, grabs the arm of the Evil Priest and leads him to the door.

> KUNDRY
Beat it, fool. You are
ruining my scene.

The Priest hastens away. Parsifal calls after him.

> PARSIFAL
Well, thanks for the tour...

Kundry gathers herself and approaches the young man. She slightly opens the top of her dress, displaying an ample cleavage.

> KUNDRY
Welcome, Parsifal. I have
waited long for this day.

PARSIFAL
But how do you know my
name? Have we met before?

KUNDRY
Don't worry your weary head.
Come, rest on my shoulder.

PARSIFAL
I'm really not tired—

KUNDRY
Of course, you are. You must
rest and reflect. Soon it
will all be revealed...

Chapter 18

The sound of a slamming door crackles through the air and eight magenta bowling pins scatter down the throbbing, aching, head-splitting back alleys of my brain. I'm left with a seven-ten split, an impossible shot, and if that doesn't perfectly encapsulate my neurological situation I don't know what does. I awaken to an indistinct Los Angeles morning. Mornings in L.A. are always the same—hazy skies, hot temperatures and the vague feeling that today will be the day that makes it all worthwhile. I'm rejuvenated by a kind of forced optimism that runs through the pipes of the ReTan Hotel. After all, if water can make it all the way up to this room, can't I write a simple screenplay that will rise to the level of a Hollywood movie? Of course, I can. I splash some water over my face and comb the neon out of my hair. It feels good. I'm in the right place at the right time. I have the right project with the right producer. It's time to take my rightful place at the table...

There's an executive shift at Paramount Pictures and I find

myself actually caring. This is what happens when I sit in the outer office of the Producer Who Shall Remain Nameless waiting for my next meeting. Twenty minutes is just enough time to peruse tomorrow's *Variety* and catch up on all the developments in Hollywood that have never had, do not presently have and most likely never will have any impact on my life. In San Francisco I'm blissfully ignorant of the inner workings of the movie business, but in Los Angeles I'm immersed in the intricacies of who's hot, who's not and what's being shot on which lot. There's a little blurb on Page Two about Bobby Littman negotiating a "very nice" deal on some hush-hush project, but details are scarce and names even scarcer. For a moment I think it must be me they're talking about, that Bobby simply forgot to mention our "very nice" six-figure deal and that all of my worries are over. Then the big black Labrador bounds into the room, drools on my pants and jolts me back to reality.

"Have you heard anything about the deal?" I ask him in dog speak.

"I'm really not at liberty to discuss anything of a potentially sensitive nature."

"No-no, of course not, I'm just wondering what the Producer thought of the script."

"Do you have any Chewy Bones for me to gnaw on?"

I dig into my pocket as if hoping to find something. "No, I don't seem—"

"I like Chewy Bones."

"I'll bring some next time."

"If there is a next time," says the Lab, knowingly.

"Well! How's San Francisco?" calls the Producer Who Shall Remain Nameless from the doorway of her office. "Do the little cable cars still climb halfway to the stars?"

"Right over the Golden Gate Bridge."

"And through the fog."

"There's no such thing as fog," I jokingly remind her. "It's just low clouds."

"Yes," she says, her smile fading. "I must remember that." She obviously doesn't get the joke. I'm not sure I do, either. She also doesn't even remember that I've been in L.A. all this time and that she is paying for it. Is she completely out of touch with anything outside her Santa Monica bungalow? She leads me into her office and motions for me to sit: "Well, I see all the new things you've added..."

"I just tried following your suggestions," I say, disingenuously. The fact is, I don't even remember her suggestions. I'm not sure she even *had* any suggestions. If she did she doesn't remember them either. It's a game that producers and writers play. Producers make suggestions and writers pretend to follow them. Then they have meetings to talk about all the changes that were never made. "Your ideas really opened my eyes."

"Yes, good," she says, paging through the script.

"Of course, it's not done yet. I just want to get your feedback before moving on."

"Let me just make sure I understand," says the producer as she runs her fingers over the title page. "You've got a hero on his way to meet an evil sorcerer, a witch is ready to seduce him, everything around the castle is exploding and all of a sudden, in the middle of nowhere, you throw in a ten minute lecture on architecture? Is that right?"

"I think it's more like six or seven minutes."

"Um-hmm. Tell me something, just for the sake of argument. What in God's name were you thinking?"

"You said you wanted sophisticated."

"Who the hell cares about the design of a castle in a medieval action-adventure?"

"The architecture is the key to the story. You lose the architecture, you lose everything."

"That's what you said about the sorcerer."

"Well, like I said, it's just a rough draft—"

The producer takes a deep breath, then drops the script upside down on her desk so that my name and the title are no longer visible. "I'm not sure this is going to fit on our production slate anymore," she says, fixing me with a stare. "I liked it better before."

"Uh-huh, good..." Wait a minute. Did she just say—

The world explodes. It's a sickening thud, kind of like a wheel falling off a car and the axle being dragged along the tarmac. Oh, yes, the world has blown right out of its orbit and is spinning into a terrible abyss. We're breaking all the laws—the speed of sound, the speed of light, the speed of speed—as this little planet of ours tumbles wildly into a whole new anti-dimension where Einstein plays chess with Madame Blavatsky and always loses, that's right, we've blasted right through into an *anti-dimension* and all because the Producer Who Shall Remain Nameless liked my script better *before*. Is she completely mad? The script is obviously so much better than before that I don't even know how to respond. "No. No-no-no," I sputter. "You need to read it again."

"I already read it."

"Look, there's obviously no way I could spend all this time writing this and wind up making it *worse*. It doesn't make sense."

She looks at me with a frozen expression. "Is this another fog theory?"

"You just need to let it sit for a day or two. Give it another read. You'll see what I mean."

"That really won't be necessary. I have other projects—"

I feel myself losing it. "Other projects? What the hell do you know about other projects? You wouldn't know a good project if it bit you in the ass."

The producer reflexively pushes back in her chair. "Listen, I need to trust the people I work with. This is a tough business."

"What are you saying, that I'm not good enough to write for you? There's a hell of a lot of producers better than you I'm not good enough to write for."

The Producer Who Shall Remain Nameless spins around in her chair, her face reddening. "You'll never work in this town again!"

"I never *did* work in this town!"

She glances at her watch and coolly regains her composure. "I have to be on the lot in an hour," she says, motioning to the hallway. "I'll call Bobby later. We'll talk—"

"Yeah, yeah, we'll talk," I say, forcing out the words. I move zombie-like to the door. My eyes are glazed. My legs are stiff. I have a strange desire to eat human flesh. The earth puts on the brakes and stops spinning altogether. We're just sitting there in space, out of kilter, out of orbit, out of whack. There will be no more seasons, no day or night, no need for clocks. It will be 11:17 A.M. everywhere on earth for eternity. The deal is dead. The movie is over. The Chewy Bones are history.

Chapter 19

I slink back to San Francisco, debased, demoralized and defeated. I feel like I've been wandering the Gobi desert for forty days, trapped on an ice floe in the North Atlantic and fed upon by a thousand rabid bats in an Incan cave. It's time to call it quits. I've finally had it. Hollywood has sent me over the edge and done me in. Here I am, Dr. Gold, I'm all yours, I'm donating my body to science—who cares if I'm not dead yet?—just wrap me up in a sheet and mail me to the nearest laboratory, go ahead, paste a couple of stamps on my forehead and drop me into a mailbox, I won't make a peep, I'll just lie there with all the other junk mail, fourth class, do not return to sender, dispose of upon delivery, go right ahead, probe my brain for a treasure trove of misplaced neurons, faulty synapses and disjointed tissues, oh yes, I'm quite a specimen, half-blind and half-deaf, asthmatic and anaphylactic, disoriented and disillusioned, go right ahead, give me the old scalpel to the forehead, dig around in there, see what delights you can come up with—

"So, how was L.A.?" asks Dr. Gold, as he flashes a pinpoint of light into my good eye.

"Oh, not bad at all," I say, calm as a clam. "Pretty good, I'd say. "

"Anything new on the movie front?"

"Well, you know Hollywood. Every day is a new beginning."

"Don't forget, I get tickets to opening night."

"Sure, sure—"

"For me and my wife."

"Front row, center—"

"I've got a couple of cousins."

"Yeah, cousins—"

"And my Uncle Pete, too."

And with that, I completely lose it. "Uncle *Pete?*" I scream. "Opening *night?* There *is* no opening night! There's nothing, understand, nothing at all, nothing but a black hole in the pit of my stomach that drains into an endless cesspool of slime and decay."

Dr. Gold looks at me with alarm. "When did you start having digestion problems?"

"This isn't indigestion! Don't you see? My whole system is shutting down! I haven't even been home yet! You're my first stop! I'm in a state of complete collapse!"

Dr. Gold wraps a blood pressure sleeve around my arm and pumps up the valve. He listens to my heart, chest and lungs and takes my pulse. "Your vital signs are all within an acceptable range."

"Are you listening to me? What I've got can't be measured with a stethoscope. Something big is about to happen. I can feel it in my bones. I'm on the verge of an out-of-body experience."

Dr. Gold leans against the stirrups of his examination table and glances out the window. "Do you know the work of Kandinsky?"

"Kandinsky, the butcher?" I say with a straight face. Even now I can't help myself. Sometimes the Jewish humor thing gets a little out of control.

"Kandinsky, the painter. He said, '*Stop thinking.*'"

"I know just what he means."

"Do you? He was a synesthete, too. Many artists are. He painted the sounds he saw. He was of the opinion that creativity comes from some part of the brain that defies analysis. If you think about it too much, you kill the creative impulse."

"I think the creative impulse is about to kill *me*."

"Did you know that many synesthetes are compulsive and can't work on a messy desk or with dirty dishes in the sink? That many report unusual psychic phenomena, like déjà vu, esp, telepathy and clairvoyance? Does any of that sound familiar?"

"What, are you kidding?"

Dr. Gold sits back on his stool and pushes his tortoise shell glasses up his nose. "Listen, I want you to take this to heart," he says with particular seriousness. "I want you to stop thinking. It's the best advice I can give you."

"How am I supposed to stop thinking? That's like asking me to stop breathing."

"If you're not careful I'm afraid that might be the next stage."

"I see, so that's how it's going to be," I say, satisfied at least to have gotten his full attention. "How long have I got, Doc?"

"How long do you want?"

"A couple of weeks should do it."

Dr. Gold pages through his notes, glances over at one of his arcane physiological charts and puts his hand on my knee. "I'll see what I can do."

Yeah, a couple of weeks should do it. That's more than enough. I don't think I could take much more of this torture, especially when I step outside Dr. Gold's office and find the big black Oldsmobile waiting for me at the curb. Has this thing got some kind of radar that spots me the minute I return to San Francisco? I approach cautiously, wondering if it's back for another game of tag, but this time the driver has something else in mind. He lowers the darkened window just enough to fling me a newspaper, which I catch with the quick hands of an old paperboy. The window rolls up, the engine starts, a black cloud of toxic smoke belches out of the tailpipes and the Oldsmobile rumbles off down the street. I glance at the front page. What is it, a coded message from Walter Horn? A cryptic warning from crazed occultists? An offer of a free subscription to the *San Francisco Chronicle*? Hardly. There's nothing there but extended coverage of the World Series, a rare all-Bay Area event in which the Oakland A's have taken a commanding 2-0 lead over the San Francisco Giants. It makes no sense.

I slip the newspaper under my arm and try to get lost in the all-too-familiar sights of the neighborhood. I walk past the deserted robe shop, glance into the window of the closed bakery, skitter past Sts. Peter and Paul Church and meander through Washington Square Park. A dog barks. A bottle of vodka falls out of the fireman's hand. A lonely harmonica plays in the distance. The notes get blown by the wind and fall in little droplets along the cold and winding path. I follow them home.

At the top of the Filbert Steps I pry open my mailbox and pull out two weeks of overdue bills, a bank statement and a bunch of junk mail. The only thing vaguely of interest is a jury summons from the San Francisco County Superior Court. Ho! That's a good one! Maybe they'll make me foreman! I rip up the whole mess and toss it into the garbage. I haven't been home in ages and wonder if the place is even still there. Any number of things could've happened to shut me down—the health department, the permit department, the apartment department—any one of them could've come by and said, "That's it, you've pushed beyond all reasonable limits and a few unreasonable ones as well. We're condemning your cottage, we're condemning you and we're condemning everyone around you, too. Begone, Caretaker, begone and goodbye."

I glance into the eucalyptus grove. There's no sign of Barbara. I glance up at the top floor of the Big House. There's no sign of That Guy. I glance at the lower limbs of a fennel plant. There's no sign of Bernard. I glance inside a passing paddy wagon. There's no sign of Kuiper. I consider these lack of signs to be a very good sign. Then I hear the big electric door of Waverly Wellington's garage clanking open and see someone in a three-piece suit ducking under the mechanism. Is Gregory Peck here for the weekend? Is the ambassador from some island nation in the South Pacific selling off his country's treasure? Is Princess Lee Radziwell arriving for a costume ball?

I walk down the path and discover that not only is the cottage still there, it appears to be in one piece. The door is locked, the windows are closed and the roof is attached to the walls. Inside I discover that the fungus is still in the shower, the animal larvae is still behind the stove and the box is still on the desk. I take strange comfort in reconnecting with these old buddies of mine—contempt breeds familiarity?—even if I'd much prefer that they were rotting away in some garbage dump in the desert.

Taking Dr. Gold's advice I try not to think about the ivy sneaking through the cracks in the wall or the hissing of the granny killer in the corner or the draft blowing under the door. Then I try not to think about how my career has hit rock bottom or how I'm going to survive another day up here. Then I try not to think about my childhood, my family or the Norman invasion of Scotland in 1066. Kandinsky the butcher would be proud of me.

In an effort to distract myself from the inner workings of my brain I page through the *San Francisco Chronicle*, wondering why someone would give me a two-day-old newspaper. When I turn to the Obituary Page, it all becomes clear:

WALTER HORN, A DISTINGUISHED ART HISTORIAN AND PROFESSOR AT THE UNIVERSITY OF CALIFORNIA AT BERKELEY, DIED TUESDAY OF PNEUMONIA AT HIS HOME IN POINT RICHMOND. HE WAS EIGHTY-SEVEN. PROFESSOR HORN, A NATIVE OF HEIDEL-BERG, GERMANY, WAS THE FIRST ART HISTORY PRO-FESSOR IN THE UC SYSTEM AND WAS A MAJOR FORCE IN THE ESTABLISHMENT OF UC BERKELEY'S ART MUSEUM. HE RETIRED IN 1974 AFTER THIRTY-SEVEN YEARS AS A PROFESSOR.

PROFESSOR HORN CAME TO THE UNITED STATES FROM GERMANY IN 1938 AS A FERVENT ANTI-NAZI. DURING THE WAR HE SERVED AS A LIEUTENANT IN GENERAL GEORGE S. PATTON'S THIRD ARMY IN-TERROGATING PRISONERS OF WAR. IMMEDIATELY AFTER THE WAR, AS A SPECIAL INVESTIGATOR FOR THE AMERICAN MILITARY GOVERNMENT IN GERMANY, HE HELPED TRACK DOWN ART THAT HAD BEEN LOOTED OR HIDDEN BY THE NAZIS. HIS MOST SPECTACULAR FEAT WAS THE RECOVERY OF CHARLEMAGNE'S CEREMONIAL REGALIA, THE CROWN, SCEPTER, SPEAR AND JEWELS OF THE HO-LY ROMAN EMPIRE, WHICH HAD BEEN CONCEALED, PRESUMABLY FOR LATER USE AS PROPAGANDA BY GERMANS WHO STILL HOPED TO REGROUP AFTER DEFEAT BY THE ALLIES. HE LEFT THE ARMY IN 1946 WITH THE RANK OF CAPTAIN.

I feel a strange sense of loss, even though my meeting with Walter Horn hadn't been very successful. He was a tough old guy, that's for sure, somebody who wasn't going to be pushed around. So what if he was a bit paranoid? He'd been through a lot and maybe things got a bit twisted. After all, not everybody gets thrown into the middle of an incredible historical event and comes out in one piece. Especially when certain people refuse to let the story die. I slide into bed and turn off the lights. God knows what Horn thought I was up to. That I was a Nazi sympathizer from fifty years in the future come to resurrect the Reich? Sure, that makes a lot of sense. At least I know it wasn't Walter Horn who was following me, but why would somebody else want me to see his obituary? And why have they been following me all over San Francisco? And how do they know where I live? I feel my mind emptying out as I begin to fall off to sleep.

I sleep all night, all morning and all the next afternoon, trying to erase any traces of my two weeks in the Southland. I finally awaken to the pitter-patter of little feet on the ceiling above my head. The raccoons have boosted their irritation level to new heights and apparently are shooting for some kind of world record. Are they training for the Boston Marathon? Around and around they go, louder and louder, clawing their way along a circular track full of cracks, curves and potholes. Each scrunch and scrape sends a new crooked pattern zooming through my brain—neon commas, pulsating asterisks, iridescent semicolons—until the light show in my hippocampus finally goes black, leaving me with a bunch of coming attractions but no main feature.

I lie in bed with a sense of panic and foreboding. I feel a rumbling in the deepest part of my stomach and a slight swaying in my head. My toes tingle. I have a strange taste of sulfur in my mouth and saltwater in my eyes. The walls move slightly, the archway over the door dips in a meek curtsy and I feel anger rising within me, anger at the world, anger at myself, anger at the whole human condition. I force myself out of bed, make my way to the bathroom, and look into the mirror. "Dad? You in there?" I call out. "C'mon, wake up, we need to talk."

"Huh?" says Dad after a long moment. "What time is it?"

"I've got to ask you something. It's important. My whole life depends on it. Tell me, once and for all, why have we been writing all these years? What's the point?"

"Beats me."

"C'mon, you've got to do better than that."

"No, really, I haven't got a clue. I've been hoping you'd figure it out."

"We've been at this forever. Me, you, your dad, his dad. Don't you think that's enough?"

"More than enough."

"Okay, well, how about I just stop writing?"

"Fine by me. I tried that once myself. You know what happened?"

"What?"

"Your mother asked me to write down a shopping list one day and I gave her fifty-eight pages of notes."

"What are you telling me, that it's out of our control? I can't believe that."

"Believe what you want. I've got no idea."

I wipe the sleep out of my eyes and look back into the mirror. I barely recognize the pale and drawn visage that stares back at me. "Man, I really look like shit."

A dog howls in the distance. There's a pregnant pause from inside the mirror, as if Dad is contemplating something important. "Hey, what ever happened with that Emma Hound woman?" he finally says.

"Emma Hound? From *The Northwest Reporter*? That was thirty years ago."

"Maybe you could still write some of those letters to the editor. You were good at that."

"You want me to write fake letters to the editor? Is that what you're telling me?"

"It's just an idea."

"Thanks, Dad. Sometimes I wonder how I ever got through life without your advice." I stare back into the mirror at my bloodshot eyes. It looks like I haven't slept in weeks.

"When are you going to do something about those raccoons?" the old man chimes in.

"Maybe tomorrow."

"Yeah, maybe tomorrow. That's you, isn't it?"

"You know me, Dad."

"I sure do, Son."

I come out of the bathroom feeling dizzy. The kitchen floor ripples as I walk back into the bedroom and I need to hold onto the walls to steady myself. The howling dog is joined by more yelping from all over the hillside. Wild geese squeal from the skies as they circle Coit Tower. Three cats simultaneously go into heat. A yellow canary falls out of an upper branch of the pepper tree outside my door and lands on the patio, dead.

I glance over at the box, the box that showed up one day like an unwelcome relative and refuses to leave. It sits there, smug as always, occupying the choicest spot on my desk, forcing me to walk around it with deference and caution. Did it ever occur to the box that maybe I'd like to put a nice plant on the desk or a photo album or a little bundle of Barbara's potpourri to freshen up the place? No, of course not, the box couldn't care less what I think. Why? Because the box has gotten the upper hand. The box has me over a barrel. I can't touch it. I can't move it. I can't rearrange it. Oh, really? Well, every man has his limits and I've just reached mine.

"Every man has his limits!" I scream at the box as I charge across the room, "and I've just reached mine!" I grab the box with both hands and pick it up off the desk. It's lighter than I expected, not so light as to be empty, but not heavy enough to hold forty pounds of bubonic plague spores either. I tap my fingers on the side of the box, then listen for any kind of echo or thud or sizzle. Nothing happens. I give the box a shake. Nothing explodes. I give it a sturdier shake, then, growing in confidence, I shake the living daylights out of it. Still nothing.

I set the box on the floor and walk around it a few times. Looking at it from this angle, from above, it seems less ominous than before. It's all in the context—I think Frank Lloyd Wright said that—and in the context of the floor, the box seems significantly less deadly than on the desk. The desk gave it a place of exaggerated importance, of nearly monumental stature, whereas the floor is the floor. I kick the box.

Still nothing happens. Then I kick it again. And again. I kick it all over the room, this fucking piece of shit box that has ruined my life for at least a month now, this box that has kept me awake at night and kept me from working during the day, this box that has assumed mythic proportions and sent me to the depths of despair, this fucking, fucking box that has become the central artifact in my life, what is it, a box of chocolates, is that what I've been torturing myself over, a two-pound box of Whitman's Samplers for my birthday? Is it a box of Kleenex to wipe away my tears of laughter for having been such a fool? Is it a box of fun? A box of tricks? A box of chicken wings? A box of cigars? A box of cereal? A box of crackers?

I look down at the label. It still says *Do Not Open*, but from this angle it looks more like a suggestion than an order. Why shouldn't I open it, is something going to go stale? Is something going to pop out of it on a spring? Will I get a stomach ache if I eat too much? I grab a pair of scissors, cut the plastic cord, slice the blade through the tape, pull back the flaps, and open the box—

"Aaaaaaaaaaaaaaaaaaaaaaaaaaaaahhhhhhh."

I feel myself being lifted right off the floor. A rocking, rolling, roiling sensation overcomes me and I hear an enormous cracking sound as if the world is being split in half. The walls shake, the windows break, the floor heaves to and fro and everything crashes to the ground. I grab onto the edge of the desk as the lake beneath the floor gurgles up and sends a wave rushing through the room, then backs up and pulls half the carpet off the baseboards. The exquisitely crafted nineteenth century European door creaks and groans and shoots right off its hinges. A brick falls through the fireplace. The granny killer blubbers, shudders and completely conks out. Then comes another rolling motion and a quick jolt that pushes right up through my spine. The mattress jumps a full six inches, then flops back on the platform with a thwack. My closet door jerks opens and empties three weeks of dirty laundry onto the floor. The refrigerator gurgles, the ice tray cracks in half and the motor dies.

Outside, day becomes night as the earth struggles to get back on its axis. Dogs belly flop into puddles of rain, birds fly upside down and raccoons rush bleary-eyed to midnight rendezvous. The ivy curls up the wall of the cottage as if to hold it in a witch's gnarly embrace. Redwoods dig in for a period of rootlessness. Nasturtiums suck their scent from the air. I stagger to the patio and watch Coit Tower swaying above me as a familiar soprano bellows her warning over the hill: "Earthquaaaaaaaaaaake!"

There's a momentary lull, then total silence. I see some smoke in the distance and hear a few sirens. Then a hundred car alarms go off in unison, simultaneously recovering from the shock. The sky looks strangely pink, as if it were preparing for a tropical sunset. The pepper tree shakes its trunk, as if to make sure it's still alive. I feel my hands trembling and my body shaking as I head back into the cottage. The box is still there, sitting on the floor with its flaps open. I approach cautiously, then bend down and look inside. There's a bunch of wadded up newspaper shoved into the bottom as filling. Blocks of Styrofoam provide some basic protection at the corners. Around the top is a haphazard array of popcorn stuffing and bubble wrap. Beneath it a blue towel is carelessly wrapped around something of apparently little value. Whoever put this package together was either in a rush, incredibly sloppy or dead drunk. I pull back the towel and find a strange metal object that's about sixteen inches long with coarse edges and a flanged base. It has a kind of a crude blade with a nail tied around its center that's held by strands of gold, silver and copper wire. On either side of the blade are cross-hatched markings that are crudely etched into the metal. There's a note inside the box with twelve simple words:

I WARNED YOU NOT TO OPEN THE BOX.
NOW IT'S YOUR PROBLEM.

The note is signed, 'Walter Horn.' Now, perhaps this is a very elaborate hoax or an extremely bad joke but it appears that on this day, October 17, 1989, at precisely 5:04 P.M., at the exact moment of an earthquake of significant magnitude, I have, with absolutely no foreknowledge of, prior involvement with, or professional interest in, and, having heretofore expressed no claim to, ownership of, or partnership in, and, averring that receipt of any such delivery was unsolicited, unwanted, and thoroughly unexpected, it does, nonetheless, appear that somehow or other, by hook or by crook, one way or another, I have, unbeknownst and unknowingly, taken full and total possession of the Spear of Longinus, the most sought-after relic in all Christendom.

Caveat emptor.

INTERLUDE

In which walls shake, floors buckle, rivers flood, bridges collapse, windows rattle, cages throb, clearings rumble, bells toll, jails open, and the anthurium shudders with bad vibrations...

Interlude

Fifty-seven thousand feet beneath the surface of the earth, the San Andreas Fault slips just slightly. It's more of a hiccup than a full-blown seismic event, a slip on a banana peel rather than a complete collapse, a shaker rather than a trembler, but this mini-cataclysm—epicenter at Loma Prieta, California, magnitude 7.1 on the Richter Scale—is more than enough to get everyone's attention if not quite enough to cause full scale panic. It is, in fact, nothing more than a chunk of earth somewhere far below the surface shearing off and falling just a bit farther below, from one dark corner to an even darker corner, but Mother Earth, occasionally being of unsound mind and ornery disposition, can't just leave it at that, no, she has to insist on consequences and ramifications, and so this little shockwave of activity courses up through the ground, through the upper mantle, the oceanic crust and the continental crust, through iron and sodium and potassium, through roots and rocks and dried up river beds, and then it moves right under the Bay, along the Embarcadero and into North Beach, and this little ganglia of energy reaches out its octopus tentacles and gives a good shake to the streets and the trees, it knocks out the phone lines, the electric wires and the TV signals, and then it moves right into the foundations, up the central beams, through the floorboards and into the walls of every single building on Telegraph Hill.

The walls of the third floor apartment in the Big House shudder like dying leaves on an autumn tree. The walls weren't all that sturdy to begin with and the panoramic windows provide even less support when everything is swaying and threatening to collapse in a pile of rubble. In the corner of the room That Guy is caught napping beneath his blanket on the floor when a jolt pushes him to his feet. The shadows that usually hide his mouth and eyes are briefly illuminated and a pinpoint of light exposes the strangest reaction: He's actually smiling! And it's not just a little smile, it's a big smile, an immodest, unwholesome, disingenuous smile that threatens to crack right through the walls and shower the streets with glass. He shades his eyes and looks out over the Bay, where a Chinese container ship with neatly stacked, hermetically sealed containers sails under the Golden Gate Bridge, around Alcatraz and over to the Oakland headlands. The windows rattle again—ho-*hoooo!*—and he gathers some kindling for his indoor campfire. He busies himself as if preparing for some event that only he is aware of. He does a couple of quick push-ups and jogs in place, then opens a bottle of condiments and slathers them on a bun, realizing there's no reason to hold back anymore. He empties the whole jar and licks it clean. *It's coming... oh, yes, it's coming.* His eyes glow mustard yellow.

The walls of the Lusty Lady on Broadway shake day and

night to the throbbing bass of Ike Turner, the throbbing vocals of James Brown and the throbbing saxophone of Grover Washington. At this moment, however, the throbbing rises to a whole new level as the cages pulsate to a different tune. It's a ragged, jagged refrain that starts and stops as the needle skips across the record, bounces off the automatic return and starts again. A ring of pink neon falls from the ceiling. A mirror cracks into seventeen pieces. An Egyptian harem tent collapses into a pile of polyester. It takes the strippers a moment to realize that the shaking isn't the usual gyrations of their clientele, no, this is something altogether different, this is massive, this is God sending His disapproval or Nature taking Her revenge or the League of Decency coming with a tractor. As the strippers dive for cover one loyal customer, a diminutive admirer named Bernard, imagines himself bouncing on a fur-lined trampoline in silk pajamas. Unable to hear the disturbance he feels only a gentle swaying and then a jolt of energy that surges up his legs, through his loins and straight into his manhood in a Nazi erection for the ages.

The walls of the eucalyptus grove shake like a hula dancer on the dashboard of a 1957 Chevy. Woven from branches, tied with bark and held up by what appears to be mastodon bones from the early Cenozoic Era, the walls offer little protection as Barbara gets bounced off her dried leaf mattress and tossed into the upper reaches of a fennel plant. When she pulls away from the scraggly foliage an elastic branch snaps back and swats her right across the forehead as if to make sure that the point isn't lost. The forest is speaking to her, all right, and telling her that the end is near. A dark shadow passes over Barbara's face as she glances up at the Big House. The structure sits silhouetted against the sky, a hulking giant that weighs too heavily on the hill. Barbara pushes away from the fennel and retrieves some freshly made balm that's baking on a rock in the sun. She holds her fingers in the shape of a triangle, then rubs the balm over her forehead for protection. Protection against what? An earthquake that already happened? It makes no sense.

The walls of Sts. Peter and Paul shake with the creaking of a stone edifice suddenly unsure of its own might. With its huge dome and broad expanse of empty space the church exists at the center of its own galaxy, a galaxy now growing dark as a cloud of dust descends from the rafters and blankets the altar, the apse and the pews. The bells in the tower begin clanging of their own accord as if resetting the time and day. *Clang-claaaang-clang-claaaang*, they intone in a wild, haphazard cacophony. It might be morning, it might be noon, it might be Christmas Eve for all anyone knows. Father Indelicato rushes into the nave, pulling up his pants and tightening his robe. His Italian loafers slip along the dusty stone floors and he struggles to stay upright as the building sways to and fro. A statue of the Virgin Mary totters on its pedestal, threatening to fall over. The priest hurries right past her and heads for the tower stairs.

The walls of the Central Police Station shake with the groan of iron rubbing against steel as the bars of the holding cells slip right out of their tracks. The locks twist, the tumblers bend and the doors swing open in an act of God that seems to suggest—no, *demand*—a jailbreak. A drunk awakens to a world of possibilities. A petty thief recognizes a golden opportunity. A pickpocket sees fortune written in the wind. As they slip through the open doors and wander the halls Patrolman Kuiper panics. He rushes into the holding area and shoots wildly—at the cell doors, at the ceiling, at the earthquake itself—and hits a 4.6 on the Richter Scale. The guy is nuts.

The walls in Sabine's apartment rupture with a sharp jolt. The walls are adorned with paisley teardrops and it looks like they're crying. It's a controlled crying, not a raging storm of tears but rather a slow, sad trickle. The walls cry for the human condition, for wars and hunger and illness, for the orphans and the dispossessed, for star-crossed lovers and long-lost friends. The walls cry for the sunrise, they cry for the buffeting wind, they cry for the bells of Sts. Peter and Paul. The walls cry for the sad violin that drifts up from the park, for the smell of lavender that wafts in from the garden, for the curls of clouds that float past the window. And now they cry for themselves, for their own mortality, for their own place in the universe, as the support beams creak, the studs buckle and the baseboards groan.

"*Scheizer,*" says Sabine as she slides into her slippers and tosses her kimono around her shoulders. She totters across the room like a tipsy debutante on a late night cruise, rolling with a succession of ever bigger waves until she finally hears a crack in the window frame and the shattering implosion of glass. The anthurium and calathea shudder to the tremors, the heliconia topples out of its vase and the umbrella plant scatters dirt all over the carpet. The rolling stops just as fast as it began and the floor feels flatter than ever before, so flat that Sabine's feet seem to glide over the surface with no effort whatsoever, almost as if she were being swept along by some unseen gravitational force released from the core of the earth.

It's strangely quiet inside the apartment and even quieter on the street, as if the aftershocks had scared the sounds right out of the air. Sabine stares out the window at a semicircular spectrum of color that reaches across the sky. Bands of red, orange and yellow shimmer at the outer edge of the arc while rays of green, blue, indigo and violet flicker on the inside. Half a mile away, in the Bay, the colors refract off the waves in shimmering columns of glistening light. Is this normal, she wonders, that an earthquake leave a rainbow as its signature?

Sabine ventures out into North Beach. It seems safer here although she doesn't know why. The stores are mostly closed except for a few with gas generators that buzz noisily from inside crowded doorways. People walk around in a kind of half-daze seeking candles, batteries and foodstuffs for the coming days. Sabine walks along Stockton Street, past the focaccia shop that's always closed, along the edge of Washington Square Park, past the Italian deli where they sell farfalle, and is overwhelmed by an onslaught of numbers that invade her field of vision. It's as if the earthquake has shaken something loose from deep within her own brain—something primal—and released an assault of numbers the likes of which she hasn't seen since childhood.

There are numbers all over the place, often where she least expects to find them. There are street numbers, house numbers, apartment numbers, electric meter numbers, parking sign numbers, license plate numbers, expiration tag numbers, telephone pole numbers, manhole cover numbers, water main numbers, pressure gauge numbers, gas tank numbers, alarm code numbers, traffic sign numbers, newspaper rack numbers, wire gauge numbers and garage door numbers. It's an endless cascade of numbers and the numbers all have different colors that blend into the magnificent rainbow, this rainbow that is everywhere, on the sides of buildings, on the front of mailboxes, on the awnings of stores. Is this the rainbow she has been chasing ever since Parchim?

Sabine turns left at Columbus and passes Bank of the

West, Wells Fargo and Bank of America, each of them taking up a corner, then come the shops—the candy shop, the coffee shop, the jewelry shop, the knick-knack shop, the knife shop—and then all the Italian restaurants, the Broadway strip clubs and the block for serious drinkers, then it's left on Pacific at the florist shop, past the chair shop, the travel agency and finally to the Café Vienna, where there's no sign of life whatsoever. The workers have abandoned their posts—no great surprise—but Sabine's sense of duty and responsibility overwhelms her sense of rhyme and reason and she steps inside. *Ach,* the curse of being German: a thousand years of obedience can't be wiped out in one shake of the earth. The skylight above the counter lets in enough light for her to see that damage is minimal and things are no more a mess than the usual muddle and clutter left by the untidy day shift. Other than a cloud of dust having been coughed up by all the shaking, everything looks pretty much as always.

Sabine sets to work straightening the tables and chairs, an exercise that clears her mind and puts her brain in a kind of stand-by mode. It's a state of near thoughtlessness where her senses can take in a wide variety of stimuli without doing the heavy work of processing them. Sounds are sounds and colors are colors and deeper explorations of meaning and fate and destiny are altogether unnecessary. It's the time of day she likes best and no little earthquake is going to get in the way.

The minutes pass. No one comes in and Sabine has a chance to line up the coffee cups, rearrange the silverware and fill the sugar bowls exactly the way she likes them. The café has become an extension of her own kitchen and it cries out for logic and order. Shouldn't the tea spoons be next to the soup spoons and the wheat bread next to the rye? Shouldn't the bacon be next to the lettuce and the whipped cream next to the strudel? The sun moves beyond the skylight, leaving the place in near darkness. Sabine lights a dozen candles, places them around the restaurant and looks around. It's all in order, every napkin, place setting and tablecloth, except for one thing: the painting of the Hofburg Palace is tilted to one side, giving the whole room a slightly tipsy look. She climbs up on a stool and reaches over to straighten the frame when someone shuffles in through the doorway. Sabine turns to see that it's the writer, the one who comes in every day. "Oh, it's you," she says in her typically flat monotone.

"What are you doing here?" he asks.

"I am fulfilling my shift. It is Tuesday."

"We had an earthquake. You realize that, don't you?"

"I thought there was something unusual about the way everyone was running around like half-baked chicken cutlets. Was that the Big One?"

"Big enough. It was a 7.1."

"It didn't seem so big. Everything in this country gets exaggerated."

"You really shouldn't be here. You never know what's going to happen. There could be an aftershock. Or worse."

"Worse?"

"Somebody could come in here. Robbers. It's not safe."

"What would robbers rob? The sprouts? They can have them." Sabine walks back behind the counter and arranges the wine glasses on a rack that hangs over the sink. A few have smudges. She pulls them down and soaks them in soapy water, then wipes down the counter for a second time.

Tobias watches her from his table beneath the painting. He pulls out a transistor radio from his coat pocket and tries to pick up a signal. There's a little burst of static, then nothing. "Do you have any batteries?" he calls out to her. "These are dead."

Sabine picks through a box of assorted junk and hands him a fresh pack without saying a word. He slides open the plastic battery cover and replaces the battery. A second later a scratchy voice comes through the speaker—

"There's a new report of damage on the Bay Bridge, with the East span near Treasure Island closed to all traffic. The fires in the Mission District of San Francisco are forty percent contained, says the SFFD. San Francisco General reports that backup generators have kept the emergency room and essential services operating. On a sadder note the collapse of a building on Gough Street appears to have taken two lives. Broad patches of the Marina District are still in flames and police and fire marshals are keeping residents at bay. Damage to Candlestick Park was limited to a few chunks of loosened concrete, but the World Series has been postponed indefinitely. Stay tuned to live, up to the minute reports from our field reporters throughout the area. This is KGO radio, your Voice of the Earthquake."

Tobias shakes his head. "I can't believe it... it's all my fault..."

Sabine looks up from the counter, bemused. *"Your* fault? I don't think you are quite so powerful."

"You don't understand."

"Of course not. I never understand."

"I never should've opened that box—"

Sabine raises an eyebrow and mumbles to herself as she goes back to cleaning the counter. "Men and their toys."

Tobias looks at her for a long moment, studying the glint of her eyes and the angle of her eyebrows. "Can I trust you?"

"Can *you* trust *me?"* she says. "This is a very funny one."

"I mean, you're German, after all. You could be an East German spy."

"Yes, I have been sent here to learn the secrets of the Café Vienna's kitchen. Once I have the formula, the world will be mine."

"Listen, we have to talk. It's important."

"Oh? Have you come up with some new insults?"

"You misunderstand—"

"I understand very well. My English is not perfect but I know what things mean."

"Good, then maybe you'll be able to help me."

Sabine shrugs her shoulders and blows some air through her lips like the French women do in the movies. "Help you? I don't see how I could help you."

"Please, just listen."

Sabine watches as Tobias reaches under his jacket and pulls a wrapped object from inside his sleeve. "What's that?"

"Something I want to show you."

"No, it's very busy at this hour—"

"There's no one here."

"Yes, but any minute now—"

"It won't take long."

"No, really—"

He carefully unwraps the blue towel and holds up the Spear for her to see. The flickering light from the candles reflects off the metal and casts an eerie glow. Sabine takes a quick glance, despite herself.

"What's that old thing?"

"It's... it's very important."

"It doesn't look very important. It looks like something you got down the street."

"No, I assure you, it's not from around here."

"Well, where then?"

"It's hard to say. It has a long history."

Sabine looks impatient. She unscrews a salt shaker and begins filling it. "I really don't have time for this. If you want to tell me, then tell me. If you don't, I need the counter space."

"It's the Spear of Longinus."

"What's that?"

"The Spear that killed Jesus on the cross."

"Okay."

"Okay?"

"I'm not very religious."

"I don't think you understand. This is the actual Spear of a Roman Centurion—"

"Is it plastic?"

Tobias takes a deep breath. "Listen to me. I didn't just buy this at the ninety-nine-cent shop in Chinatown. This is the real thing."

"And *you* have it? Aren't you lucky!"

"This isn't a joke."

"Do you think I could borrow it sometime? There are a couple of people who come in I could use it on."

"Please, just listen. I've got to do something with this. I can't just walk around with it."

"Well, you can't leave it here. Alena would never allow it."

"Look, it's getting late. We have to get out of here. Why don't you just lock the place up and call it a day?"

"I can't go. It's almost Happy Hour."

"Will you forget Happy Hour! It's not safe here."

"Then I'll walk."

"No, I'll drive you home. There could be looters on the street."

Sabine stands there for a minute, bites her lip with indecision, then finally blows out a candle. "I'd better not get fired for this—"

Chapter 20

I wait outside the Café Vienna, my car idling in the loading zone of an empty restaurant, my head throbbing in the danger zone of incomprehensibility. One conclusion is inescapable: Walter Horn had the Spear all along. He probably brought it back with all the other war memorabilia that soldiers had collected from all over Europe. Who knows exactly what happened? He could've made a switch, shoved the Spear down his boot and feigned a limp walking back to the barracks. That red-faced, schnapps-drinking old coot! It turns out those crazy occultists were right after all. The Spear really *was* in his closet or under his bed or in the linen drawer. I wonder what he did with it. Did he take it out every night and look at it? Did he run his fingers along the edge and clasp it in his hand? Did he wrap and unwrap the nail just to see what it looked like in the moonlight? No wonder he was so paranoid! He'd stolen one of the most valuable objects in the world, something any art dealer or museum curator or rich collector would kill for. And what did it say in his obituary? Something about Nazis wanting the coronation regalia as a symbol to rally a new movement around? Are you kidding me? Those weren't just occultists he was worried about, they were *Nazi* occultists. I suddenly feel like an old blues musician on the Mississippi Delta. *Oh, Lordy, Lordy, why me?* Of all the people in the world why would Walter Horn want *me* to have the Spear of Longinus? I met the guy for maybe one hour and it wasn't all that good of an hour, at that. Was the schnapps that good?

Sabine checks the doors of the restaurant one last time, then walks over and gets into the car. "Okay. It's all locked up," she says.

I barely hear her through the arsenal of thoughts pounding around my head. Am I really considering the possibility of there being Nazis in San Francisco who are searching for an old Spear that I'm carrying around in my jacket? Ridiculous. I'm a Hollywood screenwriter, for God's sake. Can't I come up with something better than this?

"Are you all right?" says Sabine. "Your face is as white as a Bavarian toboggan run in winter."

"I'm fine," I lie.

"Well, then," she says, looking at me impatiently, "take me home. I live near the park."

"I've just got to make a quick stop," I say as Sabine looks at me suspiciously out of the corner of her eye. I pull out onto the street and drive to the corner, where a labyrinth of vehicles tries to negotiate the blacked-out intersection. North-south traffic flows smoothly for a few seconds, then east-west jumps the gun and takes over the lanes. Whatever happened to the rules of a four-way stop? *I go, you go, he goes, she goes.* Was it nothing but an exercise in verb conjugation? I turn onto Columbus Avenue, maneuver across Broadway and stop in the middle of the next intersection. "I'll be right back," I tell Sabine as I jump out of the car.

"Don't leave me here!" she yells through the window.

"Just keep your eye on things."

"I can't drive!"

"Nothing's moving, anyway."

I hurry for the Bank of America, a reassuring outpost of stability in this wobbly world of ours, and come upon a burly guard holding up a big, beefy hand. "We're closed," he says.

"It's not six yet," I protest, pulling out my grandfather's pocket watch. The truth is, my grandfather's watch doesn't even know which century it's in, much less the hour.

"There's been a run on the bank. No more withdrawals. Come back tomorrow."

"I don't want to make a withdrawal. I have a deposit."

"A deposit?" he says, rubbing his chin.

I add him to my list of chin-rubbing carpenters, car mechanics and doctors, then slip through the door before he can stop me. The bank is blissfully empty but for one lonely teller manning his post. He looks happy to have someone to talk to. "Can I help you?" he says a bit too brightly.

"I need a safe deposit box."

"Very good, sir," he says, thumbing through a sheath of papers. "If you'll just fill out these forms I'll be happy to assist you. What size were you looking for?"

"Something in an extra long."

"The Executor Box is eighteen inches with padding and double hinges."

"That'll be fine."

The teller runs his finger along a long column of numbers. "It seems all of those are taken. How about the Secretarial Box? It's just three inches shorter."

"That's too small."

"It's roomier than you might imagine," says the teller, giving me the hard sell. "Are you sure you can't fold your documents? You'd be surprised how many times we get people into smaller boxes."

"No, that's not going to work. I'll try across the street."

"Across the street?" The teller looks alarmed at the possibility of blowing the sale. The bright light of the generator accentuates the creases in his forehead as he leans in a bit closer with some confidential information. "I wouldn't advise banking with our competitors. Couldn't you hold off until the first of the month? Things often open up on the first."

"I'll have to take my chances." I say, retreating quickly.

"Did I mention that the padding is virgin felt?" he calls after me as I head for the big double doors.

Across the street I see that Wells Fargo is as dark as a tomb and Bank of the West, which I never trusted anyway, appears to be on an extended bankers' holiday. I return to the car, where Sabine awaits in a monumental traffic jam. She's nibbling on a sandwich from the Café Vienna.

"Can I ask you something?" she says. "What does it mean, to sit on pins and needles?"

"I don't know, it's just an expression."

She sits back with a shudder of irritation. "I thought maybe you were robbing every bank in North Beach."

I turn on the ignition. "I have to make another quick stop."

"You think *this* was a quick stop? If this stop was any longer, my cucumbers would become pickles."

I pull into traffic and head downtown. As we drive through the Financial District we pass hundreds of business-men wandering the streets with bewildered expressions. Hotel workers have been pressed into service and are doing their best to line up mattresses and spare blankets on the sidewalks to accommodate the overflow of people. Sabine looks around in a daze. "Is this how the capitalist class lives?"

"They're trapped. The bridge is closed down."

"The Central Committee warned us of this."

I cross Market Street and pull up outside the Greyhound Bus Terminal. Dozens of people are milling around, some coming, some going, some just standing there. "Don't go anywhere," I say, leaving the car running in a loading zone.

"Where can I go?" screams Sabine. "I don't even know where we are! This is very far from my apartment!"

I give her a reassuring wave and head for the passenger depot. The terminal is jammed with people hoping to escape the chaos. Buses are lined up outside the gates bound for Fresno, Bakersfield, Modesto, Sacramento and Redding. Me, I'll take my chances on an earthquake in San Francisco over a night in Modesto any day of the week. I follow the signs to the baggage department, locate a wall of rental lockers, deposit a pocketful of quarters, glance around to make sure that no one is looking, and slip the bounty from under my jacket into the compartment. "Just stay here for now," I whisper to the Spear, rubbing my thumb along its flange as if to reassure it. "Don't worry. I'll be back." I turn the latch, pull the key from the lock, bury it inside my pocket and make a quick exit.

Halfway to the door a rolling, shaking, gut-wrenching aftershock hits the terminal like a six-day-old chicken curry vindaloo. The ceiling creaks, the walls wobble and the floor flounders like a volatile pogo stick. As everyone rushes for the exits I fight the tide and return to the baggage room. The old building threatens to collapse at any second but I have no other choice. I push my way toward the lockers, climb over some boxes and suitcases and finally locate the correct compartment. The door seems to glow very slightly, which might be a reflection from outside, some kind of magnetic geothermal reaction, an otherworldly psychic phenomenon or simple my overactive imagination. I cautiously open the door to find the Spear lying there just as I left it, although with a distinct aura of hurt and abandonment. "All right, all right," I mutter under my breath, "I won't leave you alone." I wrap it up in the ugly blue towel, slip it inside the sleeve of my jacket and head for the exit before it does any more damage.

Outside the terminal the tremor stops and the panic

subsides, at least for the moment. A mass of humanity wanders the streets, not sure what to do or where to go. Is it safe inside? Is it safe outside? Is it safe anywhere? There's a shared sense of nervousness, fear and uncertainty that both brings people together and pushes them apart. I make my way to the curb, where my old Toyota seems no worse for the wear. I open the door to find Sabine scrunched beneath the dashboard. "Was *that* the Big One?" she asks.

"Close enough," I say, trying to downplay the fact that my mismanagement of the Spear has once again nearly done us in. "Let's get out of here."

Sabine slides back onto her seat as I get behind the wheel. "I knew I should've walked home," she says, staring at the blue towel hanging from my jacket sleeve.

"Look, I'm really sorry I got you into this," I say to her as I put the car in gear.

"It was Happy Hour. I was just about to put the toothpicks into the pizza squares."

"If something happens, I just want you to know that I would've given you bigger tips for the coffee if I had the money."

"That's what they all say."

"Not that I expect anything bad to happen—"

Sabine folds her arms over her jacket and stares straight ahead. "Take me home," she says.

"Right away."

I feel something pulling at my insides, a cramping, reflexive pain that ties my intestines into knots and squeezes the breath out of me. I hurry down the pathway to my cottage, careful not to drop the Spear but desperate to get rid of it at the same time. I feel like my body is rejecting a transplant, as if the blood types aren't mixing, the platelets are all wrong and the cell count is off.

I slip inside my house, make sure no one is watching, and prop a chair beneath the handle of my exquisitely crafted nineteenth century European door. I feel better the moment I take off my jacket, turn down the lights and tip-toe into the bathroom. "Dad?—Dad?—You up?" I whisper.

"Huh? What time is it?"

"It's Showtime."

"Can I just once get a decent night's sleep? Is it really asking so much?"

"Listen, we've got to talk about something. You remember that box that was on my desk? The one that said *Do Not Open?*"

"Let me guess. You opened it?"

"Yeah. And you know what was inside?"

"The Spear of Longinus."

"You knew that?"

"Of course I knew that. What the hell is the point of being dead if I can't know a few things?"

"You could've told me."

"You could've kept me out of the nursing home."

I stare into the mirror and see my dad in my face. It's a disconcerting sight, like I'm being violated by my own chemistry. Doesn't humanity exist under the basic agreement that everybody gets to have their own face, one to a customer? I've got my face, he's got his face and that should be that, right? This is no time to be playing games. "Look, I've got this Spear and it's making me very nervous. What am I supposed to do with it?"

"That all depends. Are you feeling good or evil?"

"Dad, this isn't funny."

"No, I'm serious. You've got a choice. You can wreck havoc, like you used to do in the basement with those darts I never should've bought you, or you can create heaven on earth. It's up to you."

"It's that easy, is it?"

"I didn't say anything about easy. I'm just saying you've got a choice. It's like what your mother and I always said about your career: Do whatever you want. By the way, how's that going?"

"Lousy."

"Listen, just make up your mind and do something. The Spear's supposed to be an object of revelation. People see things in it. Take a look. Maybe it'll tell you something."

"How can you be so blasé about this? It's like it doesn't matter what I do."

"We're all a bunch of moral relativists in the afterlife."

"That's depressing."

"You want depressing? Not being able to enjoy the sleep of death, *that's* depressing. You still got those darts?"

"Dad, I am *not* throwing darts at the raccoons."

"I don't care if you throw the Spear at the raccoons. Just do something, okay?"

"Okay."

"Can I count on you?"

I force a smile—

"Well, you know me, Dad."

The mirror forces a smile back—

"I sure do, Son."

Chapter 21

The sun slips into the ocean and night falls on San Francisco. A foghorn sounds in the distance. A lighthouse flickers across the Bay. A hint of honeysuckle wafts up from the gardens below. I remove the Spear from the towel and look at it in the glimmering candlelight. It's not really all that impressive—at least not if it's the most important religious relic of the Western world, that is—and might go unnoticed if placed on some shelf in an antique shop. Not that that's an option, of course. Put this item on a shelf and I might as well kiss the whole planet goodbye. No, the Spear stays with me until I can figure out what to do with it. Then it's bye-bye, baby, catch you on the rebound.

An indistinct glow emanates from the blade and I feel an electric charge in the air, a presence that transcends the normal senses. It's as if someone is watching me, hovering just out of sight. As I stare into the Spear of Longinus, I feel my legs getting lighter, my skin becoming translucent and my hands shimmering in the candlelight. I don't know if I'm floating in air or levitating through space or dissolving in liquid gravity, but I feel myself being transported far beyond the four walls of my cottage. It's as if I'm zipping halfway to eternity as I embark upon a journey to the far reaches of the in-here and out-there.

I'm sitting on my mattress and the Spear is cradled in my arms but I could be anywhere in the universe right now. It could be day or night, yesterday or tomorrow, as everything blends together and pushes me into a whole other zone of existence. My diminished abilities to see, hear and touch leave me with a kind of pure mind with which to process my thoughts, unencumbered by the distractions of beauty, hunger and desire. I feel smarter than before, like I'm on the verge of something big, like my brain is about to break apart and recombine into one massive idea, a pure idea, something that's going to shake the cupboard and break a few dishes.

Night gives in to day. I look at my grandfather's pocket watch and see that its hands are up, as if in a position of surrender. What is time, anyway? You can't see time, you can't touch it, you can't wrap it around your shoulders. If time can't even keep you warm on a cool, autumn morning, what good is it? I stare at the Spear and the Spear tells me:

Time only exists so that everything doesn't happen all at once. The problem is, everything did *happen all at once. It all happened at the instant of the Big Bang. The history of the universe was entirely written in one great burst of celestial creativity.*

It all just exploded into being? It went straight from nothing to something?

It went from nothing to everything. It was an intergalactic evisceration, a cosmic cleansing, not the least of which was the human experience, this life which began in the Petri dish of imagination and mutated into its thousand forms. Everything happened all at once—the births and deaths, the wars and famines, the proms and weddings—they all occurred at the exact same instant as everything blew apart, and now all you're doing is picking up the pieces.

So, it's a giant jigsaw puzzle that we're putting back together?

Exactly. And until the pieces are placed just so, they'll appear disjointed, like jagged slivers of a broken mirror. Sometimes the pieces get completely misplaced and the whole picture begins to tilt. Events appear to happen out of order, sons get born before fathers, ghosts shimmer by, the future becomes the past.

What a mess!

It's a jumble of misconception and misinterpretation that can't be set right until you recognize that time simply doesn't exist. That's when order returns. It's when the desk gets cleared and the dishes get washed.

Okay, so if there's no such thing as time, then Mondays don't necessarily follow Sundays. Night doesn't have to precede day. Afternoons can pretty much materialize whenever they want.

Now you're getting it—

No wonder my dream life and my waking life have become interchangeable! No wonder the internal wiring of my cerebral cortex is hopelessly crossed! No wonder the only order I can find is in chaos! If everything happened all at once, have I simply been separating things into specific events and then rearranging them to fit into this totally fictitious scenario that I call the story of my life?

You are the author of your own dream.

If this is all a dream it's a pretty damned crazy one. The characters seem to have walked off the pages of a medieval opera. They're like biological remnants from an earlier age, like penguins walking north or bees waggle dancing to their hives.

As we get farther and farther from the source of the Big Bang, what appears to be the advancement of life forms is actually a movement in the opposite direction. True evolution is a return to the perfect state of origin. We evolve by a series of lower and lower reincarnations until we are finally reborn as one-cell amoebas.

What is it, some kind of *reverse* evolution?

It is at that time that we reunite with the cosmos.

Then these neighbors of mine are more highly evolved than just about anyone I know—

It is the richest and most handsome among us, the most highly educated and multi-degreed, who are in the earliest stages of reverse evolution. The journey before them is the most arduous. We should be patient with them and forgive them their missteps, for they have the longest road to travel.

I feel like a cork floating in the sea, ever bobbing but never sinking. What am I supposed to do now?

It bears repeating: Every family on Earth has a destiny to complete, a specific task that is passed through the genera-tions until it is finally accomplished, from father to son to grandson. Each family is responsible for a particular piece of a grand puzzle that we are all putting together. Your family's destiny is to be writers and you are the end of your family's line. You are here to write the final chapter...

The Spear falls to my side. My eyes flicker closed. The universe around me goes into deep hibernation. Time not only stands still but collapses to its knees in total surrender. Madame Blavatsky moves her Queen to King four. Einstein sacrifices his Bishop. The chessboard shimmers in some faraway sky and disappears into the infinite abyss.

Chapter 22

I awaken from the deepest sleep of the ages. The Spear lies next to me on the bed, exhausted from its own journey over the millennia. I try to digest the events of the past evening and am left with a hole in my head you could drive an Oldsmobile through. Have I been the recipient of a profound revelation or the victim of yet another hallucination? The line between perception and delusion has blurred to the point that I almost dare not let my mind wander, fearing one day it simply won't come back.

I step outside the cottage and see Barbara walking in circles. Bernard is hanging upside down in a tree. That Guy scurries up the wall next door in one of his spidery ascents. At the top of the pathway Patrolman Kuiper spies on me through a crack in the gate. They've been around pretty much all of the time since I opened the box, as if they sensed something important was in their midst, some new energy vortex they could sponge up and ring out of me. What do they want from me, blood? Sorry to disappoint you, my little coterie of fans, but you'll get no blood from me, not a drop, because I've got to harness my strength, maintain my equilibrium and get down to writing the final chapter of my personal saga. I turn abruptly and catch them all in a high-stakes game of stare-down. Barbara wraps her burlap bag around her shoulders and walks off haughtily to her eucalyptus grove. Bernard flutters a little and falls head first from his oak branch. That Guy slips on a pipe and slides down two full stories before disappearing into the shadows. Patrolman Kuiper ducks behind the gate and loses his footing on the stairs.

What a sad bunch.

I walk up the pathway feeling trapped under the weight and responsibility of my unwanted guardianship of the Spear. The fact of the matter is, I want nothing to do with this religious albatross and haven't got the slightest idea what to do with it. Won't someone make me an offer? Wouldn't it look good over someone's mantle? C'mon, ten bucks and it's yours. I'll even throw in the towel.

Barbara appears from behind a bougainvillea. Her eyes are glazed and her brows furrowed. "The camps are full," she says, leaning in close. I can smell wild boar on her breath. "They're planning something."

"Okay, I'll look into it," I say, knowing full well that I won't.

"Look for a spot where a eucalyptus branch, a redwood tree and an elderberry stalk form a perfect isosceles triangle."

"Got it."

Barbara does some kind of holy roller hula with her hands and vanishes into the underbrush. I stop at the mailbox more out of routine than expectation. I don't even know what I'm looking for—a tax rebate? A bank error in my favor? A check from Bobby?—but it's a bad habit I got into long ago, this hope thing, and I rummage through the usual credit card rejections, overdue bills and jury summons. How many trees could be saved if everyone would just leave me alone! That's all I really want, to be left alone.

An old Mercedes pulls into the driveway next door and idles while the garage door slowly clanks open. I glance inside to see if it might be Gregory Peck or Lee Radziwell or Zsa Zsa Gabor. A thin, elderly man steps out of the car. He's wearing a full-length smoking jacket with the initials "WW" embroidered on the pocket and a matching sailor's cap with the same insignia. It's Waverly Wellington, my elusive neighbor! He looks more like somebody impersonating a rich man than a rich man himself. Twenty-one years I've lived next door and this is the first time I've ever seen him in the flesh. Talk about fate playing its hand. Isn't he the proud owner of a major art collection? Isn't his mansion a secure fortress against theft? Isn't it about time I introduced myself? The garage door opens, the car pulls in and I follow right behind him. "Yoo-hoo, Mr. Wellington," I call out.

The old man turns with a start and I see his face for the first time. He has the rubbery, elastic skin of someone who once was fat but then lost sixty pounds on a crash diet. His eyes are dark and sunken, his cheeks pale and hollow, his forehead flaking and peeling. His nose is strong and his chin is weak, an unfortunate reversal of features that leaves him both imposing and completely forgettable at the same time. His shoulders are stooped, his chest concave and his arms weak and spindly. "How did you get in here?" he says with a voice devoid of timbre or tone.

"I'm your neighbor," I say, pointing next door. "From over there. The old cottage."

"Bend down."

"Pardon me?"

"On your knees." I curtsy slightly as if in the presence of royalty, hoping that will suffice. There's a limit to my subservience, after all, even if I *am* trespassing. Wellington looks at me from above, as if from a spot atop a throne. "You're the caretaker," he says, recognizing the top of my head and my shoulders.

"That's right."

"I watch you through my telescope."

"Oh?"

"You don't really do much, do you?"

"Well, on Fridays—"

"Yes, yes, the key escapades. What can I do for you?"

"I've heard you're an art collector. Well, of course you are. Everybody knows that. There's something I want to show you."

Wellington closes the door of his Mercedes and steps toward an elevator to the upper floors. "What is it? Do you have some knick-knacks you are trying to unload?"

"Not exactly," I say as I reach into my jacket sleeve. "I have something very unusual."

"Unusual doesn't interest me. The beak of a platypus is unusual. I collect the extraordinary."

"Yes, well like I said," I say as I carefully unwrap the blue towel and hold out the Spear for him to see.

Wellington stares at it for a long moment. I see his eyes involuntarily widen and his eyebrows arch sharply before he brings them under control. "Come with me," he says, his voice barely fluctuating in tone.

We enter the elevator and head for the third floor. The lift scarcely makes a sound as it whisks us to the top of the building. Wellington glances at the Spear once or twice but doesn't say a word. The fluorescent light inside the cubicle casts a ghostly glow around his head, giving him a slightly radioactive veneer. Upon closer inspection his entire body looks smooth and shiny, as if he'd been dipped in varnish. The doors open onto a private gallery that extends across the entire expanse of the room. Wellington removes his shoes, puts on a pair of Chinese slippers and leads me past a collection of bronze sculptures, wooden masks and stone figurines. There are paintings, rugs and carvings occupying every wall, recess and alcove. We pass a row of elaborately carved display cases and enter a sunroom that overlooks the city. A telescope is propped up on a stand next to one of the Bay windows. It's aimed directly at my courtyard.

"The Spear of Longinus," says Wellington the moment we enter the room.

"So, you know what it is."

"Of course I know," he says, "It's the weapon that pierced Jesus on the cross." Wellington focuses deeply on the shaft of the Spear and quotes an arcane verse from medieval lore. *"He who possesses the Spear has the power of ultimate good or ultimate evil in the universe."*

"That's the legend. It's never to leave the side of its owner."

"How much do you want for it?"

"I don't know that I want to sell it."

"I see," says Wellington as he motions for me to sit on a luxurious leather recliner. I sink into the soft underbelly of young lamb while Wellington plops onto a high-backed Louis XVI chair that keeps his spine straight, his head tall and his body a good six inches above mine. It's a position of power quite unnecessary to assume since he's he and I'm, well, me. "One might naturally ask where you acquired such an unusual object," he says, "but I'll forgo that pleasure, wondrous story though it might be. The truth is, I don't want to hear a word about your disagreeable exploits, unsavory friends or dubious connections to this artistic rarity. In matters like this the less said, the better."

"That's fine by me."

"How do I know it's real?"

"Oh, it's real," I say, staring into the shiny blade.

"A laboratory will confirm that. They'll do a metallurgical analysis and have it carbon dated. Then we'll see if it's worth discussing any further."

"That takes time."

"Are you in a hurry? Is something pressing? A car payment, perhaps? Or a debt? Medical bills piling up?" Wellington runs a twisted finger over his chin, never taking his eyes off the Spear. "In that case, I'll give you ten thousand dollars for it right now."

"For something that might not be real?"

"I'm a gambler."

"As I said, I don't know that it's for sale. But if it was—"

"Twenty thousand."

"—if it was, I'd want to know what you'd do with it. How do I know you wouldn't turn right around and sell it?"

"I'm an art collector, not an art dealer. The Spear would stay in this very room, under lock and key. You know about locks and keys, don't you?"

"Intimately."

"Twenty thousand dollars would be quite a nest egg for a caretaker, wouldn't it?"

"Like I said, it's not just about the money."

Wellington leans back in his chair and runs his tongue over his lips. "I love a good negotiation. May I hold it?"

It occurs to me that Wellington could take the Spear, bash me over the head, throw me down the elevator shaft and no one would be the wiser. Actually that doesn't sound entirely disagreeable. If the guy knocks me off *he* can write the final chapter. "You know, it's funny how we've never met before," I say, handing him the Spear.

"I rarely get out."

"Yeah, a place like this, I guess you've got everything you need."

"Almost," says Wellington, staring at the Spear and savoring its touch. "So, young man, we seem to have reached a financial impasse. Must we bargain like they do in the bazaar?"

"You forget, I haven't decided whether to sell," I say, thinking how no one has called me a young man since Bobby Littman. Apparently caretakers, like screenwriters, stay young until everything collapses around them.

"Perhaps fifty thousand dollars would hasten your decision."

Fifty thousand dollars could hasten a lot of things, but the very thought of selling the Spear suddenly makes me feel queasy. I feel a dull, throbbing sensation in my head and a clenching in my gut. I watch Wellington holding the Spear and see his reflection in the blade. There's something unsavory about the whole thing. Wellington shifts in his chair and stretches one leg over the other. One of his slippers teeters on his heel. The room seems to get darker. "I need to think," I say, staring at the shadow of his foot on the floor.

"Don't think," says Wellington with a strange glint in his eyes.

"That's what Kandinsky says," I say, trying to gather my senses. "Kandinsky, the painter." Everything seems slightly blurry. The room, the chair, the Spear—

"I'm well aware of who Kandinsky is."

"Of course you are—"

"One hundred thousand dollars," says Wellington, a number that shoots across the sky like a meteor shower.

"That's a lot of money," I say. Not that I need the dough. The only thing I need to buy is time and that's one of the few things in this world not for sale. Still, a hundred grand ought to be worth at least an hour or two, even in a universe in which time doesn't exist. "I'll take it."

Wellington's eyes light up, his skin takes on a rosy hue and his limbs twitch like frog legs on a battery charger. "Would you like cash or a check?" he says, reaching out to shake hands in an effort to quickly consummate the deal.

Before I can respond I notice that the slipper dangling from his foot is about to fall to the floor. I feel queasy again and glance back at the Spear. It seems to call to me, as if scolding me for some oversight or lapse of judgment. Once again I see the reflection of Wellington's face in the blade, only now it's distended and strangely elastic. "Listen, I don't know—"

Wellington's slipper finally flops to the floor, startling both of us. I glance down and notice that the bottom of his foot is covered with dozens of tiny suction cups. A feeling of inexorable doom rushes up my spine. I grab the Spear just as Wellington grabs his slipper. He pulls the Spear back and we struggle for a brief moment. Back and forth it goes from his feeble fingers to my shaking hands until I finally pull the Spear from his grasp. "But we have an agreement!" he says, still trying to pry it from my grasp.

"I'll let you know," I say as I quickly make my way to the exit.

Wellington follows behind, desperately trying to keep up. I hurry across the gallery and escape into the open elevator, cradling the Spear close to my chest. I punch the down button just as the old man appears from behind some masks and statues. He pushes aside a couple of tribal baskets and races for the elevator just as the door closes with a whoosh. I lean against the cage as the sickening sound of suction cups dissipates from the floor above.

Fwap-fwap... fwap-fwap... fwap-fwap...

Chapter 23

The telephone is ringing when I return to the cottage. I figure it's either Waverly Wellington with a new offer or one of his henchmen with a threat. It turns out to be someone far more dangerous to my psyche and sense of well-being. "You still alive?" asks Bobby Littman, my agent/enabler and the man whom I hold most responsible for my present state of unparalleled danger. After all, wasn't it Bobby who encouraged my screenwriting in the first place? Wasn't it Bobby whose promises led me into a deep pit of delusion and madness from which I have yet to emerge? Wasn't it Bobby who got me onto this story about the Spear of Longinus when that encyclopedia hit him over the head?

"Barely," I whisper into the telephone. "I've been tiptoeing through fields of hot lava."

"I've been trying to reach you ever since the earthquake. I was afraid maybe you fell through a crack somewhere."

"No such luck."

"You're a survivor, kid. That's what it takes in this business. Persistence and stubbornness. Oh, and it doesn't hurt to have a high profile agent to the stars."

"Bobby, this isn't a good time—"

"Did I ever tell you about the time Ken Russell tried to leave me?"

"Of course you told me."

"Now, you've got to understand something. I love all of my clients. I love them dearly. I even love you. But Ken Russell is something else. Me and Ken, we're like brothers, a couple of English blokes who came up the hard way. Me... Ken... Ken... me... you couldn't tell us apart. There were times *I* couldn't tell us apart. Take a look at *The Devils*. Who directed it, me or Ken? What about *Tommy*, what about *Altered States*, what about *Crimes of Passion*? What a team we were! Then one day, a Tuesday if memory serves me right, I got a telegram from some distant shore, a very matter-of-fact couple of lines that said that due to this and that and in light of such and such and given that so on and so forth, my services were no longer needed. Well, you could've taken a knife and stabbed me in the stomach. In fact that's exactly what I did. I took a knife and stabbed myself in the stomach. Next thing I knew, Ken was at my bedside, begging forgiveness. I played it very cool for the next twenty minutes, didn't say a word, just let him go on and on, blubbering away until I couldn't take it any more. Then, out of the bigness of my heart and out of respect for our shared heritage, I let bygones be bygones and took him back as a client. You never saw anybody so relieved. He didn't even object to the extra five percent I added to my agent's fee."

"Bobby, listen, this Spear, we've got to talk—"

"Why do you think I called you, to entertain you with my magnificent tales? I've got good news and better news. The good news is that I've got another producer interested in the project. The better news is that it's Jerry Karp!"

"Wait a minute. Isn't that who the Producer Who Shall Remain Nameless was trying to get on board?"

"That's Hollywood for you. The minute she dropped out he jumped in. Next thing you know, Mel Gibson will be begging to direct."

"This is amazing."

"He loves the architecture stuff. Says it adds a lot of class."

"I knew it!"

"If I were you I'd add every Frank Lloyd Wright reference I could find to that script. When's it going to be done?"

"Soon... soon..."

"Okay, kid, get moving. Karp's as changeable as the wind. We've got to strike while the iron is hot."

It takes me a moment to digest the news. One day I'm being booted out of Santa Monica, the next day I'm moving into the Hollywood Hills. Figuratively, that is. I'm not actually moving anywhere unless there's another aftershock, and then I'd probably wind up at the ReTan Hotel on a month-to-month lease. "It's a crazy world out there, isn't it?"

"Just another day on the frontlines of Hollywood. Shoot or get shot, that's what I always say. Now, get cracking, young man, I need some of your beautiful words on paper before you get buried alive up there."

And with that, we're back in business.

How easily I shift from events of universal importance to matters of purely personal significance. I have for reasons completely unknown to me been entrusted with the Spear of Longinus, possibly the most important cultural artifact of the last two thousand years, and one might expect that I'd develop a certain reverence for it, a feeling of transcendental duty, a sense of profound humility. After all, I might hold the fate of the world in these extremely shaky hands of mine. But then there's the Siren's call of Hollywood and its pitmaster for whom I am willing to jump at a moment's notice. Is my vanity and self-absorption so endless that I can actually be distracted from this once-in-a-lifetime hero's journey only to bask for a second or two in the elusive glow of klieg lights? It embarrasses me sometimes, the thoughts that come to my mind.

I walk down the street to clear my head. People are still milling about Washington Square Park three days after the earthquake, afraid of another aftershock. Radios crackle from every corner with the latest reports about liquefaction beneath the Marina District, the destruction of a mall in Santa Cruz and the death of forty-two people in the collapse of the Cypress Viaduct. Electricity has been restored throughout most of the city but North Beach is still intermittently blacked out. The traffic lights work, the streetlights don't and the store lights flicker on and off to the rumble of gas generators. There's a shortage of candles, batteries and Genovese salami. The hairdressing salon across from the park is closed. So too the video store, the robe shop and the corner bakery, although they've been out of focaccia so long, who knows what they're up to?

My mood brightens when I see Sabine sitting in her favorite spot on a bench. She's all alone and I feel sympathy for her plight of being a foreigner in a strange country during a natural disaster. "Feeling better?" I say, sliding next to her on the bench.

"Not really."

"It's been a rough couple of days."

"Alena has closed the café until the end of the week. The tip jar is empty."

"Maybe I could help."

"You?"

"Well, I got some good news. My screenplay has been put on the fast track. Things are moving quickly. I could use an assistant."

"I know nothing about Hollywood assistants. I have no training in this field."

"You think I do? You just jump in. You'll see, it all comes naturally."

"No, the movies hold little appeal for me. Now, if you were a famous clothes designer and required a cutter or a seamstress, maybe we could talk."

"The fact is, I can't offer you a salary right away, but I could give you a percentage of the profits once I sell the script. How does ten percent sound?"

"I am not good at higher mathematics but I believe that ten percent of nothing is still goose eggs."

"Okay, how about fifteen?" I say, moving closer.

"There are police in the park," she says. "Please remember that."

"Listen, we've got to stick together. You're one of the few people I trust."

"Trust is a two-way street. I saw the way you drove the other day. Like a truck driver on the autobahn."

"I was under a lot of stress. You don't understand how important that Spear is."

"Do not remind me. I have had enough history lessons in the last few days."

"Listen, I've got some important research to do on the other side of the Bay. What do you say you come along? It'll be like a trial offer. It might be interesting."

"Would we be back before sunset?"

"Of course. Come on, it's a chance to get out of North Beach for a couple of hours."

Sabine looks at me, at the clock on the church steeple, at the people milling around the park and back at me. *"Scheizer..."* she says, which I'm guessing either means yes, no or maybe. We leave the park, walking side by side. It's not entirely clear if I'm following her or she's following me.

⚬⚬

It's a lovely day for a drive. The sun is up, the clouds are down, the wind is steady and the barometric pressure is stable. I head across the Golden Gate Bridge with my new screenwriting assistant and, after making three or four wrong turns, arrive at the Marin County Civic Center, the very last and possibly most glorious building ever designed by Frank Lloyd Wright. Sabine has been drawn into this action-adventure as the one person with whom I feel comfortable sharing my most peculiar secret. But Sabine is Sabine, a particularly tough cookie to soften, and I decide to nibble around the edges before biting off more than either of us can swallow. We walk out of the parking lot and stop at a succulent garden to examine its collection of subtropical exotica. I read a little sign stuck into the ground: "It says here that the Bay Area has a Mediterranean climate, one of only eight in the world, and that's why succulents thrive here year-round."

"So?"

"So that's what makes it special."

"They're just plants."

"They store water in their leaves and they can go months without rain. They're like camels, only without the humps."

"They're nothing at all like camels."

"No, of course not, I'm just giving an example."

"Camels are mammals, these are plants. They are different shapes."

"Yes, you're right. I misspoke."

"You often misspeak, don't you? It seems half the things you say are not really true. And also, many of the things you do are incorrect. Like the drive over here. You kept circling around before entering the parking lot."

"I got a little lost. It's not a big deal."

"It would be if we were camels."

I think it over. "Yes, I suppose it would be—"

"I am making a small joke."

I flash a big grin. "No! It's a *big* joke! That's a good one!"

"It's because it would be very inefficient for camels to go so far out of the way."

"Yes! I get it! Very, very good!"

Sabine chuckles. "How about we look around?"

"Good idea." We head for the main entrance of the Civic Center. The building is long and low, stretching gracefully into the surrounding hills. "Life is funny, isn't it?" I say, feeling strangely warm inside.

"Not really."

"Here we are, working on a project, doing research, having fun, after months and months of missed opportunities."

"When opportunity knocks, you must answer the door."

"Yes. Exactly."

"That's what my mother used to tell me. I kept waiting for someone to knock, but it never happened."

"Until now."

"I think the doors in Germany are too unattractive for anyone to knock on them. Who ever saw such shapeless doors? Can I ask you something?"

"Of course."

"What does it mean, to be dead as a doornail?"

"I don't know, I guess it's to be really dead, deader than dead."

"There are degrees of dead?"

"There are degrees of everything. You can take pretty much everything to the nth degree."

"I told you, I don't understand higher mathematics. I also don't understand what we are doing here. What does this building have to do with a story from the middle ages?"

"Nothing. And everything. That's the beauty of it. I'm stretching the boundaries of cinema, opening people up to new experiences."

"I don't think people want to hear about architecture when they go to the movies. I think you are shooting yourself in the head."

"Foot."

Sabine pauses a moment to think. She has a worried look. "I am working for a percentage of profits, is that true?"

"Yes."

"I strongly suggest you drop the architecture."

"You'll see."

We walk inside the Civic Center and immediately get lost in a maze of corridors that weave in and out between the stairways, hallways and roadways. The floors are punctuated by atriums that rise the height of the building and stretch out into an oasis of stone gardens. Glass walls expand the open spaces, a translucent roof opens to the sky and arched walkways glow with reflected light. The whole building exists in its own kind of rhythm, one floor flowing into another, the views stretching to eternity, the hills, the sky and the patios all breathing together in unison. We step outside to a patio where a pond meanders around a garden, then falls off into endless space. "I like the shapes," says Sabine. "Everything is round and infinite."

"I thought you might like it," I say. We gaze out to the outer edge of the building, which stretches along the landscape as far as the eye can see. A thousand golden spheres extend around the circumference of the roof like an uninterrupted string of pearls. "You told me once that numbers appear to you as colors."

"As a child. And now again, since the earthquake. It's like it shook up a big bucket of paint inside my head."

"Have you heard of something called synesthesia?"

Sabine stares off into the infinite expanse of the pond. "The nurse at school said some such thing," she finally says.

"I have it, too. Do you know the odds of two people having synesthesia?"

"Fifty-fifty?"

"Not even close."

"Well, I told you, I'm not so good at higher mathematics."

"Don't you think there's some reason that we were brought together? Doesn't it seem strange how we communicate without really speaking? Doesn't it seem like our primitive brains are tied together with the same wire?"

"I don't know. Maybe we are on parallel paths going the same direction."

"Yes! Exactly! We're like two parallel lines orbiting the sun. Two parallel lines traversing an irrational universe. Two parallel lines moving in tandem."

To which Sabine says: "The beauty of parallel lines is that they never meet."

To which I counter: "Even though they move together in the same plane."

To which she reiterates: "But never actually touch."

To which I assert: "Despite walking hand in hand."

To which she retorts: "Maybe in this country. In Europe parallel lines never intersect."

To which I interject: "And you claim not to understand higher mathematics."

To which she concludes: "I know what I know."

We follow a path past the pond to a wooded area higher up in the hills. The top of the building magically hovers at the edge of the terrain and seems to stretch right into the side of the hill. A blue dome emerges from the center of the roof and a golden spire stretches to the sky. The spire is serrated with vertical channels and looks for all the world like the Spear of Longinus. I carefully unwrap the Spear from inside the sleeve of my jacket and stare into the blade. I see an endless expanse of white, not the white of nothingness, but the white of infinity. What is white, after all, but an infinite combination of all the colors? I turn to Sabine and hold it up for her to see. "What do you see?"

Sabine gazes deeply into the Spear for a long moment. A slight smile appears at the edges of her lips. "I see a rainbow. It's the rainbow I imagined as a child. It's the same rainbow I saw after the earthquake."

"I think there's a reason we met. I think there's a reason you're here. I think there's a reason for the colors and the sounds and the shapes."

"Oh? And what's that?"

I look back at the Spear, as if expecting an answer. All I can see reflected in the blade is the endless expanse of infinity. "C'mon, let's go," I say, covering it with my jacket and heading down the path. "It's getting late."

The signs on the freeway point to Sausalito, famous home of concentration camps, prisoner research centers and low security bathing facilities, according to Barbara, that is, Barbara, the least reliable witness in the courtroom of public opinion, Barbara, the least believable advocate in the halls of measured debate, Barbara, the least plausible interpreter in the chambers of rational discourse. This is who I'm getting my advice from? It makes no sense whatsoever that I should find myself compelled to turn onto the steep and winding road that leads into the little seaside town and even less sense that I keep glancing into the thick woods expecting to find rows of Quonset huts, tents and chain link fences, but here we are, driving along Bridgeway, the main road that meanders through downtown, then stopping at the docks to gaze out upon the impressive view of San Francisco where, surprise, surprise, a thick blanket of fog rolls under the Golden Gate Bridge and obscures the panorama, first the pylons of the bridge disappear, then the boats, then Alcatraz Island, and Sabine poses one of my favorite questions—*"What is fog, anyway?"*—to which I am happy to respond that it's just low clouds—*"Then why don't they call it low clouds?"*—which, of course, is my point exactly, and I decide this is a very good moment to walk

along the docks even though I'm not at all sure what we're
doing there and I'm not even sure that Sabine is actually
strolling alongside me, I mean, isn't this the moment I
usually wake up on my soggy mattress or on a park bench or
at some library table, oh yes, here we go again, the entire
excursion is descending into a thick soup of unreality and
illusion, and out of this soup what should appear but the
silhouette of one of those big Chinese container ships, the
ones with stacks and stacks of identical, hermetically sealed
containers, okay, fine, something familiar, only it's not
familiar at all, not even close, because from this side of
Alcatraz I see something altogether different, I see what
appears to be a rowboat bobbing up and down in the water
and slowly pushing away from the vessel with a bunch of
bewildered-looking guys crammed shoulder to shoulder
from stem to stern, and what could they be if not illegal
aliens—*hah!*—what a scam, they unload them under the
cover of fog, row them to shore, and the next thing you
know a restaurant in Chinatown has three new busboys, two
waiters and a dim sum chef, to which I say, fine, we need
some new blood, the country's getting stale, give us your
tired, your hungry, your poor, hell, I've got plenty of space
right at the top of Telegraph Hill if you need a place to
crash, and now I pull my jacket closer together against a
brisk wind and feel the Spear inside the sleeve, it's absolute
madness, of course, that I'm walking around with this thing,
but what else am I going to do with it, I'm afraid to leave it
out of my sight for even a second and as for stashing it
somewhere, well, the last time I tried that I almost leveled
the bus station, and now the rowboat disappears into the
fog only to be replaced by a motorboat piloted by some
goofy kid who agrees to take us up the shore because he
thinks Sabine is hot, and she's hot all right, hot under the
collar—*"Who said I am going anywhere? I did not agree to
such a plan. I am not dressed for such a journey!"*—and we

hug the edge of the shore, passing deserted docks, going down inlets that lead nowhere, skirting fishing piers that look ready to topple into the sea—*"Where are we going? What are we doing?"*—why, we're searching for a rowboat, and that's when I notice a peculiar arrangement of redwood branches, eucalyptus limbs and elderberry stalks in the shape of an isosceles triangle, and the kid cuts the engine and Sabine and I march through an opening in the forest—*"This is no place for a screenwriting assistant!"*—and we head up a path of slippery leaves and rickety trees to a clearing in the hills where I pull back a branch to discover a half-dozen buildings arranged around a training ground, a rowboat propped up at the end of a compound and a squat concrete bunker hunkered down at the edge of a field, and in the middle of all of this, in this desolate camp in the hills, twenty Chinese aliens are practicing martial arts, legs lifting, heels spinning, arms thrusting, and this seems like a very good time to get out of there since, as ideas go, this is not one of my better ones—*"Do you ever actually think about what you do?"*—and now we're heading back down the hill, slipping and sliding on a wet path that proves to be much trickier to navigate when in emergency descent mode, and what should we bump into but an observation station hidden in the hills, it's not much, really, just a concrete platform, a wood stand, and a telescope pointed across the Bay—*"If you look into that telescope I will consider my assignment terminated!"*—and I gaze into the lens and discover it's aimed directly at a house that rises up from the water and levels off into the hills and faces a frontage road, and I recognize that house, I was there once, it's in Point Richmond, and I can't for the life of me figure out why I should at this very moment be staring into the window of Walter Horn's bedroom.

Wha-a-a-a-a-a-t?

Now, I have a very calm exterior. I'm normally cool and

collected, admittedly prone to the occasional exaggeration but essentially an accurate reporter of the news, but this seems like a perfectly good moment to take leave of my senses and teleport to that blissfully pristine spot where no harm can befall me, where the sun always shines, where it's seventy-two degrees and where the mosquitoes don't bite. There's a woman next to me, a shy, lonely woman, and she blushes slightly when I put my arm around her waist and pull her close. She has a butterfly's nest of hair that brushes against her shoulders and she shudders just slightly in the cool breeze, she shudders and I shudder and the whole hillside shudders with anticipation, the leaves shudder, the branches shudder, the bushes shudder, the sky shudders, and that's when I turn the telescope to the camp and see Father Richard Indelicato walking out of the bunker and barking some orders to the Chinese prisoners, oh, yes, indeed, Father Indelicato with his big silver cross and heavy black frock takes center stage and directs the martial artists to increase their routine, legs lifting, heels spinning, arms thrusting, over and over and over, lift, spin, thrust, lift, spin, thrust, until I become dizzy just watching.

"Let's get out of here," I whisper to Sabine.

"About time," she whispers back.

Because this is just about all I can take.

In which Barbara shines as a financial wizard... Helga assumes a whole new position... Bernard provides parliamentary services... and the plot to resurrect pure evil is hatched...

Interlude

The crack of a wood mallet on a Formica table shatters the calm of evening and silences the few stray murmurs of a gathered assembly. "The meeting will come to order," intones the Leader, peeking out from the flickering shadows of a fire burning on the third floor of the Big House. He slams the mallet once more just in case anyone didn't get the message, then proceeds with the business at hand. "We'll begin with a call of attendance. Barbara?"

"Here," says Barbara with her mellifluous soprano.

"Bernard?"

"*Aaaak!*" croaks Bernard, standing at attention.

"Helga?"

"Present," says Helga with a low, throaty inflection.

"Father Indelicato?" There's a long moment of silence. *"Father Indelicato?"*

"I think he is still at the training facility," says Barbara.

"Yes, of course," hisses the Leader, slouching down along the floor and stretching his long legs. "You can count on him never to be here when we need him." He quickly pulls

himself upright and continues the roll call. "Sabine?—
Sabine Westerburg?"

There's another moment of silence and the uncomfortable shifting of arms and legs. "She did not come," says Helga at last. "I tried my best."

"She did not come?" repeats the Leader in a mocking tone. "Of *course* she did not come! She is the most stubborn woman in the Western hemisphere! How could I have chosen her of all people?"

"That's what we'd all like to know," says Barbara.

The Leader glares at her with impatience. "You dare to question me? It is all *your* fault! You have grown so old and ugly that even a master wizard cannot transform you into a presentable seductress! The very *idea* that I would have to waltz around the Berlin Wall looking for a suitable young maiden to step into your shoes! It is humiliating!"

"Well, *excuuuuuse* me!"

"The Secretary will read the minutes of the last meeting."

Helga stands up and smoothes out her fishnet stockings. She looks almost proper as she reads from a notebook, turning toward the fire every so often to cast some light on the pages. "Our Leader made a motion that refreshments would no longer be reimbursed from the General Fund but would instead be provided on a rotating basis of the membership. The resolution passed unanimously. Our Leader made a motion that meetings would henceforth be held on the second Tuesday of each month instead of the third Thursday. The resolution passed unanimously. Our Leader made a motion that the fiftieth anniversary of the beginning of World War II be the official launch date of the resurrection of the New Reich, that recovery of the Spear of Longinus be the first act of the New Reich, that the Spear serve as the unifying symbol of the Reich, that final plans for decisive action be set in motion and that October 22, 1989 be declared Recovery Day. The resolution passed unanimously."

"Are there any amendments to the minutes of the last meeting?" asks the Leader, staring out at his unsavory group of malcontents with a distasteful leer. "If not, I move that the minutes be accepted. Do I hear a second?"

"Aaaak," says Bernard.

"The resolution is passed unanimously. The Treasurer will make her report."

Barbara shifts her hefty legs into a more comfortable position and unfurls a big pie chart. "Last month saw a twenty-three percent increase in revenue from the Illegal Alien Project. Fourteen Chinese aliens were sold into indentured servitude, nine were leased to the agricultural combine and nine were sold outright to subcontractors and distributors. The General Fund is healthy and we have exceeded all economic goals and projections. Recovery Day will see us in optimum financial health."

"Excellent," says the Leader, leaning back in his chair with satisfied look. "Now, as you know, our miserable adversary, Walter Horn—"

"*Booo!*" yells the group.

"Order! The assembly will come to order!" bellows the Leader, slamming the mallet to the table. "Our old adversary, Walter Horn, has died—"

"*Yeaah!*" yells the group.

"One more outburst like that and I will have you all removed!" roars the Leader, glaring at them with blood-red eyes. The suction cups on his feet flop impatiently—nay, uncontrollably—until he finally slurps them up from the floor. "Now then, as a consequence, the Spear of Longinus has been transferred to an unworthy opponent—*a complete fool*—in a clever attempt to thwart us from the recovery. But our opponents are not nearly clever enough to pull the wool over our eyes. We are but days away from our ultimate victory!" He turns with blazing eyes to Helga. "Is the young woman ready?"

"Hard to say," says Helga, staring at the floor. "I'm doing the best I can. I've been chatting her up, dropping hints, priming the pump, such as it is. The truth of the matter is, I'm not completely certain if Sabine Westerburg has a romantic bone in her body."

The Leader rolls his eyes and mutters to himself. "How could I have chosen so poorly? Yes, it was dark in Berlin, it was late at night, I was tired, but in the old days I could've danced all night—"

"Not the old days again," groans Barbara.

The Leader fixes Barbara with a stare that could wither deerskin. "We must push forward. Do whatever it takes. She's the only one we have. Play some weepy violins. Put her under a trance. Give her some of your extra strong eucalyptus cookies."

"Butterfly Girl *is* a tough cookie."

"No more excuses, old woman! Are you prepared?"

Barbara responds with rote indifference. "I suppose."

"Bernard?"

"Aaaak!"

"Helga?"

"Of course."

The low murmurs in the room are interrupted by the sound of a gate opening outside. *"Shhh!"* says Barbara, as she glances out a window to see Tobias returning home from a long day in the country. "It's him!"

The Leader throws a blanket over the fire, hoping to douse the flames, but light still flickers off the windows. "Everybody out!" he yells.

The room erupts in activity. Helga hurries down the back stairs, her stiletto boots clacking against the wood and echoing into the night. On the porch she rips her stockings on a screen door and blindly makes her way through the darkness. She finally finds a sliver of light and follows it along the edge of the building to the gate outside.

Barbara takes the front stairs two at a time, moving from landing to landing with surprising agility for a two-thousand-year-old woman. When she arrives at the front entrance of the house she peeks out the door, looks left, looks right, and manages to slip over to her eucalyptus grove with no one noticing.

Bernard shimmies down the banister of a side staircase and disappears into the shadows. He slips outside the gate and scampers down the Filbert Steps to Kearny Street, where a big black Oldsmobile is parked at the corner. He unlocks the door, glances around to make sure no one is watching, pulls out a pair of extension rods, attaches them to his legs, swings himself up on the driver's seat, turns on the ignition and screeches off into the night.

The Leader loosens a window pane, squeezes his lithe body through the narrow opening and slips down along the outer wall of the Big House. He jitterbugs down a heating vent, stretches along a water pipe and disappears into a cold, dark crawl space beneath the foundation. Lying on his stomach he slinks under the support beams and inches along over dirt and rock, slipping in and out of fetid pools of muck and oily slicks of slime. The Leader maneuvers his elastic carcass to the edge of an underground river and then, with barely a ripple, he submerges his body into the icy water and torpedoes himself across the fast-flowing channel. He emerges beneath Tobias' cottage, where a family of raccoons tangos across a bleak plateau as if they were in a Depression-era nightclub dancing away their troubles. Shaking off the water like a mangy dog, the Leader crawls farther beneath the loose bricks and shaky beams until he comes to an underground retaining wall that separates the cottage from the mansion next door. He twists himself up along the barrier until he comes to an iron portico that is covered with cobwebs, rat excrement and rotting toadstools. Brushing away the grime he pushes open the door, crawls along the ceiling and lowers himself onto the garage floor, where a classic Mercedes 190 SL sits gleaming in a beam of moonlight. He polishes some dust off the hood with his shirt sleeve, slips into the waiting elevator and punches the top button.

Upstairs the night is black as coal. The silver wicks of a triangle of black candles cast a muted purple glow as the Leader stares at his shadowy reflection in a full length mirror. "You are so weak," he hisses to himself. "It is not like the old days. You've become a second rate wizard."

Waverly Wellington's face stares back at him in the mirror, shapeless and indistinct. In the low light the reflection shifts among his alternate personas of Wellington, That Guy and Klingsor. "Pull yourself together," says the reflection. "It's a temporary condition. Once we regain the Spear you'll feel the power surging through your veins again."

"Look how far we have fallen," says the Leader. "The last war was a travesty. We are celebrating the fifty-year anniversary? Of what? Better to bury and forget it. And these assistants of mine! I am surrounded by idiots and outcasts. Look at them. A toothless old witch! A deaf mute midget! A psychotic priest! A right-wing stripper! An army of aliens!"

"We do what we do."

Wellington's eyes blaze an angry crimson as he walks across the gallery and examines his rare collection of exotica. With barely a second thought he smashes one of the display cases with an iron poker, sending shards of glass all over the floor. Inside the case is a twelfth century bronze statue of Arihanta, the Jain Destroyer of Enemies. Showing not a trace of irony Wellington pulls out the artifact, buries it beneath some pillows and dials the telephone.

"North Beach Police Station," comes a voice on the other end. *"How can I direct your call?"*

"I want to report a robbery at the top of Telegraph Hill!"

"When did the incident take place?"

"Moments ago!"
"And who am I speaking to?"
"This is Waverly Wellington!"
"Yes, sir, Mr. Wellington, we'll send someone up there right away..."

At the bottom of Telegraph Hill, in a darkened apartment, Sabine feels confused, an emotion she doesn't much like since it throws into question all of the assumptions that have led her to this particular place at this particular time. She's confused about Tobias. She's confused about the Spear. She's confused about Frank Lloyd Wright. These are the moments she can't bear, when everything throbs and vibrates inside her head, when the garden inside her apartment stretches out and tries to embrace her and all she can do is pull away. The heliconia and protea despair for Sabine, Sabine who works too hard but plays too little, Sabine whose heart is large but mostly empty, Sabine who follows a rainbow but doesn't know why.

There's a tiny cubby hole of a room just off the kitchen that serves as her workspace. A dozen patterns are pinned to the walls along with swatches of material and a series of black and white sketches. On the table is a sewing machine, spools of thread and a big roll of denim that stretches to the floor. Sabine finds herself working late into the night, being pushed by some vague feeling of urgency. The day's events have left her tired to the point of exhaustion, an exhaustion where something else takes over and guides her unconsciously to cut, sew, snip and mend. It's as if a primitive part of her brain has been loosened and an unseen hand unleashes a design that's been buried in her subcortex for a thousand years. The design fights against everything she knows, it transforms corners into curves and edges into circles, it stretches patterns to patternless and boundaries to boundless. It's as if Frank Lloyd Wright sat down with Coco Chanel at a sewing machine and tripped the light fantastic. Sabine double stitches a seam, turns the material in a circular motion and sews a hem. She repeats the process on the other leg, then ties off the thread and pulls the pants from the carriage of the machine. She holds them up and takes a look. The waist is tight and narrow over an unadorned flat front with a simple button fly. The inner seams of the legs extend in an ever-widening arc to the bottom hem. The outer seam flairs at an extreme angle, so extreme that the legs are both rounder and squarer than before, and the overall effect is to go from the sublime to the ridiculous, from the improbable to the impossible, from the unlikely to the untenable. This is not Charlie Chaplin at a skating rink, this is Charlie Chaplin as a human parachute. These are pants that are beyond shape, they thumb their nose at shape, they take shape and turn it inside out into some kind of proletarian funhouse of fashion. These are pants that Marx could wear to the coronation of Czar Nicholas. These are pants that Stalin could wear at Trotsky's funeral. These are pants that could bury the whole politburo and leave enough material to export to Cuba for sombreros. Sabine looks at her creation with the hint of a smile. "Who would wear such pants?" she whispers to the night.

"Capitalists," the night whispers back.

Patrolman Kuiper shines his flashlight on the outer doorway of Wellington's mansion, steps inside the lobby and checks out the floors, walls and ceilings of the entryway, then aims his beam at the window ledges, baseboards, doorknobs, draperies, heating vents, alarm panels, electrical outlets, light switches, surveillance cameras, laundry hampers, thermostat coils, telephone jacks, toaster plugs, air freshener canisters, dishwasher buttons, garbage disposal toggles and dehumidifier valves that are located all over the palatial estate. When he flashes the beam on Waverly Wellington himself, standing silently in the shadows, Kuiper nearly jumps out of his skin. "Jesus!"

"Well?" says Wellington, barely moving a muscle. "What have you found?"

Kuiper assumes that the authoritative voice belongs to the master of the manor. Either that or he made a wrong turn and wound up in the Wax Museum. "I've dusted the garage, the elevator and the upstairs for fingerprints," he says. "Nothing comes up except for some round curlicues. I've never seen anything like them before. They look kind of like puffed wheat. Or pasta shells. Or miniature onion rings."

"Yes-yes," says Wellington, quickly changing the subject. "But what about the broken glass? What about the cabinet?"

"I don't know what to make of it. I'm thinking it might be an inside job."

"What are you talking about? I'm the only one who lives here."

"Well, the alarm is still set, the doors are locked—"

"I assure you, it is none of my employees."

"What about the neighbors?"

"It's mostly empty apartments next door. There's just the caretaker."

Kuiper turns slowly and faces Wellington. "The *caretaker?* You don't mean Tobias Parker, do you?"

"I believe that's his name."

Kuiper salivates with the anticipation of getting his sweet revenge at last. He's been after Tobias so long he doesn't even remember why anymore. "Parker's your guy," he says. "Oh, yeah, it's him all right."

Wellington, a man of a hundred unsavory faces, assumes the role of a kindly gentleman as he toys with Kuiper. "Oh, no, I don't think so. He seems to be the most reasonable sort of fellow."

"Believe me, there's nothing reasonable about him."

"No-no, I really think—"

"Listen, the guy boosts stereos right out the door of Circuit City!"

"It can't be."

"Oh, yes it can. He's your man. Sure as I'm standing here."

Wellington feigns disappointment at the course of events. "Well, then, I suppose you should arrest him," he says, assuming the role of beleaguered neighbor.

"If only I could. The question is, for what? Living next door? I need more than that to go on."

Wellington rubs one of his gnarly fingers over his receding jaw and ponders the situation. "Come to think of it, this Tobias fellow doesn't appear to have a discernible source of income. Have you ever wondered how he makes ends meet?"

"I've more than wondered. I've checked his tax records. What a joke!"

"And yet there are times he just flies off to Los Angeles on a whim, as if he's merely going for a quick lunch."

Kuiper begins steaming. "He's nibbling cracked crab at Sardi's while I'm walking my beat up and back through North Beach? Wait a minute... artwork... L. A.... quick trips... ten to one the guy's a fence! He's knocking off you rich guys and unloading your trinkets on La Cienega Boulevard!"

Wellington shakes his head in disbelief. "It can't be. He seemed like such a nice young man."

"I knew it! Stereos, my ass! This guy's a hotshot art thief!"

"Are you certain? I'm beginning to feel unsafe living next door to him."

"Not for long. I'm taking our wise-ass caretaker off the streets before he wipes out the whole neighborhood."

"But if you don't actually catch him in the act—"

"I've got my ways. I've never met a man yet who didn't have something to hide."

"*Yesssss*," says Wellington, unconsciously hissing the word a second too long. He catches himself before his true nature is revealed. "We all have our secrets, don't we?"

"We sure do, Mr. Wellington, we sure do."

Chapter 24

I'm curled up in a fetal position, tight like a seashell, my knees crunched into my chest, my shoulders hunched around my legs, and it occurs to me that leaving the womb isn't all that it's cracked up to be. The slap on the bum, the bright lights, the cold air, the sore throat, the runny nose, the high fever, the yellow eyes, the wet bed, no, when all is said and done I would've been quite happy staying right where I was, swimming in the saline sea. Ah, Mother, dear Mother, look what's become of your second born. I'm a total mess, a physical wreck, an unworthy heir to your noble intentions.

I pry my fingers from around my knees and force myself into the kitchen. A calendar pasted onto the refrigerator tells me it's Thursday, October 21st, the moon is waning, Mars is in retrograde, I have seven planets lined up on a collision course and, oh yes, by Dr. Gold's timetable I have approximately zero days to live. That sounds just about right given my fast-deteriorating memory, the numbness spreading into my toes and fingers, the profound loss of taste, sight and hearing, and a heartbeat so irregular I have to put my fingers into the light socket just to get out of bed in the morning.

But get out of bed I do because I'm a survivor—isn't that what Bobby said?—yes, I'm a survivor of some of the most improbable events and unlikely characters ever to have reared their disjointed heads in one place at one time. Let's see if I've got this right: I've got a two-thousand-year-old woman living in the bushes, a guy upstairs who's half-ape and half-spider, a millionaire next door with suction cups on his feet, a wannabee Nazi hounding me for quarters, a bunch of *real* Nazis watching my every move, a trigger-happy cop looking to unload his clip into my spleen, a doctor whose medical opinion isn't worth the prescription pad it's written on, a bell-ringing priest training an army of illegal aliens, and an East German waitress who's more mysterious than all the rest of them put together. Then there's my Dad, who seems to know more than he lets on but less than would really be useful, a Hollywood agent leading me down a primrose path, and a recently deceased history professor who has left me the strangest bequest of all time. Have I left anyone out? The fact is, I've become the central figure of my own action-adventure, the lead character in a story I long ago lost control of. I'm no longer the author of events but merely a hapless chronicler of someone else's tale.

Let us not forget the Spear of Longinus, the object which has become the bane of my existence. What am I going to do with this thing? I can't just continue carrying it around with me wherever I go. Maybe I could leave it somewhere in more capable hands. The police would know what to do with it, wouldn't they? Couldn't I just take it over to the station, tell them I found it on the street and be done with it? No, of course I couldn't. Patrolman Kuiper would get involved, I'd wind up in handcuffs and somebody would get shot. No, the Spear is much too important to leave to the likes of the local police. How about the Mayor, wouldn't he know what to do? Sure, that makes sense, I'll give the Spear to the Mayor of San Francisco, a guy caught up in so many controversies he'd probably stab himself in the chest just to ease the pain. No, I've got to think bigger, maybe the Governor, oh yes, that's a good idea, I'll drive up to Sacramento, camp out outside the Governor's Mansion and somehow slip the Spear inside his bedroom. Good God, the higher I go the worse it gets. How about I give it to the Catholic Church? They've got as good a claim on the Spear as anyone. Let's see, who do I know? Why, of course, Father Indelicato! He knows all about the Spear. I could give the Spear of Longinus to Father Indelicato and watch the world go straight to hell in a hand basket.

This seems like a good time to take a deep breath and let things settle down before I contemplate my next step. After all, a wrong move now could have untold consequences. I feel like I've got seventeen balls in the air that could all drop on my head at any instant. The only thing that keeps me grounded is the screenplay I'm writing, and that's a scary prospect. As someone (I think it was me) once said:

WHEN A HOLLYWOOD SCREENPLAY IS
THE MOST STABLE THING IN YOUR LIFE,
WATCH OUT, YOU'RE IN BIG TROUBLE.

Be that as it may, the little table down at the Café Vienna is my only release and finishing the screenplay the only thing that makes even a bit of sense. I need to walk, to clear my mind, to let my thoughts wander and roam. I head out the door, up the path and down the hill and there's nobody, not a soul, to interrupt my reverie. I revel in the solitude, lost in my thoughts, free for a moment from the onslaught of events, free from the weight of history and the burden of responsibility. I take a deep breath of relief only to see that big black Oldsmobile that's been dogging me ever since I visited Walter Horn. There's no relief!

I hide in the bushes and watch the car moving fitfully along the road, starting, stopping, idling and jerking back and forth. Finally it pulls into a tight parking spot and the engine sputters to a halt. Moments later the door opens and Bernard—*Bernard?*—hops out of the driver's seat, comfortable as a flea on a bloodhound. Yes, Bernard, adorable as ever in his cute little pants, darling suspenders and doll-like cravat, suddenly moves front and center on my list of prime suspects who are attempting to wrest away the Spear from my short tenure as Protector of the Realm. "Here it is!" I yell to him, ready to relinquish this most valuable of objects to this most unlikely of villains, but Bernard of course can't hear a word I'm saying and my generous offer evaporates into the low clouds rolling in from the Pacific.

I follow him on his circuitous path of panhandling to see exactly what he's up to. I lag half a block behind as he passes one likely mark after another with nary a request for change. Odd. Are my quarters so special that he would walk right past a busload of tourists without even flashing them one of his irresistible, sad-eyed stares? Bernard moves purposefully down the street and I follow him to Broadway, where he hops over the curb, edges along the sidewalk and disappears into a brightly lit girlie show. The idea of Bernard having sex never really entered my mind and even now I'm imagining all sorts of things—he's got a job cleaning the peepshow walls, he repairs the vending machines, he changes light bulbs—but then I see him standing at a peephole with at least three body parts in full salute and I can no longer deny the obvious. Curious as to who might be holding sway over my favorite Lilliputian, I drop several quarters into a mechanical slot. My very own peephole opens upon an extravaganza of arms, legs and breasts that flies past me in a kaleidoscope of naked flesh. One dancer in particular captures my attention when she bends down just inches in front of my face, spreads her legs and exposes two swastikas hurtling out of her womanhood like lightning bolts from the deep. Isn't this the woman who chatted me up at Café Vienna? The woman who encouraged me to pursue Sabine? This is the source of the Nazi salute? This is where all of my quarters have been going? This is what gets Bernard up in the morning and puts him to sleep at night? Oh, Bernard... Bernard... Bernard... what have you gotten yourself into?

I enter the café to find Sabine arranging a spice rack behind the counter. She's attired in a magnificent ensemble and looks as if she might've parachuted to work right through the skylight. Her pant legs are layered with progressively larger circles of denim that flare out like a stack of hula hoops, then gradually narrow toward the ankle. It's an airy look—like a balloon or a bubble or a dirigible—and looks as if a gust of wind could transport her right over to the next county. "Nice pants," I say.

"Is that all you can ever say?"

"No, I mean it." Sabine gives me one of her patented blank stares. It intrigues me how she can completely suspend all facial movement into a kind of molecular necrosis. I mean, there's blank and then there's *blank*. "Listen, about Sausalito—"

"Not interested," she says, turning back to her salt and pepper shakers.

"I think we should talk—"

Sabine's irritation with that little episode forces her hand to reflexively twitch just enough to topple over the spice rack. *"Scheizer!"* she screams as a dozen jars come crashing to the counter in a distinctly disorderly display. I reach over to offer her a hand but she wants nothing to do with me. "Let me do it!" she says, motioning me away.

"No, no, I'll help," I say, reaching for a bottle of vinegar that's dripping onto the floor.

"It is really not necessary," she says, bending down to sponge up the mess.

I reach for a bucket, only to splash some vinaigrette onto a tray of condiments.

"*Ach...*"

"Sorry, sorry." I grab a wad of napkins off the counter and dab at the mess which grows by the minute.

"Can you just leave it—"

I reach back for some more napkins and notice a handbill that's been shoved underneath. I pay it no attention but a couple of words catch my eye. It's something about "Bay Aryans" and a meeting of historical importance. I figure it's a misprint. Do they mean Bay *Areans?* Well, probably not. How about Bay *Arians?* Unlikely. But what would Sabine be doing with this handbill? No way she's an Aries.

I feel a queasiness in my stomach and an unsteadiness in my legs. It's a sensation I haven't felt since the anaphylactic shock episode that took place in this very restaurant. Is this the part where I lose consciousness and wake up on Dr. Gold's table? Or is this merely the next malady to befall me, the next body function to give out? I glance again at the flyer, my stomach churning, then watch Sabine cleaning the mess. "You know, there are some things that don't make a lot of sense," I say.

"Oh?"

"Like what a girl from East Germany is doing in an Austrian restaurant in the Italian section of San Francisco."

"I wonder about that myself. Everyday I ask myself this question."

"Or how you just happen to show up wherever I go in North Beach."

"Maybe I am following you," she says playfully.

I push the handbill across the counter. "Maybe you are."

She glances at the leaflet, then looks directly into my eyes and shoves it back. "Do you think I am involved with this group?"

"You tell me."

"Do you think because I am from East Germany I have been sent here as some kind of spy? Do you think I have come for the Spear? That I am interested in taking over the world? That I am a mastermind of evil forces?"

"As far as I'm concerned anything is possible."

Sabine slams a coffee cup onto the counter. "Are you *completely* crazy?"

"Maybe I'm finally beginning to see things clearly."

Sabine storms out from behind the counter and pushes me toward the door. "I must ask you to leave."

"*What?*"

"Please don't come back."

"You're throwing me out? You're actually throwing me out?"

"I believe the expression is, *eighty-sixed.*"

"Now, wait a minute—"

"No, *you* wait a minute. I have had enough. Everyone in this city is mentally disturbed. I am finished with it."

"Listen, maybe we should talk about this—"

"Out!"

Sabine grabs the telephone and dials. I hurry for the door before she calls the police. She screams into the receiver—

"Alena? It is Sabine. I am giving you one week notice. I quit!"

Parsifal Unleashed

Part IV

INT. CASTLE CHAMBER - NIGHT

Parsifal looks tired. He's wandered the forests and the hills. He's shot white swans out of the sky and been invited to feasts. He's met kings and knights and wizened priests. He's held the Holy Grail in his hand and been banished from castles. Now, having entered Klingsor's evil realm, Parsifal rests his weary head on Kundry's shoulder. The beautiful young seductress strokes his cheek and runs her fingers through his hair.

> KUNDRY
> *Rest, handsome stranger, forget*
> *your troubles and woes.*

Parsifal looks out upon the magic garden. There are plants and trees everywhere, along with a waterfall that drops off into a bottomless chasm.

> PARSIFAL
> *Is this but a dream? Am I soon to*
> *awaken to the harsh light of day?*

> KUNDRY
> *Life is but a dream, a dream born*
> *in imagination and fulfilled in love.*

Parsifal admires the expansive courtyard. A domed roof lets in reflected light, the corridors go on forever and atriums descend to the floors below.

> PARSIFAL
> *Look how the walls stretch to infinity.*
> *Note the use of circles and rounded*
> *edges. See how the construction*
> *blends into the terrain rather*
> *than drawing unnecessary*
> *attention unto itself.*

Kundry impatiently taps her fingernails along a clay vase that is overflowing with a profusion of wildflowers.

KUNDRY
Yes, yes, it is a miracle of design.

PARSIFAL
*And the use of resources is unusual
as well. The limestone is of local
variety, the marble of highest
quality, and natural materials
are used whenever possible.*

KUNDRY
So they are.

PARSIFAL
*The decorative elements provide
a real sense of rhythm and the
use of space adds to the
overall flow of pattern.*

Kundry grabs him with a mixture of lust and anger.

KUNDRY
Ach, you men and your buildings!

PARSIFAL
*Forgive me, lovely maiden,
I am starved for beauty.*

KUNDRY
*Can you not see when beauty
stares you in the face?*

Parsifal gazes at her with innocent eyes.

PARSIFAL
*So it does, fair maiden,
so it does.*

INT. KLINGSOR'S CASTLE – NIGHT
Klingsor watches the two of them from his turret, rubbing
his hands with glee.

KLINGSOR
*It is all going according to plan. Soon I
will defeat the self-righteous forces
of good and be done with
them forever.*

The Dark Knight raises his arm in a stiff salute to his master.

DARK KNIGHT
Aaaak!

KLINGSOR
*Yes, my little loyal liege. Soon enough
the path will be clear. Soon we shall
lead the world into darkness!*

INT. CASTLE CHAMBER - NIGHT
Kundry stretches out on a bed of roses. Her hair is a glorious butterfly's nest of curls that sweeps up off her forehead and brushes along her shoulders.

KUNDRY
*Lie here with me, Parsifal.
Rest your head on my breast.*

Parsifal sits at the edge of the bed. He looks troubled.

PARSIFAL
*I am nothing but a fool.
I have failed at everything.*

KUNDRY
You are too hard on yourself.

PARSIFAL
*Even my mother has deserted me.
O, sweet mother, why did you
cast me from the womb?*

KUNDRY
Now, now...

PARSIFAL
I could've made something of myself.
A mender of bones, perhaps—

KUNDRY
Leave the doctoring to the nurses—

PARSIFAL
A practitioner of the herbs—

KUNDRY
You? A balmist? No, no—

PARSIFAL
A builder of buildings—

KUNDRY
Forget the buildings! Everything
falls down in time!

Parsifal gets a faraway look in his eyes.

PARSIFAL
I feel destined for something. Something
that has been passed down through
the ages. Something that boils
in the blood.

KUNDRY
You speak with the innocence of
youth. It is time to experience
the pleasures of manhood.
Come, handsome prince,
come into my arms.

Parsifal is wracked with indecision. He leans closer to her on the bed, then stops.

PARSIFAL
I don't know...
I just don't know...

INT. KLINGSOR'S CASTLE – NIGHT
Klingsor leers down from his turret, watching the action unfold. He turns to his reflection in the magic mirror and titters with anticipation.

> KLINGSOR
> *No one can resist her charms. No one!*

He turns his attention back to the chamber below.

> KLINGSOR
> *Seduce him, Kundry, make his toes curl!*

INT. CASTLE CHAMBER - NIGHT
Parsifal rubs his forehead with pain and confusion.

> PARSIFAL
> *I am lost, dear maiden.*
> *I know not what to do.*

> KUNDRY
> *You make complicated what is simple.*
> *Follow the instincts you were born with.*

> PARSIFAL
> *My instincts fail me. I am pulled*
> *in two directions. On one hand*
> *I burn with desire; on the other*
> *I feel called to a higher purpose.*
> *There is something I am meant*
> *to do, something great and noble,*
> *but I know not what it is.*

Kundry explodes with impatience. Her voice booms out across the courtyard.

> KUNDRY
> *Kiss me, you fool!*

She pulls Parsifal to her side and kisses him deeply. His resistance falters. He takes her into his arms.

INT. KLINGSOR'S CASTLE – NIGHT
The Dark Knight can barely control himself as he thrusts his
hand inside his robe, rubs himself vigorously and watches
through a small window in the tower.

DARK KNIGHT
Aaaak!

INT. CASTLE CHAMBER - NIGHT
Parsifal suddenly pulls away from Kundry's kiss. Something
is different about him. A soft light illuminates his head. He
has an other-worldly look.

PARSIFAL
*But what is this? I feel a holy
spirit beating inside my chest.*

Kundry looks at him with alarm and thrusts herself into his
arms.

Kundry
*Come to me, Parsifal, before
the night passes into day.*

Parsifal kneels on the ground, supplicating himself as if he
were a monk.

PARSIFAL
*Your kiss has opened my heart
and shown me the true way.*

Kundry grabs him by the shoulders and tries to pull him
back to bed.

KUNDRY
*Don't you get it? You cannot resist!
I have offered myself!*

Parsifal looks skyward with a beatific glow.

PARSIFAL
Heaven, I am yours.

> KUNDRY
> *Forget heaven! Hell hath no*
> *fury like a woman scorned!*

Parsifal pushes Kundry aside.

> PARSIFAL
> *Away, harlot. I will not fall*
> *to your evil temptations.*

Kundry leaps from the bed of roses like a wild woman. Her soprano's voice crackles through the air.

> KUNDRY
> *Kliiiiiiiiiing—soooooooooooor!*

INT. KLINGSOR'S CASTLE – NIGHT
Klingsor is startled by her scream. He grabs the Spear and bounds down the stairs.

INT. CASTLE CHAMBER - NIGHT
The door bursts open and the sorcerer appears in his most terrifying form. His eyes are cold and sure. His mouth is thin and tight. His jaw is square and firm.

> KLINGSOR
> *The end has come, innocent fool! Let's*
> *see what your virtue brings you now!*

He throws the Spear at Parsifal.

EXTREME CLOSE-UP ON THE SPEAR
sailing through the air in slow motion, aimed directly at Parsifal's chest.

Parsifal stands firm and strong. He raises his arms to the heavens. A crack of lightning.

Klingsor disappears into the castle walls. Kundry ages a thousand years. The garden disappears in a puff of smoke. The Spear stops in mid-air, just inches from Parsifal's heart.

FREEZE ACTION.

Chapter 25

Today's the day. I've been putting things off far too long, blocking them from consciousness, pretending they don't exist, going on as if nothing ever happened. It makes me wonder sometimes if my whole life isn't a dream, a fabrication being played out by a disturbed brain soaking in the beaker of a mad scientist, or an extraterrestrial transmission being beamed backwards through the universe, or an opera being performed by mice. This is not the time to ponder the imponderables, though. This is the time to take action and do something positive. It's Friday, a day to tie up loose ends, bring projects to completion, answer the mail and pay the bills. Yes, indeed, today's the day. It's time to grout the bathroom.

Grout is the devil's plaything, a messy concoction guaranteed to crack, crumble, flake and peel. It's impossible to add the correct amount of water to powdered grout, just as it's impossible to spread it correctly, seal it properly or dry it thoroughly. Grout is the stone mason's revenge, the tile setter's retribution, the carpenter's final reckoning. Never has there been a love song to grout, nor a poem, not even a limerick. Grout is nature's way of saying, "Give up, you've had a so-so life, why ruin it now, why throw away every decent memory into this slow-drying pail of misery?"

I mix up the sludge, slap it onto a putty knife and start filling in the empty spaces. Then I remember that I haven't pre-cleaned those spaces so I try to remove the grout, but the grout is already drying so I decide to leave well enough alone except there's no such thing as well enough when dealing with grout, no, the best you can hope for is the barely acceptable and that's where I set the bar, at the barely acceptable, except that one man's barely acceptable is another man's total fucking disaster, and that very probably is exactly what I have cooking up in my bathroom, a disaster of unimaginable proportions, because had I read the fine print I would've discovered that grout can in extremely rare conditions create a chemical chain reaction with loose particles of fecal matter to create a massive detonation that can awaken the dead. Maybe that's why I'm hearing a muffled cry from behind the mirror: "Stop—" gasps Dad. "The fumes are killing me!"

"Stop exaggerating, will you? It's not that bad."

"Oh? Maybe you'd like to be trapped in a stone sarcophagus with quick sand drying around your feet."

"Dad, please. I'll be done in a couple of days."

"Don't you get it? You don't have a couple of days!"

I put down the grout, the bucket and the spatula and look into the mirror. "So this is really it, eh?"

"End of the line. Everybody off. Next stop: Forever."

"Yeah, I kind of figured—"

"I'm gonna miss these little chats," says Dad in an unusually somber tone. He pauses for a moment to let things sink in, then does his usual Russian two-step. "Just kidding. I'm not gonna miss them at all. Son, you've been boring me to death."

"You know, Dad, I've been thinking. You and me, we're a

lot alike. It's like we're on parallel paths going in the same direction but never quite intersecting. Maybe that's a good thing. It keeps us at a safe distance. Don't you think that's a good metaphor for our whole relationship?"

"Metaphor, shmetaphor. You handle the geometry. Leave the poetry to me."

"You, me, Sabine, we're all a bunch of parallel lines that never meet."

"Until infinity."

"Huh?"

"That's the rest of the definition. Two lines that meet in infinity."

"That's impossible. Two lines either meet or they never meet. You can't have it both ways."

"I've got news for you, kid, you *can* have it both ways. You'll find out soon enough when you come join me in the great beyond. Maybe you'll understand a few things."

"I can hardly wait."

"Tell me something. What happens if you stare down a couple of train tracks as far as you can see?"

"I don't know, I guess they merge at the end of the line."

"Exactly. Now, your mind probably tells you there's no way those tracks can come together but your eyes tell you something different. So which one is it?"

"Haven't got the slightest."

"Well, Sonny Boy, you better figure it out before you have a train wreck. Speaking of which, you know what day it is?"

"Friday."

"And what happens on Friday?"

"I water the plants."

"That's right. Anything else?"

"I put on my work clothes."

"And?"

"I check the apartments."

"Correct. Don't you think you should get on with it?"

"Okay, okay, keep your shirt on."

Dad's tone changes again. This time he actually *does* sound serious, as if I should pay attention. "Today's the day, you know," he says.

"I figured."

"We're talking about the family's honor."

"I know."

"The destiny of untold generations."

"Right."

"Try not to blow it, okay?"

"You know me, Dad."

"I sure do, Son."

I slip into my old jeans, floppy sandals and a torn *Bauhaus* T-shirt. With my jacket an unnecessary addition to my work ensemble I realize I have nowhere to put the Spear and need to find somewhere to hide it for a few minutes. I've got at least ten good reasons to exclude the bedroom, the kitchen and the bathroom, but outside in the ivy seems like an oddly perfect spot. I shove the Spear behind some branches without even thinking. Who, after all, would leave the most important historical artifact of the Western world crammed inside an overgrown patch of ivy?

My fourteen minute excursion into the workaday world begins as always with a ritualistic throwing of the keys. This is both similar to and completely different from the Chinese art of throwing yarrow stalks to divine the secrets of the *I Ching*. Just like the Confucian oracle readers I seek a pattern of recognition—for them the lines of a hexagram; for me the jagged edges of a key—in my noble attempts to unlock a door, if not the secrets of the universe. I throw the key ring onto the brick patio outside the back cottage hoping that some unknown force of magnetism will draw out the

correct key from the dozens of interlopers and point it to
the lock like a dowsing rod in the desert. I've been doing
this every Friday for seven years now and every Friday I
have failed, but today I toss the key ring a bit higher, watch
it tumble in the air and listen to the jarring clang of metal
on brick. One key, an old brass Yale with a nice patina on
the grooves, is distinctly pointing right toward the door. I
pick it up, insert it into the lock and—*click*—it opens just
like that! The door swings open, a mass of fetid air collapses
against my chest and I'm thrown like a rag doll right across
the terrace. Good enough. That's as complete an inspection
as I've given that deathtrap in years. Nothing could live in
that cottage, neither man nor mouse nor cephalopod.

I pick myself up, head up the path for Bill Bailey's old
place and miraculously find his key on the very first try.
What's going on here? Has some primitive impulse from the
subcortex kicked in and unleashed my long-buried instinc-
tive nature? Is this the apotheosis of reverse evolution, the
moment when man awakens his ability to unlock a door
without going through a dozen botched attempts? I glance
inside the tiny cabin and whistle a few bars of *Won't You
Come Home, Bill Bailey,* just as I always do. Ah, Bill, where are
you now? Painting a big red banner on those Pearly Gates?

I cross the patio, glance at the outer walls of my collapsing cottage and wonder again what exactly is holding it up.
Am I living in my own energy vortex where the laws of
gravity have not only been pushed beyond their limits but
been completely broken? I check the drain pipes, the
window frames and the heater vent, then come around the
corner of the house where my exquisitely crafted nineteenth
century European door stands proudly against the elements.
I love that door and don't begrudge it its various bungled
efforts in keeping burglars at bay. It never fails to amaze me
how lucky I am to have that door, how unlikely it is that it
should adorn this house and how much I will miss it when I

pass on to the next great adventure. A wave of melancholy passes over me as I head up the pathway. I suddenly realize that this might be the last time I inspect the houses, the last time I struggle with the locks, the last time I double-check the doors. There's probably a lot more I'll miss, things I haven't even thought of, things I need to look at and savor. I open the outer gate, walk across the stairs to the main door of the Big House, insert the key and suddenly feel a pair of hands grabbing my shoulders. I try to turn but a knee jabs into my back and a club wrenches at my elbows. I fall to the rough cement of the stairs and fight to get up, then finally crane my head to see Patrolman Keith Kuiper looking crazier than ever with his eyes bugged out in a fit of exultation.

"*Gotcha!*"

"What are you *doing?* Let me go!"

"You're under arrest!"

"For what?" I say, struggling to get free.

"Disregarding civic duty."

"What are you talking about?"

"Aren't you Juror Number 27894448?"

"Juror number *what?*"

Kuiper quotes an obscure civil code from his twisted memory: "*Failure to appear for jury duty is a misdemeanor punishable by a fine and/or a jail term pending sentencing by a judge of the Municipal Court.*"

"You're kidding, right? This is all a big joke."

"You think it's funny?" Kuiper pulls me up by my arms and shoves me against the wall. "Who's laughing now?"

"This is ridiculous! I've got things to do! I'm a busy man!"

Kuiper flashes me a look of hatred. "Sure you are." He glances up at the sunroom of Waverly Wellington's mansion, where I can see Wellington staring at us through his telescope. Kuiper flashes him a thumb's-up, then snaps a pair of handcuffs around my wrists.

I begin to panic. "C'mon, Kuiper, give me a fucking break!"

"Not a chance, buddy. You've obstructed justice for the last time."

I let out a howl that is part bird, part jackal and part ostrich. Kuiper backs off for a second as if afraid he might catch something from me, then grabs me around the scruff of my neck.

"Why don't you do that for the judge? He'll lock you up in the pound. Think you'd be comfortable *there?*"

"I'm sure it's at least as good as your jail," I say as he pulls me down the stairs. I go limp and make him drag me like a war protestor. "Tell me something, Kuiper, what exactly did I ever do to you?"

"You don't take things seriously enough. Somebody's got to teach you that life isn't just a game."

"But don't you get it? Life *is* just a game."

"Tell that to the judge, too. He'll add another ninety days to your lock-up."

And with that I add silence to my act of civil disobedience. The only sound that's heard is the muffled thwack of my heels knocking against the steps as Kuiper pulls me down the street. The guy is nuts.

With absolutely no foreknowledge of, prior involvement with, or professional interest in the judicial process, whether civil or criminal, municipal or federal, I find myself once again incarcerated in the Central Police Station, my pleas of hithertos, heretofores, henceforths and woebegones falling on the deafest of deaf ears. That's right, I'm in jail again, me, the caretaker of Telegraph Hill, the guy people gravitate to in a crisis situation, the calm port in the storm, the solid rock in a sea of molten lava, well, this is one hell of a crisis situation I've gotten myself into, I've committed the cardinal sin as protector of the Spear—*Don't leave the Spear unprotected!*—oh, yes, legend be damned, just because Otto the Great and Constantine and Charlemagne lost their empires, that's no reason for *me* to worry, no, I'll just stash the Spear in the ivy and go about my business—*Don't leave the Spear unprotected!*—and now here I am, a prisoner of circumstance, unable to meet an exorbitant bail of twelve thousand dollars, and why so much one might ask, because I'm considered a flight risk, that's why—*Don't leave the Spear unprotected!*—me, who rarely gets past the Broadway tunnel, me, who has nowhere else to go and no means of getting there, me, who no lawyer in his right mind would ever seat on a jury panel in the first place, me, who is now pacing an eight-foot by eight-foot cage, I'm in solitary confinement, I'm staring into a black abyss, I'm on a bread and water diet, and I've got one phone call to make before they lock me up and throw away the key. Is there even one person out there I can trust? One person outside these walls who can understand the gravity of the situation? One person in the universe who will heed my call?

Anybody?

In which Sabine embarks on an important rescue mission...

...meets her destiny face to face in the guise of a familiar counterpart...

...and is rewarded handsomely for creating the shape of things to come.

Interlude

Sabine cuts a pizza into forty-eight one-inch squares, festoons them with a like number of party toothpicks adorned with little red and yellow cellophane jackets, and arranges the bite-sized treats on an Austrian porcelain platter. She dries a few glasses, straightens some napkins and pans the room to make sure there are no wayward dishes to upset the delicate balance of things. Soon it will be that time of day when an odd straggler or two might wander in for ten or twenty minutes of uncontrollable fun and joy. Sabine turns up the zither on the jukebox, preparing for the worst.

Outside, Helga walks up Pacific Avenue with Bernard in tow. He walks three paces behind her, either to protect her back, guard against sneak attack or simply because he can't keep up with her brisk gait. When they arrive outside the Café Vienna Helga motions him to a table on the tiny veranda where he, and perhaps only he, can stretch out comfortably. "Keep a look-out," she says, a pointless redundancy since looking out is pretty much all Bernard can ever do.

Helga enters the café and is pleased to find Sabine alone behind the counter. "We missed you the other night," she says.

"*Ja*, well."

"There's always another chance."

"Sandwich?"

"The usual," says Helga. "Better throw in a muffin for my assistant."

"The man sitting on the patio?"

"Yes, the little man. Do you have anything a day or two old?"

"Maybe he would like some pizza. Why don't you bring him in?"

"Better he's outside. He keeps an eye on things, if you know what I mean."

"Not really."

Helga glances around to make sure no one else is there. "I guess I can tell you. You're a foreigner yourself. I got him off a ship for a song. They pack these illegals so tight, sometimes the oxygen runs out. It left him deaf and dumb but he can see like a hawk."

Sabine looks perplexed. "And this is useful, this optical ability?"

"Very. You'd be amazed at the things I've learned. Just here in North Beach there are things going on you'd never imagine."

"I'll bet."

Helga looks around again. "No writer today?"

"I have excommunicated him."

"Oh?"

"He is—how do you call it?—a bad customer."

"Every man I ever met is a bad customer. When did this happen?"

"Does it matter?"

"No-no, as long as he's gone. Keep away from him, that's

my advice." Helga glances at a tray of pastries. "Maybe you have something *three or four* days old?"

Sabine makes a tuna fish sandwich and wraps a fresh biscuit inside a bag. "The pastry is on the house. For your friend."

Helga shrugs and gives her a ten dollar bill as she gathers the coffee. "Keep the change."

Helga leaves, a middle-aged man comes in and Sabine busies herself behind the counter with his order. The telephone rings. "Hello, Café Vienna," says Sabine into the receiver. She pours coffee with one hand, mixes a salad with the other and has the phone cradled between her shoulder and ear. Her expression immediately darkens when she hears who's on the other end. "Oh, it is you," she says. "Have you called with some new insults?" She taps her fingernails impatiently on the counter as the voice on the other end goes on and on. Her eyes slowly widen with growing incredulity. "You are *where?* — The bail is *how* much? — You left it in the *what?*"

She hangs up the receiver and shakes her head in bewilderment. The customer stands at the counter waiting patiently. "Don't forget the sprouts," he says. "I like plenty of sprouts."

"Yes, I will give you sprouts. The world would end without sprouts, wouldn't it?"

"I don't know about the world ending. I just like sprouts, okay?"

"Okay," Sabine responds in her low monotone. She wraps up the sandwich, slides it across the counter and walks over to clean a table. As she gathers the dishes and straightens the condiments she glances at the painting of the Hofburg Palace on the wall. She looks at it as if for the first time, staring at the courtyard, the columns and the corridors that lead to the museum rooms inside. "*Scheizer,*" she says as she finally pulls herself away from the painting. She quickly jots

something on a piece of paper, tapes it to the door and
turns off the lights. The little sign reads:

NO HAPPY HOUR TODAY

Sabine tries to remind herself exactly how she got involved
with this crazy writer and can't for the life of her seem to
remember. All she knows is that one day she was living a
normal if perhaps insignificant life and now, at this very
moment, she is on her way to retrieve the Spear of Longinus
before the forces of evil get their grubby little hands on it
and screw up the world. Is this what all those years of
arguing over the color of numbers has been leading to? Is
this why her mother planted a tropical garden in the cold
wastelands of northern Europe? Is this why the aspidistra
tickled her toes this morning and the Buddha's Hand gave
her a thumb's up? Who knows? Not a bit of it makes any
sense to her but she gave up on things making sense the day
she moved to San Francisco and found out there was no
beach in North Beach.

Sabine recognizes the front gate of Tobias' compound
from her many evenings at Coit Tower watching the sunset.
She follows a path past the eucalyptus grove, passes the
redwood tree behind Bill Bailey's cottage and comes upon a
dilapidated structure that looks like the slightest gust of
wind could level it to the ground. This is where he lives?
What is he, a squatter? What kind of man lives in a shoe?
Sabine cautiously approaches an old, ugly door—the cheap,
poorly made kind you find all over Europe—and glances up
to the patch of ivy that hangs a bit low over the upper edge.
She can't quite reach the top and moves a bucket from the
garden to stand on. As she climbs up she can't help but
notice that the inside of the cottage is a true disaster of
design. The refrigerator stands at an odd angle, the floor

ripples like the sea and the walls pucker like leather. "He lives like a college student," she mutters to herself.

Sabine reaches beneath the ivy and searches for the Spear. There's nothing there. She moves some spindly branches aside and reaches a bit higher. Still there is nothing. She pulls back some leaves and finds a big empty space in the undergrowth. Sabine stands on her tiptoes and looks more carefully at some broken twigs and tussled leaves. She sees in the dusty remains along the wall something that looks strangely like the footprints of an octopus or a squid or a one-toed sloth—

"Can I help you?" comes a voice from the pathway.

Sabine glances down to see Barbara standing there in full Visigoth warrior attire. Sabine balances unsteadily on one foot, unsure what to do, then steps down from the bucket and answers matter-of-factly: "I am a friend of Tobias."

"I'm in charge when he's away. What can I do for you?"

"Yes, well, I'm just here—"

"You're Butterfly Girl, aren't you?"

"Pardon me?"

"You're the one he likes. I've seen you around. Come with me."

"I really don't have time—"

"I don't either. Come with me, girlie, I've got something to show you."

Sabine reluctantly follows Barbara up the path to the eucalyptus grove. She notices how the older woman keeps flashing weird little hand signals to the trees as if engaged in some kind of primeval pantomime. They step over a low brick wall, then enter what looks like a nature preserve for extinct species.

"These are my digs."

Sabine glances around at the woven walls that flow into the underbrush and up into the ceiling canopy. It looks more like a nest than a home. It's airy, this aerie. "I like it," she says.

"I thought you would," says Barbara as she brushes off a log with her deerskin sleeve. "Sit."

Sabine eases onto a section of smooth bark. It's remarkably comfortable for a piece of unrefined wood. "It reminds me of home."

Barbara reaches over to an outdoor oven where a mixture of flower petals, pine cones and fennel roots are drying in the sun. She pounds the concoction with a mallet, then forms a couple of semicircles out of the goop. "Cookie?"

"I just ate."

"Keep it for later. They're good to nibble on."

"Yes? I like to nibble. I am always nibbling at work. Alena says I am nibbling her out of business."

"You remind me of myself when I was young."

"Oh?"

"I was pretty once. Seems like a thousand years ago. I was quite the looker."

"I can see that. Why do you live like this?"

"Sometimes you've just got to do what you've got to do."

"I know just what you mean."

"You, me, we're the same."

"Maybe so."

"No, I mean we're the *same*."

"Yes, well..."

"You don't understand, do you? You have no idea who I am. You have no idea why you're here."

"I haven't understood a thing since the night I took a long walk in Berlin."

"The wall is going to fall, you know."

"So they say."

"No, it's going to *fall*. In a few days. You'll see. Nothing will be the same. Germany, Russia, Poland, they'll all be transformed."

Sabine gets up off the log. "Yes, well, I have to go. I have some very bad news for Tobias."

"I figured."

Sabine heads for the path, then turns back. "Thank you for the cookie."

Barbara nods to her and watches Sabine disappear through the gate. She pounds some more grains into balls, then flattens them into little semicircles to dry in the sun. Today's a good day to mix up a full batch. A good day to enhance the solar rays. A good day to gather one's strength.

Today's the day.

Sabine has no idea what to do. She walks the hills, up the Filbert Steps to Coit Tower, down the Greenwich Steps to Montgomery, around the dead end circle of Julius' Castle and through the Grace Marchant Gardens to the base of Telegraph Hill. Up, down, up, down, she walks with no direction and no goal, she seeks only to lose herself in some unconscious state where there are no ancient weapons, no prison camps and no rowboats emerging from the fog. She crosses Levi's Plaza, stopping for a moment to observe a flock of sparrows bathing in the artificial waterfall. What do they care that it's not real, water is water, even if it comes from a pipe, a sparrow can surely be happy without knowing everything about history, geography and higher mathematics, yes, that's what she'd like to be for her next rebirth, a sparrow, and a small one at that—

"Excuse me? Miss?" comes a voice from across the way. Sabine glances over to see an elderly man sitting at an outdoor table with a bunch of papers overflowing from his briefcase. He's staring straight at her. "Can I ask you something?"

"I suppose."

"Where did you get those pants?"

Sabine glances down to see exactly which concoction she's got on today. It's the Frank Lloyd Wright-inspired pants, the denim dirigibles. "I made them."

"Really? From your own design?"

"Of course."

"They're very interesting."

"They're just pants."

"Well, that may be but I don't recall seeing anything quite like them before. They have a very modern attitude. What we like to call fashion forward."

"I never understood this expression. How can fashion be forward? I am happy just to keep fashion from falling to my ankles."

"You're not from around here, are you?"

"I am from Germany."

"I thought I recognized the accent. That's where my great-granduncle was from. A town called Buttenheim."

"Never heard of it. You probably never heard of Parchim."

"Afraid not."

"You're not missing much. It's hot in summer and cold in winter and that's about it."

"What brings you to San Francisco?"

"Sandwiches. I am the sprout queen of North Beach."

"Sounds exciting."

"Americans are crazy for sprouts on their sandwiches, which is something else I don't understand. It's like eating *sauerkraut* without the *sauer*."

"I know just what you mean."

Sabine looks at him with surprise. "You do?"

"Not really." The man leans back against the table and motions to the cluster of buildings that comprise Levi Plaza. "You ever think about working in a place like this?"

"They would never hire me. I don't have a college degree."

"College degrees aren't all they're cracked up to be."

"I also don't have a high school degree."

"That gets a bit trickier. But who knows? Anything is possible."

"You work here?"

"Thirty-five years."

"Can I ask you something?"

"Go right ahead."

"What does it mean, to be stone-washed?"

"Just what it says. We throw a bunch of stones into the washing machines to distress the denim."

Sabine looks at him skeptically. "I see."

The man pushes back from a simple wood bench and gets up to stretch his legs. He takes a step or two towards Sabine and looks at her more closely. "Listen, those pants of yours, they're very interesting. I think we could do something with that design."

"I don't really have the time. I'm working full time as it is."

"It's not like you'd have to make them yourself. Would you consider selling the pattern?"

"I never thought about it."

"How much would it be worth to you?"

"I don't know. They didn't take long to make."

"What's the first amount that comes to your head?"

"Twelve thousand dollars."

"That's a lot of money. How about five thousand?"

"Twelve thousand dollars."

"Ten thousand?"

"Twelve thousand dollars."

"Okay, you've got a deal."

"You can just make an offer like that, out here on the terrace?"

"I'm Walter Haas. This is my company."

"You are the family of Levi?"

"The very same. Levi Strauss from Buttenheim. Small world, isn't it?"

"Not really."

"Is a check all right?"

"I need cash."

Haas gathers together his briefcase. "Okay, cash it is. Let's go to the office. There's probably that much lying around somewhere."

Sabine follows him across the terrace. "It's funny, isn't it?"

"What's that?" he says, turning back to face her.

"They're just pants," she says, shaking her head.

"You know what?" he says, leading her into the main building. "That's exactly what Uncle Levi used to say."

"I think I would like Uncle Levi."

"Uncle Levi would like you."

"Buttenheim, you say?"

"Buttenheim."

Chapter 26

The door to the cellblock clangs open and my brain unleashes a full-color montage of despair and betrayal. It's my all-time synesthetic vision, the accumulation of every paranoid fantasy, unlikely suspicion and untenable fear combining into an unsavory psychic stew. The images fly by like the coming attractions of a bargain matinee—Waverly Wellington admiring his Asian art collection, laughing demonically and toasting himself with a drink; Barbara stirring up a medieval balm and smearing warrior paint on her face; Helga throwing knives at a human target on a spinning board; Bernard ironing a crisp crease into his pants and polishing his shoes to a sharp Nazi shine; Father Indelicato gathering together his army of illegal aliens and lighting the black candles of a secret mass—and through it all a calliope of jangling sounds, the banging of iron bars, the echoing of footsteps and the clanging of keys until finally the door of my jail cell swings open to reveal Patrolman Kuiper standing there with a pen, a clipboard and a long legal form. "Sign this," he says through gritted teeth.

"What is it?" I say, wondering if he's trying to trick me into signing a confession.

"Your bail bond. You've been sprung."

"Are you kidding?"

"I wish," he says, his words dripping with sarcasm. "Why don't you just refuse to sign it? You can rot in here forever as far as I'm concerned."

"No-no, that's okay," I say, grabbing the document and signing it immediately.

"You'll be back," says Kuiper as he leads me down the corridor. "I'll be counting the days." We pass a bright fluorescent light and he looks older than his years, as if he'd aged right before my eyes. Seeing the expression on Kuiper's face at this very moment is almost worth the price of incarceration. His lips are drawn and tight. His skin is red and blotchy. His carotid arteries look like they're going to pop right out of his neck. He's like a bounty hunter who's lost his bounty, a warden who's lost his ward, a mind reader who's lost his mind. The guy is nuts.

I retrieve my valuables from Sergeant Shiaparelli's desk, a meager haul consisting of a pair of torn jeans, a couple of well-worn flip-flops, a ripped T-shirt and a conspicuously large key ring. "What's that, a key to every house in San Francisco?" says Shiaparelli when I open my envelope of personal effects.

"Sometimes it seems that way. Actually it's thirty-four keys to fourteen apartments."

"What are you, a one-man crime ring?" says Shiaparelli, looking at the keys suspiciously.

"Yeah, I'm the Key Thief of Baghdad."

"Um-hmm. Tell you what, buddy. Don't go too far. We'll be checking your fingerprints on everybody's banisters the next couple days."

"Okay, keep in touch," I say as I gather my things and head for the door.

I walk out of the Central Police Station to find Sabine waiting for me on the sidewalk. "Are you the missing juror?" she says, struggling to keep a straight face.

"Yeah, that's me, all right," I say. "Public Enemy Number One. How did you manage to get me out of there?"

"I simply followed the rules of capitalism," she says, as if bailing someone out of jail was an everyday event. "It's really quite easy once you get the hang of it."

I decide to let this particular mystery wait until another day. "What about the Spear? Did you hide it somewhere safe? Did anyone see you?"

Sabine furrows one of those exquisitely shaped eyebrows, the ones that swoop down at just the perfect angle to her temples. "Yes, we should talk about that," she says, deftly avoiding my question. "Are you hungry?"

"Starving." She pulls a paper bag from her purse and un-wraps a piece of focaccia bread. "Where did you get this?" I say, surprised to actually see one of the missing wonders of North Beach.

"I was strolling the streets at four in the morning and I saw a light on in the basement—"

I dig into the bread with gusto. That's a funny word, gus-to, a word I rarely use, especially when referring to myself. I do things with haste, disregard, alacrity, eagerness, zeal and fervor, but gusto is a bit over the top, even for me. "So, the Spear..."

"It's very important to you, isn't it?"

"Of course it is," I say as I sit on the curb across from the police station and tear off a piece of focaccia.

"Something I am curious about," says Sabine. "Do you really believe it was the sword of a Roman Centurion?"

"I suppose so."

"And it really was in the hands of all those kings and generals?"

"That's what they say."

"And that he who possesses the Spear has the power of ultimate good or ultimate evil?"

"That's the legend."

"Then I have some bad news."

"What's that?"

Sabine hesitates a moment. "The Spear is gone."

I stare at her for a long moment, trying to digest the words. Perhaps it's the olives baked into the focaccia, or the onions, but I feel a sudden case of heartburn. "What do you mean?"

"That's what I mean. It's not there. I looked everywhere."

"Tell me you're not serious."

"I think I am as serious as I can be."

"But you couldn't have looked in the right place!"

"In the ivy, above the door."

"The front door, right? The nineteenth century European?"

"Yes, the ugly one."

I can barely breathe. I jump up from the curb and run down the street, only tangentially aware of Sabine's protestations:

"But you have not yet finished your lunch!"

I feel the strangest sensation as I run up the hill—the sensation of my feet not touching the ground, the sensation of air giving no resistance, the sensation of gravity giving up its strict interpretation of the rules. It seems like no time at all has elapsed before I am digging around behind the ivy, shoving my hands beneath the tangle of twigs and leaves and pulling at the branches until they snap into brushwood. I search the crevices of the door frame and the tongues and grooves of the wallboards, then I pull down more ivy and search through the pile of undergrowth on the sidewalk. That's when I see the dusty residue of suction cups—*the incriminating fingerprint of evil itself*—and I follow those prints down along the door, across the sidewalk, over the gate and right up along the three-story expanse of the Big

House. A flicker of light reflects from the upper window. Oh, God, no.

A strange calm washes over me, a kind of serenity in which I experience a clearness of mind unlike anything I've ever encountered before. *"Don't think,"* says a disembodied voice from somewhere deep inside my brain. I feel my conscious mind emptying out as I pull the key ring from my pocket and head for the gate. Instinct alone drives me to open the outer door, bound up the first flight of stairs and race for the second floor. Only the sight of Sabine following right behind gives me a moment's pause. "What are you doing here?" I whisper to her on the third landing.

"I'm coming along," she says.

"No, you're not."

"Yes, I am."

"It's not safe," I insist.

"Life is not safe," says Sabine as she opens her hand basket and begins nibbling on Barbara's cookie.

"You're eating again?" I ask her.

"I always eat when I'm nervous."

I pull a key from the ring. "You've got to get out of here."

"Too late."

"This is your last chance to leave."

She defiantly takes a bite of the cookie. "Open the door!"

Arguing with Sabine is pointless. I slip a key into the lock and hear the tumbler pins clicking, the cylinder spring turning and the deadbolt latch sliding. *Don't think,* I tell myself, *don't think, don't think, don't think—*

My adrenaline is pumping so hard I nearly pull the door right off its hinges as I burst into the apartment. I leap into the room like a gladiator ready to do battle, a warrior facing his ultimate challenge, a knight confronting his destiny, and am immediately hit in the face by what appears to be a hundred rounds of ammunition. They slap across my skin—*rat-a-tat-tat-tat*—and my knees weaken in shock, but I soon determine the onslaught to be nothing but the tiny glass raindrops of a beaded curtain. I push through the baubles, my muscles taut, only to discover that the apartment has been transformed into an exotic indoor garden. The floors, walls and ceilings are overflowing with a wild profusion of flowers. "What's going on here!" I demand of no one in particular.

Sabine steps into the room and gazes upon an arrangement of orchids blooming along the base of the windows, bromeliads flourishing in the shaded hallways and succulents blossoming in the sunny recesses of the walls. "It's beautiful, isn't it?"

"Where are you, Wellington? Where's the Spear?" I yell out as I search the room. I upend pots and planters looking for any sign of life. "C'mon, show your face!"

Sabine follows right behind me straightening the plants. "Do you have to make such a mess?"

As I take a closer look around the room I discover that what had been a bare, open space is now furnished like a medieval harem den. In the center of the room are billowing carpets, plush cushions and silk-covered pillows. Surrounding them are brocade tapestries, satin duvet covers and fine Persian rugs. At the far end of the apartment a waterfall appears to drop from the porch into an endless abyss. It's as if Frank Lloyd Wright had been hired by the Sultan of Brunei to spruce up his summer palace. "I don't understand... what happened here?"

Sabine tosses her basket onto the bed and nibbles on the cookie with a faraway look. With each bite she seems to transform a bit farther from the shy German country girl into a more knowing woman of the world. "There is nothing to understand," she says with a matter-of-fact disclaimer, surprised that anyone would question the architectural upgrade.

"Where did all of this come from? How could someone just move all of this stuff in here without my even knowing?"

"What's the difference?" she says, a hint of irritation in her voice. "Why do men have to question everything? It's just some plants and pillows. Can't you accept a little change in your surroundings and leave it at that?"

I walk through a misty, enchanted forest and am suddenly struck by a fanciful notion: Did Sabine do this while I was away? Was this her plan all along, to seduce me at the moment of her own choosing?

"Come, sit down," she says as she leads me to the edge of the bed. "You've had a long day." I follow her in a daze. If this were a dream it would be laughably unrealistic, but this is not a dream, at least I don't think it is, no, this is much too bizarre to be anything but real, this is the culmination of months of pursuit, the pot at the end of the rainbow, the moment when the guy finally gets the girl, the long-awaited climax when the pheromones kick in, the chemicals react, the magic potions take over and the blessed lovers are whisked to a cloud on the breath of a breeze. Yes, it's finally happening, nature is taking its course and offering its cornucopia of delights and all we need do is to give in to the moment, give in to countless years of destiny, give in to this most divine of interventions. Sabine sits close to me on the bed. "You can put your head on my shoulder if you wish," she says.

"Yes, I would like that." I lean into her long, thin neck and can feel her porcelain skin against my cheek. I feel a surge of electricity passing between us.

"Cookie?" she says, offering me a bite of her snack.

"Maybe later," I say as she chews the organic oddity with a faraway, glassy look in her eyes. It's a look I've never seen before. What can it be but the look of seduction?

Sabine runs her hands up along my arms and brushes her fingers against my neck. "Come to me," she says.

My skin tingles. A blush. A glance. A race of the heart. "Sabine... the Spear..."

"Yes, yes, the Spear."

Sabine leans into my arms and our lips slowly move together, two bodies in space finally moving as one. It's a kiss that's been months in the making, a kiss that's been hibernating, gestating and now finally bursts to life. Our lips meet with an exchange of elemental energy, an unleashing of an eternal vital force that turns day into night and color into sound. The entire power of the universe is found in this kiss, it's a kiss that makes the bonds of atoms rupture and causes molecular structure to unwind, it's a kiss that forces electrons to break loose of their orbits and head willy-nilly for the hills, it's a kiss that causes the magnetic pull of the poles to reverse and send shooting stars into the sea, it's a kiss that stretches into eternity and circles around for more, it's a kiss of the falcon that nuzzles so deep into the soul that nothing remains but the flick of a wing against the warm purple sky.

And then—

The falcon flies deep into my brain. It flies through time and space and comes out on the other side where nothing remains but a single sensory experience, it's a sense beyond hearing, a sense beyond sight, it's what we're left with when everything else shuts down, it's when evolution reverses and strips away the cerebellum and parietal lobe, it's when all that's left is the primitive subcortex, the home of instinct, impulse and telepathy, the place where generations meld and fathers speak to sons, the place where destiny meets desire, where the future precedes the past, it's the whole hobglob of being, the warm, milky sea of existence where every family's fate is determined and where every family in the end returns, and maybe it's a tiny speck of understanding I'm being granted right now as I kiss Sabine, a little glimmer of light that tells me we've been brought together not as lovers but to share a mission, that each of our families holds in its hands a piece of the puzzle, our contribution to the master plan, we've been here all along to perform one act in history, to be in this particular place at this particular time to engage in one crucial performance, to move the Spear from Here to There, to be the Protector, the Conduit, the Spirit, the Force, and it's about to happen, our families are about to finally take their rightful places as pieces #1,444,387 and #1,444,388 of the puzzle, right next to all of the other families that have already fulfilled their destinies and just ahead of those still struggling to find their own, and soon it will happen, the puzzle will be complete, each and every one of us will hold our little piece and we will see again what it all looked like before the moment of the Big Bang, that last moment of understanding when the whole thing got blown apart and sent into the infinite expanse of space.

I pull away from Sabine, feeling as if something inside me is unalterably changed. "Sabine... I finally understand..."

"Good," says Sabine. "It's about time."

"Yes, it's about time... and family... and destiny... and space... and history—"

"What is this, another one of your half-baked theories?"

"Please, listen to me—"

"Because if I want half-baked, I can go back to the café."

"We're here for a reason," I say as I move off the cushion and sit on the floor. "You, me, we're agents of history. Our destinies are being fulfilled."

"Yes, yes, come back to bed."

"Don't you see? That's why the chemistry between us always pulled and repelled at the same time. It was never about romance. We were brought together for something completely different."

Sabine looks annoyed. "What are you talking about?"

"We're all part of a giant puzzle that we're putting back together piece by piece. My family, your family, our jobs are done. We're finally going back to the moment of origin."

"Maybe *you* are, but I think I'll hang around a little longer."

"You'll see, you just need a little more time—"

"Enough of this craziness!" she says, reaching over and grabbing my hand. "Come back to bed!"

"All those generations of failed writers, all those years of plants and gardens, it was all leading to this very moment. It's all about our unique moment in history."

Sabine tries to pull me back on top of her. "Don't be a fool!"

I push her away and leap to my feet. "Maybe a fool is what I'm meant to be."

Sabine lets out a blood-curdling scream. *"Waaaaaaver-leeeeeeeeeeeeeeeey!!!!!!"*

There's a momentary lull, a silence beyond silence, and then a crack that shears right through my skin. The big bay window overlooking the ocean crashes open with the explosion of a thousand shards of glass and Waverly Wellington bursts through the jagged edges of the windowpane howling in a voice that is part animal, part demon and part phantom. "The end has come, innocent fool!" he screams as he throws the Spear of Longinus directly at my chest. "Let's see what your virtue brings you now!"

I watch the Spear moving inexorably toward my heart and I know there's not time enough to move nor parry nor even react. No, this is just me and my own mortality meeting head on, it's the last hurrah, the moment when my life passes before my eyes. The Spear sails through the room in slow motion and shakes loose a memory of not so long ago, just a few nights or a few weeks or a few months ago when I first held the object in my hands. What was it the Spear told me, that there's no such thing as time? Because if that's true then there's no such thing as this moment and there's no such thing as this Spear and there's no such thing as the death that surely awaits me. The Spear—this ambiguous object, this *apparition*—suddenly stops in mid-air, just inches from my heart. If the Spear can so brazenly defy the laws of motion, what would stop me from just walking away and choosing my own ending?

With everything frozen in the moment, I think about the Doctrine of Maybe and wonder if I myself am not the embodiment of the Sevenfold Paralogic. Maybe the Jains were right. Maybe within this fragile mortal coil is every imaginable permutation of reality. Maybe it's true that I live next door to a socialite who has suction cups on his feet, maybe it's false that I live in a cottage where the laws of physics cease to exist, maybe it's unknowable if I ever went to Hollywood and had a meeting with an agent, maybe it's true that I wrote a screenplay and false that I ever sold it, maybe it's true that foxes live in trees and unknowable if they fall dead at my feet, maybe it's false that aliens are living in my shower and unknowable if they are stealing my dreams, maybe it's true that colors are numbers and false that fog is just low clouds and unknowable if Dad is really behind the mirror. Who knows? There's one maybe I'm pretty sure of though, the maybe that the Spear is lingering there in space just inches from my chest, and I wonder if I might have one scene still left inside me, one last scene in this incredible action-adventure known as my life, one last gasp to bring it all to an end...

Parsifal Unleashed

Part V

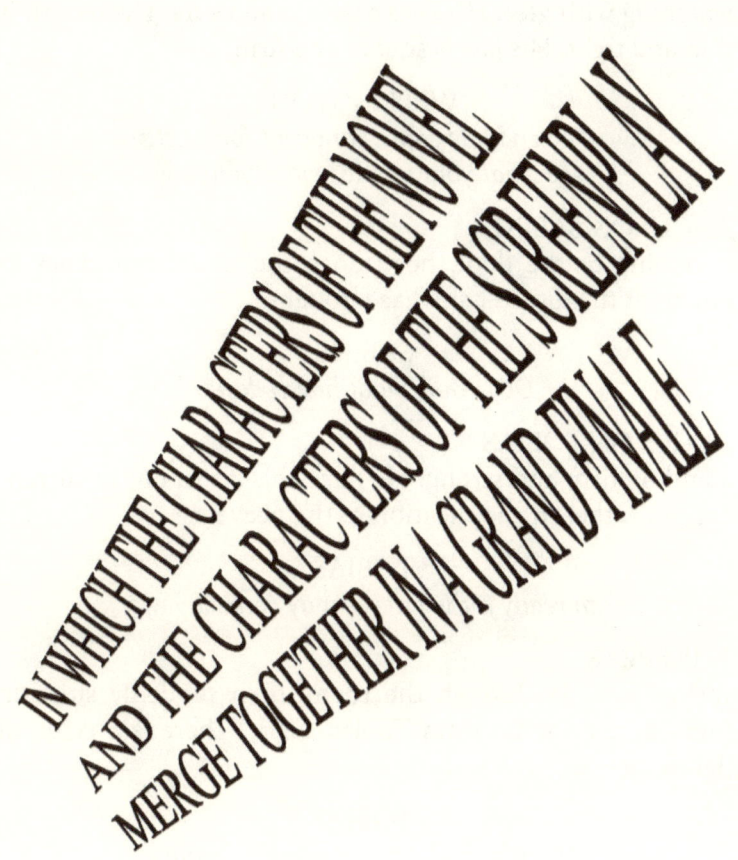

IN WHICH THE CHARACTERS OF THE NOVEL

AND THE CHARACTERS OF THE SCREENPLAY

MERGE TOGETHER IN A GRAND FINALE

INT. THE BIG HOUSE – DAY

The Spear sails through the air in slow motion, traversing a room filled with plants, pillows and brocades. It's aimed directly at Tobias' chest.

ANGLE ON WAVERLY WELLINGTON

watching with glee. His eyes are cold and sure. His mouth is thin and tight. His jaw is square and firm.

> WELLINGTON
> *The end has come, innocent fool! Let's*
> *see what your virtue brings you now!*

ANGLE ON SABINE

swooning to the floor, her trance broken. She watches in horror at the disaster she has wrought.

> SABINE
> *Dear God, what have I done?*

ANGLE ON TOBIAS

standing firm and strong. He raises his arms, not in surrender but rather in supplication to the heavens.

> TOBIAS
> *I am ready for whatever may come my way...*

THE SPEAR

moves steadily through the room, then suddenly stops in mid-air, just inches from Tobias' heart. There is a crack of lightning.

> TOBIAS
> *What's this? Am I witnessing reality*
> *or are my eyes playing tricks on me?*

Tobias reaches out and grabs the weapon from its frozen place in space. Wellington wipes the grin off his face and leaps into the fray.

> WELLINGTON
> *The laws of motion conspire against me!*

A SERIES OF QUICK CUTS:
Wellington grabs for the Spear... Tobias pulls it back... Wellington lurches from a chair... Tobias leaps off the bed... Wellington lunges for his arm... Tobias shoves him away... Wellington flails... Tobias blocks... Wellington kicks... Tobias evades... Wellington attacks... Tobias counters...

MEDIUM SHOT
With the Spear in Tobias' hand Sabine fully recovers from her trance and watches them grapple for the weapon. She sees Wellington kick off a shoe and unleash one of his long tentacles around Tobias' ankle.

SABINE
Tobias!

Tobias flies into the air as the tentacle upends his arm, his leg and the Spear. Wellington grabs the weapon and swings it wildly as he retreats to the window. He quotes the prophesy of the Spear as if to mock them.

WELLINGTON
He who possesses the Spear has the
power for ultimate good or ultimate evil.
Now we shall see which is stronger!

Wellington crashes through the window, showering the room with broken glass.

EXT. THE BIG HOUSE – DAY
The half-ape, half-spider escapes down the side of the building, his tentacle-like legs flopping wildly against the walls.

INT. THE BIG HOUSE – DAY
Tobias and Sabine crawl over the broken glass and make their way to the door. As they race down three flights of stairs to the street, Tobias calls back to her.

TOBIAS
Please, just once, do what I tell you.

SABINE
We'll see.

EXT. FILBERT STEPS – DAY
Wellington pushes his way through a group of tourists and heads down the hill. A woman notices his suction cups leaving a thousand circles imprinted along the steps and faints dead away.

EXT. KEARNY STREET – DAY
Tobias and Sabine sprint around parked cars and leap over a rubbish bin as they follow Wellington's trail down the hill.

EXT. UNION STREET – DAY
Wellington shoves an elderly couple out of the way as he slinks along the sidewalk.

EXT. GRANT AVENUE – DAY
Tobias and Sabine follow close behind.

EXT. WASHINGTON SQUARE PARK – DAY
A guitarist strums a tune. A Yorkshire Terrier chases a ball. Three Chinese women practice Tai Chi.

ANGLE ON WELLINGTON
digging his way through the bushes. He half-runs and half-limps along the path. The dog begins chasing him. A boy calls to the dog.

BOY
C'mon, Chaucer, get back here!

Chaucer keeps running, yapping at Wellington's ankles. Wellington suddenly swings around and transforms himself into a vicious, snarling wolf. Chaucer scampers away.

EXT. STOCKTON STREET – DAY
Tobias and Sabine pass the bustling shops of North Beach, looking for any sign of Wellington. They approach Washington Square Park, searching the alleyways, dead ends and shadowy paths of the surrounding neighborhood.

TOBIAS' P.O.V. – WELLINGTON
slips through some trees, crosses the road and heads
directly for 666 Filbert Street.

> TOBIAS
> *It's him! I should've known*
> *he'd head for the church!*

ANGLE ON TOBIAS AND SABINE
following Wellington across the street.

INT. STS. PETER AND PAUL CHURCH – DAY
Tobias and Sabine burst through the big double doors of the
empty church and search the apse, the pews and the altar.

> TOBIAS
> *He's in here somewhere.*

Sabine sees that the door to the steeple is slightly ajar.

CLOSE-UP ON FAMILIAR SIGN ABOVE THE DOOR

> SABINE
> (reading it aloud)
> *Evil is done here...*

INT. STEEPLE – DAY
Wellington climbs the steep stairs of the campanile with a
crazed look in his eyes. His suction cups slip along the
polished bricks as he climbs higher and higher.

CLOSE-UP ON THE STEEPLE DOOR
swinging open with a loud creak. Tobias and Sabine appear
at the bottom of the stairs.

> WELLINGTON
> *Welcome to my world...*

INT. BELL TOWER – DAY
Wellington lunges for a big steel cable, gives it a mighty pull
and sets the clapper into motion. The giant hammer pounds
into the side of a bell, emitting a jarring, bone-shaking ring.

Lower down the stairs the bell reverberates through Tobias' ears. His whole body shudders.

TOBIAS
That bell's completely out of tune!

SABINE
Just put it out of your mind, will you?

TOBIAS
I can't! Dissonance drives me crazy!

EXT. NORTH BEACH – DAY
The atonal church bells ring out over the neighborhood, delivering evil from every nook and cranny.

A SERIES OF SHOTS:
Bernard snaps to attention and ties his tiny cravat tight... Barbara vacates her lair and heeds the Siren's call... Helga grabs her knife kit and stashes it inside her stockings... Father Indelicato awakens from the lower dungeon of the church.

INT. BELL TOWER – DAY
Wellington unsheathes the Spear and charges for the spot where Tobias is holding his ears against the cacophonous eruption.

WELLINGTON
Now we shall see for whom the bell tolls!

ANGLE ON BERNARD
appearing in a tiny peephole of the bricks. He shimmies down behind Tobias with the oldest trick in the book.

REVERSE ANGLE ON BERNARD
hunching behind Tobias while Wellington attacks. Wellington lunges at Tobias with the Spear. Tobias tumbles over Bernard's prone body and falls to the ground.

TOBIAS
Ask me for another quarter,
Bernard, just try it!

WELLINGTON
It's useless to fight me, innocent fool.
Come join me on the dark side.
We will rule the world!

Tobias rolls away just in time as Wellington lunges at him again.

TOBIAS
The world deserves better.

INT. STEEPLE – DAY
Barbara appears in the campanile with her bag of balms. She pulls out a cookie and approaches Sabine.

BARBARA
Come, pretty one, join me for a little snack.

SABINE
Get away from me, you old witch!

Barbara glares at her with a wicked grin. She unsheathes a long stick from her deerskin garb and lunges at Sabine.

BARBARA
En garde!

Sabine grabs a bell clapper and parries Barbara's thrust.

SABINE
En passé!

INT. RAFTERS - DAY
Father Indelicato and his twenty Chinese martial artists come flying through the air with flying daggers, whistling bullets and incredible dance steps.

FATHER INDELICATO
Hail Mary this!

The army of illegal aliens takes up positions along the inner walls of the tower, awaiting Indelicato's signal.

INT. STEEPLE – DAY
Helga awaits Wellington's signal higher up the stairs. She pulls out her set of knives and readies herself for action.

INT. BELL TOWER – DAY
Wellington and Indelicato see each other across the tower.

CLOSE-UP ON INDELICATO
waving to Wellington.

CLOSE-UP ON WELLINGTON
nodding to Indelicato.

ANGLE ON THE MARTIAL ARTISTS
thinking the wave is their signal.

ANGLE ON HELGA
thinking the nod is *her* signal.

BATTLE MONTAGE:
The army of kick boxers, kung fu fighters and aikido combatants flies into action... Helga flings her hundred knives into the black void of the stairwell... a mass of confusion... arms, legs and chests being skewered by Helga's assault.

INT. STEEPLE – DAY
Father Indelicato sees his army being destroyed. He rushes to stop Helga but trips over his long black frock and tumbles down the stairs.

CLOSE-UP ON FATHER INDELICATO
landing with a thud. Lying in a pool of blood he struggles to turn over and sees that his heavy silver cross is embedded in his chest.

WELLINGTON'S P.O.V. - FATHER INDELICATO
struggling, collapsing and taking his final breath.

                    WELLINGTON
              Who said irony is dead?

INT. BELL TOWER – DAY
The combatants converge on a narrow platform. Sabine's bell clapper is no match for Wellington's Spear and Helga's knives. Wellington lunges at Tobias... Tobias barely avoids his thrust... Helga flings a knife at Sabine... Sabine does a circular move that spins the knife to the ground.

EXTREME CLOSE-UP ON TOBIAS' HANDS
grabbing the handle of the Spear and grappling with Wellington for control.

ANGLE ON WELLINGTON
kicking a huge vat of candle wax into the pit below.

INT. STEEPLE – DAY
Barbara and Bernard barely avoid the tumbling vat as it smashes to the floor. The candle wax seeps out and begins oozing toward a burning flame. They race for the door.

CLOSE-UP ON THE FLAME
igniting the wax.

EXT. STS. PETER AND PAUL CHURCH – DAY
Barbara and Bernard get blown through the big double doors as the wax behind them explodes.

INT. BELL TOWER – DAY
Tobias and Sabine are trapped at the edge of the platform. Wellington closes in and swings the Spear in a circle that comes closer and closer. At the last possible second Sabine grabs Tobias' hand and leaps into the abyss.

SABINE
Hang on!

They fly through the air and grab onto a bell clapper. The big iron pendulum swings right for the platform.

ANGLE ON WELLINGTON
assuming the stance of a medieval swordsman.

WELLINGTON
The moment is here.

ANGLE ON TOBIAS
twisting on the clapper.

TOBIAS
Hold on, Sabine.

BATTLE MONTAGE:
Wellington lunges... Tobias parries... the clapper swings around... Wellington thrusts again... Tobias spins away... the Spear misses his chest... but stabs his arm... Wellington twists the blade deeper... Tobias grabs his wound...

ANGLE ON SABINE
hurtling the bell toward the platform.

ANGLE ON HELGA
trying to claw herself free.

WELLINGTON
Watch out!

HELGA
It won't hold!

The bell swings back again and hits the landing with such force that the tuning is changed. Wellington and Helga are thrown into the air. Tobias grabs the Spear from Wellington's grasp. The platform collapses.

ANGLE ON WELLINGTON AND HELGA
falling to their deaths in the abyss.

EXT. STS. PETER AND PAUL CHURCH – DAY
Barbara and Bernard slowly come out of their trances.

BARBARA
Bernard, are you all right?

BERNARD
Aaaak...

BARBARA
The curse has been lifted.

INT. STEEPLE – DAY
Tobias and Sabine climb to the highest part of the steeple. Their hands entwine around the handle of the Spear as they hold it to the heavens. A drop of blood falls from Tobias' wound. The clapper clangs against the bell. Miraculously the collision with the platform has reset its tuning to a perfect 440 cycles per second.

EXT. NORTH BEACH – DAY
The beautiful sound of church bells rings out over the community. Good conquers evil. Right triumphs over might. There is consonance, at long last.

FADE OUT.

Twenty Years Later

Chapter 27

Time, like a jittery quarterback running for life and limb, passes. My ability to turn a phrase, however, remains intact. Old screenwriters, after all, never die, they just fade to black. Or a very dark gray. I'm presently living down at the bottom of Telegraph Hill, if you can call this living, that is. It's more a state of existence, or a state of non-existence, a kind of self-imposed limbo that is both better and worse than all those years I spent at the top of the hill. It's better because I've been relieved of all my duties as caretaker of a parcel of land that didn't need any taking care of and I can now fully pursue my bohemian lifestyle without any compromise whatsoever. It's worse because I seem to have developed a myopic view of the world in which my perceptions range from vague to vaguer, a state I can best compare to looking at an indistinct cloud in a hazy sky through a translucent eye patch. Take right now. I'm gazing out at a room that appears to be choking itself to death with an overabundance of plants, trees and flowers. There's aspidistra hanging from the ceiling, Buddha's hands stretching out along the wall, and banksia, jasmine and lobelia sprouting from every other available surface. I'm not sure if there's too much oxygen in here or not enough but the accumulation of smells is creating a perfume time bomb the likes of which hasn't been encountered since all those society ladies showed up for opening night of *Parsifal*.

Sabine enters the room and I strain to see her clearly. She looks a bit flat—two-dimensional almost—and it appears as if she hasn't slept much. She works too hard, that's for sure, but suggesting to Sabine that she change anything is as always utterly hopeless. No, if there's one thing I've learned it's that you have to accept certain things. Live and let live. Let bygones be bygones. Que sera, sera. "Nice pants," I say in an even, non-confrontational tone. I've learned that by keeping my voice flat and unemotional I reduce the chance of her completely misinterpreting my attempts at casual conversation.

Sabine stands at the bathroom sink. She's filled the basin with water and is gently rubbing Dr. Hauschka's Rejuvenating Crème into her forehead. She glances up, narrows her eyes and stares into the mirror. "Oh, it's you again."

"Nice to see you, too."

"I don't have much time. I'm late for work."

"How's the job going?"

Sabine shrugs. "Do you know what it means to be Senior Vice President of Women's Apparel? There is a denim shortage in Germany and it has somehow become my responsibility. I tell you, it was easier under the communists. No one even knew what denim was."

"Too bad the Berlin Wall had to fall down."

"Sometimes I think it was all a big mistake. November 9, 1989 is a day that will live in infamy."

"And to think it was all our fault."

"*Ach*, you think you are responsible for everything. The earthquake, the fall of communism, God knows what else. The power of that Spear may have been exaggerated.

Sometimes I think it all would've happened without us."

"You know, I've been thinking."

Sabine backs away from the mirror with a look of concern. "This is not a good thing," she says. Her face appears distorted again through my two-dimensional view of her, the room and anything else I can get a glimpse of.

"No-no, don't worry," I reassure her. "I'm retired. I'm in full-time relax mode."

"What do you do back there all day long... behind the mirror?"

"Not a hell of a lot. Reminisce mostly."

Sabine raises one of those perfectly shaped eyebrows into a mocking arch. "*Ja, ja, the good-old-days.*"

"Well, they *were* good. I felt really alive."

"Maybe it's because you *were* alive."

"I was just thinking about all those crazy characters, that madman priest down at the church and the rich guy up in the mansion—"

"Please, don't remind me. For twenty years I have been hearing this story."

"And how I got that infection from when the Spear nicked my arm—"

"*The Jesus bug—*"

"And how Dr. Gold said it was incurable—"

"For once he was right—"

"And how Dad convinced me to go back to Milwaukee so that I could die without causing everybody too much trouble—"

"Very thoughtful—"

"And how I took a long drive around town just to remind myself why I left in the first place—"

"It's like Parchim with breweries—"

"And how I somehow wound up on Blue Mound Road heading west—"

"Right past the cemetery—"

"Well, I'm just trying to remember one thing."

"What's that?"

"What the *hell* was I thinking?"

"Hard to say. Anyway, you just sit there and think about it. Why don't you rewind that film in your head, the one you're always going on about? I don't have time to entertain you."

"Yeah, I'll do that. Be sure to send Levi's my regards."

Sabine leaves and I settle into a comfortable seat behind the mirror. She's right, I'll watch that movie again, the one that's still playing on an endless loop inside my head, the one I wrote, directed and am starring in. Maybe it'll remind me how I ever wound up here, behind Sabine's mirror, of all places. All I can really remember is feeling woozy, getting on a plane in San Francisco, getting off in Milwaukee and renting a brand new 1989 Chevy Nova at the airport. Let me fast forward through all the boring parts—the baggage claim, the Avis counter, the gas station—ah, here it is, let's just slow things down and take a look...

I head west on Blue Mound Road, right past the cemetery, and give it a passing glance. No need to dwell on this particular piece of scenery since I'll be taking up permanent residence here soon enough. No, this too is part of my destiny, that much I've accepted, and the idea of being buried in Milwaukee doesn't seem quite so dreadful after all. Sure, the smell of stale beer still wafts over the city and the ground freezes solid in winter, but these are small prices to pay for successfully wrapping up my mission. Still, there is the small matter of what to do with the Spear of Longinus. Wrestling it away from the forces of evil was a brave and noble endeavor but keeping it out of the hands of the next group of crazed occultists is just as important. Because if there's one thing you can count on in this endlessly effervescent life of ours, it's that some miscast group of tea readers will misinterpret the leaves and leave some old cranky professor holding the bag. Didn't Walter Horn in his own oblique way—*"Drei Litre!"*—as much as tell me what to do? The Spear, the beer, the beer capital of America, where else but in the shadow of a brewery should I seek the Spear's—and my own—final resting place? Yes, indeed, it's finally clear to me that in the moving of the Spear from Here to There, the There is right Here in an orthodox Jewish cemetery in Milwaukee, the last place anybody would ever think to look for one of the world's most important historical artifacts.

I follow Blue Mound Road through Elm Grove, Brookfield and Waukesha, nondescript suburbs of a city I now barely recognize. It's been years since I was here and it doesn't really seem quite so bad as my stilted memories of growing up in some musty backwater outpost. No, Milwaukee is pretty much like anywhere else, a city with nice homes, a baseball team and a European-style café or two where you can sit and write. I keep driving, up through Pewaukee, Nashotah and Okauchee. If it weren't for some car blasting its horn behind me I'd feel downright serene. I'm dying, after all, and I might as well see the blossoming of the trees and the flocking of the birds and the goosing of the geese before they turn out the lights. And it's coming soon, that much I know. In addition to my myriad of other ailments—the eye, the ear, the brain—I now have a sharp shooting pain that reaches from the wound on my arm into every vein, artery and organ inside my body. Given that my body parts and these car parts are essentially indistinguishable, I wonder if I might not be able to shove a couple of muffler pipes into my chest and call it a day. The sad fact is, no car mechanic would waste a good muffler on my beat-up frame.

I continue up along Highway 16 through Oconomowoc,

Lac La Belle and Ixonia, town names that seemed laughable in my youth but now sound downright exotic. What goes on in Oconomowoc—other than more honking of horns—are there tribal dances and teepee sleepovers and buffalo stews to warm the soul? Is the great American past hiding in some sweat lodge just north of town? I turn down a country road and come upon a sign—*Waterloo, 12 Miles*—and think back to years ago when I swore that the only Waterloo I'd ever visit was the real one, in Belgium. Now Belgium seems a full lifetime away but if ever there was a time in life to compromise, this is it. The car flashes its headlights behind me and I find myself actually speeding up, almost anxious to get there. Sure, why not? What delights might Waterloo, Wisconsin, hold for the unwary stranger, what secrets are buried in Firemen Park, what intrigue awaits at Cindy Lou's Diner?

I pull up on a dusty gravel driveway, walk across an empty parking lot and squeeze through a screen door that barely creaks open. My arm is hurting, I'm feeling dizzy and I take the first table next to the door. "What's good today?" I say to a buxom blonde who harrumphs herself over to my table. She's got her hair in a bob, a bowling shirt with *Cindy Lou* sewn over the pocket and bell-bottomed pants three sizes too tight.

"The tuna fish won't kill you," she says through pops of bubble gum.

"Can you melt a slice of cheese on it?"

Cindy Lou narrows her eyes, wondering what she's getting herself into. "Suppose so. Never heard of that one, though, and believe me, I've heard plenty."

"I can imagine. Let me ask you something. What do you do in Waterloo?"

"Wait."

"For what?"

"If I knew that, I wouldn't be here. Potato chips on the side?"

"Sure." I look around at the Formica tables, red Naugha-hyde booths and a life-size bowling pin clock. In San Francisco this place would be a theme restaurant with a maitre d', a sous chef, and people lined up around the block waiting to get in. Funny what people will wait for. I'm waiting. Cindy Lou is waiting. The cemetery is waiting. "Nice little town you've got here."

"If you say so."

"Reminds me a little of Spring Green. You ever been there?"

"Nope."

"It's another fifty miles down the road. Frank Lloyd Wright grew up there."

"Wright, the podiatrist?"

"Wright, the architect. He's buried there at a place called Taliesin. It tells you something, doesn't it, a guy like that coming back to his roots? He was too big for New York and Chicago and Los Angeles, but just right for Spring Green."

"Lemme see how that cheese is doing."

I glance out at the craggy hills, the low sky and the uninspiring horizon. What was it in this kind of terrain that sparked Wright's vision, what provoked his great outburst of imagination—

A cold, hard voice interrupts my reverie and hangs in the air like week old cigar smoke. "Okay, pal, step out of the booth real nice and easy."

It takes me a moment to realize it's me who's being spoken to, a moment longer to grasp the seriousness of the situation, and another moment still to connect the voice to an all-too-familiar face. "Kuiper?" I say, slowly turning to face my adversary.

Patrolman Keith Kuiper is crouched down in full combat position, gun drawn, armed locked, ready to fire. "Thought you could get away, didn't you?"

"To tell you the truth, I never thought about it at all. Not even for a second."

"Jumping bail is a federal offense. Did you really think you could just get on a plane and fly off to Shangri-la?"

"This isn't exactly Shangri-la. Do you realize that you just followed me two thousand miles for missing jury duty? Doesn't that seem a bit excessive to you?"

"Tell it to the judge."

"You're serious about this, aren't you? You're going to take me back to San Francisco?"

"Plane leaves in two hours."

Cindy Lou comes out of the kitchen with a platter of food. She doesn't seem to notice there's a guy pointing a gun at me. "Anything else, hon?"

"A glass of wine."

"Red or white?"

"Red."

Cindy Lou walks over to the bar, pours a glass of wine and brings it back to the table. Kuiper watches carefully as I pick up the glass. "No funny stuff."

I take a sip. "No funny stuff."

"Lemme know if you need anything," says Cindy Lou as she heads back to her spot behind the counter.

"I've got to hand it to you," I say to Kuiper. "You take a vendetta just about as far as it can travel."

Kuiper slowly moves around the table, never taking his eyes off of me. "I nearly lost you in Pewaukee."

I take another sip of wine and feel my face begin to redden. "I knew I should've blown through that stop sign."

"And then again in Oconomowoc."

"That could be a good song."

"What's that?"

My breathing quickens. *I Lost My Con in Oconomowoc.*

"I don't get it."

I sip the wine, take a couple of quick breaths, then sip some more. "Doesn't matter."

Kuiper sits down across the table and scans the menu.

"That tuna melt any good?"

"First class."

"Well, I suppose there's time—"

"Let me," I say, tapping Kuiper's arm. I take a couple of quick gasps of air, then call over to Cindy Lou. "Can you bring my friend one of your specials?"

"You gonna want more cheese?"

"If it isn't too much trouble," I say, taking a bigger drink of wine. I can feel my face taking on a deeper blush.

"Hey, you all right?" says Kuiper, watching me closely.

"Sure... sure... I'm fine," I say, leaning back against the booth, feeling light-headed. The room takes on a strange hue as if the edges of my line of vision are burnished. The tables and chairs become indistinct, the counter too, even Kuiper and Cindy Lou begin to fade in intensity, but the bowling pin clock looms larger than ever. The second hand ticks from pin to pin while the hour and minutes form a perfect seven-ten split, tick, tick, tick, faster now, faster than it really should be, how long should it take for the tick of the second hand—a second, right?—but this is much faster than a second, this is five to a second, maybe ten, ticktickticktick*tickticktick*—

"Hey, no fooling. You need something? Glass of water?"

I remember something: *When time starts moving so fast that you can barely distinguish one thing from another, watch out. You're about to die.* The bowling pins fly right off the clock, faster and faster, the pins, the balls, the alleys, the shoes, the powder to keep your fingers dry, the scoring sheets, the dots on the floor, *tickticktickticktick,* they're all flying by so fast that I duck, I duck right off the seat and hit the floor—*"Call Nine-One-One!"* screams Cindy Lou—and now things are really moving fast, somebody's lips are on my mouth, somebody's hands are on my chest, a siren, an ambulance, a stretcher, an oxygen mask, an emergency room, a doctor, a nurse and even then, at this darkest of moments, the tiniest flash of awareness that life, when all is said and done, is nothing if not absurd. It would appear that I, Tobias Parker—*tickticktick*—failed screenwriter—*tickticktick*—the end of a long line of failed writers—*tickticktick*—have met my Waterloo—*tickticktick*—in Waterloo.

I can hear voices from somewhere down below. I'm hovering in the air, half here but mostly gone. I see a few images slipping in and out of my third eye, right from the exact spot where the synesthesia always erupted. I feel strangely calm as I watch Kuiper pacing the waiting room of the Waterloo Medical Arts Clinic. A man in a white smock slowly walks out from the emergency room with a grave expression. He looks like a doctor. Or a barber. Or a car mechanic. "Are you a friend of his?"

"Not even close."

"I see. Family, then? I'm sorry. We did everything we could do. He never regained consciousness."

"What was it?"

"Anaphylactic shock. Do you know if he had any medical history, any particular allergies?"

"Far as I know, the guy was allergic to everything."

"Um-hmm. We'll have to ask you to sign a few papers. Are you the next of kin?"

"I don't think he's got much left in the way of kin."

A nurse comes into the room carrying a Hefty Bag. She hands it to Kuiper. "I thought you'd want to have these. There's not much here. Just his clothes, his shoes, a leather jacket. Oh, and some kind of a collector's weapon. You'll see to it?"

"I'll see to it," says Kuiper, flinging the bag over his shoulder. He follows the nurse to the admitting desk, signs a few papers and heads out the door into the cool, crisp, Wisconsin night.

I feel both here and not here, aware and not aware, connected and disconnected. Part of me is in a nondescript pine box that's slowly being lowered into the ground, a box, I should add, that someone has cleverly labeled *Do Not Open*. I like that, a little after death humor to lighten the mood. Another part of me is somewhere else in a kind of indistinct, wayward orbit beneath a little puff of a cloud on an otherwise clear and sunny day. The oddest thing is that I can see in both directions, from above and from below, and if you were to draw lines between these two points to an infinite spot on the horizon, you'd have a perfect isosceles triangle, the sum total of whose angles, I should add, equals precisely 180 degrees. I'm already learning new things and I'm really looking forward to investigating some of those mathematical relationships that never fully made sense to me. Like how two parallel lines meet at infinity. What the hell does that mean? For now, however, I should probably get back to the matter at hand, which is that they're lowering me into the last vacant plot in this corner of the cemetery. I'm next to my brother, who's next to Dad, who's next to Mom and there you have it, we're all back together, just like at the dinner table. I expect an argument to break out any minute now.

There's not much of a turnout but everyone seems to be in a properly somber mood. Barbara is there, humming a Visigoth fugue that sounds perfectly fine for thirty seconds but then begins to deteriorate into a broken mess of soprano warbles. Bernard is next to her, cute and cuddly as ever, all dressed up in a black mourning suit. Bernard looks so sad that I'd give him every quarter in my pocket if I still had pockets. That's something I think I'm going to miss and qualifies as one of my first post-mortem observations:

DEATH HAS NO POCKETS.

On the other side of the grave is Sabine, who's sniffling into a Kleenex, and Bobby, who just keeps nodding to himself as if confirming some secret piece of wisdom that he and only he is privy to. Behind them is the Green Street Mortuary Marching Band, an unexpectedly nice touch, and a little ways farther is the Green Street Mortuary Marching Band Bus, its radiator steaming, hoses dripping and battery dead. Looks like the whole bunch of them took off on a cross-country tour. As for me, hovering about in this highly disembodied state, I'm not planning to hang around too long. I've always found funerals overly morbid but I feel it's my responsibility to at least make an appearance and pay my final respects. I see that the casket is finally settling in at the bottom of the grave and I can hear the sound of dirt hitting the upper lid. First it's just a couple of grains, then a few handfuls and finally whole shovels full. Okay, that's it. I've had enough. See you around, buddy. Nice to see ya, wouldn't wanna be ya—

"Hold on, not so fast," says a stentorian voice filtering down from some kind of celestial mahogany pulpit.

"Bobby? Is that you?"

"Who were you expecting? Mel Brooks?"

"No-no, I wasn't expecting anybody."

"It's all part of the package. The box, the band, the agent to say a couple of nice words."

"I'm honored, Bobby, really I am."

"You should've heard me at David Niven's funeral. There wasn't a dry eye in the house. Especially mine. God, he was a money-maker for me."

"I guess you couldn't say that about me."

"You were okay, kid. As a writer, you were a good actor. Listen, I've got to get back to L.A. before I lose the whole day on this. Anything you need to know?"

"There *is* something I've always wondered about. Remember when I was in your office that day and the encyclopedia fell off the bookcase and opened to a page about the Spear of Longinus? Was that just a coincidence?"

"Of course not. I had that planned for weeks."

"And that meeting with Walter Horn? Were you behind that, too?"

"Don't get me started on Horn. What a pain in the ass! Can you believe he wouldn't even trust Eisenhower with the Spear? Said he didn't comprehend its importance. That's why he replaced it with a fake, the one that's still in Vienna. He walked down into the caverns, made the exchange and brought it home in a duffel bag."

"But why get *me* involved? Why me, of all people?"

"Horn knew he was dying and he had to move the Spear to its next caretaker. He needed to check you out, see if you were up to the task. I already knew from before."

"Before when?"

"When you sent me your first screenplay. The one about Frank Lloyd Wright. I remember thinking, who in God's name would actually believe that Hollywood would make a film about Frank Lloyd Wright? Only one person: A completely naïve fool. Just like the guy in that opera."

"Wait a minute. You never took me seriously as a screenwriter?"

"Not for a second."

"I wrote script after hopeless script just to entertain you?"

"Believe me, they weren't that entertaining."

"Bobby, you ruined my life!"

"Look, kid, this is what it's all about. Your family's destiny was never to be a writer, your destiny was to protect the Spear."

"What are you talking about?"

"That theory of yours, what did you call it? Mystical genetics? That was a good start. You see, every family has its own particular obstacle to overcome, an epic battle that pits you against powerful forces that are out to crush you. You fight the same fight as your father, he the same as his father, and what gets passed along is the same obstacle that will be fought over the years to its final conclusion."

"To be lousy writers for an eternity?"

"What's the difference? An obstacle is an obstacle. All that matters is that it strengthened you for the final test. And that's what you've accomplished. You've wrapped it up. You've added the piece of the puzzle your family was responsible for. A couple million more and we'll have the whole picture again, like in the beginning."

"The Big Bang—"

"That's right. What a mess. Sorry to put you through so many hoops but you needed to be a failed screenwriter in order for us to get together."

"Bobby, I even failed at that! Don't you realize that the Spear isn't in that casket? I even managed to screw that up in the end."

"What are you talking about? It's with Kuiper, isn't it? That was always the plan. Who better to give it to than an officious, self-righteous cop? Nobody will ever get it away from him. The guy is nuts."

"What, you're going to tell me *his* family has a thousand year destiny, too?"

"Crazy, isn't it?"

"So, what am I supposed to do now?"

"Whatever you want. Stay here, hit the road, it's up to you. Find yourself a nice mirror for all I care. You need to take a little interlude."

"Every time I take an interlude it turns into a geometric form I can barely keep on the page. I don't know what all of these triangles and circles are supposed to mean."

"They're steps along the way. When your piece of the puzzle settles into the big picture, you'll understand. It's all about the shape of the universe. You're about to take the ride of your life, my boy, a nonstop roller coaster ride that keeps looping around and around. That's when you finally become one with the universe."

"Bobby, I just don't get how you know all this stuff."

"Yeah, well, you know what they say, kid."

"No, what?"

"*Bobby Littman is God.*" He gives me an exaggerated wink, then disappears into the reddish-orange leaves of autumn.

The grave is filling up with dirt, the mourners are walking back to the bus, and the Green Street Mortuary Marching Band strikes up a nice rendition of *Won't You Come Home, Bill Bailey.* I'm kind of floating around above it all, and by above it all I don't mean in any kind of an arrogant, egotistical way, because the fact is, I am humbled, I'm in awe, I feel a part of a big puzzle that's being put together, and I take a certain pride in the fact that I've done my job, I've made my Dad proud and his Dad, too, and now I'm heading up over a single lane road that winds through the cemetery and up here, high in the air, I get a whiff of something peculiar to Milwaukee—*hops! That damn brewery is fouling my air!*—I head past the graves and the headstones and the little shed where they store the shovels, and then I slip out past the gate and turn high above Blue Mound Road, where I merge with some other ephemera that appears to be heading west, and I guess that's where I'll go, too, at least for a while, west to where the sun shines, west to where the aspidistra grows, west to where I can finally relax and reminisce and make sense of a few things. I get pulled into some kind of reverse jet stream and am really making good time now, the plains, the mountains, the deserts fly by in a kind of kaleidoscopic whirlwind, and then I notice what looks like skywriting, some big, bright, beautiful letters that illuminate the atmosphere like klieg lights, they're coming from everywhere, shining up from Hollywood and down from Heaven, and I fly right through them and for a moment, at least, my reflection adds to the glistening message in the sky and I realize, absolutely, positively, that I'm going to have plenty to mull over on those cool, foggy, San Francisco nights, oh, yes, it's going to be an eternity before I get this image out of my head, it's writ large, really large, like the coming attractions for some big holiday blockbuster splashed across the screen:

TOBIAS PARKER,
FAILED SCREENWRITER,

FULFILLS HIS DESTINY
AT LAST

MORE PRAISE AND REVIEWS

"After reading *The Bone Man of Benares,* many of us hoped to hear more tales of adventure from Terry Tarnoff. He has done it again with his customary gusto and we don't need to worry about waiting for *The Thousand Year Journey of Tobias Parker* to be made into a film because when reading this delightful new book, you have a front row seat and are already in the movie itself. Terry Tarnoff has the gift of making the reader feel that he or she is part of the story. This is the gift of great story tellers."
—David Amram, author of *Off Beat: Collaborating with Jack Kerouac*

"*The Thousand Year Journey of Tobias Parker* is a tour de force. Hilariously funny, thoughtful and multi-dimensional, it's a roller coaster ride up and down San Francisco's Telegraph Hill and around Washington Square, fueled by a Hollywood action-adventure retelling of Wagner's biblical opera, *Parsifal.* Evoking the likes of *Confederacy of Dunces* sprinkled with *Ask The Dust,* Tobias Parker also brings to mind the movie hero Barton Fink as Tarnoff deeply mines what he knows, for laughs, romance and a little enlightenment on the side."
—Jody Weiner, author of *Prisoners of Truth*

"The great Polish poet, Czeslaw Milosz famously said, 'When a writer is born into a family, the family is finished.' In Terry Tarnoff's brightly colored, hilarious novel, *The Thousand Year Journey of Tobias Parker,* we witness an extended line of DNA imploding in a failed screenwriter's mind. Tobias Parker is the ultimate lone wolf, dismembered from society, he functions as a caretaker of a set of ramshackle cottages overlooking San Francisco. By day he roams the hills of North Beach, like the lost son of Kerouac and Ginsberg,

attracting a panoply of characters worthy of a Fellini circus. By night his mind folds in on itself as he examines his insides. On his last gasp of inspiration, he hooks up with a legendary Hollywood agent who leads him on a serpentine odyssey through the depths and heights of an existential dilemma—how to combine artistic nuance with the demands of a commercial endeavor. Smitten with a condition in which he "sees" sound as exploding colors, and burdened with an attraction to an aloof East German waitress, the complications which arise from his research for the screenplay gather an amalgam of strange denizens of North Beach into a whirlwind of events that cascade from one unpredictable outcome to another. As Tobias is being sucked into a larger story with seemingly fateful implications which could affect mankind itself, we see the world through his eyes— it's a delightful intellectual soup, a stream of consciousness which distills everyday reality into a series of convoluted yet wonderfully logical philosophical observations that only a stridently original mind could conceive. There is laugh-out-loud humor which rings true in almost every line. As a reader, one feels inside the mind of a razor-sharp genius character who, while constantly misfiring with the outside environment, has an alluring nobility of purpose and a startlingly frank self-awareness. His effort to leave a writer's impression on the world and complete his family's destiny creates an overwhelming empathy with his quest to untangle the bizarre twists his life has taken. As things come together and fall apart, Tobias' story hurls toward a climax that is so spectacularly perfect it will knock your socks off. Terry Tarnoff writes sentences that burgeon into paragraphs with internal rhythms that dance off the page in twisting, labyrinthian melodies redolent of Henry Miller's musical cadences. *The Thousand Year Journey of Tobias Parker* is a revelation that spills from page to page in a joyous song."
—Michael Danzig, screenwriter